GUARDIANS: A SECRET SOCIETY

WINGS
OF THE
SECRET
REALM

K.E. DEYARMIN

Developmental Edits by Maryssa Gordon
Cover and Formatting Design by Authortree.co

To every aspiring author holding a story close to their heart but wonders if it is good enough. Your voice matters. Your story matters. And it needs to be told.

PROLOGUE

Sheriff Jones was standing at the door fiddling with his black hat. "Hi, Amy." He hesitated as he continued to spin the hat between his hands. "Is your mom home?"

"Mom," I yelled behind me. I could feel a rock forming in the pit of my stomach. Police visits were not an uncommon sight at our home. But this time, there had been no fighting or yelling. For once, there had been peace. Something was wrong. His face was sullen.

"Hi, officer." My mother answered with the same confusion I had, "Please come in."

He followed my mother into our living room. The tension hung in the air making it almost suffocating. My eyes kept looking at her for reassurance that this was okay. That there was nothing to worry about, but her own body was rigid as she moved.

"Amy," My mom was the one to break the silence. "Go to your room."

"But Mom…" I tried to protest. My stomach churned. I didn't want to be sent away, I wanted to know what was wrong.

"Go." Her tone was sharp, and my body tensed more. She

1

was always so soft with me and my brother Cole. She was rarely the one who raised her voice to us. My dad, that was a different story.

I reluctantly obeyed. I bounded up the wooden staircase, but that is where my obedience stopped. I huddled behind the half wall. Out of sight, but still close enough to hear the voices. This was a spot Cole had found early on when our parents' fights were bad. Out of sight, so he wouldn't get caught in the crosshairs, but close enough to hear the venom spewed from our dad. Phone in hand ready to call the cops if he felt our mom was in danger.

I pushed my ear against the wall. I could feel the cool of the wall against my cheek. If I pressed any further, I was sure there would be an indent left of my face.

"Mrs. Evans," the voices finally resumed, the officer's voice was cracking so he cleared his throat. "It's about Cole."

"No!" my mom screamed. Ringing filled my ears as my own panic rose. I slid to the floor as the hallway was beginning to spin.

Howling followed, as if a wounded animal had broken in. It took a moment to realize the sound was coming from me.

The room went dark, and now my own personal nightmare begun. My brother was dead. That was all I knew.

ONE

FOUR YEARS LATER

S tanding outside the glass door, I lifted my hands to my cap tugging hard on the sides, in hopes that it would hide even more of what was left of my hair. Stupid internet! Why did you give us such hope that if we watched a simple instructional video, we could accomplish anything. My poor hair was a direct result of how false that was. I now looked like I had gotten in a fight with a weedwhacker and lost.

My chest swelled as I took in a big breath of air. My palms were starting to sweat as I reached for the door of the salon. Not ready to face the shame of my stupid attempt. How many times would I have to explain my thought process. Because the multiple times I replayed it in my head, the worse it sounded.

"Amy, what the hell did you do to your hair?" My friend, Grace, gasped as I walked in, my head dipped trying not to make eye contact. Of course she was the first person I would run into, since she typically worked weekends at the front desk.

"I wanted to try something new." I could feel my cheeks burning as the redness spread across my face.

"Caroline is finishing up now. You better pray for some

type of miracle." Grace sighed as she typed my name into the computer.

"It's not that bad," I muttered under my breath as I sat in one of the plush chairs. I grabbed one of the gossip magazines from the table and flipped through it. Pictures littered the pages, some of happy couples, others of people disheveled, either pumping gas or running to a store. Matched with headlines concerned with their wellbeing. I didn't know there was a dress requirement at the gas station. Shoot, what would they think after spending a day in our town?

As I sat staring at the page, waiting for my name to be called, I could hear the shrill noise of the phone. "Strandz n' Curlz, Grace speaking!" Grace answered in a sing-song voice.

I peeked up from the magazine and watched her finger tapping on the desk. She listened intently to the person on the other side. Nodding her head, as if the person could actually see her response. Her black curls bounced with the motion. Her fingers furiously typed on the keyboard as she tried to capture all the necessary information needed for their appointment. Her nails caught the light, always perfectly manicured, and in my opinion, always a little too long. How she was able to type so quickly with those talons was a talent of its own.

"Amy?" a young woman called as she walked to the front of the salon, her heels clicking with every step.

"Here," I said as if I was answering a teacher doing roll call. I could feel the heat returning to my cheeks, half expecting a horrified gasp when she saw me.

Without a word she turned and headed toward her chair as I stumbled to keep up. How could a woman in three-inch heels walk so fast? She motioned for me to sit, and as I did, she pulled the cap off my head.

"What were you trying to do here?" She asked, picking at my hair as if it was a dead animal. It sure looked like one. Fumbling, I pulled out my phone and showed her the picture that had started this mess. The silence felt like an eternity. Maybe she was doubting her ability to save my hair. Just don't shave it, I silently prayed.

"It won't be easy… but I can fix this." I heard the flap of the black sheet before she pulled it around me. I wasn't fully convinced as I stared at the mirror, gawking at the blue streaks in her platinum blonde hair. I usually left the decisions up to the stylist, but I was really hoping I wouldn't walk out with a rainbow on my head. And before I could say another word, she was leading me to the hair wash station.

What felt like an eternity later, she was fluffing my hair and inspecting her work. After cutting off another two inches of hair and adding highlights, my hair actually looked decent. Though I wasn't initially thrilled with the highlight idea, I was glad she pushed it. Snapping off the black cape, she turned the chair, escorting me to the register.

"Wow Amy! Your hair looks so good!" Grace said, punching buttons on the computer. "I hope you know how lucky you are." I stared, still shocked at how quickly she could type with those nails. As I looked closer, I could see silver sequins on a few of them. "That will be two hundred and fifty dollars."

"How much?" I choked out.

"Two hundred and fifty dollars," she repeated, clearly annoyed. "One hundred for the haircut, wash, and style, and one fifty for the full highlights."

Reluctantly, I handed over my debit card. This is why I always opposed highlights. "And how much for a tip?" she asked. "Twenty percent is typical," she quickly added, afraid I would embarrass her with my response.

"Twenty percent is fine," I said, taking my card back. I

quickly signed the receipt, silently saying goodbye to the three hundred dollars.

"You'll need to come back in six weeks for a touch-up. I scheduled you for Sunday at the same time," she said, handing me an appointment card. "See you tomorrow at school!" Grace shouted as I headed out the door. I raised my right arm and did a quick wave before leaving. I will say one thing about Grace, she took her job very seriously and took no time for chit-chat.

I internally screamed as I walked out. There was no way I was coming back in six weeks to dump another three hundred dollars. People will just have to get used to brown roots. That was coming back into style… right? I headed toward the bus stop, still mumbling.

I glanced at my watch. It would still be another ten minutes before Bus 8 would arrive. I pulled out my notebook where I kept track of our family finances. I could've gone to a cheaper place, but every time I tried in the past, I would be greeted by Grace's disappointed face the next day. Which would then lead to a lecture about the importance of having a good relationship with a hairstylist and not chasing the best deal. That was the main reason I tried to cut my own hair. I guess I need to go back to watching some more online videos before I can try that again or find a simpler hairstyle.

Flipping through the pages, I finally found the one I was looking for. My goal for college. My chance at a better life. To leave this place behind and never look back. I let out a large sigh as I had to write down the new expense. Being fifteen, I was only able to work a couple days a week. At roughly $8.50 an hour, on a good day with tips and taking out the typical taxes, this haircut cost me at least two weeks of work! Plus, the monthly bills I contributed to, there was no way I was going to put anything away again this month. At least, for now, I wouldn't have to pull anything out of savings.

I could hear the rumble of the bus pulling toward the curb

and closed my notebook, placing it back in my bag. Two more years. I have two more years until I can go to college. This is just a little setback, I keep reminding myself, but if I continue working hard and tracking my finances, I should have no problem reaching my goal.

I climbed up the stairs of the bus and slid my card across the reader. That familiar beep chirped, signaling the transaction was approved. I carefully walked down the aisle, trying my best to avoid the bags and legs sticking out in different directions. I was able to find a seat next to the window. I sat down, gazing out as we pulled away from the curb. I could see the faint reflection of myself staring back. I pulled on my short hair and could feel the tears forming in my eyes. The whole reason I tried this dumb haircut was to distract myself today. It was four years ago today we got that fateful knock on the door. The day that our whole lives changed.

Cole, my older brother, was at a party with his friends. They had gotten into an accident on their way home. We still had very few details about what caused the accident, but the crash had damaged the gas tank, creating a leak. Something had sparked in the engine, which initially started a small fire, but combined with the spilled gas, it was only a matter of seconds before the car was engulfed in flames. Everyone inside was killed, and they claimed it was my brother's fault. It had been determined that he was under the influence while driving, so in layman's terms, drunk.

I could feel my hands starting to clench. It happened every time that thought crossed my mind. It didn't make any sense. I recalled all the lectures he would give me about how alcoholism ran in our family. The image of my dad passed out in the recliner popped into my head. Because of that fact, we had to be extra careful if we were ever around it. His voice echoed in my head. He always hated how our dad got drunk at home and the fights it caused. He vowed he would never turn out like him. How could he make those declarations and then go to a party and do the same damn thing?

Because of the fire, everyone had closed caskets. I couldn't even say goodbye to him. And since the accident, it has felt like an ongoing nightmare that I just need to wake up from. My mom couldn't take it. Between the growing fights between her and my dad and the whispers around town, as everyone blamed my brother for the accident, she only lasted a couple of months before she left us and never looked back. She abandoned me at eleven to take care of Dad. After she left, my dad also vanished, but he left me emotionally, though he wasn't much of a support system before everything happened. He checked out and turned to his only relationship that supported him, alcohol. That is when I realized if I wanted anything in life, I had to do it on my own. It was also up to me to take care of what was left of our life that my family had deserted.

I didn't even notice the tears starting to run down my cheeks. I glanced around, hoping no one noticed, before brushing them away with my sleeve, blinking hard to make them stop as I continued to stare out of the window.

Two more years.

Two more years, and I would be able to leave this place. I would be the first one in my family to go to college. I won't be stuck in this town alone. I won't be a nobody like my dad. I'm going to leave and not look back. I let out a brief chuckle with that last thought. Maybe I was more like my family than I tried to admit. My response was also to leave, but what other choice did I have?

As we approached the library, I quickly pulled the cord, and a ding echoed, signaling the driver someone needed off. The best way to get through today would be there. I used the back exit of the bus and walked toward the tall brick building.

The library was my place to escape because it was a reminder of simpler times. It reminded me of when I was little, and my mom would take me and Cole to pick out our weekly books. We would enter the glass doors before we took off, running toward the kid's section. We spent what felt like hours searching for the right book, and if we got there at the right time, one of the librarians would have a section set up where they would read a chapter from one of the books that were popular at that time.

I pulled on the familiar doors and let the smell of old books hit my face. This was one of the places that made me feel closer to not just my childhood, but my brother, a good place to be today. I walked past the first row of shelves. The walls were brightly colored with the ABCs sprawled over them. The sound of a baby crying echoed in the background. My hand spread out over the books as I walked down the aisles, feeling the slick bindings. I walked around until I made it to the perfect section.

The sci-fi section my brother always ran to. He was big into those fantasy books. He liked the ones with superheroes, men who took on the troubles of the world to save some type of damsel in distress. I walked to the back of the aisle, stopping at the back wall. I turned my back against it, feeling the coolness of the painted bricks against my shirt. I slid my back against the wall, bringing my knees to my chest. Laying my head on my knees, I finally let the full extent of my tears escape, letting all my memories of us together flow. The memories I worked hard every day to banish. I would allow this one day for them to return.

TWO

"Amy! What did you do to your hair?" Alicia half yelled across the parking lot as I walked toward the school. Her bright blue eyes looked as if they had doubled in size as she stared in astonishment.

I pulled at my hair self-consciously as I felt myself turning red. I knew people would notice since it was a pretty drastic change, but did she have to announce it so loudly. "Oh, you know, just wanted a change."

"Well, I think it looks AMAZ-ing," Grace said proudly, brushing a dark curl out of her face. "You should have seen what she looked like when she came to the salon. She's so lucky Caroline was working."

"Hey, did ya finish your math homework? I got stuck on question ten," Alicia said, pulling us to our normal picnic table.

I couldn't help but smile. She had the attention of a goldfish, but at least the topic was off my hair. "Hold on, let me find it." I opened my backpack and pulled out my math binder. The metal rings flipped open as I pulled out the homework.

"You're a lifesaver!" Alicia squealed, grabbing it as she

pulled out her own copy. I glanced over at her paper, which was only a third complete. It looks like she was "stuck" on number ten plus the rest of the assignment.

"I would prefer if you called me when that happens. I can walk you through it, or you could meet me at the library, and we can do it together," I said, peering over my shoulder, afraid a teacher would walk in and catch us. "You won't learn if you keep copying my homework."

"Yeah, yeah." She waved the pencil she was holding. "But Mike wasn't working for the first weekend in months, and we just got busy." Her eyes were not leaving the papers.

"Okay, just watch how you write out the equations. Don't make it obvious you just copied it." I watched as she stopped and rubbed her eraser in a few spots, smudging the paper to look like she had erased and made a few attempts.

She finished just as the first bell rang. We all waved goodbye as we went our separate ways. I scooped the assignment off the table and stuck it in my binder. Luckily, we all had lunch together, so it wouldn't be long before I saw them again. I was a little glad we didn't have many classes together. We all had different perspectives when it came to school.

Math was my first subject, so I decided to carry my binder instead of putting it back in my bag. This would be my first mistake. Then came my second. I should've been paying more attention as I walked toward math because before I knew it, I hit something, and it was hard. The force caused me to propel backward, losing everything in my hands. I fell flat on my back, the wind instantly escaping from my lungs. Then came my binder. All I heard was the loud slam. My binder exploded as soon as it made contact with the floor, and I watched in horror as my papers flew everywhere. For a minute, I thought I had walked into a door by how solid the object was, but after the initial shock, I looked up. My eyes locked with one of my classmates.

"Are you okay?" Derek asked, extending his hand. He stood there unfazed. Dang, how weak was I?

My face was on fire. "I'm so sorry, I wasn't looking." I was on my knees at this point, keeping my eyes on the ground. Praying I would just disappear. I felt like an idiot grasping at the loose papers.

I could hear the giggling behind me. Typical high school students, embarrassing moments were the lifeblood of their amusement. Derek knelt down next to me as he tried to gather the papers that had turned the small space around us white. I had given up on trying to put them in my binder and instead was aimlessly grabbing and shoving them into my backpack. As soon I grabbed the last paper, I mumbled out an apology as I made my quick exit toward the open door. Thankfully, I was right in front of my classroom, so I was able to quickly fumble out of view.

After taking my seat, I took a quick breath before opening my bag. Through the chaos of crumpled paper, I was able to locate my homework. I earnestly rubbed my hand over the sheet, trying to smooth out the wrinkles. I should've taken time to put it away before leaving. No, I thought again, I shouldn't have let Alicia borrow it.

This period wasn't my favorite class. Usually, I enjoy math. I liked how everything was constant. Two plus two would always equal four. There was logic behind it. It wasn't subjective to people's interpretation. However, my teacher, Mr. Bellows, he was another story. He was a younger teacher and cared more about trying to fit in with his students than the actual subject. He would quickly teach the lesson, then as we did independent work, he walked around the class so he could talk about the newest movie or the latest gossip. The gossip usually consisted of who may have recently broken up or who was dating whom.

I felt bad for the students who were struggling. Maybe this was one of the reasons Alicia never completed her assignments. Mr. Bellows walked around the class, picking up our homework and shaking his head after picking up mine.

"Folders, students... remember to use folders," he mumbled as he continued to shake his head, walking to the next row. Convinced that my face was going to stay bright red the rest of the day, I dropped even lower in my seat. He discarded the papers onto his desk and then walked to the whiteboard to start the lesson.

FORTY-FIVE MINUTES LATER, THE BELL RANG, AND WE ALL rushed out of the classroom. My next class was Spanish with my overly enthusiastic teacher. It was on the other side of the building, so most days, I had to run in order to make it before the tardy bell rang. An obstacle course of dodging students and open lockers. Who needed the gym? This was my daily workout. I reached the door and opened it, exposing the excessively decorated classroom.

The rest of the day flowed as normal, with history following next and then gym. The only thing I liked about gym was having lunch after. This way I had time to shower without the fear that I was going to be late to class. I always brought my lunch anyway, so I didn't have to worry about the lunch lines, and Grace and Alicia always saved us a table.

"Ugh, I hate Mondays!" Grace whined as I sat down. "I always forget the assignments from Friday and end up missing something."

"What happened to your planner? They give us a new one every year," I asked, pulling out my lunch.

"I lost it. Plus, it was so tacky." Her long nails tapped against the table. "I should stop at the store this weekend and get a pretty one. Alicia, what do you think?" She always sought her approval.

"Why waste your money on a planner? You have your phone. Just download an app. There are some cool ones that help you organize your assignments." Alicia pulled out her phone. She always had the newest model, but I highly doubted it was her assignments that she was organizing.

I took a big bite out of my sandwich. I didn't want to get involved in this conversation. My phone was probably around four generations behind Alicia's. It did what I needed it to. I could make phone calls, receive texts, and have access to the internet. Plus, the cost of phones was getting insane. People were spending close to a thousand dollars every year for the newest generation. It acted more as a status symbol for people at the school than actually providing any additional service.

Alicia half asked, half shouted, as the voices in the lunchroom were becoming deafening as more people settled in with their lunches "I can't wait until Tyler's party. You're all going right!" It was more of a statement than a question. "Have you guys picked out your costumes yet?"

"Yes! Mine is almost done! I'm going as a vampire. I tried to talk my mom into ordering these ceramic teeth, but she told me no," Grace said, looking through her phone for a picture.

"You need to get fake blood to incorporate into your makeup!" Alicia said, wiping a strand of her long blonde hair that slipped from behind her ear. "I'm going as a nurse, I know a little cliché, but Mike wants to go as a doctor. I thought it would be cool if we did it in fifties style. That way, we could stand out!"

"So cute! They had some really cool hairstyles back then," Grace gleefully added.

"Really?" Alicia stopped to think, tapping her chin. "How about if you do my hair, then I'll do your makeup!" Alicia had taught herself to do makeup by watching videos online. And I had to admit she was pretty good, which was one of the reasons I thought I could cut my own hair. "Amy, you're coming too, right?"

"I don't think I'm going to go." I stared at the lunch table behind Alicia and Grace, partly to avoid eye contact, but it was also amusing to watch a group of students try and cram as many people as they could on the bench seating

"Oh, come on. You have to come. Tyler is throwing the party, and his are always the best! His parents are super chill." She paused. "Is it because you don't have a costume? I could help you find one!" Alicia urged. "I know! Let's go to the mall this weekend."

"I don't know. I think we have a math test that Monday after the party. I haven't even started studying for it yet." I pursed my lips as the words left my mouth. It was a pretty lame excuse, almost up there with I have to wash my hair.

"Okay, how about we make a deal. If we don't find you a costume, then you don't have to go." She smiled at herself, proud of the idea, skipping over the whole math topic.

"Okay…" I knew this would be a losing battle, but it could give me the perfect out. I hated shopping and usually annoyed Alicia and Grace so much that they would typically give up on my indecisiveness, and the focus would end up back on them.

"Perfect! Let's do Sunday! Mike is working that day, so we can stop by the food court and see him after. He'll probably get us some free food for lunch!"

Grace and Alicia continued to make the plans as I zoned out. Which was easy to do as I let the sounds of the lunchroom wash over their voices. The slamming of lunch trays echoed behind me where the empty trays collected. I should go to the party. I haven't been to one yet this year, and this way, I could get Alicia off my back about going to the next few. I just wished she wasn't pushing a Halloween party. Sometimes, I wish they were a little more sensitive. Neither Alicia nor Grace reached out to me yesterday. I thought it was best to not bring it up to them. I made that mistake last year, and they both were genuinely shocked I was still "mourning."

Alicia even made the comment, "Shouldn't you start to move on? It isn't healthy to dwell in the past."

At that moment, I decided to keep these things more to myself. That day would forever be a black mark on my calendar, but to everyone else, it was becoming a distant memory.

The shrill bell pulled me out of my spiral. Lunch was over.

My last class of the day was English. Even though English was never my favorite subject, this year, I loved the class. It was all because of our teacher, Ms. Fuller. This year, we were focusing on literature, but Ms. Fuller really tried to make the books we read relate to us. She was a favorite amongst many of the students. She would also be a constant subject in my math class as my fellow students were shipping Mr. Bellows and Ms. Fuller. Trying to find ways to get the two teachers to run into each other. Though internally, I was against it. Ms. Fuller was too good for him.

I quickly entered the classroom and sat in my seat. This is one of the few classes where we didn't have assigned seating. I always chose the second row. It was close enough to be involved in the discussion but didn't give the appearance of being a teacher's pet or an overachiever.

I was placing my bag on the back of the chair when I froze. I watched as he walked in the door. The day had flown by so quickly that I forgot about my run-in with Derek today. Would he bring it up? I didn't realize I was holding my breath, and I let out a heavy sigh when he took his seat. I shouldn't have been surprised he didn't acknowledge me. He never acknowledged anyone. He and his friends held a low profile at the school. They barely left their social circle and never went to parties or school events. They were the type of students who sat in the back and fell asleep half the time. They weren't bad kids. Other than getting in trouble for sleeping, they never caused problems. However, you could tell coming to school was low in their priorities, but that seemed to be the case for most students.

However, at times, it was hard to look away. He was one of the hottest guys in our school. He had dark brown hair, always kept short. He also had soft brown eyes. Not the brown that blends with the black iris almost looking like they were one color, but the rich and soft color of hazel as the brown slowly turns to amber, then green. He was also very tall. He had to be over six feet, so he towered over the other boys, as most hadn't finished hitting puberty.

Freshman year, all the girls in our class swooned over him, along with some upperclassmen. However, he always had an air of indifference. He soon started dating Becca. Who was, of course, another girl from his small circle of friends. The type of girl every other girl envies, with her long blonde hair. She was skinny but curvy in the right areas. Puberty was definitely kind to her.

"Alright, class," Ms. Fuller started, pulling me back into class. "Today, we are going to review the assigned reading. Can everyone please pull out their books?"

After a long discussion about symbolism, the bell rang, ending the school day. I picked up my book and placed it back into my bag. I tugged at the black plastic bag inside, pulling it to the top. It held my work uniform. Luckily, the diner I worked at was only two blocks from the school, so I could walk instead of catching the bus.

I debated changing into my uniform before or after getting to the diner but decided on the latter. Alicia would be working tonight, which helped the evening go faster. Alicia had turned sixteen at the beginning of the school year, so when she worked, she typically gave me a ride home. Which would save me from the bus. I wonder if she wanted me to wait for her. I pulled out my phone to text her but saw her message pop up first. My heart sank for a moment. Was she ditching work again? The air rushed out in relief as I read the text.

With Mike. Cya @ work

Walking outside, I pulled my jacket closer. The weather was starting to get colder. I was wondering what that meant for Halloween. Would we get snow? If we did, that would limit some of the girls' costumes. They may have to add some layers to their skimpy outfits. I shook my head. They would rather catch pneumonia first.

"Hi, Amy!" Mr. Johnson called from the kitchen as I entered the diner. He was training a new cook on the grill.

"Hi, Mr. Johnson. I'm going to go change really quick!" I called back, gesturing to the bathroom. He nodded and went back to talking about the importance of waiting for the right combination of heat and oil before placing the meat on the hot grill.

I reached the bathroom at the back of the diner and pushed open the blue door. There was a total of three stalls. I shuffled to the first one closing the door behind me. Fumbling in my backpack, now hanging on the small hook, I juggled pulling out my uniform and putting my school clothes away.

Finally, after some quick footwork, as I tried to keep balanced on my sneakers avoiding touching the floor at all costs, I was in my uniform. It was a pretty simple uniform but definitely unflattering for any girl. A white button-up shirt with black slacks. Some of the waitresses added accessories to dress it up. Alicia liked to add a belt to emphasize her waist, while others added cute ties for a pop of color. That was all too much work. I never got the gene for fashion, which was probably attributed to not having a mom during those key years. If I was still able to manage tips and hours, I didn't care how I looked.

"You're in the green section today," Beatrice, one of the

managers, announced. "And Alicia, you're in yellow." I looked behind me and saw Alicia walking up to the counter.

"Ughhhhh, I hate the yellow zone! It's always full of kids," she whined.

Beatrice rolled her eyes, though sometimes I felt she got amusement out of seeing Alicia whine. "Hurry up, you have tables waiting to be bused."

THE AFTERNOON STARTED LIKE NORMAL, FILLED MOSTLY WITH classmates who were stopping in for snacks before heading home. Then, at 4:00, the band kids would file in after their daily practice. Their tables tended to be large, with very few meals being ordered. Which caused their bills to be low, and they always asked for them to be split individually, which was a pain. The tips were also small, but this was also attributed to the fact people categorized the diner as a fast-food place, so any tip was a nice gesture, whether it actually met the 15% rule. People were generally shocked when they found out that wasn't the case, and 15% was supposed to be the minimum.

Finally, around five, the dinner crowd started as parents were beginning to pick up their kids from their extracurricular activities, and we would be busy until Alicia and I left at 7:00. Unfortunately, during the school months, we couldn't work too late, but the crowd usually died down quickly, so we didn't miss out on too many tables.

"Want a ride?" Alicia asked.

"If you don't mind," I said, breathing a sigh of relief. I didn't mind taking the bus places, but I always felt uneasy taking it after work with a wad of cash in my pocket from tips.

Her eyes rolled as she threw her hands into the air. "I wouldn't offer if I did. But I still don't know why you haven't applied for your permit yet. My cousin can find you a car for cheap to practice in!" Alicia blubbered on as we walked to her car.

"We're lucky to have a good bus system here. I also don't know when I'll be able to practice, so I was thinking of waiting until this summer and taking driver's ed." It was kind of hard to practice driving when your adult figure was either drunk, passed out, or both. "Plus, I would have to pay for all the upkeep. It's already pretty tight with the bills and trying to save for college."

"Amy…" Alicia stopped, with a sullen tone to her voice. "I know how much college means to you, but this is the time for us to make our high school memories. I don't want you to miss out or look back years from now and regret not enjoying this time. Just try and remember that, okay?"

"I will." I half grinned at her trying to give the illusion I was taking her message to heart. I hid my clenched hands behind my back.

It was easy for her to not have to worry about money. She came from a loving family. She worked because she wanted to and liked having the perks of extra spending money. When it was time for college, her family would help her in any way they could. I didn't have that luxury. What didn't go to bills at home was all I had for college. I knew when the time came, I wouldn't have the same support. It would probably go the opposite direction with my dad begging for me to stay and help him. This was my only way to a better life. I couldn't lose focus now.

We reached the car, and Alicia cheerfully talked about her weekend with Mike on the way home. I would give the occasional one-word answers to show I was interested. It worked, and she continued the conversation until we reached my house.

"I'll see you tomorrow. Don't forget to call me if you get stuck on your math homework!" I said as I closed the door.

I watched her drive off and pulled my coat closer. I turned

to the dark house. I pulled my backpack around and fished out the house key. I must have just missed Dad. He probably headed out early to grab dinner before his shift started.

I unlocked the door and walked into the quiet house. Luckily, Mr. Johnson allows us to take food home after our shifts. I walked to the kitchen, turning on lights as I walked by, hoping the extra light would make up for the stillness of being alone. I walked over to our black microwave to heat up my meal and yanked on the door to open it, as the button had stopped working years ago. I flipped on the television to drone out the creaks of the old house.

I pulled the burger and fries from the microwave and headed to the table to start my homework. I sat there for the next two hours, working and listening to the distant sound of the TV drifting into the room.

THREE

CRASH!

I sat up ramrod straight, panic spreading through my body, my hand clutching my chest as my heart raced. All I could see was shadows all around me as I was still half asleep. Was my room normally this dark at night? I tried to slow my breathing, hoping the panic would dissipate while straining my eyes to find my clock, but I froze when I heard another sound.

Grughhhhhh… CRASH.

Something was in my room. Every single muscle in my body froze. My chest was tight as my heart fluttered erratically. "GET DOWN!" I heard someone shout, and before I could react, there was a bright light that filled the room. I screamed when I saw it, or at least I think that sound came from me.

My eyes widened when I finally saw it. A black creature stood over my bed. Its eyes were bright red. The type of red you would normally see on Halloween decorations. Bright as if it was being powered by two red lightbulbs. The rest of the body looked almost fluid. Like at any moment, its flesh would start melting off its bones. But the part that held my gaze was its mouth. It opened into a sickly grin where its white fangs bared. Fangs that I swore were the size of my fingers, but that wasn't the worst part. I watched as drool poured from its lips.

"MOVE!" I heard the voice yell again, and almost as if the voice took control over my body, I flung myself off the bed onto the floor. My shoulder caught my fall, and I muffled a painful whimper as the pain from the impact shot through my body.

Then I saw him. A man across my room where the light was coming from. But the light wasn't coming from my room. It was radiating behind him. From bright wings. Not the feathery wings from a bird or what we would imagine angels to have, but wings made of bright yellow fire. He flew across the room toward the creature wielding a long sword. With one slash, he sliced the monster into two. I covered my ears as the creature let out a piercing shriek as it seemed to vaporize.

I stared in shock, my eyes not leaving the man, "… Derek?" I gasped. He turned at the sound of his name being called. It was Derek, but he wasn't the same boy from my class. Those soft brown eyes were replaced by the same yellow that made up his wings. Fiery wings that stretched out of his back and extended the length of his body.

Before I could say another word, everything went black.

I WOKE UP COVERED IN SWEAT AND GASPING FOR AIR. My stomach was churning, shit I was going to puke. My ears were ringing, and my vision was beginning to blur as I looked around my room for the trashcan. I felt the first moment of relief as my eyes locked on. I leaped off the bed just in time to hurl into the basket. I sat with my back pressed against the cool wall next to it, holding my head. Was that a dream? It had to be a dream! I slowly moved my head, making sure the movement wouldn't cause me to get sick again. The streetlights lit up my room. I knew it wasn't pitch dark in here. Another sign that it had just been a weird dream. As I turned to look at the clock, I twisted my shoulder, and it was on fire. I choked out a moan. I slowly got up, still afraid any movement would trigger my still struggling stomach. I stumbled to my light switch, flipping it on. My room was untouched. Nothing out of place. Nothing broken.

I sat on the edge of my bed, rubbing my shoulder. I felt to make sure everything seemed normal, at least what I thought my shoulder should feel like. I must have slept on it weird. Now it was making sense. That's why it hurt so much in my dream. I rested my head back into my hand. These damn dreams! It's been going on for months, waking up covered in sweat with a sense of panic in my chest, but tonight was different. Normally, I wouldn't remember the dream. So, was this it? Was this the dream I was having? But it felt so real, and why was I finally able to remember it, and why would Derek be in it?

I opened the door and headed to the bathroom. My clothes stuck to my body against the sweat. Stripping off my clothes, I turned on the shower. I needed to clear my head, and everything felt sticky. I stood under the water, letting it hit my face, but every time I closed my eyes, all I could see was that creature. No, not a creature that was too kind... a monster.

I stood under the stream until the hot water started to turn cold, then turned the knobs off and opened the shower curtain, grabbing my towel. I let out a long sigh. There was no way I was going to be able to fall asleep now. Wrapping the towel around my body, I walked down the hall toward my room. The light was pouring out against the darkness of the rest of the house.

In my room, I walked to the tall wood dresser. I ran my fingers over the top, feeling the grooves from the wood. I grabbed the handles from the top drawer and yanked it open, electricity shot from my shoulder as my body winced against the pain. I pulled out some new pajamas as mine were soaked in sweat on the bathroom floor. I could feel my heart starting to race in my chest as I felt like someone was still watching me. My body was beginning to shake as the panic continued to spread. *Nothing's there.* I tried to reassure myself, but it didn't help. I quickly pulled on my pajamas and left my room. My hand hesitating on the knob. I half wanted to lock the door behind me. This was one of the few times I wished my dad didn't work nights. Where it would've been nice having another body around.

My mind wandered to when I was a kid. To those nights when I woke up crying from a bad dream. My mom would rush in almost instantly, as if she had a sixth sense when it came to her kids and nightmares. She would crawl into bed with me and stroke my hair until I fell asleep. I could feel the tears pricking in my eyes. I quickly banished the memory away. I tried everything in my power not to think of her. The person who so easily abandoned me.

I slowly made my way downstairs. My good arm reaching out, my hand tracing the wall right beneath the hanging pictures. I couldn't bring myself to look at them. Pictures of our life when we were a family. Instead, I looked toward the living room. I guess that was where I would spend the rest of the night.

The carpet in the living room felt thin against my feet. Worn from neglect and high traffic, as it was one of the few rooms that was actually used on a regular basis. I climbed into one of the oversized chairs, flipping on the television. Fortunately, because of the time, I was able to find a channel that played some old sitcoms. I curled my good arm around my legs and rested the other on top. I sat focusing on the canned laughter slowly pushing the images out of my head. It was a dream, I kept reminding myself, but the last thing I remembered was Derek flashing in my head again, but not the school Derek. The Derek with the fiery wings and piercing eyes.

I awoke to the sound of the unlocking of the door. My whole body was stiff from trying to sleep in such a small area. I don't know how my dad is able to sleep in these chairs night after night.

"Amy? What are you doing down here?" I heard my dad ask with genuine surprise in his voice.

"I couldn't sleep," I said, rubbing my eyes. My right shoulder screamed in pain with the movement. The chair hadn't helped, but was I really expecting it to?

"Oh… maybe you should stay home today. You look terrible," he said, standing in the living room, shifting his weight from one foot to another, clearly uncomfortable.

Thanks, Dad, I thought, but instead responded, "I'll be okay. I have a couple of big assignments due today." That was a lie, but I knew that would deflect any objections. I looked at the clock. Crap, it was already 6:30. I needed to start getting ready if I didn't want to miss the school bus. Thank goodness for that late-night shower!

"Okay… but call me if you feel like you can't make it," he said, rubbing his arm. This had to be the longest conversation we've had in months.

"Thanks, Dad. Do you want me to make coffee or anything?" I asked, making my way to the kitchen.

"No, I'm going to just head to bed." I could hear him starting to climb the stairs.

"Night, Dad." Well, this was an interesting start to my day.

EVEN WITH THE ROUGH START, I MADE IT JUST AS THE BUS pulled up to the stop. My backpack hung on my left shoulder since my right still ached whenever I tried to move it. Maybe I could stop at the nurse's office before class and see if she could take a look. I shook my head at the thought. Her style was more placing a Band-Aid and having you lay down for thirty minutes.

"Amy! You look terrible!" Grace said as I slumped down at the table.

"Thanks... I got no sleep last night, and I did something to my shoulder." I winced as I rolled it, still hoping I could just rub it away.

"If I was you, I would've stayed home," Grace said. "I think you had a pretty good excuse."

I was starting to think she was right, but if I missed school, I would have to call out of work, too. "I'll be fine," I said, plastering on a grin.

Thankfully today I had study hall, so maybe I could sit in the back and get a little nap in. The teacher normally didn't care what we did as long as we were quiet. I pulled my bag around and laid it on the picnic table, making a makeshift pillow. I felt like I barely closed my eyes before Alicia nudged me signaling the bell had gone off. I didn't even notice she had joined us. Today was going to be rough.

The morning was a blur. Hopefully, none of the topics were important because if I had been given a surprise quiz on the last four classes, I would have failed. Gratefully, my gym teacher was having a good day and let me sit out of the planned activity because of my shoulder. It helped that we were practicing catching in our baseball/softball phase of the class, so it was going to be even more of a strain on my shoulder. Unfortunately, that meant organizing the storage room.

When the rest of the class made their way to the gymnasium to begin warm-ups, I went across the hall to the small closet. When the door opened, the smell of sweat and rubber balls engulfed me. Everything was shoved haphazardly on the shelves. Bins tossed in the aisle, making it almost impossible to walk in. What was I supposed to accomplish in a period? This room needed a month of work at least.

It took about fifteen minutes to really gain momentum, but I had finally made a path inside and was starting to work on detangling the jump ropes. They were more twisted than the Christmas lights you pulled out of the attic every year. My attention was focused hard on all the knots. I jumped as someone yanked the door open. My heart thumping hard, I was convinced it would break through my chest, like one of those horror movies where the alien bursts out. I must still be on edge from last night.

"Oh, sorry..." a familiar voice muttered. "Coach sent me in to get some more balls."

"Hi, Ben," I said, glancing around before finding the basket of baseballs. "Here, do you think this is enough?"

He just shrugged. "Who knows, everyone keeps losing them over the fence. I think Coach Davidson is starting to regret today's activity. By the way are you okay? Why aren't you out there with us?"

"Ugh... long story, but I hurt my shoulder, so I thought it'd be best to baby it a little bit today." Again, rolling my shoulder to emphasize. I don't know why that was my go-to move, it would instantly cause a bolt of pain through my body.

"Ouch! That sucks," Ben said, grimacing. We stood awkwardly in silence. We were about the same height, but that was normal as the girls were almost done growing, and the boys had just started. "So..." he began running his hand on the wire basket, "are you going to Tyler's Halloween party next weekend?"

I let out a quiet sigh. I guess Alicia was right. This seemed like an important party this year. "I don't know yet. I'm supposed to head to the mall this weekend to look at costumes. But I'm not big into parties." I hesitated for a minute, then thought I should probably return the question. "What about you?"

"Yeah, I think we are going to go. If it's lame, I heard they are doing some monster movies in the park, so that would be cool to see," Ben said.

When he said we, he was referring to his soccer team. They always went to parties together. The different sports teams tended to stay together. The only people who would cross social circles were the players who played multiple sports. Other than that, the only time they would interact was to trash-talk each other about which sport was superior.

"You should go, though. We are dressing up as a team of zombie soccer players. Gabe found someone who does monster makeup, so we are going to look badass." A grin appeared on his face as he thought about their costume, not very original, but it was nice to see him excited about it. "I better head back before coach sends in a rescue team. This closet really is a disaster zone."

I laughed and waved bye with my good arm as he left. I turned around and just rubbed my face with my hand. Ben was right. This should be roped off as a hazard zone. Though I would think more biohazard. I had found one of the big culprits of the sweat smell as I found a ball of used uniforms had been thrown in the back corner.

TWENTY MINUTES LATER, THE BELL RANG, ENDING CLASS. I WAS actually pretty proud of my progress. I was able to organize one whole wall. Maybe I could talk Coach Davidson into letting me finish this project and not have to suffer humiliation with my lack of hand and eye coordination. But I highly doubted he would go for it.

"Oh look, it's Ms. I'm Too Good to Play Ball," I heard someone mock as I walked into the locker room.

What the hell? I thought when I opened my locker. I hated high school, one change from the normal, and you were an instant target. I tried to just ignore them as I pulled off my clothes, but I knew if I looked in the mirror, I would see the pink start appearing on my cheeks. Stupid cheeks, why couldn't I have more control of you!

"Didn't you hear... *her shoulder hurts,*" someone responded in a mocking tone.

I couldn't help it. I glanced over to see who it was coming from. I was shocked to see it was Becca, Derek's girlfriend, and her friend Samantha making the commotion. They tended to stay to themselves. What the hell did I do to piss them off?

Becca was part of Derek's small circle. There was a total of ten of them that stuck together. I'm not sure why they were all so close. They weren't a part of a club like the soccer team, but they had been that way since they entered high school. But that wasn't totally abnormal. They had gone to the same middle school and, like a lot of kids, had formed friendships then that probably helped them through the beginning year of high school. I thought of Alicia and Grace. We were the same. If it wasn't for our early friendship, would we be friends now? We didn't really have much in common.

Becca was stunning. She was one of the reasons girls hated gym. One of the few girls that required gym clothing actually looked good on. While the rest of us looked like we were wearing cloth bags. Becca's friend Samantha wasn't much different. She had wavy brown hair and green eyes, versus Becca's long blonde hair and blue eyes. Even though they were both pretty, if Becca was ever around, her looks would always fall second. I was always surprised that neither of them ever tried out for cheerleading as they both looked like your typical gymnast.

Actually, now thinking about it, their whole group was very attractive and fit. If you came across them, you would think they were all a part of some sports team. One with some type of contact sport like football or wrestling. There were seven boys and three girls that made up their group.

I slammed my locker door, trying to get them out of my head. Quickly changing and skipping the shower since I really didn't work up a sweat. Though I hoped I didn't absorb the smell, I left, heading to the cafeteria. I couldn't get away from them quick enough. I was only able to breathe a sigh of relief when I spotted Alicia and Grace. What would I do if we didn't have lunch together?

"Feeling any better?" Grace asked as I sat down.

"A little, I'm hoping lunch will boost my energy," I said, sliding onto the bench.

"Do you want me to cover your shift?" Alicia asked as she stabbed her salad. Alicia always bought her lunch. She thought it was tacky to carry a lunchbox and wouldn't be caught dead with a brown paper bag.

"No, worse comes to worst, I'll grab an energy drink at the gas station on my way in. But thanks, though." I could see her breathe a sigh of relief. She was only offering to be nice, but I knew she didn't want the hours. She only worked the bare minimum to keep the job, and even then, I usually covered her callouts at least a shift or two a month.

I pulled my peanut butter and jelly sandwich out of my lunchbox. I didn't care if it was tacky, as Alicia commented most of the time. I would probably be eligible for free lunch, but I didn't want the judgment that came along with it as the cashier asked for your ID number and wrote your name on the pad before waving you on. The sign that your family is poor. A PB&J sandwich from a lunchbox was just fine.

I just sat in silence as Alicia and Grace babbled on about some gossip from earlier. Something about someone breaking up with someone else because they had walked in on them kissing their brother. Or was it their sister? I just shook my head. The scandals of high school.

Chemistry was a disaster. It was lab day, and my lack of sleep was catching up with me. I read the ingredients wrong. Instead of five milligrams of baking soda, I put in five grams, and the chemical reaction we were supposed to observe in our beakers ended up covering our desks. Luckily it wasn't any dangerous chemicals, and we didn't have to jump into the chemical shower at the end of the room. But Sally, my lab partner, was pissed.

Most days I was thankful I was teamed up with Sally. Unlike other lab partners who thought it was hilarious to see what chaos they could cause, we both cared about getting good grades in class. We both worked hard, but this class was Sally's passion. She was taking this class as her prerequisite for next year when she would take AP Chemistry. It was all a part of her plan to go on and be a pharmacist like her father. Another person who had the next ten years perfectly planned out. Who couldn't afford any misstep to derail it.

I was a little annoyed at how much she overreacted. This was my first mistake all year. I wonder if this is how Alicia and Grace felt whenever I went off on finances and my goals for college. Maybe I should think a little bit more about what Alicia said and slow down a little and, as she put it, enjoy the little things.

The bell rang just as we finished cleaning up our station, so I took that opportunity to swiftly exit. Leaving Sally and her mini meltdown, as she was trying to redo the assignment, but correctly this time. I headed to the class I was looking forward to all day. Study hall. Fifty minutes to breathe. I usually took advantage of this time to catch up on any projects or assignments, but today, I was going to put my headphones in and sleep.

I walked into the lecture hall. It was three times the size of one of our classrooms. The room was built on a slant, so each row of seats was a little higher than the next. The chairs were right next to each other with the half desks you would swing up. For study hall, they would tend to combine two to three classes together depending on what liberal arts class you were in.

I was fortunate, and our study hall was only made up of two classes, so we were able to spread out more and had the ability to change up our seats. I quickly signed the sign-in sheet, which was how they took attendance and headed up the ramp to the second to back row. I tugged my backpack off, laying it on the small desk, and pulled open the zipper. Laying safely inside was the old MP3 player. Most people used their phones to listen to music. I doubt they still made them. But I couldn't part with it. It had been Cole's when he was younger. When I listened to it, I always felt a little closer to him.

Just when I put the headphones in my ears, I suddenly sucked in air. The door opened, and Derek walked in, pausing at the desk to sign his name. I never realized we shared study hall together, as we didn't share the same art class. He turned to head up the ramp, and all I could see was the vision of him from my dream. Blazing yellow eyes with large fiery wings. I could feel the fear begin to rise in my chest as my mind went back to last night. The monster flashed in my head. I quickly shook my head, bringing myself back to reality. I took a few deep breaths to help calm myself.

I watched as he stopped and turned his head back to the door. Of course, Becca was also in this class. Unfortunately, she *was* in my art class. I could feel myself sliding down my seat. Hoping she wouldn't see me, and she was over gym class. We linked eyes for a quick moment, and I swore she was throwing me daggers. Seriously, what did I do to piss her off?

I could feel myself holding my breath as Derek walked up the ramp to his seat. What was I expecting, him to recognize me? To look at me and be like, yeah, that dream was crazy! Or was I expecting him to grow the wings I imagined and fly around the room? I rested my head on my hand and rubbed my forehead. "Snap out of it," I quietly told myself.

Self-conscious, I couldn't sleep. I pulled out my English book. Maybe I could read ahead. This way, I could get a jump on the assigned reading. But that didn't work. I read the same line twenty times before putting it down.

"Hey, Amy! You never sit back here." I heard the familiar voice call behind me.

I turned to see Ben sitting diagonally from me. "I didn't know we had study hall together."

"Yeah, I typically stay back here with the delinquents," he said, winking. "How's the shoulder?"

"It's feeling a little better." I had stopped at the nurse's office before chemistry, and she gave me some green gel to put on it. "Ms. Nelson doesn't think I did any permanent damage, just a minor strain."

"Good. I would hate to see it keep you from going to the party." He winked at me. I could hear a loud shush coming from the front. He just rolled his eyes. "What are you doing after school?"

"Oh, I have to work," I whispered, glancing at the front. I was always terrified of getting in trouble. Alicia and Grace always made fun of me for it.

He brought his volume to the same whisper. "Where do you work?"

"Charlie's Diner," I responded.

"I love that place. They have the best milkshakes!" He responded a little too loudly, which caused a stern look from Mr. Steely, but Ben just ignored him, probably because he was also the soccer coach. "Maybe I should stop in sometime when you are working."

I could feel my cheeks starting to burn. "Yeah, that would be nice," I said, signaling to my book as I turned around. Well, that was new. Guys rarely gave me the time of day.

The time went quicker after that. Once the bell rang and

we were gathering our stuff, a piece of paper fell on my bag. I saw Ben get up and wink as he walked out of the class. I quickly opened it and saw his number written down with the words *'text me'* next to it. I folded it and stashed it in my book before putting it in my bag. I couldn't help the smile spreading across my face.

I was still thinking about the note when I walked into English. The class that I always looked forward to, but this time, I walked in, and my heart sank.

FOUR

"Hi, class," the nasally woman announced from the front. We were all huddled against the back of the room as we had been instructed. A few boys were tasked with moving the desks.

I slowly raised my hand. "Yes..." the woman responded looking at her sheet but not sure how to put the names to faces.

"Amy," I started awkwardly, pointing to myself. "Where is Ms. Fuller?" As I asked, I felt a sudden feeling of dread wash over my body. This didn't feel like the typical substitute situation. This lady had a bigger presence to her than most substitutes. And a substitute wouldn't dare to change up the desks in a classroom.

"Oh... Ms. Fuller had to unfortunately take a leave of absence. I will be taking over the class until... or if I should say *if* she returns," she said as her attention snapped to the desks. "Now, when I call your name, you will go to your desk, and that will be your assigned seat moving forward."

To make matters worse, I was seated in front of Becca. Normally, this wouldn't bother me, but after today, all I could feel were her eyes driving holes in my back. Every snicker and whisper made me self-conscious. I never took her for a mean girl… or maybe I was just lucky enough to never be in her sights. That changed today. Did she somehow know I had a dream about her boyfriend last night? My cheeks warmed as his face popped into my mind once again. I slightly shook my head, as if the movement erased memories like those old sketch boards we used as kids.

"Psst…" my new neighbor Jimmy murmured. "Did you read the book?"

I slid lower in my chair. My favorite class was fading into my least. All I could think was I hoped Ms. Fuller was okay.

"Now what were you guys learning?" Based on what she wrote on the board, her name was Mrs. Haines, she never made a formal introduction. She was an older woman whose hair you could tell was graying, covered by a cheap hair dye. What was supposed to be auburn just turned a weird shade of red. Her face would be the poster child of the statement 'don't make that face or it will freeze that way' as it stayed in a constant grimace. The type that makes you wonder when the last time she smiled. Maybe in 1962?

A boy who sat in front of her desk handed her a copy of the book we were reading. She quickly snatched it out of his hands before tossing it onto her desk.

"Ugh… I hate that book. Change of plans, class. I have some articles with me. I'm going to pass them out, and I would like you all to pair up with the person sitting next to you. I want you to read it together and then prepare a presentation for the class, and we are going to go around the room so you can summarize what you read," she said, pulling photocopy pages out of a folder from her bag.

I was shocked at how quickly she discarded what we had spent weeks reading. This was the time for them to introduce us to different types of literature. Instead, I was handed a six-page article on "*Reading the Room – How to Make a Successful Presentation.*" This was just busy work.

The rest of the time fumbled on. Everyone was reeling from the change. I could tell the people who were most likely getting their information from the book from the internet were happy about the change. But everyone awkwardly went around the room half-heartedly presenting an article we spent twenty minutes reading.

The bell rang, and we anxiously started to put our stuff away, ready to leave the awkwardness presenting usually brought behind us. We all jumped when we heard a loud smack echo from the room.

"Excuse me," the nasally voice echoed again. This time, she was holding a ruler, which explained the loud noise. "The bell does not release the class. *I do*. Sit down and wait for my direction to pack up." Everyone slowly lowered themselves down. After waiting in painful silence, she finally spoke, "Okay, you may be excused."

We filed out of the class feeling like we were back in elementary school. "What was that about?" I could hear a student mutter to a fellow classmate.

"I don't know, but I hope Ms. Fuller is okay," another student chimed in.

"I heard she got fired because she was dating a student!" someone whispered.

Oh great. Here goes the typical high school rumors. I quickly made my way through the hallway that led to outside. I decided to skip the gas station. Surprisingly, the shock from the last class pulled me out of the daze.

I walked into the already full diner and quickly headed to the bathroom to change.

"Amy, can you clock in a little early? We are slammed this afternoon. Apparently, there was a conference down the street that just got out," Beatrice asked as I walked behind the counter.

"Of course!" I said cheerfully. Any excuse to get more hours and more tables meant more tips.

"Perfect, you can take the red section today. Your first table is being seated now." She gestured to a large group of students being seated.

I nearly dropped my badge as I was swiping to clock in. What was Derek and his group doing here? And out of all the luck, why was I assigned to them. I couldn't help but think of Grace's comment today. I really should have stayed in bed.

I took a deep breath and walked toward the table. Keep smiling, I told myself. If you talk when you smile, it makes you sound cheery. The pep talk in my head wasn't helping. "Hi, my name is Amy, and I will be your waitress today." I felt so stupid introducing myself. Of course, they all knew who I was… or at least I thought they should.

"We will have ten waters," Becca answered for the group. *Free waters*, I wrote on my pad. "And do you guys have bread or chips or something we can have?"

I had to quickly catch myself. Bread? Where did she think she was? Would a pack of hamburger buns do, I smugly thought. But I smiled as sweetly as I could muster and responded. "No, I'm sorry, but I could put an order of fries in?"

"Are the fries free?" she shot back.

"Um, no, it's two-forty-nine for a large fry." Was she serious? I really hoped this wasn't going to be a group that thought they could get free food because we went to school together.

"Then no, the waters are fine. We need a few minutes to look at the menu." She waved her hand, dismissing me. I could feel the anger starting to burn inside, and I'm sure my cheeks were starting to turn red. But I held my composure. All I could think of was how lucky Alicia wasn't working today.

She probably would've jumped across the table already. I smiled, walking back to the order screens as I imagined the scene playing out in my head.

I stopped at another table to get a drink order in before returning to their table, hoping the extra time would be enough for them to decide on their orders. The less I had to go to the table, the better.

"Finally, we thought you forgot about us." Becca sighed. "I guess not all waitresses work for tips."

"I'm sorry for the delay," I said through clenched teeth. "Are you ready to order?"

I quickly took their orders as I went around the tables, then immediately left. I didn't want to spend any more time than I had to around Becca.

"Becca, why are you being such a bitch?" I heard someone mutter as I walked away. Okay, so this wasn't her normal behavior. What the hell did I do to piss her off?

"Dominic, shut up," she snapped back.

I put their orders into the computer. Four burgers, two salads, one soup, and three chicken tenders. I was surprised they all ordered meals. Everyone even ordered a shake.

The rest of their meal went without any more outbursts. I checked on them a few times, and I was equally shocked when they ordered dessert. They seemed to have a bit of a sweet tooth. As expected, I had to split the check ten different ways, which was pretty normal for the high school crowd, but it was still a pain.

After they all left, I went back to the table with the busing tray and cleared the table. I sighed when I picked up the tip. Three dollars off a hundred-dollar bill table. Also, pretty typical of the high school crowd. But it didn't help when my area was mostly larger tables. I probably wouldn't make my usual $8.50 an hour tonight. I tucked the money into my apron and finished clearing the table.

I was exhausted. It ended up being a late evening. The

dinner crowd never slowed, so no one had time to pitch in with evening prep. Everyone worked up until their shift ended and then clocked out. I felt bad leaving Beatrice alone to close, so I decided to set up in one of the back booths that we normally closed off to the customers, as the cushions were super worn and had quite a few tears in them. I had dinner and spent the time working on homework until she was ready to close. It made no difference being alone in a booth or alone at home. I still made sure to clock out at 7:00 so Mr. Johnson wouldn't panic in the morning.

After the last dish was washed and put away, I waved to Beatrice and headed out. I walked to the bus stop, wishing again Alicia had been working tonight, but knowing if she had, she wouldn't have agreed to stay late.

When I finally reached the bus stop, I slumped onto the dimly lit bench. My shoulder was beginning to ache again, the rush from work allowing me to keep my mind off of it, but now it felt worse. Probably because of the trays I was carrying back and forth. I glanced at my watch. I couldn't believe it was already ten. I had to count back from my usual bus route to determine how long it would be before the bus arrived. About twenty minutes, not terrible. I pulled my jacket closer and slid further down until my head could rest on the back.

Again, I was feeling that sense of panic that I had felt in my room. It was normal for me to be sitting at night waiting for the bus. I did this every time I worked alone. I could feel the hair rising on my arms and feeling as if I was being watched. My body jerked as I noticed two red eyes out of the corner of my eye. My shoulders slumped when I realized it was the back of a car. Damn dream! Just get out of my head!

I put my headphones into my ears and chose one of Cole's favorite playlists on my MP3 player, and let the music drown out the outside world. If I just focused on the words, I could stop envisioning that creature. I was half expecting it to leap out from behind the trees. I was so wrapped up in my internal battle I didn't even notice the car pull up to the bus stop curb until it was parked in front of me. Their windows were so dark I wondered if they were street legal. At the same time, that thought was passing through my head, the window started to go down.

My heart pounded as a new type of panic started to fill my body. My fingers tightly wrapped around my backpack as I pressed it as close as I could to my body. I forgot to remove my tips from my wallet the last few nights, so there had to be at least a hundred dollars in tips in there. The pounding of my pulse was deafening in my ears. If someone was next to me, would they hear it as well? What if this was a kidnapper or robber? Should I run? I took a quick glance to my left. It was lined with buildings. I looked back at the figure that was finally visible against the light. As if someone had hit a switch, my whole body seemed to release from the tension. It was Derek. He was leaning across the seats so he could talk through the open window.

I popped my headphones out of my ears because all I could see was him mouthing something. "I'm s-s-sorry. What did you s-s-say?" I stammered as my body was still recovering from the unnecessary panic he had caused. Did he not think how creepy he was being?

"Do you want a ride?" he asked, motioning to the open passenger seat. He drove a black car—what I think they call a coup? It was shiny and very new. I'm guessing one of the newer models. If not this year's model, then I would be shocked if it wasn't last years.

"Oh…" Again, when I looked at him, all I saw were the blazing yellow eyes. I quickly blinked the image away. "Thanks for the offer, but I'm okay. The bus should be here soon."

I could tell he didn't like my answer, but I didn't know him. I didn't feel comfortable sitting in a car alone with him. Especially after all my run-ins with his girlfriend today. If she was as nasty as she was today, what kind of guy would put up with that?

"It's pretty late. It isn't safe for you to be out here alone." I could see the disapproving look on his face.

"I'm okay, really," I tried to reassure him. "I take the bus all the time. I'm not worried. Thanks, though." I gave an awkward smile, hoping that would ease him.

I could see him let out a labored sigh. He quickly rolled up his window and pulled out of the bus stop. I was expecting to see him pull down the street, but instead, he did a quick U-turn and parked in the diner parking lot. He got out of his car and walked toward the bus stop. He clicked his keys behind him as he walked toward me, and I could hear the beep from the car, signaling it was locked.

Without a word, he slid next to me on the bench. I could feel my cheeks starting to flush. I really have to start wearing makeup if I keep this up.

"I'm really okay," I said, staring at my hands, but he was sitting so close I could smell him. He had a soothing smell, a mix of leather and some nature scent. I thought of the candles I collected at home, trying to match the scent. Maybe sandalwood? For some reason the smell put a sense of calm over me, giving me the feeling that everything was going to be okay. I hadn't noticed how on edge I was.

He shrugged next to me. "I can't in good conscience leave you alone out here. I would rather be driving home in my warm car, but I guess the bus will do." He typed something quickly into his phone and then placed it in his pocket. "Oh... by the way, this is for you." He held up three fives in his hand. "We didn't know until after we left that Becca swiped the money off the table. I'm sorry for how she was acting. I have no idea what got into her today. She is usually never that... moody."

"Oh... that's okay. I really wasn't expecting anything more," I said awkwardly, taking the money.

"Why not?" he asked, cocking his eyebrow.

"Oh… well… usually when classmates come in, they typically don't follow the normal fifteen percent rule," My hands moving frantically as I spoke, which usually happened when I was flustered. I didn't want it to sound like I was complaining.

"Well, just because other people don't, doesn't make it right," he said matter-of-factly.

We sat in silence as we waited for the bus. I couldn't lie. It was kind of nice having someone with me so late at night. I did feel a little safer, even if we were practically strangers. I was shocked when I heard the bus pulling up to the stop. I couldn't believe twenty minutes had already passed. It let out a loud hiss as the bus settled and the driver opened the door.

"Well, thank you for staying with me," I said. I could feel the grin spreading on my face, which I quickly tried to hide.

I watched as he stood up and stretched. I was half waiting for him to say something back, but I was afraid the driver was going to get impatient, so I turned and boarded the bus. I nearly froze when I heard steps follow me. After swiping my card and waiting for the typical beep, I quickly shuffled to one of the benches that faced the opposite windows. This time, Derek took a seat opposite of me. I awkwardly stared at my hands, afraid to make eye contact. Why was my heart beating so hard?

"Umm… what about your car?" I asked as the bus pulled away.

He just shrugged. "I'll come get it later." He stopped for a second. "Like I said, it isn't safe for you to be out so late on your own."

"Heh… well, it is nice to have someone to keep me company. Will you be my escort on all my late nights?" As soon as the words were out, I wanted to pull them back in. I sounded like an idiot. My heart was beating so hard, I swore Derek could hear it, but all my mind kept jumping to was my dream.

"Can I see your phone?" he asked, extending his hand.

"Um… sure." I fumbled it out of my bag. I was starting to feel self-conscience about the age of my phone. I'm pretty sure my screen had at least three cracks. I watched as he saved his phone number.

"If you have to work late again, text me. I'll always be available to escort you," he said with a grin, handing back my phone. I think that was the first time I ever saw him smile. Most of the time, he had a look of indifference on his face. "Just do me a favor and send me a quick text so I know who's texting me."

"Okay."

I texted "hi" with a smiling emoji. Already overanalyzing my message. I heard his phone faintly chirp as it received the message.

He turned his face, so he was looking out the front windows. My heart hadn't slowed since we sat down. I hadn't stopped thinking about him since the dream, and now we were here alone together. Well, mostly alone. There were a few other passengers scattered through the bus. Even in the cold, my hands were starting to sweat.

I glanced outside and realized I was about to miss my stop. I pulled the cord, hearing that familiar ding. The bus came to a quicker-than-normal stop due to my short notice. As I got up, I noticed Derek also rising from his seat.

"Oh, no. It's really okay. My house is literally right down the road. I can make it from here." My words fumbled out at the chaotic speed I was speaking. My mind flashed back to my house, and all I could think of was a haunted house with all the dark windows.

He gave me a stern, but warm look. I closed my mouth and exited the bus with him close behind. Once we exited the bus, I noticed he was texting someone. He turned and looked at me again.

"Where's your house?" he asked.

I turned and pointed down the street. "It's five houses down. I'm really okay."

He was lost in thought. His eyebrows furrowed as if he was doing some complex calculation in his head. I wonder if he was calculating how fast he could run in that distance if someone jumped out and tried to mug me. I laughed quietly, picturing him taking the runner stance and taking off down my road. "Okay, are you sure you don't want me to walk with you?"

Yes, yes, yes! I didn't want this to be the end, but instead, I shook my head. "No, I'm okay from here. But how are you getting home?"

"Oh, don't worry about me. One of my friends is close by. He's going to pick me up."

"Do you want me to wait until they get here?" Was it right for me to leave him alone after everything he did for me?

I was surprised at the look of confusion on his face, but the look was brief. A smile replaced it. I could get used to seeing his smile. "Unless you want us to drive you to your door, I'll be fine." Then he did something even more surprising.

He winked at me.

"Yeah, I'm good." I turned to walk away, but I hesitated. "Thank you for tonight." Before he could respond, I briskly left. Something between a jog and a fast run.

Using my key, I opened the door and locked it behind me. For the first time in a long time, when I walked through my house, it felt a little less lonely.

FIVE

I walked to the kitchen table and placed my backpack and jacket on the chair. As I was heading to the bathroom to change out of my uniform, I felt my phone buzz. I forgot to take it off vibrate after work. I pulled it out and turned on the screen. It was probably Alicia asking about some homework assignment. I stared at the notification for a minute before opening it. It was from Derek.

My rides here. Have a good night.

I could feel the stupid grin taking up my face as I placed my phone into my back pocket. I quietly unpacked my bag, thinking about what I needed to bring tomorrow. Thankfully, I finished all my homework in the diner. I felt sadness wash over me as I pulled out the English book, knowing we wouldn't finish it. It was starting to get interesting. Maybe if I have time, I'll just read it on my own. As I was moving it to the kitchen table, I saw a piece of paper fall out of it.

I knelt down, picking it up off the ground, and curiously I opened it. Ben's number. I totally forgot he gave this to me. It felt like days had passed since study hall. I stared at his handwriting for a few seconds. His number with the words *text me* next to it. My eyes flipped to the clock. Was it too late to text? It was already after eleven. But he might get offended if I didn't respond. I decided to send something short, hopefully he kept his phone off at night.

> Sorry for the late text. Just got home from work. Long day! This is Amy btw... from study hall

I felt dumb for sending the last part, but I wasn't sure if he knew a lot of Amys. Maybe he was in the habit of giving out his number? As I continued to debate my message in my head, my phone pinged back.

> Man that sucks! If your shoulders better tomorrow partner with me in gym I think we are graduating to bats.

Wow, I not only spoke to two boys in one day, but they were also texting me. I couldn't remember the last time a boy took notice of me, let alone held a conversation with me. I ran my hand through my hair. Maybe this hairstyle was good luck. I was trying to remember where I put that stylist's card. Maybe I would keep that appointment.

I thought more about the day and started to overanalyze as I typically did. Well... I guess one boy took notice. Derek was in a relationship with Becca. He was probably just feeling guilty for how she treated me at the diner. His words rang in my mind, 'If you have to work late again, text me. I'll always be available to escort you.' I could feel my heart drop a little. He didn't mean that... he was just feeling guilty, kind of like damage control.

But Ben, from what I knew, was a nice guy. He was leaner than Derek, still muscular, but more like a runner than a football player. He asked if I would be going to the party. Was he hinting at going together? Maybe I would ask Alicia and see what she knew. She was close to the soccer players since her boyfriend used to play on their team, and she went to almost every game.

Alicia's boyfriend ended up quitting after losing a spot on the varsity team. Alicia said something about favoritism on the team, but from the few games I attended with her, I noticed he spent most of his time on the bench.

No, I decided it was best to wait before bringing it up to Alicia. This was the first boy who I think was even somewhat interested in me, and knowing her, she would blow it out of proportion. I would see how gym went tomorrow. I wasn't even thinking of where I was going until I was in my doorway.

I stood, gazing into my bedroom, which was illuminated by the hallway light. Well, I better get this over with. I walked in and flipped on the light. It felt like ages since last night and that dream. I sat on the end of my bed taking in my surroundings.

Why was I letting this dream get to me? I've had many nightmares in the past. They were bad after Cole died. During that time, I would have two types of dreams. The first type, I was typically a passenger in the car the day of the accident. I remember how frantic I would be as I tried to get out of the car before it was engulfed in flames. The second was even worse. I would be following Cole that day, but no matter how much I screamed or tried to stop him, he wouldn't hear me. I was a ghost watching our last moments together, knowing what was going to happen. I would always wake up feeling helpless and lost. I shivered thinking about them. I could also feel the familiar pain in my chest whenever I thought about him. I forced the dreams and him out of my head.

I lay on my back, staring up at the ceiling. As I watched the ceiling fan rotate, I pulled out my phone and opened the CircleUp app. It was a popular app all the kids used at school. A way to stay in touch with each other and post the highlights of peoples' days. Also, it was another way to track the school romances that constantly change. The screen loaded quickly bringing up all my friend's activity. The first notification was from Alicia and Mike. It looked like they checked into the theater tonight. I wondered what movie they saw. I quickly tried to take a mental note of the movies I had seen previews for. Most likely, they were seeing some new horror movie, just in time for Halloween.

As I kept scrolling, I saw a new album Grace had recently posted. Pictures, most likely from the salon, of girls with wild-styled hair and unique coloring. It reminded me of the hair-stylist who did my hair. I think her name was Carol, or was it Cathy? I really had to find that card. I let out a sigh of relief when I noticed my recent haircut wasn't on the list. I wouldn't be surprised to find myself on one of those before and after advertisements.

I knew exactly what I was going to look for before I even opened the app. I clicked on Alicia's profile and went to her list of friends. Her profile would be the best to use as she had more friends than Grace and I combined. I typed Ben in the search bar. Of course, it brought up five matches. How does she know so many Bens? I've only met two in my life and only one I would be comfortable adding as a friend. I scrolled down until I found our classmate.

I shouldn't have been shocked when his profile loaded. As luck would have it, it didn't have any privacy settings, so I could see all his pictures and posts. The majority of his pictures were of him and his teammates on and off the field. The most recent was from their game against our rival school. I clicked through the pictures until I saw a close-up of him. He was preparing to kick the ball into the goal. His left leg was planted firmly as his right leg was extended back preparing to bring it forward to make contact. I wondered if he made the goal.

Next, I clicked on his profile pictures, flipping through them. I smiled as I saw the lack of girls in any of the pictures.

That didn't mean he never had a girlfriend, as people were pretty petty after breakups and tended to delete all traces of each other on their accounts. Again, the majority was him posing in his uniform either solo or with his teammates.

I was about to close the app but then stopped and went back to Alicia's profile. I hesitated for a moment before typing the name in the search bar. Derek. What was I doing... why was I obsessing about him? He had a girlfriend for one. And second... well, second, he had a girlfriend. The search brought up three matches, but none were the right Derek. I then clicked up in the main search bar and typed his name again. This time, I searched for his full name, Derek Adler. That seemed to work as it brought up fifty results. I scrolled down until I found the one I thought was his.

When I clicked it, I first thought maybe it was set to private because it was so bare, but as I navigated through the page, I could see the signs that the security settings were off. The only messages on his profile were the ones he was tagged in. Same with his photos. His profile picture was one of the few of just him, and even that one looked like it was snapped quickly by someone else. I stared at his photo for a few minutes. It was a little out of focus, but he was sitting on what looked like the school bleachers. His face held his normal dismissive face. As if he was annoyed with everything that was happening that day.

I moved on to his tagged pictures. I smiled as I saw more pictures of him and his friends. A lot of times, they gave the impression that they were too "mature" for high school matters, but in these photos, I could see them laughing and, well, acting like the rest of us. While I was flipping through the pictures, the corner of my phone caught my attention as it almost shouted the time. One thirty! I was going to be regretting this tomorrow, especially after two nights in a row with little sleep.

I placed my phone on my night table and picked up a

clean pair of pajamas. Taking them down the hall to the bathroom, I reached for the switch and flipped it on. My reflection stared back at me as the light flickered on. Out of everything about me, I always thought my eyes were my best feature. They were a deep green color, but this time, they were accompanied by dark circles. Instinctively my fingers ran through my hair as they were still processing the new length. Shaking my head to pull myself away from analyzing every detail, I grabbed my toothbrush and brushed my teeth.

Before I entered my room, I did one last glance. The closet caught my attention. I chewed on my lip as I walked across the room. I felt like a baby as I flipped on the light and closed the door. Pulling the cord from the middle of the room turned the light off but kept the fan turning. I liked not only having the feel of moving air but also the sound of the motor turning the blades. I then flipped one of the switches on the wall, turning off the floor lamp. Even with the door closed, the light through the cracks of the closet left a warm glow in the room. Much better than the usual murky black. I pulled up the covers and laid my head on the pillow. That was the last thing I could remember.

"UGH..." I SWUNG MY HAND OUT FROM UNDER THE BLANKET, blindly slapping the nightstand, trying to find my clock as the alarm blared, finally making contact. I lay there for a few minutes, listening to the quiet creaks of the old house.

"The sun isn't up. I shouldn't be," I mumbled to my room, kicking off my blanket and cursing at my past self for staying up so late. My future self always got punished for my past self's actions.

I just let my body go through the morning routine, taking note that tonight, I was going to go to bed early. Fortunately, I didn't have work today. I heard the toaster pop, signaling my toast was ready. Snatching them out of the toaster, I grabbed my backpack and jacket and headed out the door.

I guess being on autopilot was more efficient than my usual self because when I made it to the bus stop, I was one of the first people to arrive. The early morning fog still hung on the ground, making it feel a little eerie. I stood on the outskirts, kicking at a stubborn stone in the cement. After about five minutes, more people started showing up, and soon, there wasn't much room to move around unless you wanted to stand on someone's lawn or in the middle of the street.

The flashing white light approached, signaling the bus. I guess everyone on our schedule somehow changed their clock five minutes early because, for once, our route was running early, or the fog was making everyone else late. By the time our bus made it to school, it was the second one to arrive when, on normal days, we were typically in the last round. We stepped out to a quiet building. My eyes located our normal hangout and saw our table bare, which meant neither Alicia nor Grace had arrived. I shifted my backpack and headed toward the table anyway.

I decided to help pass the time. I would take the seat facing the buses and just enjoy people-watching. Most of the students, I noticed, stumbled off the bus, still half asleep. I understood the reason for having us start so early, as the elementary school and middle school shared the same buses, but it didn't make it any easier. Then, you had the wave of students who drove to school instead. They had more energy, probably because of the coffee in their hands as they took detours first. I wonder if any of them stopped at Charlie's looking for the diner to go cups but not seeing any. It seemed most fancied the popular coffee shops.

The air caught in my throat when I saw the black car pull into the parking lot. Guess that means Derek got his car last night. Which made sense. He said his friend was picking him up, so he probably had them take him back to the diner. I wonder which friend picked him up. I watched as three other people exited his car. No surprise, Becca. She stretched as she opened the passenger side and stepped out, her shirt riding up, showing off her bare midriff. She flipped her hair over her shoulder before turning around and popping forward the seat.

Aiden and Hannah crawled out of the backseats. Aiden's hands almost touched the parking lot as he pulled himself out from behind the raised seats. It was surprising he could fit back there. He walked next to Derek, and I noticed he stood a little shorter than him, but still taller than most of the boys in our school. Hannah, however, made climbing out of the back seem effortless. She looked completely different from Becca, with her short black hair, the type that was almost shaved on the sides but still had length at the top. The hairstyle you would picture in those ends of the world movies that's usually donned by the badass woman.

"Wow! I can't believe you beat us!" I heard Alicia call, pulling my attention away from the car.

"I know, I guess all the stars magically aligned on our route today," I responded as they both took their seats.

"So… about math…" Alicia started, I just shook my head, pulling out the math homework. Some things will never change.

THE REST OF THE WEEK FLEW BY, AND LUCKILY WITH NO OTHER notable instances. I held the discolored rag in my hand, leaning against the counter. The Saturday rush had finally ended, leaving the awkward three o'clock slump. Too late for lunch and too early for the 'early bird' dinner crowd.

"Any fun plans this weekend?" Beatrice asked. She sat

opposite the counter, systematically pulling the clean utensils from the bin and wrapping them in the paper napkin.

"Just the mall with Alicia tomorrow. We're looking for some costumes for next weekend." I dunked the rag into the blue liquid, wringing it out before placing it on the counter again. It was supposed to be a disinfectant, but my nose scrunched against the smell of the chemicals.

"Oh, that's right! You're both off next weekend. I was afraid you guys were getting too old to celebrate Halloween."

"We aren't trick-or-treating, just a party where people are showing up in costume." The chirp of my phone caused me to jump. "Sorry, I thought I silenced that when I came in." I fumbled with the ringer, flipping the toggle to silent, but then I saw her name pop on the screen. My heart dropped as it only meant one thing.

> I'm sooooo sorry to ask… can you cover my shift 2day? I'm at the beach and it's pouring! I don't think I'll make it back in time! Thx cya 2morrow

"What's wrong?" Beatrice asked, reading my face like a book. I was never good at hiding my emotions.

"It's nothing." I flashed a smile. "Do you mind if I actually take my thirty-minute break?" I was trying to quickly calculate my hours in my head. In the beginning, Mr. Johnson was strict about us sticking to our schedule, but after about a month of Alicia calling out, he wavered and allowed us to shift our schedules between each other only if we stayed at eighteen hours.

I was only supposed to work five hours today, 10:30 to 4:00, with a thirty-minute break, but I usually skipped it and left early. This way, we weren't short-staffed during our rush. However, I could only pull that off if I worked under five hours. Alicia was working from 3:30 to 7:00, so with our combined hours with a thirty-minute break, I would be at eight hours. Luckily, this week, I was only scheduled for two four-hour shifts, so I wasn't close to my hours. I did need the extra time to make up for my hair cut at least.

"Yes, we are pretty slow." She froze for a minute before picking up a fork. "I'm guessing this means you are working late today." Damn, she didn't miss anything.

"I actually need the extra hours, so it works out perfect." I dropped the rag in the bucket, causing the water to splash on the counter. I grabbed a paper towel to clean up the drops.

"Okay… but just make sure she doesn't take advantage. It isn't your job to cover for her. You need to enjoy your week-ends as well." I appreciated her concern. That was one of the reasons I enjoyed working at the diner. Beatrice had taken a motherly role over Alicia and me. Sometimes a little overly doting, but every time she did, I could feel a warmth grow in my chest. I missed having someone care about me.

The breakroom in the diner was tiny. It had one booth against the wall, the cushions were torn and faded as it was retired from the dining room. There was also an old TV hung on the wall. I guessed it was from the early 2000s, as it was a large box, nothing like the flat screens, which were all you could find now. The remote was long gone, so unless you were willing to find a chair and try and change the channel, you were stuck watching whatever the last brave soul had put on. I sighed, watching the sports announcers sitting at the long desk bickering back and forth about some infraction a player had made.

Thank goodness for the year of the phone and employee WiFi.

> Bummer! Yeah I got you covered…tips sucked today.

I texted back, though I knew she wasn't concerned. I rarely turned down her request, especially if I had to see her the next day. It would be torture listening to her complain about the inconvenience work had on her day. Or worse, not even showing up, pissing off Mr. Johnson. He tended to loop us together, so if he didn't see the need for Alicia, I was afraid he would also get rid of me.

My phone vibrated, I was shocked, as Alicia usually never texted back.

A laugh escaped, a little louder than I would have expected. Ben was dressed in an old soccer jersey that had been cleverly torn. Any bare skin showing was painted a yellow-green, and his arms were sticking straight out with his head cocked, the iconic zombie pose.

> BRAINS!!!

I texted back with a GIF of a popular movie character pumping their gun.

> Eek! Where's my shotgun!

> Have you found your costume yet?!?!

> I'm going to the mall 2morrow. Hope all the good costumes rn't gone

I had told him Wednesday I had decided to go to the party, and since then he had been texting me updates about his costume.

> If you can't find anything I'm sure the guys wouldn't mind you joining with us! We have some girls dressing up as victims!

> Sounds tempting... I'll keep it in mind...well my break is ending ttyl

I could feel the smile spreading on my face. It felt nice to have someone checking in on me. Maybe I should put more effort into finding a costume tomorrow. I would hate to disappoint Ben.

"I'm about to head out. Do you need anything before I leave?" Beatrice craned her neck through the door. "Norman will be here for seating assignments, but I wrote on the schedule for you to just stay on your current section."

All I felt was dread. I hated it when Norman was shift-lead, but it wasn't fair to complain to Beatrice. I plastered on, what I was hoping was a convincing smile. "Thanks! I'm good, have a great weekend!"

Ten minutes later, I was back in the dining room. "Amy, I'm putting you on milkshakes tonight," Norman called from the kitchen as I was clocking back in.

"I thought Beatrice put me in the yellow zone." Dread filled my body. This was normal when Norman was in charge. He would pull someone from tables to oversee all milkshake and dessert orders, and that person was normally me. Which would be great if our wage was supplemented during that time, but we still received waiter wages and now no tips. Plus, it wasn't allowed. All waiters and waitresses oversaw their own drink orders. This relieved the kitchen for cooking and didn't affect our tips.

"And I'm taking you off and putting you on milkshakes. I have two orders coming in, so when you're done clocking in, hop back."

My hands were bright red and numb at the end of the night. I must have made over a hundred shakes. I also knew a lecture was going to be waiting for me on Monday. It was nine before I was able to clock out, way past what my departure time was supposed to be. But there was still a mountain of items that needed to be done to prepare for the opening crew.

It was great to see how busy the diner was getting, but it looked like it was time for Mr. Johnson to start hiring some more waiters. I just hoped that didn't mean replacing his high school crew with full-time employees.

The cold night air did not help my frozen hands. I mentally added gloves to my list of things to pick up tomorrow. The cold weather did not detour the desire for milkshakes. That's because there is nothing that goes better with a big, greasy burger and fries. I froze at the bus stop, cursing at myself. I was such an idiot. It was Saturday, so the last bus ran at 8:30. How could I have forgotten? Oh yeah, because this wasn't my normal shift. Now I was stranded.

My brain raced thinking of solutions. I could call Alicia. This was partially her fault… but if she was still with Mike, she would be pissed and blame me for working too late, even though I wouldn't be in this predicament if I wasn't initially covering for her. My dad was no use. He was probably halfway through a case of beer by now. Who else had their license? Derek? He did offer to help if I was ever out late. I shook my head. I could imagine how that conversation would go. "I know we only really talked once, and I refused to get in your car, but would you pick me up?" My hand rubbed my now sweat-dampened head, and I felt the panic start to take over.

I opened the GPS app on my phone. It would normally take about fifteen to twenty minutes to drive, so walking home shouldn't take that long, right? Maybe an hour? That wasn't terrible. The sidewalks here were at least lit by the streetlamps. Now I was thankful I didn't work tables the whole night. At least I didn't have too much cash on me. But did that help or hurt if someone tried to rob me? And I did stand out as a waitress in my uniform. What about the cops? Would this count as an emergency? No. I could walk. It would be fine.

Every sound or car light made me jump. This was ridiculous. Nothing was going to happen. I really needed to cut down on the crime shows I watched.

"Hey, cutie!" someone catcalled and let out a shrill whistle from their car when they sped by. I felt as if I had an out-of-body experience, my insides feeling as though they had leaped out of my body.

"You okay?" a low voice asked from behind. My body instinctively whipped around, holding my bag close to me.

A robber wouldn't ask if I was okay, I lectured myself. I gave a weak smile in response. "Yeah, sorry, that car scared me."

"I don't understand the allure that comes from screaming at people from a car," the man responded flatly. His voice was so low it was a bit of a strain to hear it against the sound of the road. I was also having a hard time making out his face, but I could picture the look of annoyance from his voice. He stood just out of the streetlamp, and a cap was covering his head, adding to the shadow. "What are you doing out on the street so late at night?"

"I missed the bus." Wait, should I be making up a lie? I wasn't sure how to handle the conversation. He didn't seem dangerous, but I still had a pit in my stomach, probably from being on edge this whole time.

"Do you know how to get home?"

"Yeah, I have my GPS on my phone." I flashed my phone at him.

"Can I see?" My hand froze in place with his request. Should I give him my phone? I felt completely out of my element. I was already breaking the stranger danger rule, but if he really wanted it, he could just take it from me, so asking was a good sign. Before I had a chance to answer he had tugged my phone free.

"Uh... okay," I sheepishly responded, though it was already too late. I looked at his hands as he held it. He had nice leather gloves covering his hands. Actually, his whole arm was covered, not an inch of skin exposed. While here I was clutching a thin jacket, my hands turning from red to white. How much time did it take to get frostbite?

"You have it set to driving. If you change it to walking, it will give you better shortcuts to reduce the time. It looks like if you turn down that trail up there, you can cut a couple miles." He handed the phone back to me.

"Uh… thanks." I said staring at my phone. He shrugged as he turned and walked away.

He was right. The GPS had changed from highlighting the designated roads, to more diagonal lines around the buildings. The time also changed, from the fifteen minutes it had previously shown, to now forty-five minutes with a walking person icon highlighted. But that also took me away from the main road. I flipped to the alternate route I was taking. The change increased my time from forty-five minutes to a little over an hour. I mean, how bad could it be? Plus, I would be home faster. I started down the sidewalk again and decided I would try the shortcut.

After walking at least ten minutes down the road, I knew this was a mistake. The streetlights were farther apart, so I was walking in the dark more than the light. There were also fewer cars, which means if something happened, there would be less of a chance for someone to drive by and help. It also felt colder. I think the lights tricked my mind into thinking I was getting some kind of warmth. Now the only warmth was my eyes, as the warm water started to cloud my vision. I was on the verge of tears. I just wanted to be home.

"Amy?" someone called from behind, the voice familiar. "What are you doing out here?" It also sounded very angry.

I turned on my heels, and my body stiffened as our eyes met. Out of all the people to run into, of course it had to be Derek. The last two years of high school we barely crossed paths, and now I couldn't go a couple days without running into him. Even though I was frozen, my face instantly flushed red. "Uh... I'm... uh..." and I couldn't even put a sentence together.

"Are you walking home? Are you insane!" He was so furious his eyes were burning. I was half expecting them to turn the golden yellow from my dreams.

"Yes, I'm walking home! I missed the bus, and I would rather not be stuck on a cold bench all night!" I lifted my chin in defiance; I could feel the anger also rising inside of me. Who did he think he was lecturing me? Did he think I was just out for an evening stroll?

"I thought I gave you my number if you ever needed a ride?" His gaze held, not faltering.

I couldn't stop the tears. I was exhausted, tired, embarrassed, and worse, scared. "You're right, I could've texted, but why would I? I don't know you, and we aren't friends! I'm tired, my hands are frozen from making a million milkshakes, and I just want to be home. So, if you are done lecturing me, I'm leaving!"

"Wait..." Derek reached his hand out but stopped in mid-air before clenching it into a fist and dropping it back to his side. "You're right, I'm sorry. Let me help you find a way home." His gaze softened, but his posture was still very rigid.

All I could do was nod as I tried to swallow back the sob threatening to escape, but the tears had won the battle and did not show any signs of letting up.

"Let's just head to the main road where it's lit better." He shook off his coat and draped it over my shoulders. The warmth engulfed me. The familiar smell of leather and sandalwood also flooded my nose. I followed him like a lost puppy. He walked unfazed by losing his jacket. I noticed him sending a text on his phone.

"Is the jacket warm enough?" He asked, stopping under a streetlight. I was thankful for the sound of cars again. I just nodded, still not trusting my voice.

We stood in awkward silence before he started again. "I'm

sorry... you were right. We don't know each other, so I guess that offer was pretty dumb sounding." He paused for a moment as if he was debating how to continue. "It's just not safe being out alone at night. I would hate for something to happen to you." He hesitated again. "So, can we be friends?" He extended his hand.

"Friends." I grabbed his hand to shake, feeling a little silly, like we were elementary kids making a pact. I jumped at his response.

"Holy shit! Your hands are freezing!" He grabbed my other hand, grasping them between his, in an attempt to warm them. His hands were rough, what you would expect from someone who did hard labor. I wonder what he did to get all those callouses.

A light honk came from behind, and Derek dropped my hands. We followed the car to the side street so they could pull over. Derek walked over and opened the passenger door. I could see his friend Dominic sitting in the driver's seat. I could feel the pit reform in my stomach. I didn't want to seem ungrateful for the help, but I also was not ready to get in a car with a stranger alone. Derek must have noticed my hesitation because before I could walk to the door, he slammed it shut and walked to the driver's side. I could see them having a heated discussion.

"Seriously?" Dominic responded. I tried not to eavesdrop, but it was so quiet their voices were hard to ignore.

"Everyone is on Fourth Street. I need you to meet them there and let them know I'll be back soon and to keep looking." Derek had the door open as Dominic stalked out, apparently not happy with the change of plans. His eyes were ice when they met mine.

"Hop in," Derek called as he climbed in. The warmth hit me first when I entered. "Put your hands in front of the vents." He cranked them up higher.

"Thanks." This car was different than Derek's. It was a lot

flashier, and the smell was different. More metallic? The inside glowed orange from the backlight on the dash. "This is a nice car."

Derek smirked to himself as if I was telling a funny joke. His whole body was finally relaxed. It was odd to see him smile, but it felt nice. I jerked my head forward at that thought. What was I doing? "Yeah, this is one of Dominic's babies. He was not happy to hand over the keys, so next time, it'll have to be my lame ride."

"Oh, I didn't mean... I mean, your car is nice too..." I glanced quickly over, afraid I offended him, but instead, he was smiling to himself. Damn, he was hot. He had one hand stretched out, grabbing the wheel while the other was leaning against the door. Though he was wearing a long-sleeved shirt, you could still see the outline of his muscles. It was still shocking he wasn't on one of the sports teams. I imagine he would dominate on the wrestling team. His jawline had the sharp angles you would picture on a movie star, with a slender nose guiding your eyes to his lips. I snapped my head forward again. I hoped he didn't realize I was staring. "Shoot, I didn't give you my address!"

"I know where it is," Derek responded, turning onto the next street. "From our bus ride, remember?"

"I forgot." I hadn't, but I wasn't expecting him to remember from one visit. It usually took me four to five times, at least, before I remembered how to get to a place.

We rode in silence the rest of the way. By the time we reached my house, I felt like I finally defrosted. I almost didn't want to leave the car. We awkwardly sat in front of my house for a few minutes. I wasn't sure what I was expecting to happen.

"Listen, I want to apologize again for earlier." Derek was looking straight ahead. It was hard to register what emotion he was feeling.

"It's o—"

He cut me off, "But I need you to understand you can't be out by yourself like that. There are things out there that will hurt you." His hand was clenching the wheel hard, his knuckles starting to turn white.

"Things?" Was he one of those people who thought monsters were real? It made me shudder when I thought about my dream. If only he knew what I was thinking, but if he did, maybe he would think I was the crazy one.

"I mean people with bad intentions. Just promise me you won't do that again. If you need help, just reach out. If I can't help, I'll at least help you find someone who can. We are friends now, remember."

"Sure… thanks again." I shrugged off his jacket, handing it to him before I left the car. He sat in front of my house until I was inside. Once I closed the door, I could hear the car rev and drive away. Well, that turned out to be an interesting day.

For once, I was happy to be home.

Six

"Y ou guys would not believe the day I had yesterday." Alicia whined from the driver's seat as she drove toward the mall. "It was supposed to be a relaxing day at the beach, just me and Mike, and before we knew it, we were stuck in a torrential downpour."

"That's terrible." Grace matched her tone.

"Isn't it a little cold for the beach?" I echoed from the backseat, not hiding my annoyance. She had yet to say thank you for taking her shift yesterday. Who goes to the beach in October anyway?

"We weren't going in the water. We just wanted to walk the shoreline." Alicia either ignored my tone or didn't notice. "You guys know Mike likes to take his metal detector out. Remember that time he found that really cool bracelet? Anyway, we were stuck at that tacky restaurant for like three hours before it finally stopped, and at that point the tide had come in, so we had to call it a day."

I stared out the window and let them drone on. Alicia giving every detail while Grace lapped it up. Knowing the perfect time to ask for more details or give sympathetic responses. Their conversation continued until we finally reached the mall.

The Sanctuary Square Mall stood as a drab reminder of its glory days. The gray stone building sprawled out with six main entrances, four leading into department stores, while two led into the main hallway, which was lined by the smaller stores. When I was little, the mall was where everyone wanted to be. Parking was always an adventure on its own. Cole and I would try to bet what store we would end up by. Now the parking lot resembled an apocalyptic scene. Trash littered on the ground, cars scattered around haphazardly, light poles missing or bent from being hit by cars and never replaced or fixed.

The mall used to have what I thought was over a hundred stores, but it was probably closer to fifty. The mall was two stories, with escalators going up and down in different areas. Cole and I would constantly race up and down, trying to see which route and escalator was fastest. The food court was the best! Mom would usually give us each a ten-dollar bill and let us go to whichever restaurant we wanted. I typically kept it safe and bought the kid's meal, which consisted of a burger and fries, but not Cole. He would always try new things, and for the most part, they smelled amazing. Depending on Mom's mood, she would sometimes take us to get ice cream afterward. Fast-forward to today, the food court had two popular restaurants, but the rest continued to cycle in and out. The mouth-watering aroma of freshly baked pretzels was replaced by the smell of stale oil.

We pulled in front of the south department store entrance. The store was long gone, and you could almost make out the name of the store from the outline the sign left, almost as if a nuclear blast had gone off leaving the creepy outline. A scene that matched the parking lot perfectly. Half covering the ominous space was a tacky orange and black banner with a picture of a ghost holding a trick-or-treat bag.

Halloween Fun Spot! Your place to find the spookiest costume to knock anyone's socks off!

Grace was the first to get to the entrance and pulled open the glass door. They had covered the glass with black paper to give it an ominous look. The smell of plastic and rubber filled the air as we walked in.

"Holy SHIT!" Alicia screamed, as she walked in first.

A crackly laugh followed as a plastic witch started to descend back into the box right inside the entrance.

"Why do they think that is funny!" Alicia shouted. Red spreading across her cheeks and her hands balled as if she was about to punch the next person who got in her way. She stomped off while Grace and I muffled our laughs. The witch sprung up again when we passed, but unlike Alicia, we were expecting it.

"So, where should we start?" Grace was tugging at my arm like a kid does to their mom.

"How about a bunny?" Alicia pulled a plastic bag off the rack.

"How is that a bunny?" I picked at the corner, holding it at arm's length. The girl in the picture was bent forward, her hands resting on her legs. Her butt extended out, displaying the white cotton tail pressed on it. On her head were two floppy ears held together by a headband, but that was the extent of the bunny. It was followed by a body suit, similar to what a gymnast would wear, and a bow tie. "And why would a bunny be wearing a tie? It makes no sense!"

"I know." Grace proudly displayed her find. "You should be a pirate!"

This time, the girl on the package was actually standing up. She held a sword in her right hand, her arm bent in front of her as if she was about to fight someone. The actual costume looked like it belonged to an eight-year-old in size. The top of the dress really "emphasized" the girl's chest, while the skirt at least covered her bottom half when she was standing. Then the boots, or at least the scraps of fabric that clung to her legs, tied at the knee.

"I think I'm looking for something with a little more… coverage." I created a hemline on my legs with my hands. "I'm thinking at least to here."

Alicia rolled her eyes as she went back to the racks. "You can't be too picky. All the good costumes are probably gone by now."

There was a Cleopatra, too much makeup to pull off. A witch, unoriginal. A French maid, pass! I was starting to lose hope. Maybe this was a sign I shouldn't go to the party. I probably should've waited to say anything to Ben until I at least had a costume. It felt hopeless as we walked to the back of the store, or at least the back of what they had corralled for the store. I was never sure why these Halloween stores sought out the old department stores. They barely took up one section. We were standing in what was once the kids' section. I knew that because on the floor were painted feet with the different kid shoe sizes that you could use to measure your feet.

When I looked back up, something caught my eye. White stood out against the rows of black, intrigued I picked up the package. The girl on the package was standing straight, with her left knee slightly bent. Her left hand resting on her hip. She wore what looked like a white tunic. It was still pretty short, but it would at least make it to my mid-thigh. As long as I didn't bend over, I wouldn't have an issue. But what had drawn my eyes in was what she wore on her back. Small yellow wings extended from her back. The wings weren't bulky. They extended maybe six inches from her shoulders. It was a simpler costume, but I couldn't pull my eyes away.

"What did you find!" Grace squealed as she bounded over. "Could this be the winner?"

"An angel?" Alicia's nose scrunched as if a bad stench was coming from the costume. "Are you sure this is what you want? I mean, you could get something super wild!"

"Aren't you going as a nurse?" Grace's eyebrow rose. "I mean, isn't that super cliché for Halloween?" Wow, I think this was the first time Grace ever spoke back to Alicia. Looking at her face, I think Alicia was just as shocked.

"Fine, whatever. If that's what you want, then can we check out and go? I told Mike we would stop by for lunch." Before we could answer, she was making her way to the register.

"Don't you want to try it on first?" Grace whispered. "We can wait."

I flipped the package in my hands until I found the sizing chart on the back. My finger scrolled down, looking for my size, then running over to the right color. "Nope, it's purple, so it should be fine." Plus, I didn't really want to change here. Instead of using the obvious dressing rooms in the store, they had constructed their own. PVC pipe covered with black plastic. Who knew what they actually covered, or who may or may not be around them.

I nearly choked at the register. "I'm sorry, how much?"

"Eighty-nine-ninety-nine," the cashier huffed as her eyes rolled.

"They are more expensive when they come with accessories." Alicia sighed. "Do you want me to grab the ninja one? That's just fabric?"

Damn, I really didn't want to spend that much today, but I was too exhausted to try and find something else. "No, it's good. Sorry, I just didn't think it was going to be that much." If I had to be honest, I was starting to get excited about the costume.

"Cash or card?"

"Oh, sorry here." As I handed my card, she pushed the card reader forward. I hated using those things as I could never remember if I was supposed to inject or slide. Panicked, I slide the card. Nope, wrong choice as the machine beeped back. I could feel my cheeks getting warm.

Finally, the receipt started to print. Ripping it off the reader, she placed it in the bag, dropping it on the counter. "Have a spooktacular day." She followed in the most monotone voice. If words could grow eyes and roll them, it would be off that phrase.

"Now, who's ready to eat?" Alicia almost jumped up and down as she led us toward the entrance to the inner mall.

Mike stood at the counter with a bright purple shirt and black visor. The visor had a large chicken drumstick stamped on it, signifying the restaurant's famous food. This was one of the few restaurants that actually held up time after time, and surprisingly, it usually had a decent line. Probably because it was a popular fast-food chain, and the only other one in town was at least another twenty to twenty-five miles away.

"What's Clucking? Can I interest you in some wing-tastic food?" Mike peered over his shoulder, probably looking to see if his manager was nearby. "Ugh… we have to say the lamest stuff here!" On his shirt was a large gold button with the words 'How about a round of drumsticks!' with a picture of two chicken legs mimicking actual drumsticks hitting the top of a drum.

Alicia giggled. "We're hungry! How about some nuggets?"

Mike cautiously looked to the side again while quickly clicking a couple of buttons on the register. The drawer popped open, then after closing it, he handed Alicia a receipt, winking. "Your order will be up shortly, miss. We hope you have a wing-da-ful day!" He shook his head in response, but a smile covered his face. I'm sure it felt good to be able to do something special for his girlfriend.

Another great thing about Mike's restaurant. They were fast! Before we could even make it to the end of the counter, the food was already coming out. Mike had also rung up some drinks, so empty soda cups were also waiting on the tray. I volunteered to get Alicia's drink from the machine so she could find us a seat.

I wasn't surprised at where she chose. She sat on the opposite side, so she had the perfect place to watch Mike.

"So…" Alicia started after we had all sat down. "I heard someone has a crush on our Amy!"

"What!" Grace nearly choked on her drink. "Who? Amy, do you know?"

I could feel my cheeks burning. "And I heard he wants to meet up at Tyler's party!" Alicia continued playing with a nugget in her hand.

"Seriously? Stop with the suspense! Who is it?" Grace was nearly off her chair, leaning onto the table.

"Amy, why don't you tell us! I heard you guys have been texting back and forth." Alicia gave a sly smile before biting into the chicken.

"Ummm…" Why was I having a hard time answering? I knew who she was talking about, but why was I doubting it. I shook my head to get him out of it, there was no way she would be talking about him. Right? Of course, there was no way Derek liked me. Why was I even contemplating the thought? "Do you mean Ben?"

Alicia nodded with satisfaction. Happy she was the one who had the insider information. I wasn't surprised she knew, though. Mike had been on the same soccer team, and even though he didn't play anymore, I'm sure he was still close to a lot of the players.

"Alicia, how did you know?" Grace was clearly impressed by her ability to obtain the latest gossip. I was not.

"I have my ways! Anyway, I heard he is going with his soccer team. They are doing some type of group costume, but he is really hoping to run into you." She stopped to take another bite of her nugget. "So, I was thinking after school Friday, you both should come to my house, and we can get ready together and go! This way, we can get Amy ready for her first date!"

"I can do your hair! I'll look up some fun angel ideas!"

Grace grabbed her phone, already starting to search for images.

"And I'll do her makeup! This is going to be so fun! Then, after the party, we can spend the night at my house so Amy can tell us all the juicy details!" Alicia smiled to herself, obviously happy with her plans.

It would've been nice if they asked my opinion somewhere in the mix. I know we had started talking, but I don't know if I actually liked him in that way. What if I was giving Ben the wrong signals, and I ended up hurting him? Now that I know Mike is getting insider information, how close were they? If things ended badly with him, would that cause problems with Alicia and me? I gripped the Halloween bag in my hand. Plus, this costume I bought. I chose it for another reason. Why was my heart fluttering when I thought of him?

"Ready?" Alicia asked as she started to stack her trash on the tray. I barely touched my food. The topic caused me to lose my appetite.

"Ready." I followed her lead, but that was normal in our friendship. When Alicia was ready to move on, she wasn't looking for objections.

Before we left, Alicia bounded back to the counter. They exchanged a few words. Even though Grace and I stayed by the tables, I knew exactly what they were talking about. She pointed in our direction, and both laughed. I was sure she was relaying the plans we just made. As if to confirm my suspicions, Mike made eye contact with me and winked.

We headed back to the Halloween shop. It was the closest exit to our car. "Does anyone need anything else before we leave?" Alicia called over her shoulder as we almost reached the store.

We both shook our heads as we followed behind. A shrill scream came from the shop when we entered, followed by the crackle of the witch. Sounds like another victim of the clever placement. Alicia pursed her lips, still not amused with her earlier run-in.

The girl, still unamused, barely looked up from her phone when we walked by. The witch jumped up with her same crackle as we left the store as if to wish us a final goodbye. Maybe I should come back and pick that up as a thank-you gift for Alicia. I chuckled, just imagining her reaction.

The parking lot was, surprisingly, busier when we left. All the last-minute people running to get costumes. I pulled the costume out of the shopping bag once we were in the car. I wonder what I would look like. Maybe it would be nice to let Grace and Alicia go wild.

SEVEN

"Alicia, that looks amazing!" Grace stood staring at my face. "I love what you did with her eyes!"

"You're doing my hair next, right?" Alicia responded, standing back and analyzing her work. "Those curls you did are perfect!"

The suspense was killing me! Alicia and Grace refused to give me a mirror as they worked. They wanted me to wait until the final reveal. "Well! Can I see?" My leg was bouncing from the anticipation, and I had been scolded on multiple occasions because it would cause my head to move. Apparently not a good thing when someone was pointing something near your eye.

Alicia pressed her pointer finger to her lip, and her thumb rested on her chin as she did one final look. A smile followed as she pulled my arm, dragging me out of the chair to the full-length mirror on her wall. I stood in silence. The person staring back at me was pretty. I couldn't believe that was me. Grace had put extensions in my hair to give back the length I had chopped off. I was starting to regret my decision to cut it. Alicia had not only done my makeup, but she also applied gold glitter from the edge of my eyebrows to my cheekbones. "Wow…" was all I could say.

I could hear the high-five behind me. "Wait until Ben sees!" Grace squealed.

"Okay, we have to hurry! We have less than an hour before we have to leave!" Alicia was pulling out her costume and accessories as Grace reset her impromptu hair station preparing to do Alicia's hair.

"Is Mike picking us up?" Grace asked as she unplugged her hair dryer and curling iron.

"No, we're going to meet him there. My mom requested a car to take us there and back. This way, we can all have some fun." Alicia winked, but I knew what she meant. I'm sure there would be a ton of alcohol. A shudder ran down my back. I couldn't help but think of Cole. Were he and his friends this excited before leaving? I quickly blinked away the tears. Alicia and Grace would be mad if I ruined my makeup before the official reveal.

Alicia's phone dinged, alerting us the car was there. We all filed in the back seat as Grace confirmed the address with the driver. We could already hear the music before we reached the house. This would either make for a great party or a quick one, depending on the neighbors' tolerance.

I couldn't stop staring at all the people. They really went all out! Halloween makeup has really gotten popular in the last few years, with more and more makeup tutorials becoming available online for people to try. One girl's face was covered in sequins complimenting her mermaid costume. Another person's face looked as if pieces of their skin were cracking off, revealing a completely difference face under-neath, as if their human face was the fake mask.

"Alright, so we will meet back here at eleven?" Alicia was staring at her phone, probably checking to see if Mike had arrived yet or not.

"What if we need to leave earlier?" I first didn't want to

come to this party, and now they were ready to ditch each other.

Alicia shot me a warning look. "Keep your phone on, and we will text each other if plans change, but I hope that doesn't happen." I knew that last part was directed at me. I could suck it up. They all spent so much time on my costume. Worse, I could find a quiet corner somewhere to hang out in until they were ready.

We walked to the front door before we went our separate ways. Alicia left us to head back toward the street. I'm sure Mike was almost here, and she wanted her true reveal to be on his arm. Grace found a couple of her friends in what looked like the dining room. I decided to try the kitchen. Hoping there was some food somewhere. Everyone was so focused on the costumes and being ready in time that we didn't plan for dinner, and my stomach was not happy about that decision.

"Amy? Is that you?" someone called out from behind. I turned, and our eyes met.

"Oh my gosh, Ben, your costume looks amazing!" He looked just like the picture. Sure, his makeup was more comic than scary, but they had done a great job.

"And you look... wow..."

I started to feel self-conscious. My hand tugged at my skirt. I really should've tried it on in the store. It was much shorter than I thought. What I would give to have it grow a couple of inches.

"I want you to come meet my friends." He grabbed my hand and led me away from the kitchen toward the back patio. Sorry, stomach, we will get something soon.

His hand was so soft in my hand. Nothing like Derek's. It was almost childlike. I shook my head. Why was I comparing them. I need to get him out of my head! Ben led us to the back of the house. Out the glass French doors leading to the backyard.

As grand as Tyler's house was, the outside was just as

magnificent. In the center was a large pool with a beautiful stone waterfall across the back. On the one side, there was a diving board, and on the opposite, a zero-entry with a couple of lounge chairs scattered. Ben's friends stood under the covered patio, sitting in the plush lounge chairs, a fireplace in the middle, helping to combat the cold. A shiver moved through my body, staring at it. The snow held off, but that didn't make it any warmer. I wasn't expecting to be hanging outside, so I hadn't brought a jacket. Worried I would be stuck holding it all evening.

Ben led me to the fire, which I was thankful for, though he probably heard my teeth chattering. At least that drowned out the gargles of my stomach. He went from left to right, going around the circle and calling out to the guys. "Guys, I want to introduce you to Amy! Amy, this is…" I know he was intro-ducing his friends, but there were so many, and they were all in costume, I wasn't able to keep track.

I wished we had met before the party because, to be honest, I probably wouldn't be able to point them out in a crowd after tonight. They matched in their torn jerseys and yellow-green skin with large dark circles around their eyes. Their hair was different, but most of them were wearing sweatbands. If I were Alicia, she would've gone on CircleApp before the party and gotten the intel on this group. I'm sure Ben had group pictures of them.

"Then there is Krissy, Lacey, and Abigail." Ben went back around, naming the girls in the group

They were a lot easier to recognize. They were pretty much wearing normal clothes. They had made their faces pale, and each had giant bite marks in different places. The victims of the soccer zombies. Maybe I should've taken up Ben's offer to join. I stuck out like a sore thumb.

"Hi, Amy," one of the girls chimed in. Lacey, I believe. She looked very familiar. I wonder if we had a class together last year. Most of Ben's teammates were a year or two older.

That's what happens when someone makes the varsity team early.

"Come sit with us!" Abigail had already started scootching over, making room for me on the couch. The couch was directly in front of the fire, so I was not about to turn that down.

"I'll get us some drinks. Do you want anything in particular?" Ben had a huge grin on his face, happy his group was welcoming me in so quickly.

I looked around the group, but everyone was holding red cups, so it was hard to determine what people had. "Maybe a soda?" My stomach twisted. I felt like such a child, but it didn't seem to faze Ben.

He quickly returned with a red cup. My heart sank. I would've preferred a can. "Sorry, they didn't have any soda. See if you like this."

I half stood, taking the cup from him before sitting back down. It looked like punch. I took a sip. Surprisingly, it wasn't too bad. It wasn't as sweet as I was expecting, with a bit of a weird aftertaste, but still refreshing.

"So, how do you know Ben?" Abigail asked.

"Oh," I hesitated, taking a sip of my drink. "We have a couple classes together." I took another sip trying to act casual. I was glad to have something in my hand for the awkward moments, though I wished it was a burger instead.

The wind whistled as we sat in awkward silence. I rubbed my hands up and down my arms, trying to warm them up. Whose bright idea was it for Halloween, the holiday where it is sexier the less clothes you wear, to be in October.

"Have you been to any of the games?" It was Krissy's turn to ask. Her hands were stretched out towards the fire trying to warm them. I'm sure they were just as hardcore into soccer as the boys. I wonder if they played on the girls' team.

"I haven't had a chance yet this year…" Shoot, I didn't want them to think I wasn't interested in soccer. "But I went to some of the JV games last year. My friend's boyfriend, Mike, used to play." A grimace appeared on Lacey's face. Okay, noted, Mike may not be as influential with the group as Alicia made it out to be.

"Ah, Mike." Krissy swirled her cup, but didn't say anything else.

"You will have to come with us to the next game!" Abigail anxiously pulled on my shoulder. "Nothing is hotter than watching our boys play."

"Oh, are you guys—"

"Yeah," Krissy cut me off. She seemed to be the leader of this group. She pointed to each girl explaining which guy they were dating. Shit, I probably should've paid better attention to Ben when he was making the introductions.

I wasn't sure if it was the fire or the girls, but I was actually feeling relaxed. I was even laughing at their jokes. I was already on my third cup of punch. At least that was filling up my stomach for now. "Oh great, she's here." Lacey sighed.

I turned my head to see who they were talking about, and the whole room spun with the motion. I had to grab my head to get it to stop. "Whos-s-s-e here?" I asked, why were my s's sounding funny.

"Kayla, she uh… used to be a part of the group," Abigail fumbled out.

"Nice costumes, girls." The new girl stood to the right of the fire.

"The bunny!" I blurted.

She was wearing the bunny costume Alicia had first grabbed at the Halloween shop. It looked just as ridiculous as it did in the picture. The only difference was the added white tights on her legs. Probably to add a little more coverage against the cold. My hands covered my mouth to hide my dropped jaw. I can't believe I just said that out loud.

The girl—Kayla, I think? —gave me the dirtiest look. I

couldn't blame her. The rest of the girls erupted in laughter. That probably didn't help. "And you are?"

"This is Amy!" Abigail smacked my back, still laughing. I really liked her. Her bubbliness was very addicting. "She came with Ben."

If looks could kill, the good feeling was evaporating from my body. "I see," was all she said.

"Why are you elbowing me?" Abigail whined.

"Amy… Amy…" Kayla started again. "Oh, I know who you are!" I didn't like how she said that. "An angel, that's pretty fitting."

"Kayla…" Krissy now spoke. She was giving her a warning tone.

"You're an angel of death, right?" She smirked to herself. "I mean, your brother did murder his friends."

"I said enough!" Krissy leaped from the couch, which caused a chain reaction. As she leaped up, she pushed Lacey toward Abigail, who collided with her arm, which was holding her cup of punch. Following the chain reaction, the punch followed the course of momentum falling from her hand, spilling over the front of my tunic.

"Oh no! Amy!" Abigail was up grabbing napkins, trying to dry the large red spot on the front of my costume.

Krissy and Kayla were locked in a heated argument while Lacey was trying to figure out which group she should come and help. The boys had left at some point to go inside, apparently there was a foosball table inside. Whatever that was.

"It's okay…" I stumbled, trying to get up, pushing Abigail's hands out of the way. I tried to get off the couch but almost ate it on the floor. The whole horizon was tilting. With the sounds and laughter spinning in my head, I barely made it to the door leading back into the house.

"You aren't looking very good." Abigail was next to me again. I did really like her. I hoped we could still be friends after this. "Do you want me to call a car to take you home?" All I could do was nod. Was the floor always that close?

She helped me to the front porch and sat me on the porch swing while she ordered the car. How cliché was this house? A front porch swing on a wraparound porch, a massive house, and an incredible backyard. Must be nice to live in such a beautiful place. "Do you want me to get your friends?" Abigail asked, handing me my phone.

I shook my head. "No, please don't tell them, I don't want to ruin their night." Plus, I could picture their disapproving looks at my ruined costume. All their hard work destroyed. "Damn, I feel like shit. I think my sugar is low from not eating."

Abigail paused. "It's probably the alcohol from drinking on an empty stomach. You know you get drunk faster from not eating."

"Drunk?" Wow, was that as loud as it sounded? "I didn't drink. I only had punch!"

A couple dressed in pirate outfits walked by us. Abigail watched them go inside, probably half-wishing she was going with them. "Yeah, the punch's spiked."

"I think I'm going to be sick." I dropped my head into my hands. I just needed everything to stop spinning. My feet planted firmly on the ground to prevent the porch swing from moving. Which was probably not the best place to be sitting when your horizon is trying to do summersaults.

"Amy." I felt a nudge on my shoulder. "The car's here."

Abigail helped me off the porch, guiding me slowly down each stair, to the waiting car. The crunching of the gravel under my feet was deafening as we walked towards the car.

The driver was not thrilled with his new passenger. "How old is she?" The driver stared at me.

"Eighteen," Abigail lied. There was an age requirement to use their services. Alicia's mom had ordered our first car, but we didn't have any adults here.

"Do you have any ID?" Clearly, the driver wasn't convinced, his hands gripping tightly on his steering wheel.

"She doesn't, but I do." Abigail handed him her license. She wasn't eighteen... did she have a fake license?

The driver was still not fully convinced, but he wasn't going to argue. "She isn't going to hurl, is she?"

"No, she's just tired." No one was believing that lie, Abigail. "Amy, what's your address?" I mumbled out a reply. She helped me in the car, closing the door behind me.

"There will be an extra clean-up fee if you get sick," the driver called over his shoulder before pulling away.

I leaned against the window, watching the scenery spin by. It was definitely a different experience when your horizon was doing flip-flops. The trees and homes were blending together as the car rumbled down the road. At first, I didn't recognize any of my surroundings. I wonder how much of that had to do with the amount of alcohol I had consumed. I gripped the car door as he took a corner rather sharp. My stomach curled against the movement. I silently prayed I wouldn't get sick. I looked back out the window, trying to distract myself, and that was when I saw my first familiar landmark.

My breath caught in my chest when I realized where we were heading. Almost as if it was fate. After a few more minutes, my heart dropped as we came closer. "Stop here!" I yelled out. The car jolted from the driver's shock. He quickly recovered and pulled over to the side.

"Miss, we are still a few miles from your destination." He was not in the mood for sightseeing.

"No, it's okay. Just let me out here." I was already tugging at the door.

I could tell he was debating his options. He wanted me out of his car as soon as possible, but I could tell he wasn't sure about dropping a drunk girl off in the middle of a bridge. He was about to protest again, but I finally found the lock and flipped it, pushing the door open. He was not about to chase me down, so once the door closed, he sped off.

I froze on the sidewalk, staring at the plaque:

In Loving Memory
Isaac Pierce, Ken Wilson, Brent Cassidy, and Cole Evans
Gone but never forgotten

A collection of flowers and teddy bears were leaning against the post. Someone must have been by recently. I could feel the anger bubbling inside me.

"How fitting. Here I am the night of a Halloween party, wasted just like you, but the difference is I didn't drive. I didn't drive!" The anger rising in my voice as I spoke to the sign. "You didn't have to get into that car that night. Did you know you were drunk? Or were you stupid like me and just trusted the first drink given to you. Not asking any questions!"

"How could you do this to me!" I screamed. "You were the only one I had! Now I have no one!" My knees hit the concrete. I didn't even register the pain.

"*Who would stay with you?*" a voice crept into my head. "*You're useless, a nuisance. You're probably the reason he drank. He couldn't handle being your brother.*"

"STOP!" My hands gripped the sides of my head, trying to squeeze the voice away. Was I going crazy? I turned and leaned against the guardrail. Resting my head.

"*It should've been you. If you were the one who died, your mom would still be around.*"

"Just please stop..." my voice weakly cracked. But it was true. I was the screw-up in the family. I was always the one making mistakes. I was the reason my dad got mad. I caused the arguments. Cole had to work extra hard to make up for me. He was the pride and joy of the family. He succeeded in sports and always brought home good grades. And what was I? Nothing. No wonder everything crumbled when he left.

"*You are just a waste of existence. Would you give up your life to bring him back? Maybe then your mom will come home. Your dad wouldn't drown himself every night.*"

"Of course! If I could trade places with him, don't you think I would!" I yelled back at the voice in my head. I could feel the tears filling my eyes. Why couldn't it have been me? Why did you have to take him!

"*What if there was a way?*"

Almost like magic, he was there. "Cole?" I tried blinking the tears away. I had to be hallucinating.

For once, everything was clear again. The horizon wasn't spinning anymore, I could see everything crystal clear. It was him. He was standing in the middle of the road. His brown hair tussled erratically, and his piercing blue eyes, that matched our mom's, which always bore straight through me. Always aware when I was lying. His hand was reaching toward me, waiting for me to take it. I stood up, stretching my hand out to him.

"*You can be with him. He's been waiting for you. There is nothing left here for you. Just go to him.*"

I couldn't do this alone anymore. Could Cole really be here? Could I really reach him again? My feet started moving forward. I was getting closer to him, his warm smile spread across his face. I'm almost there, Cole. I made it to the curb, taking that next step, but instead of moving forward, strong arms wrapped around my body, yanking me back. Was that my name being yelled? The force lifted me off the ground, spinning me back to the side of the bridge. My body slammed into the concrete wall as a moan released from my lips.

A car's horn blared as it sped past. It was going to hit him! "Cole! You have to get Cole!" I screamed.

"Amy... there isn't anyone there." Warm hands cradled

my head, lifting to make eye contact as I thrashed to get free. "You have to focus. He can't be there, right?"

Dread. The now normal feeling came back. He was right, he couldn't be there. He was dead. The tears started to flow now. "Derek?" I whispered as our eyes connected. His arms dropped from my face, wrapping around my body and pulling me close. "I'm here. You're going to be okay," he whispered into my ear.

"How disappointing." The voice that had been echoing in my head interrupted the embrace. Derek spun, keeping me behind his back as if he was shielding me from something. Was there someone really there? "*We were just having some fun,*" the voice rang, once again, in my head.

"I'm warning you… leave now." Derek's voice was sharp. The hair on my arms stood as the tension grew heavy. Did he hear that voice, too?

The other voice laughed. Not a light chuckle, but a deep belly laugh, as if Derek was cracking jokes. The voice was finally out of my head. There was someone there. "You are out of your league, young one. And we both know you aren't going to do anything, not with an audience." The voice was getting louder, not because he was speaking louder, but because I assumed he was walking closer. "Now, why don't you be a good little soldier and leave that one with me. She was much happier a few minutes ago." Something he said struck a nerve. I could feel Derek's body tense.

"Amy…" Derek turned his head so he could make eye contact.

"Yes…" My voice cracked. Was he going to leave? Who was this person he was speaking to? Did I envision his voice in my head because he was here all along?

"You have to trust me. No matter what happens, I'm going to protect you, so you don't need to be afraid." I nodded, not trusting my voice to be able to answer. A smile spread across his face. Not the type of smile that someone had when they were happy or heard a joke, but like a football player about to start the last play of the game. The smile of determination.

He stepped forward, and I dropped my hands to my side, releasing his shirt, that I wasn't even aware I was grabbing. He broke out in a run toward the voice. As he picked up speed golden wings erupted from his back, the same fiery wings I saw in my bedroom, but how could that be? That was a dream. Another golden flash lit up his hands, and in its place was a golden sword. That's when I saw the other person. A shadowy figure a hundred yards back. I couldn't make out any distinguishing features because he was immersed in the shadows, but this was different. There wasn't a disgusting monster. It was a normal person.

Derek leaped forward, filling the gap between the two, his wings propelling him forward, covering a distance no regular human could match. It looked like they were going to collide, but at the last moment, the other figure leaped back at the same speed, narrowly missing each other. Before Derek could respond, two other figures flanked him with the same blazing wings.

"I think this is my cue to leave," the figure annoyingly announced. In the same tone as he spoke earlier. You wouldn't know he was in the middle of a fight. Even though he was farther down the bridge, his voice sounded as if he was next to me.

"We will meet again, Amy."

And as he spoke the last word, the figure jumped over the edge of the bridge toward the raging river below. I ran to the side and peered over, expecting to see him crash into the water below, but there was nothing. As if he had disappeared.

"Damn!" one of the figures next to Derek yelled. "What a coward! I was looking forward to a fight tonight!"

"What brought that on?" the other figure asked.

"It was him," Derek responded.

As quickly as the wings had appeared, they were gone.

"Shit! Derek, someone's watching us!" They all turned to face me now. The other two must have been focused on Derek when they flew in. Flew... did they really just fly in? This couldn't be real.

When they had turned, the light lit up the new faces, and that's when I recognized them. The one cursing was Dominic, while the other one was another boy from their group, Emery. Derek ignored the questions as he walked back, closing the distance between us. I don't know what I was expecting, but it wasn't what happened next.

As soon as Derek was in front of me, he wrapped his arms around me, pulling me against his chest. I hadn't realized how cold I was until I felt the warmth of his body engulfing mine. My body started to shake uncontrollably in response. "Emery, give me your jacket. I think she's going into shock."

That's the last thing I heard before everything went black.

EIGHT

I could hear the sound of a car engine. Was I moving? I was leaning against something, or was this someone? I could feel it moving, like a chest lifting and falling as they breathed. I think their arm was also around me, keeping me secure. I wasn't ready to open my eyes. I was still trying to remember what happened. Was it another dream? Had I passed out in the car? No, it couldn't be… but it couldn't be real. Despite my protest, I opened my eyes. My eyes slowly adjusted between the darkness of the backseat against the light glow from the front dash.

The orange glow is what I noticed first. So, we were in Dominic's car. Without turning my head, I knew who was sitting next to me, Derek. I heard someone in the front starting to speak. I quickly closed my eyes, pretending to still be asleep. If they knew I was awake, I was afraid they would stop.

I was trying to keep my breathing steady, but I could feel the panic coming back. I almost died tonight. If Derek hadn't arrived when he did, that car… no just push the thought away.

"Do you know how much trouble we are going to be in

when they find out!" Dominic's voice boomed. Maybe he didn't care if I was awake or not.

Derek's voice was much quieter. "I will handle it. It was my decision. It won't affect any of you."

"Derek, you know we are behind you no matter what." The second voice had matched Derek's volume, that must have been Emery.

They were quiet again. Dominic must have taken a sharp corner at high speed because the turn had caused my body to jolt toward the door. Derek's arm tightened to steady me, but instinctively, my right hand gripped his shirt.

"Amy? You awake?"

I tried to muffle my voice, to sound as if I was still groggy from waking up. Though my confusion was genuine. "Derek? Wh-where are we?"

"You fainted..." He hesitated. "What happened to you tonight? How did you end up on the bridge?"

The party flashed back into my head. I was suddenly reminded of my attire. The white robe was stained red from the punch. The smell of alcohol finally hit my nose. How did I not smell it before? I could feel my cheeks begin to burn. I didn't want to remember it, and I wasn't going to talk about it. "The bridge... who was-s-s that man? You had wings-s-s... and a s-s-sword?" I slurred out. My speech still hadn't recovered.

"Oh great!" Dominic boomed from the front. "I guess her memory's fine, drunk and all!"

"I'm not drunk-k-k!" I shot back, though my voice wasn't helping.

"Yeah, right! You smell like a bar." Dominic bantered back.

At that moment, the car pulled into a driveway. I turned, expecting to see my house, but it wasn't. "Where are we?" Panic started to creep in. Where did they take me? Did I see too much? Were they going to do something to me? Ensure that I didn't talk? They did say they were going to get into trouble.

My pulse was so loud I could hear it in my ears. It was almost deafening. I was trying my best to sit still, but my whole body was beginning to shake. It wasn't until Derek squeezed my arm that I think I took my first breath.

"Relax, we're at Hannah's," Derek whispered, I'm sure he read the panic on my face. "I thought she could help." I could feel his eyes drop. He did notice my outfit. I peered down, my skirt barely covering my legs while sitting.

I quickly wiped my damp hands on my dress as we stood at her door. Dominic impatiently rapped on the door. As we waited, I could feel my head starting to spin again. This was the first time I was going to be in one of their houses. Their… what were they? I wondered what was going to be inside. I don't know why, but my mind started to imagine entering some type of medieval home.

"Derek!" Hannah answered the door with a huge smile on her face. "Come in!"

I stood awkwardly in the doorway. Her house was normal… To the right there was a staircase leading to upstairs, and family photos lined the wall, similar to my own house. You could hear the distant sound of a television playing in the other room.

Derek's voice interrupted my thoughts. "Hannah, I was hoping you could help Amy."

All eyes immediately turned to me. My cheeks, if they weren't red enough already, flushed even deeper. "Oh my! Your poor dress!" She tapped her chin, pondering for a moment. "Come with me. I think I have something you can change into." She bounded to the stairs that I had just been staring at, pulling me behind. It was almost a miracle that I not only kept up, but didn't trip over the stairs with, I was still unwilling to admit Dominic's choice of words, my stability issues.

Her bedroom was at the end of the hall. Again, I wasn't sure what I was expecting, but it definitely wasn't what we walked into. Her room was a light pink color. On the wall was a couple posters of a popular boy band. I couldn't remember their names, but many of the girls at school gushed over their music. Her bed was covered with a floral quilt with frilly pillows. It didn't match the typical tough exterior she wore at school.

"Let's see what we can find!" Hannah was flipping through her clothes in the closet. I slowly sat on the bed, clasping my hands together.

"I'm not sure if you have anything that will fit me," I nervously responded. I was at least five inches taller than her.

She stood pondering, tapping her finger against her lips. I don't think the height difference had originally registered amongst the group, though in my current attire, maybe they assumed I liked smaller clothes. She suddenly froze before dashing out into the hall. She returned holding black yoga pants and a blue tank top.

"Try this!" she said, ushering me across the hall to the bathroom. "There are clean towels under the sink and a hairbrush in the top drawer if you wanted to take shower."

"I don't want to impose with a shower." I mumbled, partly because it felt weird to take a shower in a person's house I only met, officially, for the first time.

"Oh." Hannah hesitated. She was chewing on her bottom lip before she leaned in to whisper. "You smell a bit of alcohol. I wasn't sure if your parents would be upset."

"Good point." Almost immediately, as if it was her words that triggered my nose, the smell of alcohol flooded in again. "Maybe a quick one would be a good idea."

She happily pushed me into the bathroom, closing the door as she left.

I took a deep breath before looking in the mirror. My face winced back. The first thing I saw was the large red stain that covered the front of my costume. There was no hope of saving this. Black streaks covered my face from my running eyeliner and mascara. Waterproof my ass. The only thing that held up was the gold glitter. Almost all the curls had fallen. I carefully pulled the extensions out. They were like a twisted jungle in my hair.

I walked over to the shower and turned the silver knob allowing the water to run. Stripping off my clothes, I stepped inside. I stood, letting the hot water run down the back of my neck. This was not how I expected this evening to go. My heart was racing as my head spun with all the questions that were swirling in my head. One thing I knew, Derek and his friends were not human, but what were they? Were they good or bad? Should I be scared of them? And more importantly, what were they going to do now that I knew?

My mind then went back to that night in my bedroom. It was the same Derek I saw then. Did that mean that wasn't a dream? So, if he was real, what about that creature? I shook my head again trying to erase that thought from my mind.

Maybe what I saw wasn't real. I was, under some influence at the moment, maybe they had flashlights, and my blurred vision was exaggerating the situation.

The shower was heavenly. With the shock from the evening, I hadn't realized how cold I was, until the hot water hit, warming my body. My head also started clearing as my horizon started to stabilize. I popped open the shampoo bottle, breathing in the floral scent. The aroma engulfed the shower as I rubbed it into my hair, banishing the smell of alcohol. The hot water rinsed it out, the last of my curls dropping. The matching conditioner made my hair feel so soft as I ran my fingers through it. Ending too quickly, I turned the knob shutting off the water. I picked up the fluffy white towel I had laid next to the tub. Wrapping it around my body. I picked up the second one to dry my hair.

"Much better," I quietly told myself as I ran the brush

through my hair. I was pleasantly surprised by how well the clothes fit. I was able to get most of the makeup off, my face still shimmered from the glitter, but I kind of liked it. I took a big, deep breath before opening the door. I was half expecting to see Hannah waiting, but the hallway was quiet. I could still hear the TV drowning in the background. They must be in the living room.

I ran my hand against the wall as I walked back toward the stairs, similar to what I did at my house, but the difference was that I actually looked at their pictures. I took my time looking at them. They looked so happy and normal. If what happened tonight was real… I wonder if that meant they all had the same powers Derek did. Maybe Hannah was different and human like me. I shook that thought away. Based on Dominic's reaction, my knowing about them was not good. Which only confirmed what I knew deep down. They were different. I continued to follow the sound of the TV until I reached the room. All four of them were sitting on the two couches in silence. I slowly cleared my throat, unsure how to best acknowledge I was back.

"Oh, Amy, those look great on you!" Hannah was the first to respond, jumping to her feet. I was starting to really like her. Her energy was so intoxicating it was hard not to feel happy around her. Similar to how I felt around Abigail this evening. "You look pale. Can I get you anything? How about some food?"

My stomach responded first. "Actually, that would be wonderful, I haven't eaten all evening." The shower had really helped clear my head. The horizon finally stopped moving, and my words weren't getting stuck in my mouth like before.

"Well, that was a smart thing to do when going drinking," I heard Dominic sarcastically comment.

"I didn't go drinking," I shot back, spinning to face him. That was a mistake I stumbled forward. Derek was next to me in an instant steading me. "I mean, I didn't know I was drinking. I thought it was just punch."

"Maybe I should take you home," Derek said, his arm still wrapped around my waist.

"So, no food?" I whimpered back.

"I'll make something quick!" Hannah skipped out of the room past the stairway, I'm guessing toward the kitchen. Derek led me to the couch he was sitting on across from Dominic and Emery.

Hannah came back with a spread. I tried everything. There were chips, cheese, and meat to make sandwiches. Even the boys made something.

Everyone was quiet. I'm not sure if that was because everyone was so hungry, or they were afraid to say anything, at risk of letting out more secrets. I popped the last chip in my mouth, my stomach finally content.

No longer distracted by the food, all I had was the million questions bubbling up inside of me. Should I ask one? Would it be weird if I didn't? Like whom in their right mind would see what happened tonight and not have questions. I opened my mouth to speak, but Derek, as if knowing what was coming, cut in.

"Well, I better take Amy home." Derek stood, stacking the plates on the coffee table. Dominic grumbled under his breath as he fished the keys out of his pocket, tossing them to Derek, not happy to give up his car again.

Wait. If Dominic was giving Derek the keys, how were they getting home? Yellow flashed in my head as I thought about their wings again.

Derek turned and started walking toward the door, and I followed like a lost puppy. I paused at the door, turning back to the group. "Thank you, Hannah, for the clothes. I'll give them back at school Monday."

"Oh, don't worry about that! They look great on you so just keep them." Hannah responded with a wide smile.

My heart warmed in my chest at the gesture, but not wanting to delay any further, I followed Derek out the door.

We awkwardly sat in the car as Derek fumbled with the keys. "Amy…"

"Yes?" Was that my in? Was he going to let me ask some questions? I opened my mouth to speak, but nothing came out. My mind was spinning on what to ask, as I was still trying to figure out what was real and not. It would've been easier if I had been sober at the time.

"I know a lot happened tonight. But I need you to promise you won't tell anyone."

"Oh… OH! I promise I won't say anything! But…" I hadn't realized I was rubbing my arms nervously and quickly clasped them on my lap. "I do have some questions."

He nodded in response. "I promise I'll answer any of your questions, but just not tonight. I need to…" He stopped for a moment. I could tell he was trying to determine what to say and not.

"It's okay. I understand." I didn't really, why couldn't he tell me now? But I was too scared to press any more questions. What would happen if I made him angry?

We rode in silence for the rest of the trip. I didn't live that far from Hannah, so I was pleasantly surprised when we reached my house. I nervously bit my lip. I wasn't supposed to be home tonight. I was supposed to be back at Alicia's house. That's where my backpack and house keys were. I think I returned the hide-a-key back after the last time I used it.

"Everything okay?" Derek asked.

"Oh yeah, sorry!" I'm sure Derek would take me to Alicia's if I asked, but that would cause so many questions to be asked, and I wasn't the best liar. Plus, who knows what my departure did at the party. Though, drunk girls stumbling away, I think, was a common scene.

"Wait…" My hand froze on the door handle as Derek spoke. "Tomorrow at the library. Meet me there?"

I nodded and opened the door. This time, he didn't wait for me to get inside before leaving. Which I was thankful for because I had not returned the key the last time I had used it, and I had to creep around to the back. Luckily, the back door was left unlocked. Dad usually forgot to check it.

Inside was quiet, so my dad was either already asleep or not back from the bar he visited on Fridays. I climbed the dark stairs leading to my room, my energy quickly draining.

NINE

A shrill sound woke me.

"Hello…" I groggily responded into the phone, my head pounding. So, this is what a hangover feels like. I hate it.

"Amy! Oh my God, you had us both so worried! What the heck happened to you last night?"

"Alicia…?" I could barely think.

"I thought you were coming back to my house, so when we got home, and you weren't here, we were so worried!" she continued, either not picking up on the fact I sounded like death or not caring.

"I'm sorry. I left the party early and didn't want to ruin it for either of you, so I just went home." The lie left my lips so easily.

"Well, what are you going to do about all your stuff? It's all still at my house." The worry from earlier was replaced by annoyance. Not sure if it was because I had ditched them, or the lack of excitement from my adventure.

"Oh crap." She was right. We had left school and went straight to her house. "Actually, I have to go to the library today… do you think you can meet me there?"

We agreed to meet at 1 PM before I hung up the phone. This would hopefully give me enough time to talk to Derek first. It would also mean I would only have to take the bus there. I'm sure Alicia would take me home.

But first, if I was going anywhere today, I needed a large glass of water and a bottle of aspirin. If this was the result of getting drunk, I vowed right there, to never touch another glass.

THE LIBRARY WAS QUIETER THAN NORMAL, WHICH, FOR TODAY'S conversation, was probably going to be for the best. I sat at the table farthest away from the librarian's desk, though it didn't really matter where I chose. The place was vacant. That would be changing soon as finals at the nearby college would be starting soon. Once they started, you couldn't find an empty seat in the three-story building, as students try to cram more than ten weeks of learning into one. I could feel the nerves building in my chest. My hands ran up and down my thighs, trying to dry the sweat that was starting to form. I wonder what Derek would say.

I opened my phone again, staring at the text that Derek had sent me last night.

Library @ 12

The time was now 12:30... maybe he changed his mind. Alicia would be here soon, any longer and we wouldn't be able to talk alone. I was debating texting her to see if she could come later, when I heard my name being called. My whole body jumped. Man, my nerves were shot. My heart felt like it stopped when our eyes met.

"Where's Derek?" I meekly responded. Emery and Dominic were standing by the table.

"He's getting his ass chewed out," Dominic snapped, his fists clenched to his side. Something was wrong. "What did you think was going to happen when…"

"Dominic!" Emery cut him off.

"What!" He turned his anger toward his friend. "What is with both of you! Why are you going out of your way to protect…"

"Enough!" His sharp tone made both me and Dominic stiffen. Dominic started as the aggressor, but one word from Emery made him pause. "I think it's best if you wait outside," he continued, his tone drastically softening.

"Whatever…" Dominic mumbled as he sulked out. We didn't move until we heard the whoosh of the automatic doors closing behind him.

"I'm sorry, Amy, it probably wasn't the best decision to bring Dominic, but I couldn't leave him behind. He can be a little… hot-tempered, and I don't need him making things worse." He pulled the chair on the opposite side of the table, so he was sitting across from me. It forced us to make eye contact unless we intentionally looked away.

"Is Derek okay?" A pit was forming in my stomach. Why wasn't he here?

"He's fine." Emery froze as uncertainty spread across his face. Almost as if he was having some internal debate. "How are you feeling? You had quite a bit to drink last night."

I shrugged. My pounding headache was still present, the gift from last night. "I'm fine, though I think the shock of last night sobered me up pretty quickly." It felt as if we were both feeling each other out. "But why isn't Derek here? He said he was going to explain what happened last night. You know…" I leaned closer to Emery. "Your wings?"

Emery's hand rubbed his face before he sighed. "So, I

guess you remember? I was hoping you were going to chalk that up to the drinking, but I guess Derek's text didn't help."

"Where is he?" I didn't like that he was tiptoeing around the question.

"Well, Dominic was right, though his choice of words could've been better. Derek has a lot of explaining to do. The elders are not happy about our cover being blown last night."

"Is he going to be okay?"

"Yes, he wasn't expecting the news to travel so quickly, but he was also worried about you, especially since the shock from yesterday, so he asked me to come instead." Emery clasped his hands as they lay on the desk.

I just sat in silence. It made sense. It would probably cause an uproar if it was found out that there were people flying around with flaming wings, swinging swords, and fighting... something.

"So, what are you?" I was leaning across the table. If there was a volume below a whisper, I was achieving it.

Emery shook his head. "I can't answer that."

"Why not?" I sat back in my chair, my arms crossing in front. "Derek said he would answer my questions." I felt like a brat. They didn't owe me anything, especially an explanation. I'm sure coming here was breaking a lot of their rules, but that didn't help my frustration.

"Okay," I started again, seeing Emery wasn't going to budge. "How about explaining what happened on the bridge last night?" I could feel a chill run down my spine as I remembered the voice in my head.

I watched his body tense. "I think I can answer that question. Or at least shed some light." He hesitated for a moment, probably trying to find the right words. "It was a Tamer."

"A tamer? A tamer of what?"

"Shadow Reapers." Emery responded, as if that answered everything.

"Wait... is that like the Grim Reaper?" I was picturing the

hooded figure, grasping his scythe with his bony hands. I shivered again, but that was tied to dying. Was I actually trying to kill myself last night, and the Reaper was just waiting for my soul?

"Not quite," Emery cut in. "They like to cause havoc, and let's just say we are here to keep them in line."

Could he be any more vague? His answers were creating even more questions! "Okay, so then how do I play a part in all this? Why was he messing with me." If I could even call that thing a he.

His lips pursed. "Well, you are kind of their food."

"Their food!" I said a little louder. Emery looked around nervously, making sure we didn't catch anyone's attention.

"Not physically," he quietly responded, trying to bring the volume down. "More like they feast off of your presence."

Feast? This sounded like some sort of sick fantasy. I was more lost than ever. "What do you mean?"

"Well... how best can I explain this." His hand slowly rubbed his forehead. "Okay, maybe this analogy would be better. So, think of humans as sheep. We are the shepherds, ensuring the flock stays safe and oblivious to the dangers around them so they can live their happy lives." He turned to see if I was following, satisfied with my expression, he continued. "But as you know, the main enemy of the sheep is the wolf, which in this case will be the Shadow Reapers. They will feast on any sheep that they can separate from the flock. Out of the shepherd's view. You all emit energy, which you all refer to in different ways, souls, qi, life force. We like to refer to them as your soul energy. But that energy isn't enough. It can also be changed based on your emotions. Shadow Reapers will eat any type of soul energy, but they get the strongest when they devour souls that have been infused by fear or deep sadness."

"I don't understand. What do you mean infused? I was picturing those hipster restaurants that prized themselves for creating those unique dishes. They tended to throw the word infused around.

"Think about a time when you experienced extreme sadness or even happiness. Do you remember how your body felt? How it buzzed with that emotion? Those deep emotions effect your body's energy, so the Shadow Reapers will use their power to influence your feelings to get your soul energy at their perfect liking."

"Influence?" Infused, influence, this wasn't sounding any better, but he was also comparing humans to food, which was already unsettling.

"The easiest way they can do that is by manipulating dreams."

This felt like something out of a sci-fi show. First, we talked about creatures eating humans, and now we are talking about our dreams. And is he saying they can control them?

He stopped, examining my expression. Trying to see if he had lost me yet. "Have you ever had a time where you had a bad nightmare, and when you awoke, you felt more exhausted than when you went to sleep?" I nodded in response. "That was most likely the effect of a Shadow Reaper."

A shiver spread across my body leaving behind goose-bumps on my arms. Then, that night flashed in my head. The creature that had been in my room, his fluid skin and large fangs, but that wasn't the same creature from the bridge. Tamer, did that mean they controlled the monsters? "So, what, you all go around breaking into peoples' homes to battle these creatures?"

A smirk spread across his face as he leaned back in his chair. His arms crossed across his chest. "Putting it in simple terms, we make sure they don't get out of control." He didn't leave room to elaborate.

"So how do we fight them? How do we protect ourselves?" We couldn't be as powerless as he was making it sound. I mean, we were humans. We were the most powerful things on the planet. We were at the top of the food chain! At least, that is what I thought before last night.

"Can the sheep ever defeat the wolf, Mya?"

My heart stopped. "What did you say?"

I watched the confusion spread across his face, trying to pinpoint what he had said that elicited my reaction. "I'm not here to scare you. This has been going on for a long time. Longer than any of us, our parents, and even their parents have been alive."

"No." I grabbed the table. I felt like they were going to snap the edge off. "What did you call me?"

The color drained from his face. He knew what he had done. How did he know that name? There was only one person who called me that. 'Mya.' That was the name Cole used for me. He always said it was because I was "my-a" (my Amy). He rarely used that name outside of our family.

"What do you all just spy on us? Is that how you all get off on your free time?" The anger boiled in my chest. I don't know why I was so angry, but it was that small connection with him. The special bond we had together. Something only we shared.

"Amy, relax." Emery's eyes darted around the room. I wonder if he was afraid my outburst was bringing unwanted attention. I also took a quick glance. The librarian was busy scanning books at her computer, clearly unfazed.

"Don't tell me to relax," I spat through gritted teeth. "How did you know that name?"

"You really don't remember us, do you?" Sadness filled his eyes as if he was remembering a distant memory.

"What are you talking about? Remember who?" I was even more lost. Why was he playing these mind games? Just come out and say what you are thinking.

"Cole and I were best friends. We used to hang out all the time. Just like you and Derek." He was getting uncomfortable as he started to fidget in his seat.

"You're kidding, right? Derek and I have never been friends." That was a little harsh. "At least not before now."

"Your special friends with wings? Try and remember. I know your memories are there," Emery whispered, leaning closer. He reached for my hand, but I pulled it back.

"I have no idea what you are talking about! I think I would remember if Cole and I were friends with you! It's kind of hard to forget someone with wings!"

"It's there, Amy, just try." His eyes suddenly changed, the gold eyes boring into my soul. He was doing something to me. Flashes started appearing. Slight memories of my past, but instead of Cole and me, there were others appearing, almost as if they were covered in a fog. I noticed two other boys were also there.

This time, the color drained from my face. "What are you doing to me. Stop manipulating my memories." Did they have the same ability as the Shadow Reapers? Could they influence our thoughts? Or maybe worse. Were they the Shadow Reapers?

"I'm not manipulating anything." He lifted his hand up, palms facing me. "They made you forget about us, but I know we are still in there."

"Who?" I felt like I was losing my mind. His mouth snapped shut. He knew he said too much.

I was trying to think back to my childhood. What was he talking about? I froze in my chair. That must be it. Oh my God, I have lost my mind. When I was little, barely in elementary school, I had a problem inventing imaginary friends. I was told I had an overactive imagination. But I don't remember anything about them. I just forgot about them. But did they just come back? Was I having a psychotic break? Maybe the stress of everything had finally pushed me to the limit. But what was my breaking point? What finally made me crack?

"That's it! You're not real." Laughter exploded from me.

Here I was, inventing this whole new world of these shadow creatures taking over the world. I lost it. I've finally gone crazy. "None of you are real!" This must be hallucinations from being hungover. Is that what alcohol did? I turned and with all my strength, pushed myself from the table running toward the exit. The automatic doors barely opened in time.

"Watch out!" I almost collided with Dominic who had been standing right outside the doors. "Shit, what did Emery say to you? You look like you saw a ghost!"

"Go away... go away! You're not real!" I screamed. Before he could react, I jumped around him and ran toward the parking lot.

"Amy?" I heard someone call my name. I spun to see where it came from, and for the first time today, I felt relief.

"Alicia!" I ran to her car.

"Yeah?" She was eyeing me wearily. "You told me to meet you here to give you your things."

"Yes, right." I couldn't stand still. My whole body was jittering, and I just wanted to get away. "Can you take me home?"

"Sure... is everything okay?"

"Yes, sorry, I just didn't want to take the bus." I pulled the passenger handle and jumped in.

Alicia pulled out from the parking spot and headed toward the road. I closed my eyes and tried to take deep breaths, hoping to clear my head or at least try and calm myself. Of course they weren't real. People with wings, how absurd was that! Maybe Cole's anniversary was my final trigger. That's when everything started happening again.

"What happened between you and... what's his name... D-something... Dean, no... uh... Donald..." Alicia was stopped, waiting to pull out into traffic.

"Dominic?" There was no way.

"Yeah, it looked like you were yelling at him. It looked

pretty intense." There was finally a break, and she pulled out, her tires screeching from the tight turn.

"You're seeing Dominic." My voice barely a whisper as my mind started spinning again.

"What! No! I'm seeing Mike!"

"No…" I was rubbing my forehead. My headache was coming back. "I mean, you could physically see Dominic at the library?" It wasn't possible… if what I just learned today was true, only I could see them.

"Yeah… he wasn't hiding. You both were right in front of the library." Alicia's eyes shifted, looking at me wearily before turning back to focus on the road. "Amy, are you okay? You are acting totally weird. You didn't, like, take anything at the party last night, did you? I mean, I heard about the drinking. Which is totally not like you."

"No, I mean… I don't know. I think I'm just tired. I just need to get home." We drove in silence the rest of the way.

I closed my eyes. I was starting to see more memories. Derek and I at the park. Cole and Emery playing swords, but these were flashes. Almost like trying to watch a movie, but the film had been cut into small bits, and I could only see a couple short scenes at a time. What was happening to me?

Then I remembered that night. I was in our living room. Mom, me, and Cole. I was being told I needed to stop with the imaginary friends.

"Derek and Emery aren't real!" My mom said, as she gripped something in her hand. It was some kind of paper. Was it something from school? "You are too old to have imaginary friends."

"But Emery is Cole's friend!" I shouted back. "Cole, tell her they're real!"

"Amy…" he was always serious when he used my name, "I was just playing with you. I didn't want to hurt your feelings if I told you they weren't real."

"You're lying! Why are you all lying? They are real!" I ran to my room, slamming the door behind me.

Cole, like the good big brother, followed me and softly knocked on the door. I let him in. We just sat in silence on my bed. "They are real, right?"

"I'm sorry, Amy. I shouldn't have encouraged it for so long, but you were so happy. But don't be sad, you are going to make new friends, we both will, and they will be even better!"

The memory faded.

"Amy?"

I felt something nudge my shoulder. Did I fall asleep? Was that all a dream? What was a real memory, and what was fake?

"Alicia…" I responded dryly. I hope I wasn't snoring. She already thought I was going crazy, so what were a few more questions? "Do you know Derek?"

"From school? Yeah… he's dating Becca, right?"

"Yeah, and Emery? He's a senior, I think?"

I could tell she was thinking. "I think so. Don't they all hang out together?"

This made no sense. Did my imagination take real people and twist them into those things with wings. What was real and what wasn't? I pushed my hand hard into my chest as if it would calm my frantic heart. I went there to have my questions answered and now I was questioning my own sanity.

We finally reached my house. Alicia sighed in relief, she wanted me out and quick. I grabbed my bag and rushed to the house. I don't think we even said bye to each other.

I leaned against the closed door. Blinking hard, I was trying to stop the tears from forming in my eyes. I was thankful for the quiet. My dad must have stayed out all night with his drinking buddies. Sometimes, they would crash at whoever's house was closest to the bars. Hopefully, he will be gone until Sunday. For the first time, in I don't know how long, I walked past my room and went into

Cole's. Anger started to rise again as if someone had taken over my body.

"Why couldn't you be here?" I yelled. There was a ball sitting on the shelf. I picked it up, throwing it across the room. That felt good. I reached out again, throwing whatever my hand could touch.

I grabbed the books off the bookshelf and flung them to the ground. I kicked over boxes that had been in the corner. I picked up a small wooden box on his dresser and I hurled it. With a loud crack, it hit the opposite wall, the contents exploding on the ground. I stood in the center of the room, catching my breath. The room around me started to come back into focus. A pit in my stomach replaced the anger as I looked around at the damage I had done.

I walked over to the box that was now splintered and knelt next to the contents. They were random knick-knacks, but things that were special to him. There were a couple of dice, a few of his favorite monster and spell cards, foreign coins, a lighter, and a photo. I froze as I held it. It was a picture of me and Cole when we were little. I remember that day. It was our first day of school. I was going into kindergarten. My mom wanted to capture the memory, so she had us line up on the steps. Just Cole and I. The picture was creased and ripped down the middle. I tucked it in my pocket before taking a deep breath. I wish I knew what was real. Why did I have those memories?

Leaving the mess, I ran out of his room and retreated back to mine. I dove my head into my pillow and cried. I cried until there was nothing left.

I awoke to pounding on the door. I don't even remember falling asleep. I really hope I wasn't turning into a narcoleptic. I looked at the clock, how was it already seven! I stumbled out of my bed toward the stairs. It must be Ms. Swartz, our neighbor. I wonder what we did this time to warrant her visit. I don't think I left the garbage bin out again.

"Ye—" I stopped in mid-sentence when the door opened. I was not expecting him.

Derek was leaning against the front doorway. He looked exhausted, as if he hadn't slept in a week. I knew that was my fault. How long did he have to meet with the... elders, I think they called them? How much trouble did he get in for helping me?

"Can I come in?" Derek asked, even his voice sounded raw.

"Of course!" I moved out of the way so he could come in. However, I quickly jumped to his side when he stepped in. I was afraid he was going to collapse. He stumbled in, and I led him to one of the overstuffed chairs.

"Thanks." He winced as he slid down.

"Are you okay?" I sat on the couch, just staring at him. What did they do to him? Before I could say anything else, more pounding erupted from the door. My whole body froze. My eyes were probably the size of dinner plates. Who was at my door now? What if someone was after Derek? Could I do anything to stop them?

"Amy?" I heard someone call out, I sighed a breath of relief. I fumbled with the door opening to Emery and Dominic standing on my porch. There was another guy with them as well. Aiden, he was the one who was in the car with Derek at school.

"I think something's wrong." My voice was shaking. They didn't wait for an invite before rushing inside.

Aiden was the first one to speak. "Derek." Worry was the only expression on his face. Emery was stoic, which seemed normal to him, while Dominic was pissed.

"Guys... I'm okay." Derek tried to get up but stumbled again. All three were by his side immediately. Their speed was incredible.

"Amy, is there someplace he can lay down?" Emery asked.

I was cursing myself under my breath. Cole's room

would've been perfect before I trashed it. "Let's get him to my room." Aiden and Dominic hoisted him up under his arms and effortlessly brought him upstairs.

"In here." I opened my door, and I was suddenly self-conscious of my room. Emery stood in the doorway. I wonder if it brought back memories. Imaginary friends or not, he had made it clear he had been here before.

"Amy," Emery's hand was on my shoulder, "can you give us a few minutes?"

"You aren't going to hurt him, right?" I couldn't look away. He looked so broken.

"Of course not." He led me out the door before closing it behind me. I leaned against the wall and slid to the ground. I brought my knees to my chest, hugging them close. A scream erupted behind the door. My stomach twisted, I felt like I was going to be sick, and my head spun. Was I going to pass out?

Another scream erupted, followed by a yelp. I couldn't take it. I stood up, grabbed the door handle, and flung the door open. "Stop," I screamed, "you're hurting him."

Derek was lying shirtless on his stomach. Deep red marks covering his back in a crisscross fashion. There was more red than skin. My hands were over my mouth again. "Derek…" I whimpered. It was too late. I grabbed the trashcan to my right, hurling. This was becoming a common scene for me.

"Amy," Emery was by my side again, "I promise we are taking good care of him."

"What happened?" I coughed out, my throat raw.

"It's his punishment. He's actually lucky. It could've been worse."

Dominic laughed, it wasn't a humorous laugh, but the disgusted one. "How is this lucky? They could've killed him!"

"This is all my fault." I couldn't break my eyes away from him. He was passed out from the pain. "Why didn't he just leave me be? Who cares if something happened to me!"

"Amy, don't say that! Don't diminish what Derek did."

Emery's words were cold. He paused before starting again, this time softer. "Do you want to help?" All I could do was nod in response. "Perfect. Can you get us some clean towels, warm water, and hydrogen peroxide?"

I pushed myself off the floor and rushed to the bathroom. I started to fling all the cabinet doors open looking for the supplies. Towels, check. Hydrogen peroxide, check? I tried to find an expiration date. Did this stuff go bad? I also found an old first aid kit shoved in the back. I popped it open. Inside were a variety of band-aids and ace wrap. I returned my spoils to Emery before heading to the kitchen. I found a large pitcher and filled it up with hot water. It would cool quick, so I probably ran it hotter than I should. I also grabbed a couple large bowls, I'm sure they were going to need to wet the towels, so hopefully, that helped.

"Perfect, thanks, Amy." Emery handed the items to Aiden and Dominic. "Now, go downstairs and turn on the television. We'll come get you when we're done, okay?"

I nodded again.

I followed their instructions. I didn't want to be in the way again, so I sat in the living room with the television as high as it would go. It was an action movie playing, which was perfect because it would match the screams from upstairs, so if anyone walked by, they would assume it was all coming from the TV. Hopefully, Ms. Swartz wouldn't stop by, but the fact she hadn't already probably was a good sign.

At least an hour passed, if not longer, before the three of them emerged again. They all had a defeated look on their faces.

"Well?" I stood from the chair.

"He'll be fine. He just needs some rest." Emery hesitated as I watched his hand rub up and down his arm. "I know this is a huge ask, but can he stay with you tonight? I'm not sure if that will cause problems with your dad," he asked.

"It should be fine, I don't think Dad will be home tonight

anyway, and if he does, he won't come to my room." I rubbed my hands anxiously.

"Thanks, we should go. If you need anything, call me." Emery extended his hand for my phone. I fished it out of my pocket, handing it to him. He entered his phone number and sent a quick text to himself before handing it back. "Thanks, Amy."

I just nodded. Dominic and Aiden didn't say a word. I knew they blamed me. I should've just stayed in the car. No, I shouldn't have been such a naïve idiot. Who gets drunk by accident? I started up the stairs once they left. No, he needed to sleep, so I went back into the living room, flipping back on the TV. I couldn't tell you what was playing. I just sat there numb, lost in my own self wallow.

I jumped at the sound of the door. Who was there?

"Oh, Amy," my dad slurred as he stumbled in. Of course, out of all days, now he decides to come home.

"Uh… hi, Dad." I nervously glanced up the stairs. Please, Derek, stay asleep. "Are you hungry? I was about to make some food," I lied, but it wasn't a bad idea to bring some food to Derek, then I could excuse myself upstairs for the rest of the night.

"I'm good, but I could take a beer." Sure Dad. I think that's a great choice. I headed into the kitchen. I think burgers would do.

TEN

The burgers sizzled in the pan. I couldn't lie. They smelled amazing. I think the sandwiches last night were the last thing I ate. I flipped them one last time before placing them on a plate. I made three burgers. Hopefully, Dad wouldn't notice, though once he had that beer in his hand and the game on, he ignored everything else. I could probably have Derek sitting in the living room, and he wouldn't even notice.

I grabbed a couple cans of soda, the plate of burgers, and a bag of chips clenched in my teeth. I slowly made my way up the stairs, carefully balancing the precious food. The last thing I needed was for the burgers to end up on the floor. My mouth was already salivating. I entered the room backward, using my elbow to turn the knob. I froze in the doorway.

Derek was still asleep, lying on his stomach. I'm glad I found the ace bandages because they were wrapped around his body, covering the majority of the gashes. Whatever was still exposed was covered by large square bandages. Damn, even wrapped like a mummy, he was still hot. Muscles rippled down his back, his broad shoulders creating a T. Snap out of it! I was thankful he didn't stir and find me staring. I slowly set the food down, sitting cross-legged on the floor, my back against the bed. Right when I was about to take a bite, I heard his voice.

"That smells amazing," he weakly said.

I spun my head around, and our eyes linked. "I'm sorry I didn't mean to wake you."

He groaned as he turned his body, the muscles in his arms flexing as he used them to support his weight. Slowly, he pulled himself up, leaning his body against the headboard. It creaked against the added weight. "Actually, I would die for one of those burgers." A grin spread across his face. My heart almost flipped in response. I was so used to seeing dismissive Derek at school. I'm not sure I remember seeing another emotion from him.

How was he smiling at a time like this, and here I was wide-eyed staring like some lovestruck girl. Stop it. You can't use the word love. I placed the two burgers onto the second plate. After dumping a generous amount of chips, I handed it to him. I also cracked open one of the cans of soda and placed it on the nightstand, so it was easy for him to reach. We sat in silence as we ate, but that was partially due to the fact we were inhaling the burgers as if we had gone months without food.

"Damn, those were some great burgers. Did you learn how to make them from the diner?" Derek took a sip of his soda, and the plate almost licked clean.

"Yeah, I try and help out wherever I can, and sometimes I need to cover the grill." I was glad I decided on burgers. It was nice to get complimented on my cooking. That rarely happened when I cooked for Dad. I stood shocked trying to recover. "So, now what?"

"To be honest," he rested the back of his head against the headboard, staring at the ceiling, "I'm not sure."

"I don't remember you." I stared at my clasped hands. Sure, I had some memories return when talking to Emery, but they were fading just as quickly as they had returned. As if something was forcing them away.

"I know." I could hear the sadness in his voice. A lump formed in my throat. Did I disappoint him? It wasn't anything new. I disappointed everyone in my life. Then he surprised me. "But I've been waiting for you to welcome me back." Our eyes met again. That half grin was back, and there went my heart.

"I've never had a sleepover before," I said jokingly. That was true. With my less-than-picturesque home, I never wanted to bring anyone in. Then, once my mom left, it made it easier. Parents weren't keen on letting their daughters stay over at a house with a single dad. That sucks that there is that stereotype, though in my case, it was pretty warranted.

"So what? Face masks and cucumbers?" He chuckled at his own joke. What a dork.

"Sorry, fresh out. I'm sure I can mix some mud out back if that's what you had your heart set on." I peeked over. Success. Joke landed.

"Stop!" Derek gripped his sides. "Don't make me laugh." He still chuckled to himself, but I could see the pain on his face. My chest tightened. He was in pain because of me.

"Can I get you something before I go?" I was on my knees now, my arms against the bed, scared to touch him and make it worse.

"Where are you going?" Why did his eyes turn so sad all of a sudden?

"I'm not going far. I'll crash on the couch tonight." It wasn't the most comfortable couch, but at least it was better than sleeping in the recliner.

"Please stay…" Without finishing his sentence, he tugged my arm, pulling me into the bed. He winced as our bodies collided.

"Sorry!" I jumped back, almost falling off the bed, but

before I could blink, his arm was wrapped around me, holding me from falling. How could someone be so fast?

I compromised and sat next to him on the bed. There was still distance between us, but it was enough to satisfy him. My elbow rested on my knee while my hand supported my head. I couldn't stop staring at him. His skin had a perfect tan, as if he spent most of his day without a shirt on. Which I mean made sense if he randomly had wings exploding from his back.

Wait, his back. I thought back to when he was lying face-down on the bed. Sure, he was pretty bandaged, but I didn't see anything that would signify having wings. Scars, slits, baby wings? Nothing, it looked like a normal boy's back. I mean a normal back of someone who was a professional weightlifter. No, that wasn't a good description. He didn't have a large muscular body. Not like the ones where you can't figure out how they can put a shirt on every day. His was balanced. Muscles you would get from doing hard labor, not just lifting weights at the gym.

"What are you thinking about?" His eyes bore into me, as if they were trying to solve a hard riddle.

"Nothing." I'm sure my cheeks were turning red. I wasn't about to admit I was having an internal debate about his muscles.

"Liar." He wasn't letting me off that easy. "Girls can't think of nothing. You all aren't wired that way."

"And how would you know that?" Sure, my brain didn't like to take holidays, but that was a pretty broad statement.

"Because you all are always scheming on something." I knew he was joking, but I wonder how much of that was in reference to Becca. My nose scrunched just thinking of her. Shoot! Hide your reactions, girl!

"This isn't right." I shouldn't be in bed with another girl's boyfriend. I mean, I shouldn't be in bed with a guy, period, but this situation was just wrong.

"Wait." He grabbed my wrist. Not in a mean hard way, but more gentle just to get me to pause. "I'm not ready to go back to the way things are. Can't we just spend one night like old times. When it was just you and me against the world?" Almost like magic, he aged in front of me. He wasn't that mysterious guy always in the back of the classroom brooding. He was a little boy, pleading.

"But I don't remember those days. I don't know what the old times were like. And regardless, we were kids. It's different now."

"Different, how?"

Really? He couldn't think of any reason why this wasn't a good idea? Well, I did. "How about Becca?"

"Becca…" I could tell that struck a nerve. His gaze turned hard. "That's complicated."

I threw my hands up in the air. "Exactly."

"No." He reached out but dropped his hand and rested his head against the headboard, staring at the ceiling. "I mean, there's more there than you know. There's politics you wouldn't understand." He stopped again. "That's why I liked being here." He was drifting back to the past again. "Here with you, it was like I could forget all those responsibilities and expectations, and I could finally just be myself. You were the one person I could be myself around and who wouldn't judge me for not being perfect."

My heart was racing now. What I would give to remember who we were. That carefree, innocent kid I pictured he was. Is that what he needed from me? If that's what I could return to him for protecting me. For those wounds on his back, which were punishment for helping me. I could do that. He winced as he sat up straighter. My chest tightened. Was he going to leave?

"Wait!" I said a little too loudly. "Stay," I nearly whispered. I noticed dark bags were forming under his eyes. This conversation was taking too much out of him. "You can sleep here. Don't worry, I can sleep downstairs tonight."

His hand was on my hand, his fingers wrapping around the edges. My heart felt like it went on pause in response. My chest also tightened as my breath caught in my throat. "You can stay. Don't worry, I'm too hurt to try any funny business." That half smile returned. "What, this bed is a king? I think there is enough room for both of us. Plus, do you know how many sleepovers we've already had?"

My face turned beet red for the last statement. Moments ago, I had told him this was probably my first sleepover, and now he is telling me we had them in the past? Regardless though, there was a difference between a little kid's sleepover and a teenager's. I rolled my lip, moving it between my teeth. It would raise questions if I tried to sleep somewhere else, and the last thing I needed was for my dad to come into my room. The only other piece of furniture in my room to use was a wooden rocker that wouldn't be comfortable. "Okay, but no funny business." I tried to give my sternest look. "I'm going to go change… do you need anything?"

He just shook his head in response. His energy was obviously draining fast. I was actually surprised we held as long of a conversation as we did. I stopped at my drawers, suddenly self-conscious of all my clothes. None of my pajamas seemed appropriate. Why didn't I take up Alicia's offers all those times we were out shopping. Why did I care? I wasn't trying to impress him. I closed my drawer. Who was I kidding? Yes, I was.

I headed to the bathroom to brush my teeth, and then I saw them. The clothes Hannah had lent me. They could pass as pajamas. A lot of girls wore yoga pants to bed, and the tank top had enough coverage while not being too hot. I took a cursory sniff. I only wore them for a couple hours, and it was after a shower. After running a brush through my hair, I gave myself one final look over before heading back.

Derek was back to laying on his stomach on top of the blankets. He had moved to the right side of the bed, farthest from the door, but closest to the windows. I just stood in the doorway, staring for a few minutes. If I could give him a place to feel safe, I would do everything in my power to do just that.

Before heading to bed, I walked to the rocker. On the back was an old quilt. I remember how proud my mom was when she found this at the thrift store. She bragged about how she haggled down the price. My mom loved going to those places. I walked back to the bed and covered him with it. He didn't even stir.

I crawled under the blankets on the left side. I turned to face him, just to stare at his face. Those normal sharp angles on his face had softened. His lips were still very tempting. Stop, Amy. What are you doing! I flipped on my back. And this is why sleepovers are different! Why did the air feel so heavy? My whole body was buzzing. I'm not going to be able to sleep. I turned my head to look at him again.

"Goodnight, Derek," I whispered.

ELEVEN

I was so comfy. I didn't want to open my eyes. My arm was wrapped around something warm. What stuffed animal did I have in my bed? I tried to do a quick run through my list... no! My eyes sprung open. That was no stuffed animal. My arm was draped across Derek's chest as I was pressed against his side. As if a bomb had just gone off, I propelled myself to the other side. A chuckle was the response.

"Well, good morning, sleepyhead." Oh God... how long had he been awake?

"Morning," I mumbled back, I was not a morning person, and now I was horrified.

He propped himself up against the headboard again. I was surprised by how quickly he moved, and he didn't have any hesitation when he leaned back. Actually, now looking at him his ace bandage was gone. There were still patches from the bandages on his sides that signaled they were still on. I wonder if he was uncomfortable in them last night.

"Do you need me to change your bandages?" My stomach flipped just thinking about it. I wasn't sure how I would get through it without throwing up or passing out, but I would at least try.

"Actually," Derek stretched his arm across his chest, pulling it at the elbow with his other arm to finish the stretch, "I think I'm feeling pretty good. They can probably come off."

"I don't think that's a good idea... you should really keep them covered. You don't want them to get infected." My stomach flipped again, infected wounds. I was going to lose my breakfast before I even ate it.

Derek jumped out of the bed facing the window, so his back was in clear view. My jaw dropped, not a slight drop, but if my jawbone wasn't attached, my chin would probably be on the bed right now. I was right. The square bandages were still on his back, but where they didn't cover because it was originally covered by the ace bandage, the wounds that had been so deep and wide were now faint lines. Still healing as they had scabbed over, but instead of being at least a half to an inch wide, now they almost resembled cat scratches. There was no redness around them, what you would picture the final days before they disappeared.

"Wait... how in the... I mean, yesterday they were..." I couldn't finish a thought.

He looked over his shoulder, gave that half grin, and winked. As if that was the perfect answer to explain how he magically healed in less than twenty-four hours. I sat on the bed dumbfounded. I mean, he had fiery wings. Why should this surprise me?

"What are you?" I couldn't help asking again. My conversation with Emery left me with more questions than answers.

Derek joined me back in bed. Sitting so we were facing each other. "We call each other Guardians."

"Guardians?" That sounded official, though I guess it made sense based on what Emery described. I guess in their eyes, they guard us.

"And you aren't human?" That question felt stupid. Of

course, they weren't human, what human could randomly fly. Maybe they were aliens?

"I guess you could think of us as some ancient race. We have been on Earth as long as humans, but we don't really co-exist."

"Like the Greek gods?" I blurted. I don't know why my head immediately went to them.

He shut that question down quickly. "We aren't gods."

"Yeah... you're closer to angels." I pictured my costume. Wait... maybe they were angels! That would make sense. Wings, protectors against evil.

"We are NOT angels." He had a disgusted look on his face. Why was that a trigger? "Sorry... I just mean that you all have a picture of what angels are and trust me, we aren't anywhere close to them."

I feel like I'm starting to annoy him. I didn't want to make him angry, especially since yesterday, I elected to be a safe place for him. I was trying to think of a good change of subject.

"I think your dad left about an hour ago." He was staring out the window again.

Not surprising, it was Sunday, so he was probably on his way to the track. He liked to go there on Sundays. He would probably have a few bets going already, hopefully, he didn't lose too much money. It was going to be tight around here this month after my haircut and the Halloween costume. I would most likely have to pull from my college savings. Thank God for that. I probably had a little over five thousand saved. Nowhere close to my goal, but enough for emergencies.

"So, what's the plan for today?" He sounded like an anxious kid.

"Shouldn't you be resting?" And I sounded like an annoyed parent.

"Pshhh," was his response. "I'm good as new. Come on,

let's go out!" Apparently, our conversation hadn't phased him. But I was no closer to figuring out what they were.

"Well, I need to get some homework done, so I was thinking about hitting the library." His face dropped by my response. "What? You don't have any?"

He rolled his eyes. "Fine, you're lucky I have my stuff in my car, but we're at least getting breakfast first!"

IF I COULD MELT INTO THE CHAIR, I WOULD. OUT OF ALL THE places for us to go, we had to go to Charlie's Diner. I picked at the breakfast special in front of me. Two pieces of toast, two eggs over medium, with a side of hashbrowns and sausage. I wasn't a huge breakfast person. I usually grabbed the quickest thing out the door at home. Derek, on the other hand, ordered a little boy's dream breakfast. A stack of chocolate pancakes, did I count five? Doused with what had to be a whole bottle of syrup and whip cream. How did he stay so fit with a diet like this? A metabolism every girl would envy.

A little boy, that was the perfect description for him today. He was nothing like the Derek I've known for the past year. He has been almost jumping off the walls with excitement, and that usual look of disdain has been replaced with pure joy.

"How is everything tasting?" The waitress asked. She was one of the college students that worked here. She kept shooting me looks as if to say, 'we are talking about this later!'

"Very good," Derek responded with a mouth still full of food.

She couldn't help smiling in response, as if she had slaved over the grill making the meal rather than just punching it into the screen. *Alright, you can stop staring and go,* I thought. Why was I getting jealous? We weren't an item… I don't even know what you would call us. She finally left to check her other tables. I was right. Charlie's was getting busier.

"How set are you on going to the library?" Derek leaned back in the chair, clearly satisfied with his meal.

"I really need to get my homework done." I was already nervous that I hadn't started anything this weekend, I wasn't bluffing earlier to Alicia and Grace about the math test on Monday. "But if you don't want to, it's no problem. You can drop me at home."

"No, we can still work on homework. I just think I have a better spot." That sly smile was making me nervous.

"Okay… as long as we actually work on homework." My heart was beating like a drum on a drumline. He needed to stop looking at me like that!

Derek grabbed the check and headed to the counter to pay. As soon as he left, the waitress was back at the table. "Oh my God! Where have you been hiding him?" She slid into the booth, conveniently in perfect view of him.

"Oh, I just know him from school." She was talking to me as if we were close friends. I think this was the longest sentence she has said to me since we've been working together.

"Are you guys…" she drifted off, not wanting to say the word, as if saying it would make it true.

My jaw clenched to avoid a snappy remark from escaping. Why did she care what we were? "No, just friends. We just ran into each other this weekend, so we decided to grab breakfast." That was kind of true. Her eyes widened in excitement. Why did that reaction make me so angry? "But he does have a girlfriend," I added. Did that make things better or worse?

"He seems open to hanging out with other girls." She smirked before sliding out of the booth. She walked to the cash register, almost pushing poor Sandy out of the way to help.

I took that cue for me to join them. I had declined to take

leftovers since we weren't going home. They probably wouldn't be good for long. But I did feel guilty for barely eating half of my meal. Maybe Derek would let me pay him back. Or if we are out for a long time, I could offer to pay for lunch.

"Ready?" Derek asked as I joined him, I just nodded. I noticed him stuffing the receipt in his pocket. It was enough time to see a number written on it. Did she ask if he wanted her number or just gave it? Maybe Derek liked to play the field. I was starting to feel bad for Becca. It must be hard to be with a guy who girls throw themselves at. Was I becoming one of those girls as well?

We rode in silence. Surprisingly, it wasn't an awkward silence. Derek was focusing on the road, remembering where to turn, while I was tracking the landmarks we were passing to try and figure out where we were headed. I got it! At least, I hoped I got it. There was one place I loved going that was past the train tracks. But how would Derek know that? Or was this his favorite place, too.

"Are we going to the museum?" I was a little too giddy.

He gave that stupid half-smile in response. Did he know what that did to people? He probably did. I squirmed a little in my seat, thinking of the receipt. Did he give that same smile to the waitress? We pulled into the parking lot which was empty. That was typical. Most of their traffic happened during the week with school trips from elementary school to high school. They also did specials on Saturday where college students got in for free, but just like the mall, the museum had suffered from the change in the times. With more access to the internet, people stopped frequenting these places. Why drive to the museum and pay admission when you could google anything at home for free. They also offered virtual tours of the famous museums in Europe from your living room!

The automatic doors slid open as we approached, revealing the beautiful marble lobby inside. There was a large replica of a mammoth standing in the middle of the lobby, cave men surrounding it holding spears. Now older, I realized that probably wasn't the most inviting image to greet you since they were trying to kill the poor thing.

As we walked in, Derek pulled some paper out of his pocket, crinkling it up before tossing it into the trashcan. I smiled when I realized it was the receipt. Did he do that for my benefit? To show he didn't care about her number. I shook that thought away. Of course not. He was probably throwing it away because of Becca.

I stopped at the ticket line. The path was guided by cloth zigzagging back and forth to use the most space for the expected crowds. Except, there were no crowds. There wasn't anyone else in the lobby besides Derek, me, and the lonely clerk at the ticket window. Should we go through awkwardly, making our way to the front as the person watched us, or just walk around to the entrance? I think Derek was reading my mind because he led us around the perimeter to the front.

Wait… was reading minds another one of their abilities? I could feel my eyes widen with that thought. I peered over, but Derek's expression was focused forward. I'm sure if he could read my mind, he would be laughing at my hysteria.

"Welcome to the Atticus Museum. We have a special right now on annual passes, buy one get three free months."

I glanced at the sign above the ticket booths. Day passes were twenty dollars, while the annual passes were one hundred and thirty dollars. This would be the reason I would get a car, just to come here, but the bus system out here wasn't great. I probably wouldn't be able to make it back unless I could convince Grace or Alicia to go, and that was never going to happen. I started to pull my wallet out of my purse, but Derek was faster and slid his card on the counter.

"We'll take two annual passes."

"Oh no!" I grabbed his arm. "That's very nice of you, but I probably won't be able to use one."

"Why?" His brow furrowed as he asked. He was acting like this was as normal response. Like I'm the crazy one here! First off, who just randomly pays over a hundred dollars on someone they barely know? And second, we've never mentioned of the museum before this moment.

"Because my friends aren't big into the museum, and I would have a hard time trying to get here." I was glancing at the lady on the counter, afraid our indecisiveness was annoying her, but instead, she just wore the same plastered smile she had when we walked up.

"Then I guess we will come back. I'm your friend, right?" Without pausing, he turned back to the clerk. "That'll be two annual passes, please." My hand dropped. What, was this turning into a regular occasion?

The clerk took our pictures and once our passes were printed, we signed the back. The gray pixelated pictures were hard to see, so I wasn't sure how this was a good identification system, but I was happy to have one again. We used to have annual passes when I was young. My mom would try and take Cole and me here at least once a month. Cole loved seeing the dinosaurs, while I loved the African section. They had a variety of stuffed animals from Africa. I would pretend I was sitting on the savannah on safari.

Derek grabbed my hand and led me past the ticket counter. There were two floors to the museum. The lobby had two large staircases on opposite sides to take you up. There were also elevators for anyone who couldn't or didn't want to climb them. Upstairs led to the geology room, where they had different rocks, gems, and crystals. They also housed the

Egyptian room, which had mummies and different artifacts. Along with an art exhibit, that held some popular old and up-and-coming artists. The bottom housed the dinosaur and the animal exhibits.

Derek took the hallway to the left, and my heart leaped. He was leading us to Africa! It was just as I remembered. There was a herd of zebras, half grazing and half watching for predators. Elephants, antelopes, and giraffes were some of the other animals littered around. They had big cats like the cheetahs and the pack of lions.

"Is here okay?" Derek stopped at the bench facing the zebras dropping his backpack to the ground.

"Derek…" I whispered, looking over my shoulders to make sure no one else was around. "Can you read minds?" It sounded as stupid leaving my mouth as it did in my head, but how was he able to guess this was my favorite spot, on top of everything else today?

He erupted in laughter. My cheeks flushed. "No, what makes you think we can read minds?" he asked, catching his breath.

"Well, you knew I wanted the annual pass, then that the African area was my favorite spot, and now having us sit in front of the zebras."

"Of course, I knew. When we were little, we couldn't get you to leave this place when we visited. Remember how mad Cole would get because he was afraid we wouldn't have time to see the dinosaurs?" His eyes glazed over as he was thinking of those past memories.

I dropped to the bench. Yes, I remembered those visits. It got to the point where Mom would let us split up when we came because she was tired of the arguing about which exhibits to see. But why didn't I remember Derek in them? It's as if he was erased from them. How many other people have I forgotten from my past?

"I don't remember that." I said, my voice defeated. Was

that going to anger him? Is he mad I forgot him so easily? I wonder if Emery told him I was starting to remember them, and this was his attempt to help me remember.

"It's okay." Derek slid next to me. "Just means we can make better ones."

"Wait." I held up my hands in protest.

Confusion spread across his face, and for once today, his smile started to diminish.

"I appreciate everything you've done today, I really do, but you're a stranger to me. And I'm afraid you are expecting more."

"You're right." Derek stood, staring at the zebras. "It isn't right for me to just assume we can go back to how we were. I was just excited. I've missed you, well, missed us."

My heart swelled at his words. Someone missed me. Not just someone, but Derek. I wish I could remember, but maybe he was right. Maybe this was our second chance. I stood next to him softly nudging my shoulder into him. "But I'm all for new memories."

The breath caught in my throat as his eyes shined back. "Now didn't someone say they had a lot of studying to do?" His smile returned to his face.

WE SPENT THE REST OF THE AFTERNOON IN THAT ROOM. Derek dropped me off at home after grabbing some burgers in the drive-thru, which he refused to let me pay for again. It was getting late, and I'm sure he needed to get home. Were his parents going to be mad that he was essentially missing all weekend? Or was that normal for him? I wonder what his parents were like. Had I met them before?

The television was droning on from the living room. My

dad had his cans littered around him. He didn't acknowledge my presence, and I didn't his. Instead, I walked up the stairs to my room, dropping my bag inside the door. I was exhausted. I collapsed in my bed. I didn't even change before falling asleep.

TWELVE

"Amy!" Grace called from our normal spot. "So? How was the rest of your weekend? Did Ben call you after the party?"

I chewed on my bottom lip for a moment. To be honest, Ben was the last thing on my mind this weekend, but I wasn't about to let them know that. "No, we texted a little bit, but that's about it." Ben had texted me when I was at the museum on Sunday. I gave quick responses and didn't ask any questions back, so the conversation was short. I was afraid Derek would ask questions or get annoyed. Though, why should I even care? His phone had been vibrating the whole time as well. I'm sure it was Becca also checking in.

"I was so bummed you didn't come back to Alicia's after. I wanted to hear how it went!" Grace whined as I sat down.

I guess Alicia hadn't shared with her how my evening actually ended. I was surprised and grateful. I was expecting her to spread the juicy details of my drunk escapades. Maybe I didn't give her enough credit as a friend.

"I need to go talk to Mike!" Alicia pushed herself off the bench. Avoiding eye contact with me. I guess she was still not over our exchange on Saturday.

"That was weird." Grace eyes squinted as she watched Alicia almost stomp away. I just shrugged, hoping to avoid any further questioning.

Then I heard his car, how pathetic that I could already pick out the sound. I couldn't help but look over. The same crew jumped out. Derek, Becca, Aiden, and Hannah. I wonder why that specific group carpooled. Were they the closest to each other? I watched as they walked toward the entrance. Our eyes met. I couldn't help but crack a smile. His response? He looked away, no emotion or sign that he even noticed me, as if we were strangers again. My heart felt as if it dropped to my stomach. Becca grabbed his arm, whispering something in his ear. He smiled in response as they walked into the school. I stood there confused. Why spend all that time with me this weekend, bringing up all those memories from our past, to just ignore me? Calm down, don't jump to conclusions. Maybe he didn't see me.

The bell rang, and I headed to math. I sat staring at the paper on my desk. All I felt was dread. I should've studied more. As much as I tried, I couldn't focus yesterday in the museum. When I tried, I kept reading the same equation over and over again. I couldn't stop myself from looking over at Derek. Did he get annoyed at how much I was staring at him? I didn't think he noticed.

At least there was multiple choice. Some of the questions I was able to work backward with the different answers. I'm not sure if they were right, but I could make the equation work. Maybe I was a secret mathematician and was creating new unknown math equations. Could I win a Nobel prize for that?

"Ten minutes remaining," Mr. Bellows announced, interrupting the acceptance speech I was internally writing. I stared back at the test. Shoot, I still have five questions left!

I finished the last problem as the bell rang. I did not feel confident turning it in. I wonder how Alicia would do. Walking to Spanish, my phone vibrated.

> How was the math test?

Alicia must be nervous, but at least she was talking to me again.

> I think I failed...

I added a crying face at the end.

> Crap!

"Want to be partners?" Ben asked in gym. We officially moved to bats. One person had to throw the ball while the other person tried to hit it. Couldn't we do T-ball style and try and hit it off a stick. I feel that would be safer for all parties.

"Sure... but I have to warn you. I have no hand-eye coordination, so if I injure you, your soccer friends better not come after me." He may think I was joking, but I wasn't. I could imagine the uproar from his crew if he showed up with a black eye, or worse, crutches.

He just laughed, leading us to one of the corners of the gym. It actually went better than I thought. He was very gentle with the ball and lofted it to me when I was at bat. It was almost as if he caused the ball to fly in slow motion, so I was even able to make a couple hits. Then, it was my turn to throw. One word could sum it up. Disastrous. The bat turned more into a shield, its goal just to deflect any ball that would cause bodily harm. But he kept good spirits about it.

I was winded after. It took more effort than I thought to throw and hit a ball. And we weren't trying to run bases. I could start to see the allure of the batting cages people went to. Though, that didn't mean I wanted to go to one.

"Sorry, I wasn't able to say bye at the party." Ben stared at his feet as he was attempting to wipe away a black smudge with his sneaker. "I was a crappy date ditching you like that."

"Oh no, it's okay! I had a lot of fun with the girls." Shoot I could only remember Abigail's name. I wonder if she told him about my drunken exit. I also felt a little uneasy having him call it a date. He never officially asked me to the party.

"So, I was wondering if you wanted to come see our game this weekend?" Excitement filled his eyes as he looked up from staring at the floor. "It's a home game, so we will be playing at the school."

"What time?" I had to work this weekend. I hope he didn't find that as a lame excuse. A loud squeak echoed across the gym from someone's sneaker stopping abruptly against the wood.

"Five, I know it's a little late, but they have lights on the field, so you can see even when it gets dark." His face had turned towards a laughing group of boys. That must have been where the sound had come from, as they were running around swinging the bats. Another reason why this idea of gym was a bad idea.

"Oh. That's actually perfect. I should be done with work by then."

"Really? Awesome! I'll tell Krissy and the girls to save you a seat!" Ben's voice came out fast. We were briefly interrupted as the coach shouted across the court scolding the boys. "I better get to the lockers before Coach Davidson pops a vein." He smirked at his joke and then headed out with the rest of the boys. I followed suit.

"You're going to the game?" Grace almost screamed. I

looked around the cafeteria, afraid all eyes were going to be on us.

"Yeah, but do you think that's a good idea?" Maybe I shouldn't go. I wonder if I could find a good excuse.

"Of course it is!" Grace nodded to her response. "It shows you are interested in something he likes!"

"Bummer! I work Saturday night!" Alicia whined. "I wanted Mike and me to go with. It could've been a double date." Again, the word 'date' made me squirm.

I was a little thankful they couldn't come but felt guilty I hadn't asked her about it first. She was closer to the soccer group, but after the girls' reaction to Mike's name, were they really on as good of terms as Alicia thinks? I wonder what happened between them. Though, it would've been nice to have someone to ride with. I'm sure I could find someone to take me home if it ended after the buses stopped running. I immediately thought of Derek, then shook my head.

"By the way, that math test was terrible! I thought Mr. Bellows was cool. Why would he give us something so hard?" Alicia continued to whine. I wanted to lecture her on how doing her homework would've helped, but I wasn't any more confident that I didn't fail either.

I was almost late to English. In art, I knocked over my paint as we were cleaning up. The blue paint exploded over my desk and floor. Though, I had to admit it had a better design than what I had on my canvas. Maybe I could be graded on that instead? The school paper towels made it worse. Instead of soaking up the paint it almost repealed it, spreading the mess out even more. Ms. Kelly, who was the only teacher who had us call her by her first name, finally told me to just go. She was going to call the janitor instead.

When I walked into the room, I was the last person to show up. My whole body stiffened when I walked by his desk. I glanced out of the side of my eye. Would he look at me? Give me that half smile that drove me crazy? Some type of recognition from our weekend together? No… nothing. He didn't even glance up from the paper he was conveniently reading. My heart dropped. Did I do something Sunday to make him mad? I thought we ended on a good note. I glanced at Becca. Maybe she found out about this weekend, but she wasn't paying attention to me either. Which I was thankful for.

The class was fine. We had more articles to read, but this time, it was the same article for everyone. We just had to answer questions at the end. I'll take these over presentations any day. The bell rang, and we all froze in our seats, waiting for Ms. Haines to release us. We quickly learned to stay put after that lecture on her first day.

"Alright, class, if you can pass the articles forward, then you may leave." The sound of papers shuffling filled the room. "And Amy… if you can, please stay after."

My heart skipped a beat. I was trying to think back to what I might have done to warrant staying after. The class erupted in oooooooooohs. Which was quickly silenced by a glare from Ms. Haines. I just wanted to vanish.

"Y-y-yes?" I stammered standing at her desk.

"I just wanted to check and make sure you were okay." For once, Ms. Haines didn't have her normal grimace on her face.

"Uh, yeah, I'm good." What was she talking about?

"I just heard you had an eventful weekend."

There went my stomach. Did she know about the party? Oh my God, was I going to get in trouble for drinking. I didn't even know it was alcohol. Would they call the police? My thoughts just spiraled out of control. Quick, I had to respond with something. "Oh no, I'm fine."

"Okay, just know you can always come talk to me if you ever have something you needed to share." She smiled. She was trying to be reassuring, but her face was awkward with the expression as if she hadn't cracked a smile this century.

"Uh yeah, thanks." I waited for a minute, not sure if there was more before leaving. Well, that was weird.

I was hanging the new promotional material in the diner. *Turkey dinners only 5.99! Gobble them up before they're gone.* Who comes up with these phrases? At least I didn't have to say stupid catchphrases like Mike's work. We also had specials on pies. We had pumpkin, pecan, and apple in preparation for Thanksgiving.

"How many?" I heard one of the waitresses ask at the door.

"Ten," a voice responded. Oh, please, not him.

I almost dropped the sign I was hanging. At least not in my section. I refused to turn around and look.

"Amy, I just seated a ten top in your section," The waitress announced, walking back to the front door to greet the next group of customers.

Why! I internally yelled.

I grabbed the menus, not hiding my frustration. I took a deep breath and plastered a smile on my face before walking to the table.

"Welcome to Charlie's. Can I get you started on some drinks?" I prayed the smile trick worked and hid my irritation.

"Seriously, are you the only waitress who works here?" Becca groaned. Well, that answers the question of how she still feels about me.

"Knock it off, Becca," Dominic snapped back. "Can we not piss off the person handling our food." He met my eyes and tried to give me a smile. I would count it more a quarter smile, a small tug at the corner of his mouth. Not the half-smile I wanted from Derek, but I appreciated the effort. My eyes darted over to Derek who was of course sitting next to Becca. His face buried in the menu.

They all ordered milkshakes again. Followed by a split between burgers and chicken tenders. I put their order in, dreading having to do all those milkshakes. My hands still hurt when I thought about the other night.

"I'll get your shakes started. Can you run that food to table four for me?" Beatrice said from the drink counter, pointing to the kitchen window.

"Have I told you how amazing you are?" If I could kiss her, I would.

I grabbed the burgers from the kitchen window, bringing them to another table of high schoolers. They barely said thank you before shoving them in their mouths. I was starting to think it should be a requirement for everyone to be a waiter if they wanted to eat out. It was crazy peoples' lack of manners. I dropped the tray back at the window before joining Beatrice in the back at the milkshake station. She was almost halfway through the order. I couldn't help but stare at Derek's table. He was stoic showing no emotion, just like he had been at school. It took all my self-control to not walk over with a milkshake and dump it on his head!

"Is everything okay?" she asked, not looking up from the blender. She was holding the metal cup, careful to make sure the edge of the cup didn't make contact with the blades.

"I'm fine." Shoot, I shouldn't take my frustrations out at work. Was I going to get in trouble? Did she know what I was thinking just now?

"You sure? You seem upset." She could read me like a book.

"I'm fine, really. I just had a bad day at school." That wasn't really a lie. "I had a test in math that I think I failed and I'm still beating myself up over." See, that's true, I mean, that was a true statement, but that wasn't the reason I was irritated. However, I was not about to talk boy drama with Beatrice. "But I'm sorry, I didn't mean to let it affect my work."

"You aren't in trouble. I was just worried about you. Here's the last milkshake. Do you want help taking them over?"

I nodded. "That would actually be great."

We dropped the milkshakes off, and luckily, their food followed quickly after. Not surprisingly, they all ordered pie. This group had a serious sweet tooth. I checked on them a few times over their meal, and each time, Derek ignored me. If our eyes met, he stayed expressionless. Must be nice to be a boy. To just turn off any feelings for someone. Who was I kidding? There were never any feelings there. At least this time, when they left, the appropriate tip was on the table. Becca may still not like me, but at least she wasn't being as vindictive as before.

I FINISHED MY SHIFT ON TIME. IT SEEMED LIKE MR. JOHNSON was scheduling more people per shift to keep up with the crowds because even though we stayed busy all night, we were still able to finish our tables along with taking the time to do the night prep. I sat on the bench, waiting for the bus. I was still irritated with Derek. I had fished the museum card out of my wallet and was staring at it. As if it would magically answer all my questions.

Why buy me an annual pass to the museum, say we are going to use it together, and then ignore me all day? The only person to really acknowledge me in a positive way was Dominic! And from our interactions, I was obviously not his favorite person.

I stewed the rest of the way home. Standing in front of the door with the keys in my hand, I made up my mind. Forget

Derek. He can live happily ever after with Becca. At least she was honest with her feelings. Lost in thought, I wasn't paying attention and almost ran into Dad as he was heading out.

"Watch it, kiddo," he said, catching me in his hands before we collided. "Everything alright?" He smelled of his after-shave. Man, he really doused himself in it. Which was one of his tricks to hide the alcohol smell.

"Sorry, I was just thinking about something. I should've been paying attention to where I was going." I awkwardly smiled at him.

It sucks how uncomfortable these moments were. I wish we were closer. At least have some type of father-daughter relationship. But I couldn't blame these past years on that. We were never close. All my memories growing up were of the three of us, Mom, Cole, and me. Dad was rarely home, and when he was, all they did was fight. So, once my mom left, we just coexisted together. The opportunity to bond over the double loss was wasted on us. Would he even be sad if I left? Of course he would. Who would help with the bills?

Talking about bills, I pulled the mail off the table going through the envelopes. There was a red stamp signaling a second or third notice on a few of the bills. I better pay these. I walked into the kitchen. Staring at the peeling cabinets. I wonder how hard it would be to sand and repaint them. I'm sure I could find a video on how to do that. Maybe if I put in a little elbow grease around the house, it wouldn't feel so cold everywhere. I pulled open the first drawer where I kept my checkbook.

I wrote out a total of three hundred and fifty-three dollars. That covered the water, electricity, gas, and internet. How many hours of work was that? For once, I didn't want to do the math. At least we would have them for another month. I flipped the light switch before walking upstairs.

I sat on my bed with my homework. Luckily, there wasn't much tonight. The in-class assignments in English and the test in math eliminated homework in those two subjects. That just left chemistry, history, and Spanish, which didn't take long to complete.

Now what? I tapped my lips, trying to think what to do. I could go downstairs and watch TV, but there wasn't anything I wanted to watch. Oh, I know what I should do. I grabbed my phone and opened the CircleUp app.

If I was going to a soccer game Saturday, I was going to do what I should've done before the party. Research. I hadn't noticed I had some notifications pending. Probably because I had alerts for these apps off. I was annoyed with them going off all the time, so I muted everything besides calls and text messages. I clicked the alert button to read them. I surprisingly had a couple friend requests.

Abigail was requesting to be friends! I guess I didn't weird her out too much at the party. I was really looking forward to getting to know her better.

Ben also sent a request. I waited for a few minutes before hitting accept. I needed to decide how I felt about him. What if he did ask me out on a real date? Would I say yes? I mean, this soccer game wasn't considered a real date, right? It wasn't like we were going together. He just invited me to watch him play. My mind immediately went to Derek. How would he feel to learn I was going to watch another guy? Ugh, stop! He's taken!

I went to the next notification. I was tagged in some photos. I clicked the link to bring up the pictures. They were from the party. Wow... I looked so different. For a moment, I did look angelic in that costume. I wish it didn't get ruined, and I lost those wings in the car when I stumbled out. Oh well... I flipped through them. This is exactly what I needed. Each picture had other people tagged, and I followed them to their pages, trying to memorize the names of the non-makeup faces.

Krissy, Lacey, and Abigail were the girls at the party.

Krissy was dating Gabe, Lacey was with Zach, and Abigail was with Lee. The other girl, who caused that fun scene before I left, was Kayla. I decided to not click on her profile. I wasn't interested in learning more about her. Though I wonder what her problem was with me. A shiver went down my spine when I remembered her comments about Cole. I heard a lot of those comments when he first passed, but just like everyone's memory of that event, as it faded in importance, so did the remarks. I wonder if she knew one of his friends. I didn't want to think about that. I went back to looking up Ben's soccer team. At the end of the night, I felt better about going. I wonder if I should write a cheat sheet to hide in my purse, but would that be worse if people saw it? Was this considered stalking?

I turned my phone off and washed up for bed. I crawled under the covers. Before I could stop myself, I looked over and imagined Derek lying next to me. Stop it! I can't be planning on going to see one guy while thinking about another. Especially one who clearly doesn't want me around and, even more importantly, is already dating someone he has no intention of leaving. What a mess. I closed my eyes, willing myself to sleep so I could stop thinking of him. Instead, I pushed him into my dreams. Derek with the golden eyes and matching wings.

THIRTEEN

"That's cute!" Alicia commented as she was punching in.

"Thanks, though I'm going to be bundled up in my coat." I agonized last night over what to wear. I finally settled on tight jeans, a burgundy sweater, and my tall black boots. I had a tan, green, and red plaid scarf.

I had to get dressed at the diner. Between my shift ending at four and the game starting at five it left little time to get ready. There was no way I could make it home on the bus and back. So, I also had my big side bag to hold my clothes. Alicia agreed to drop it off at home for me, so I didn't have to bring it with me.

"I'm still so bummed I'm missing out!" Alicia pouted, not even trying to hide her disappointment. I was actually surprised she didn't try and call out.

"Me too." It wasn't a full lie. I think Mike being there would be interesting, to say the least, but it would be nice to have someone I know there. Especially to ask questions about the game. I tried searching soccer terms, and I have to admit, I was more confused now.

I glanced at my phone. It was 4:30. I should probably start

heading over to the school. "Let me know how it goes!" Alicia called back. "You should try and convince them to get burgers after!"

"Uh, yeah, I'll see." I pulled my coat as I walked into the cold. Why couldn't he play an indoor sport? I was already regretting my pant choice as I walked toward the school. They could've been made out of paper for the amount of protection they provided. I'm going to start investing in long johns. That was added to the list next to the gloves I was supposed to get.

THE BLEACHERS WERE ALREADY STARTING TO FILL UP. THERE were some dedicated soccer fans at this school. There seemed to be an invisible line separating the teenagers from the typical soccer moms. The opposite side exploded in red as the away team's families also came to support. All wearing their school colors. Was I supposed to wear ours? I thought that only applied to football, plus I didn't have many gold or yellow outfits. Again, if I did, it would've been lost under my jacket.

"Amy, over here!" Abigail waved from the back of the bleachers. I would've assumed they would want to be in the front row. I thought that was where all the die-hard fans always sat. Plus, the air was getting colder as I climbed up.

"Hi." I sheepishly waved when I arrived. I wonder if anyone would mention the party. Instead, all they did was scoot down to make room for me.

A loud whistle rang in the air, and the game began. I now realize why they picked these seats. You could see the whole field from up here. The only position I could remember from last night's study session was the goalie. He was easy to pick out since he stayed in the net. They also wore neon yellow outfits, which were different from the red and gold the other players wore.

Ben was one of the starting players. The little I knew, I was still impressed by him. He stayed inches from the ball, driving it down the field. How did he not trip over it as it bounced around his feet? I was already on the edge of my seat in anticipation. He suddenly stopped, extending his right foot back farther than he had so far. He brought it forward, colliding with the ball. It propelled forward, angling perfectly toward the goal as if he were controlling it with some type of remote. The goalie leaped to the side but just missed as the ball entered. The stands erupted in cheers. I was so caught up in the moment I didn't realize I was standing and shouting with them.

Now, the opposite team had the ball. Even with all the boys' effort, they unfortunately made it down the field and drove the ball into their net, tying the score. This set off a back-and-forth for the first half. Once one side scored a goal, almost immediately, the other team would score. It kept everyone on the edge of their seats.

This time, Gabe had the ball. Similar to Ben, he somehow kept the ball in between his legs. Ben was close by, running a little ahead before stopping in front of one of the red players, blocking them from Gabe's path. The stands got quiet as Gabe got into position to make the final kick into the goal. We all exploded when the net swished with contact. A whistle broke out, and the players migrated to their side of the field.

"Alright, it's halftime!" Lacey was up stretching. "I don't know about any of you, but I need something hot to drink! I'm freezing!" Krissy followed, taking mine and Abigail's money so they could bring us back something as well. This way, no one would try and take our seats.

"Well? What do you think so far?" Abigail was pulling the blanket she had brought closer to her body. I was super jealous of it. I was surprised how many people had brought blankets or other items to stay bundled. Some people even brought cushions to sit on. I'm not sure what I wanted more because I could not feel my lower half anymore. I wasn't sure if that was due to the cold or just the fact that metal bleachers were super uncomfortable.

"I'm having a blast. I didn't realize how intense this sport is!" I could tell Abigail appreciated that answer. Soccer didn't always get the recognition at the school that I was now seeing it deserved. It was normally dominated by football, with basketball being a close second.

"We come with warmth!" Lacey announced when they returned. They handed the Styrofoam cups to each of us. I was thankful for the thin walls as I was able to hold it like a mini heater. Holding it close to my face, the steam also provided moments of warmth, but that wasn't as rewarding as the added moisture to my face quickly turned cold, and I had to keep wiping my face dry.

"I heard you can buy electronic hand warmers online," Lacey commented, also holding her cup tightly. I wonder if this was their halftime routine.

"Really? That would be perfect for these night games," Krissy said, cautiously sipping hers.

The whistle shrilled again, resuming the game. It took me a few minutes to catch up because the teams had switched sides of the field. Abigail had explained this was to ensure a fair game so that one team couldn't say the other had an advantage based on the field structure. I appreciated her game-by-game narrative. I think she liked having me there. From how she interacted with the other two girls, it looked like she was the newest girl in the group, so it was almost as if she was passing that hat onto me.

The second game was a lot rougher. The red team, I wish I knew the school's name, had come back and scored against our boys, tying up the game again. After that, they were in a deadlock. They were also getting a lot rougher with each other. I'm sure it was out of frustration of not scoring. I couldn't imagine the adrenaline and testosterone occurring right now. And in front of all these people, expecting a win. The ball was momentarily stuck between three players. Right before the referee blew his whistle, one of the red players slid into the group, knocking all the players over. Boo's erupted from our side as the whistle blew. The referee was also holding some type of card in his hand.

"Oh dang!" I heard Abigail call out.

"What? What does that mean?"

"So, the referee is holding a red card, which ultimately means the player who did that dirty move is being expelled from the game," Abigail explained.

"Which he should! That move is illegal. You can't purposely try and injure someone! Think if someone's leg broke, they would be out for the season." Krissy was steaming in her seat.

The player was not reacting well to being thrown out. He was starting to argue with the ref. A couple of his teammates rushed in and pulled him back to the sidelines. That's when his coach seemed to take over, lecturing the guy. But it seemed like that disruption was just what our team needed. Because after that play our team scored two more goals winning the game.

"Wow! That was great!" I said. I genuinely had a good time. We sat in the bleachers, waiting for the crowds to file out. The boys had to go back to the locker rooms to change, so it was going to take a bit for them to return.

"Are you coming to Miguel's house after?" Lacey asked.

"Umm... I don't know if I'm invited." Ben had only mentioned the soccer game. I didn't want to assume I was invited to everything. I looked at my phone. Wow it was only seven. The buses were still running, so I wouldn't have any problems getting home.

"Everyone is invited after a win. It's a tradition we go to his house to celebrate. He has this awesome lake house we use.

Ben probably didn't mention it for fear of jinxing the game," Krissy explained.

"They usually get a ton of pizza. It's a lot of fun," Abigail chimed in. "Us girls usually ride over together, as the boys are usually pretty hyped after, and they want to replay every minute of the game as if we didn't just watch it."

It did feel good that they wanted me to go. Plus, I was a little nervous if I turned them down. I didn't want to ruin the relationship we were building. If it was pizza and hanging out, I'm sure it wouldn't be too long. Plus, all the guys are probably exhausted. "Sure, that sounds fun." I hope Alicia wasn't too disappointed about us not going to the diner.

"Let's get out of this cold!" Krissy stretched.

We followed her to the parking lot. Most of the cars were now gone. People were anxious to get out of the cold. I flipped the toggle on my phone, putting it on silent. I'm sure a lot of them would end up at Charlie's and I wasn't ready to answer Alicia's texts. Krissy had a cute little red car. It was definitely an older model, but she had added her own touches on the inside. A fluffy pink steering wheel cover and the front two seats had a pink zebra print car seat cover. Lacey called shotgun, so Abigail and I were in the back.

I was already regretting my decision before we even made it to Miguel's. When they said his house, I assumed it was going to be close by. I should've been tipped off when they said lake house. The closest lake was at least forty minutes away. It was over an hour before we pulled in.

The house was beautiful. It was a two-story house with a wraparound porch. The majority of the walls were made of glass. I'm sure it was built that way, so it didn't take away from the view of the lake. But that gave little privacy, as the lights inside against the dark made it super easy to see everything happening inside. The house had a more modern look with sharp angles, almost as if it was made of multiple triangles. You could see a dock on the back, with a large pontoon boat tied to it. There was also a sand volleyball court on the left side of the house and a large fire pit on the other side.

Cars were already starting to arrive. Two of the boys were carrying a stack of pizzas. A pit formed in my stomach when I saw another bringing a keg in. How did people get alcohol so easily?

"His parents must be super chill to let all the players come out," I said, half-fishing to find out if they were going to be there or not.

"Oh yeah, they are super cool. They give Miguel full reign of the house to use on the weekends. We just have to make sure we clean up afterward. And in the morning, they have a cook that shows up and cooks everyone breakfast." Abigail was already opening her door to head in.

"Breakfast?" I must have understood her incorrectly. They weren't expecting us to sleep here. That would be crazy.

"Yeah, we'll crash here tonight. Since it's so far, we don't want to have people driving so late, so it's just safer this way," Krissy said matter-of-factly.

Wasn't this information you shared before inviting someone? That is what I wanted to say, but instead, I said, "Oh, cool." I was trying to sound enthusiastic, but I was afraid I was failing.

"Let's go, they have the biggest fireplace inside. I need to defrost." Lacey anxiously led us inside. Either Krissy's car's heater was broken, or she didn't like to turn it on, so we were all still ice cubes.

They were still setting everything up when we walked in. Bottles of different types of alcohol covered the kitchen counter while the boxes of pizzas sat on the island. One of the boys was by the media center trying to hook up his phone to the speakers. To the right was a large sitting room. One wall was covered in stone, exposing the largest fireplace I had ever seen. Wood was already stacked, just waiting to be lit.

"Okay, who's lighting the fire?" Lacey called out. She was on a mission to find warmth.

"On it!" One of the boys from the kitchen grabbed a long blue lighter from one of the drawers before running over. He was still wearing his soccer clothes. He must have skipped the lockers and come straight here.

"Miguel, you're awesome as always," Lacey cheered as the dry wood started to crackle under the growing flame.

Okay, so that was Miguel. He was the host of the party. I noticed he wore a cloth brace around his knee. Was he injured? I thought I recognized him from the field, but they were all so far away I could be wrong.

"Amy!" I heard Ben call out when he arrived. "Wow, I can't believe you came! I'm going to be honest I was bummed I missed you when we finished."

"Oh, I hope it's okay I came. The girls invited me." I probably should've texted and asked.

"Of course! So, I have to ask. What did you think of the game?" It was kind of cute how excited he was to hear the answer. Maybe this night would go okay.

"It was so cool! You are so good!" He was clearly impressed with the compliment. His face was beaming.

"Let me get us some pizza! Pepperoni, okay?"

My stomach gurgled in response. "That would be perfect."

He brought two plates, both with two slices of pizza. I was grateful he didn't assume I was one of those girls who ate only enough to keep a baby bird alive. He was also carrying two red cups. I could smell the beer before he handed it over. My strategy was going to be different tonight. As long as I still had liquid in my cup, no one would offer me anything else. Gabe, Zach, and Lee also joined us, and we all sat around the fire as we ate.

Abigail was right. The boys talked non-stop about the game. Which I didn't mind, as it allowed me to eat my pizza without fear of being asked a question with my mouth full.

They clearly did not like the red team. Between complaining about the players and all the calls the refs missed, it definitely gave a different outlook on the game.

"So, Amy. What was your favorite part of the game?" Gabe asked. I was so glad I looked them up before coming.

"Oh. I have to say Ben's goal in the beginning." Was that stupid to say? I thought it was appropriate for me to give him a compliment since he was the reason I was here. My cheeks flushed as I started doubting myself.

"Awe, look, she's blushing!" Zach hollered. "Ben, I think someone has a crush on you!" My face had to be the color of a tomato now.

"Leave her alone," Lee chimed in. "You don't want to scare her off, or Ben's going to throw you in the lake." I peeked over at Ben. He was also starting to get red, except I noticed his ears turned brighter. Ben quickly turned the subject back to the game.

When we were done eating, the boys started heading upstairs. Apparently, there was a theater room on the second floor, and Miguel had a few famous soccer matches taped. "Do you need me to grab you anything to drink before I head up?" Ben asked.

"Oh no I'm okay. I'm still working on mine." Success, my plan seemed to be working.

Abigail and the girls had scattered to mingle with their other friends. I was shocked at how many people showed up. How did they expect all these people to sleep here? Maybe there was still hope of finding a ride back into town with someone. Although, the later it got, the harder it was to find a sober person. This also meant the party was getting a lot rougher as the time passed.

I gave up on the fireplace room as it turned into make-out central. I was afraid if I was still there, and Ben came down, he would get the wrong impression. The boys, who were now holed upstairs watching the games, were getting extremely rowdy. Some were also getting pretty vulgar as they started to pick on some of the girls who were sitting by themselves. I assumed their dates were upstairs as well. I was having a hard time finding the girls.

I found a quiet corner for now, next to a tall window. It was pitch dark outside, and no matter how hard I tried to look out, I couldn't make much out. The lights inside almost turned them into mirrors. I looked at my phone. I couldn't believe it was already midnight! I was right. I had a few missed texts from Alicia. First, asking if we were going to the diner, then how it was going, ending with an order to call her tomorrow with all the details. How would she feel about me being invited to a party without her? Especially one that was overnight. I wonder if they had these types of parties when Mike was on the team. I doubt it, or Alicia would've warned me about it. At least, I hope she would've. A sigh escaped my lips as I put my phone away. I just wanted to get home.

If only I was eighteen, then I could just request a ride, but I didn't have a parent like Alicia or a fake ID like Abigail. If I could find Abigail, maybe I could convince her to order me one again. I still had my cash from work today to reimburse her. Another girl entered the room as I was midthought. She seemed relieved to find a quieter place as well.

"Hi," I said. Maybe she could help. "You haven't seen Abigail, Lacey, or Krissy around, have you?"

"Oh, they're probably upstairs, you know, with their guys." She winked.

That's weird they didn't seem interested in watching the game. Wait... Oh God... she wasn't hinting at them doing that? I ran my hands through my hair. Of course, I mean, I guess people did that in high school. The pizza in my stomach felt like a rock. I stared at my phone, wishing for a solution. I opened my text messages again. Well... there was one.

I probably debated a good ten minutes before texting him.

Can you come get me? I'm stuck at a party and I have no way home...

Where are you?

I was surprised by how quickly he responded. I was afraid he would ignore my messages. It wasn't a far-off fear since we didn't say one word to each other all week.

Idk...

I felt like such an idiot. How did I not know where I was. Why didn't I think to look at a mile marker or at least a road sign on our way up?

A notification popped up on my screen. *Derek wants to share locations.* I clicked accept.

What are you doing all the way up there?!

My heart dropped. How did I expect him to come? It was at least an hour's drive up here.

I know... I'm sorry. It's ok I'll be fine. I shouldn't have asked.

We are coming to get you. Are you ok until we get there?

Yeah, I found a spot for now. Thank you...

We'll be there soon

FOURTEEN

After a little waiting, I migrated out to the porch. Some boys had found our quiet space and were starting to make uncomfortable comments. Once one of them sat next to me, I took that as my sign to leave. I had tried to find Ben to let him know I was leaving, but upstairs all the doors were closed, and I was afraid what I would discover if I opened the wrong one. I decided to send him a text instead. I knew it was going to be a bit before Derek arrived, but with the cold, I doubted many people would venture out here.

I pulled my jacket tighter, wishing I was still by the fire. I looked at my watch. It had been forty minutes since we texted. He should hopefully be here soon. That's if he left after we texted. I wonder if he was going to be mad. I mean, this was probably one of my more stupid ideas. Ranking up there with trying to walk home alone at night. Who doesn't ask about details before accepting an offer to go to a party?

My heart dropped when the car pulled into the driveway. There was no way Dominic would have lent his car out for such a long drive. What did Derek mean when he said we are coming? The car pulled to the front of the house. The driver's door opened. Yup it was him. Dominic was standing, staring me down. He was clearly not happy he was assigned this task.

"Are you coming or what?" he barked out before climbing back in. I obediently walked down the stairs to the waiting car. I opened the door, and the warmth of the heater hit my face. Well, at least I could warm back up. Even if my driver was giving me the cold stare-down.

I tried to do a quick scan of the car, still a little hopeful that Derek would chime in as well. But he wasn't there. I tried to hide the disappointment on my face, I didn't want to seem ungrateful to Dominic. At least I was going home.

"Okay, let's get a couple things straight before we go." Dominic glared back. "First off, we are not making this a habit. Callie is not a taxi service."

"Callie." I couldn't help but smirk. He named his car, which was kind of cute. Dominic glared back. I pursed my lips to hide my amusement.

"Second, you will not make fun of Callie's name or any part of her." I could tell he just added that in. "And finally, if you have to hurl, you better give enough warning for me to pull off. There better not be one drop of bodily fluid in here when you leave. Understood?"

"I'm not going to throw up." I could feel my cheeks starting to burn again.

"Yeah, that's what every drunk says." He placed his car, or should I say, Callie, in gear.

"I'm not drunk!" Now, he was starting to annoy me, which seemed to be his special ability. Did he even know how to be pleasant? This wasn't my first choice, either.

We rode in silence. I sent another text to Ben, letting him know I left. I didn't want any of them to be worried about me. I said a friend I knew was actually nearby, so I decided to hitch a ride back with them. I was starting to get annoyed with him now. I know he didn't invite me to the party, but if he liked me, how could he just desert me tonight.

"So..." I tried to break the awkward silence. "Thanks for coming to pick me up."

"You're paying me back for gas," Dominic responded. I guess that's his version of you're welcome.

"Oh yeah... of course. Just let me know how much I owe you." Now it felt even more awkward. I should've kept my mouth shut.

His hands tightened around the wheel. I'm sure he was uncomfortable, too. You could feel the tense air around us. It wasn't that same tense feeling when I was around Derek. That was more electric, as if our bodies were sparking off each other. This was that claustrophobic feeling, your body just wanting to break away. I noticed a glint coming from his hands.

"Oh wow! Those are some nice rings!" I didn't take him for a guy to wear jewelry. He had one on his right ring finger and another on his left thumb.

Dominic squirmed in his seat. Was he self-conscious about them? If so, why wear them. Maybe a girl gave them to him. "Uh, thanks." As I sat there thinking about it, Derek had a similar ring on his right ring finger.

"Derek has one like that, too, right?" Maybe I could branch the Derek subject with Dominic, and I could get clues from him on why he was ignoring me.

"Yeah... What do you have a problem with guys and rings?" he shot back. Nope, that didn't help.

I stared back at the window, my eyes starting to get heavy. How was it almost 2:00? The combination of the warmth from the heater and the constant rumble from the tires spinning against the highway was putting me to sleep.

A gentle voice interrupted my nap. "Amy?"

I sat up, rubbing my eyes, trying to clear my vision. My heart skipped when I was greeted by that smile. How I yearned all week to see it. That warm feeling spread through my body, but as my mind started to clear, it vanished just as quickly as it came.

"Oh, so now I exist!" Why was I being so rude? He did just help me get home. But my feelings were still hurt from being ignored all week. I was also hurt he wasn't the one to come get me.

His voice dropped. "Amy..." I couldn't tell if he was sad or annoyed. From what I could tell, it wasn't the reaction he was expecting.

"Ride's over," Dominic chimed in, clearly ready for me to exit his precious car.

"Oh yes, thanks, Dominic. How much do I owe you?" I was fishing my wallet out of my bag.

Derek shot him an icy look. Clearly not happy with that question and the source that it came from. "What? Do you think gas just magically fills my tank?" Dominic responded. "Ugh... don't worry about it. I'm *happy* I could help."

Yeah, clearly, you were thrilled.

Where the heck was I? I stepped out of Callie, looking around the unfamiliar area. Oh God... I was now calling the car Callie. We were in a very fancy neighborhood. Huge houses flanked the road. The homes looked more colonial, a little like mine, but much larger. The owners also gave them the attention they needed over time. They looked as new as when they were first built. The driveways were also littered with expensive new cars. I wonder which neighborhood this was. With how grand it was, you would think it would stand out in our town.

Dominic didn't waste any time. As soon as I was out, he pulled out of the driveway, squealing away. I cringed, expecting a row of lights to come on from people waking from the noise. Nothing happened, and the neighborhood seemed to stay asleep.

"Do you want to come inside?" Derek was between me and the front door.

I stood with my feet planted and arms crossed in front of my chest. "I thought I was being taken home." I sounded like such a brat, but we were not going to pick up as if nothing happened. Plus, I was not about to enter some strange house I knew nothing about.

He was clearly uncomfortable. Good. "I thought this would be better than trying to sneak into your house at almost three, but if you want me to take you home, I can."

My lip moved in between my teeth as I thought. He had a point. It was a gamble if my dad was home or not. "Hey!" The front door opened. "Are you coming in or not? You both look like a bunch of creepers just standing in the driveway!" Emery was in the doorway.

"This is Emery's place?" Well, that was unexpected. I'm not sure if that made me feel better or not.

Derek looked back at me. "Fine!" I stomped past him to the open door. "Hi Emery."

"Crazy night?" He smirked as I walked in.

"Something like that." I stopped in the doorway. I stood in a huge entryway with beautiful marble tile on the floor.

As you continued to walk in, it transitioned to beautiful wood floors. Not the fake kind that most houses now use, but genuine wood. To the right was a formal dining room with the largest dining room table I've ever seen. Even the chairs looked as if they came from a museum, beautifully polished wood with fabric stitched where you would sit. There was a living room to the left. A wooden staircase, the same wood that matched the floor, spiraled upstairs to a hallway that broke off to the right and left, I'm sure, with a handful of rooms out of view.

"Wow, Emery, your house is gorgeous!" I wondered how many people lived in this house. Did he have siblings I didn't know about? Are you kidding? I didn't know about any of their families.

"Thanks, it's been in my family for a long time."

"Emery, can you hang with Amy for a few minutes? I'm going to run to my room and grab my keys?" My eyes followed him as he bounded up the wooden stairs. Wait... I thought we were at Emery's house. Did both their families live here? Maybe that was why their homes were so big. It held multiple households.

"Sure, Amy, come have a seat." He led me to the living room.

The room was huge. A beautiful L-shaped couch hugged the wall facing a large flatscreen TV that hung on the opposite wall, above a brick fireplace.

"Wait... I thought this was your house." I sat on the couch. I couldn't believe how comfy it was, as I sunk down.

"It is." That was it. Okay, this group needs to learn how to elaborate.

"But Derek lives here too." I was going to get at least one answer tonight.

"Yeah, he moved in last week. You know. After what happened, he needed some space." He was rubbing his hands, clearly anxious for Derek to return. That's when I noticed it.

"You have a ring too!" He wore his on his right pointer finger.

That caught him off guard. "This?" He twirled the ring around his finger. It looked just like Dominic's. They weren't your normal bands. They were a little rougher looking, as if someone had taken a piece of metal and bent it around their fingers. They were perfectly round, but they had distinct ends that ended above and below each other. I wonder if they went to a farmers' market or one of those medieval fairs that happened once a year, where they were hand-crafted.

"I noticed Dominic had a couple too. They all look similar. Did you get them at the same place?" I wonder what the story behind them was. Did they wear them all the time?

Before Emery could answer, Derek returned. He did not

hide his relief at the distraction. "I can take you home." Derek had his keys in his hand.

I bit my lip again. Yes, I was mad at Derek, and I wasn't exactly thrilled to be in someone else's house, but I didn't want to lose the opportunity to try and get some questions answered. If he took me home, would this be the last time we spoke?

"Actually… you were right. It might be a good idea to stay here tonight. I can't imagine the questions my dad will have if I stroll in so late. He probably assumes I'm at Grace or Alicia's house right now." That was somewhat true. I didn't want to risk waking my dad, and depending on how much he drank, his reaction could be unpredictable. But I highly doubted he knew or cared where I was.

"You sure?" Derek looked back between Emery and me. Surprised at my quick change of heart.

"Yeah." I hope I didn't make him mad, and he was now regretting his offer.

"Well, now that that's settled, I'm going to bed." Emery got up, stretching. "Derek, you can set her up in one of the guest rooms. See you all in the morning." I was a little disappointed. I was secretly hoping I would be able to crash on the couch. It was so comfy that I didn't want to move.

Then, it was just Derek and me alone in the room. "Do you want me to show you to your room?"

"Can we talk first?" I wanted to take advantage of us being alone. I wasn't sure if we would get this same opportunity in the morning.

"Sure…" Derek took a seat on the other side of the couch. Since it was an L-shape, we still were able to comfortably look at each other.

"Did I do something to upset you?" I blurted out. I had to have done something to cause such a drastic change.

"No… it isn't you." Again, no elaboration.

"Okay… then what's with the one-eighty! If I recall, you

were the one to show up at MY house. You were the one who wanted to spend ALL Sunday together. Then what? You just blow me off?" I could feel my anger rising. I moved my hand over the fabric to try and distract myself, hoping it would calm me down. I'm not sure what kind of guy he was, but I was in no mood to play games. Especially ones that wrecked my emotions.

"You're right. That was all a mistake." His face was void of emotion as he stared at the TV with as much focus as if it was actually on. That happy kid from last weekend was gone.

Tears filled my eyes. I tried blinking them away. I didn't want him to see how that hurt me. "I see. I'm sorry. Maybe this is another mistake. I should just go home." Before I could stand, he was kneeling in front of me. His eyes locked with mine while his hand brushed a tear away from my cheek. I wasn't successful at holding them back. But my heart was crushed. Those words hurt more than I thought they would. I felt like a mistake in many peoples' eyes, my mom, my dad, and now Derek.

"Wait… I'm sorry. I shouldn't have said that." Derek paused. Clearly rethinking his choice of words. "I just don't want you to get trapped in our world. It isn't safe for someone like you."

"Someone like me?" My voice was cracking against the tears. I felt a sharp pain in my chest almost as if I was stabbed. The feeling of not being good enough was starting to take over.

"A human." That sounded weird coming from him. It was hard to remember they were different from us.

"I can't say I understand. But I don't want to cause you more problems. I won't bother you again after tonight." My mind couldn't stop flashing to him with those gashes on his back. I wonder how his back was now. Does he now have scars as reminders? I was being selfish. I didn't understand his world, so what right did I have to make demands on our relationship... I mean friendship. "I guess we can head to bed." Why did I have to sound so defeated?

"Wait." Derek was rubbing his forehead. Why did he look so pained? I wasn't fighting him. I'm willing to accept his request, to go back to how things were.

"You have to stop blowing hot and cold." My heart can't take this back and forth, but I wasn't going to say that. "You have to figure out what you want."

"I know. I know what the right decision is. We need to leave tonight and not cross paths again. You live your life with your friends, so you have the ability to live a long and happy life. But why do we have to be such selfish creatures! I hear that choice out loud. I want to say screw it and keep you with me forever, but I could destroy your life."

"Can't there be a compromise?" I dropped my head so we could make eye contact again.

"Which would be?" I could see he wasn't convinced.

"Can't we just try and be friends? It can be on your terms. If it becomes too much, we can end the friendship, but you have to tell me. You can't just ice me out of nowhere again." I stuck my hand out just like he did when he asked to be friends. My heart felt like it froze, waiting for his answer.

"Ah screw it." My heart went at double speed. His half grin was finally back as he shook my hand. "Friends." He turned serious again. "But the moment I see you in danger because of this. I will end it."

"Deal." I know I didn't know much about his world, but what danger would this really bring? I mean, I've already been attacked by two creatures, and he's been there to save me each time. If anything else, I'm safer because of him.

FIFTEEN

I lay on the bed staring at the ceiling. The light was already pouring in. I wonder what time it was. My phone had finally died last night, and there didn't seem to be a clock in the room. One thing was for sure, this bed was amazing. When people say it felt like sleeping on a cloud, they must have been talking about this mattress. I scooted farther into the covers. I wasn't ready to leave the warmth, but was I being rude? I wonder if Emery was waiting for me to come down. Were they waiting to have their house to themselves again? Oh God… did his parents even know I was here? I hope I didn't run into them.

"Goodbye, comfy bed," I whispered, pulling the covers off. The temperature drastically dropped. It wasn't cold in their house, but with the ceiling fan going, it felt cool against my bare skin.

Since I didn't have any pajamas, I had stripped to my underwear. I grabbed my pants and sweater from the chair I had hung them on last night. I wrapped the scarf around my neck, creating two long loops, almost like a new type of neck-lace. I slowly opened the door, craning my head out, trying to see if I was about to run into someone. Coast clear.

I shuffled down the hall toward the bathroom that Derek showed me last night. Emery had laid out a towel and a new toothbrush for me to use. The pink toothbrush was sitting in a cup next to the faucet, still damp from being used last night. Thankfully I had grabbed my hairbrush, in case I needed to fix my hair before the game yesterday. The hairbrush tugged at the knots, trying to smooth out the terrible bedhead I had. I must have slept hard. I wet my fingertips and did a quick swipe under my eyes to remove the smudged eyeliner that currently made me look like a raccoon. Okay, I didn't look terrible.

Again, I peeked my head outside before heading toward the stairs. With a house this big, who knows how many people lived here and who I might run into. Noise drifted up from downstairs followed by clashing of dishes and running water. Whoever was up was in the kitchen.

"She lives!" a voice boomed when I entered. I moaned internally. Was there ever a day where he wouldn't show up?

"Hi, Dominic." I tried to put on a welcoming smile, but I'm afraid it turned more into an annoyed smirk.

"How'd you sleep?" Emery was stacking pancakes onto a plate, preparing to bring them to the table of waiting boys. Wait... who all was here?

"Good... thanks again for letting me crash here." I was still standing in the doorway, rubbing my arm nervously.

"Come get some breakfast." Emery was signaling to an open chair with his spatula before pouring more batter onto the hot skillet.

I walked toward the chair nervously, eyeing the table. There were three boys sitting around the pancakes. Dominic was already stabbing the stack with his fork. No shocker there. The other two I wasn't as familiar with. I recognized them from their friend group. I think they were a year younger than us.

"Amy, have you met Kyle and Luke?" Emery didn't even

look up from the skillet when he asked. Okay, that's it, I'm convinced they can read minds.

"I don't think so." I slid into the chair, still uneasy. Did they all live here?

"Hi! I'm Kyle, and this is Luke." The boy sitting directly across from me chimed in. He had a little too much energy for someone this early in the morning. He had three pancakes sitting on his plate. They were doused with syrup and a large tower of whip cream on top. The other boy, Luke, sheepishly smiled before taking a bite of his.

"Are you okay with pancakes?" Emery asked as he placed two on my plate before replacing the stack. Probably afraid they would be snatched by Dominic before I would have a chance.

"Oh yes, thank you. These smell amazing, by the way." I picked up the syrup, pouring the sticky liquid on top. Oh my God, they tasted even better than they smelled. Dang, Emery was a good cook.

"Dominic keeps eating all the pancakes!" Kyle whined. I coughed, nearly choking on a piece of pancake I had inhaled while trying not to laugh. Dominic had taken half the pancakes and added them to his plate. Where was he putting everything!

"If you all start fighting, I'm going to stop cooking!" Emery called over.

"Kyle, shut up, or none of us will eat!" Luke smacked Kyle's elbow, which was holding up his pouting face. His head almost face-planted on the pool of syrup left on his plate.

That was it. I couldn't hold back anymore. I burst into laughter. I was thankful this time I had swallowed my pancakes, as I'm sure anything in my mouth would be halfway across the table by now. I'm not sure what they were, but they definitely acted like normal humans. I was even starting to doubt they were in high school with the amount of bickering they were doing. They were acting more like elementary school boys.

"Oh great, now she's laughing at me." Kyle's arms were crossed on his chest, and a huge frown filled his face.

"I'm sorry." I covered my mouth to hide the smile. "This just reminded me of how me and my brother would act when my mom cooked us pancakes. Except my brother was always the pancake thief."

"Who are you calling a thief?" Dominic grumbled.

"Alright, alright, I've got more." Emery dropped another stack down. "Dominic, please let the others grab some first." Dominic just mumbled in response, taking another large bite.

Everyone sat in silence, enjoying their full stomachs. Emery had finally joined us at the table eating his pancakes. A stack still sat on the counter untouched. I wonder if he was saving those for Derek. Speaking of Derek, I was surprised he wasn't down already. It was already ten. I think when he was at my house, he was up by at least nine. He didn't seem like the type to sleep in, but I guess we didn't get to bed until almost three thirty.

"When's Derek going to get here?" Kyle wiped his finger across his plate before sticking it in his mouth to suck the syrup off.

"I'm sure he'll be here soon." Emery was gathering the dishes, taking Kyle's first before more fingers made their way onto the plate, but you could see the worry on his face.

"Get back? Where did he go?" I guess he was an early riser. I wonder who he would be seeing so early in the morning.

There was silence again. They all seemed to squirm in their seat at my question. As if they said a little too much already. Well, everyone except for Dominic. He just sat wearing his normal annoyed face. If I was going to get any answers, I would have to try prodding some more.

"Wait." I could feel a knot forming in my stomach. "This isn't like last time, right? I didn't get him in more trouble again, did I?" I could feel myself starting to hyperventilate. I silently prayed, please don't let him get hurt.

"No, it's nothing like that." Emery had dropped the dishes in the sink and knelt next to my chair. His warm hand was squeezing my arm trying to add some comfort. "He'll be back soon. He just wanted to…" I could tell he was trying to find the right word, "make sure there was no confusion."

Confusion? Confusion on what? I wanted to ask more but decided it was best to not continue to prod. Everyone was squirming in their seats with the conversation. Thankfully, Kyle broke the silence.

"I can't believe Hannah wouldn't let us help them last night!" He was leaning back in his chair rocking on the back legs as he changed the subject. Clearly, he was upset over whatever he missed out on. "I wish we could've helped. They never let us join! How are we going to learn if we're always stuck at home!"

"Kyle…" I could tell Luke was already over this topic.

"What? They're only a year older than us, but they treat us like we're little kids! Plus, they have no problem letting Samantha and Chris join. What makes them better than us?"

"You can't even last ten seconds against me!" Dominic boomed. A little prouder of that statement.

"No one can last against you! You're a tank!" Kyle's chair made a thud sound against the floor as he brought it back on its four legs. He threw his hands up in frustration. Dominic's smile plastered across his face. He clearly appreciated the comparison.

"Kyle, Dominic's right, you need a little more practice. We take it easy on you. They won't." Emery seemed to be the one to take on the fatherly role of the group. Wait… they did have parents… right? I realized once again I was in one of their houses and still hadn't met a single adult.

Luke cleared his throat, his head tilting slightly toward me, trying to remind them they weren't alone at the table. They seemed to take the cue, and Kyle folded his arms again, clearly not happy, but ending the conversation.

So, I was right. Luke and Kyle were a year younger than us. Though now seeing them next to Emery and Dominic they seemed a lot younger and smaller. Don't get me wrong, they were still in really good shape, but they seemed like they would fit better with Ben's group of friends. No wonder they couldn't last long against Dominic. He looked like he could snap either of them in half. I couldn't stop picturing them on a wrestling mat, Dominic pinning Kyle in a chokehold. Was that what they were talking about when they said they wouldn't last against him? I wonder what their brawls looked like. My thoughts flipped from the typical scripted wrestling to MMA.

"What's with all the whining!" Derek stood leaning against the doorway. Damn, he looked exhausted. Did he sleep at all last night? I wonder what time he left this morning.

"Derek!" Kyle jumped up from his seat. He looked as excited as a boy seeing Santa around Christmas. I'm not sure what their dynamic was, but they all seemed to have a lot of admiration for Derek.

"Come take my seat." Luke scooted the chair out from the table so he could give Derek his seat. For being younger, Luke seemed to have better manners than Dominic who sat unfazed.

"Emery made pancakes," I meekly said. Why was I suddenly so nervous. I couldn't help tugging at the sleeve of my sweater. I noticed Derek and Emery locked eyes as if they were having some type of internal conversation, but it lasted just a few seconds before their attention was back on the group. I wonder what that was about.

"Doesn't he make the best pancakes!" Luke brought the stack over, placing it down on the table.

Not surprisingly, Derek grabbed the syrup, pouring more

than half the bottle out. I wonder how many bottles they went through just today. The table was silent while he ate. Kyle continued to stare at him like he was meeting his biggest idol.

"So… what did I miss?" Derek asked before taking another bite.

"Kyle was complaining about—"

"I wasn't complaining!" Kyle cut Dominic off.

"Did you just kick me?" Dominic grumbled, leaning down and rubbing his shin.

"Not so tough, huh?" Kyle mumbled under his breath. If looks could kill, Dominic's would've put him six feet under.

"Enough, you two! I would prefer my kitchen table to stay in one piece!" Emery sat forward in his chair, crossing his arms on the table. "Dominic, isn't it getting time to take Luke and Kyle to practice?"

"Practice?" I couldn't help but ask. Maybe they did play sports! What did they play? Was it with a group of kids? Maybe it was one of those leagues outside of school. Ones that weren't restricted to the school you attended but allowed any kid in the area to participate.

"Amy, you should come watch!" Kyle perked up. Excited at the opportunity to have an audience. Luke, on the other hand, was glancing at Derek, waiting for his reaction.

"What? Private humiliation isn't enough for you?" Dominic smirked back.

"Shut up!" Kyle huffed back.

"Well?" Derek pushed his plate aside. "Do you want to go?" This time, he was looking at me. Oh God, that half smile was back. I'm not sure if that was a good thing or not.

"Is it okay?" I was trying to hide my excitement. I couldn't wait to watch them play. With how athletic they were, I'm sure any game would be exciting. Though, did they hold back so people didn't get suspicious?

"Yeah… is she allowed?" This time, it was Luke chiming in. He clearly was uncomfortable with the idea.

Dominic threw his arms up in the air. "She's already seen us. I don't think anything we show her now is going to shock her!"

"Don't worry, Luke. They already know about her." Emery stood, grabbing Derek's plate and putting it in the sink with the rest of the dishes.

"Who's they?" And why did that sound so menacing?

"You have a lot to learn." Dominic smirked, pushing his chair out. "But can we save the clan dynamic lecture for another time? It's going to fill up if we don't head out now! And I need to put this little pipsqueak in his place." He grabbed for Kyle who jumped out of reach at the last second.

"Save it for the gym!" Emery pushed them both out of the kitchen. I think he was more worried if they stayed any longer something in his house would end up breaking.

Derek and I sat alone at the table. "Are you sure it's okay if I go?" I couldn't help thinking about last weekend again. How much trouble he got in for protecting me, now he was openly inviting me into his world. What would be the punishment this time? And how did we make another 180 in less than twelve hours? I was running my hands over my arms to try and calm my nerves.

"Don't worry, like Emery said, they know about you. This isn't like last time."

"And they are okay with this?" Even though Derek was trying to be reassuring I couldn't imagine they would so quickly accept me.

"I wouldn't say they are happy about it." Derek looked as if he was replaying some scene in his head. He smirked at his thought. "But like I just explained to them. It's better I answer your questions than that inquiring mind of yours going some-where or to someone else about them."

So, was that who he went to see? Did he leave right after I went to bed? Is that why he looked so exhausted. He looked okay, so it didn't get... physical. He also seemed like he was in a good mood. Maybe this friendship of ours was actually going to work.

"Ready?" Derek was already up. His hand was extended, waiting for mine. My heart was beating erratically.

Well, I wanted to learn more about them. I guess this was my chance.

Sixteen

I still couldn't place their neighborhood, but I'm not sure how I would've missed it. It was huge! It almost seemed to be its own town. Once we left Emery's house, we followed the windy road toward the front of the neighborhood. There were large black iron gates protecting the entrance. These weren't the typical flimsy gates you normally saw in those gated neighborhoods. The ones where you knew if the wind blew wrong, they would fly open. These seemed like a stampeding elephant couldn't even knock them over. They had to be over eight feet tall, and nearly reached the ground, only giving a couple inches of space before scraping across the pavement.

Before we reached them, Derek took a sharp right turn as he followed closely behind Dominic. The houses started to thin out as we headed toward a group of commercial buildings. As we got closer, I noticed it was a small shopping plaza. When you saw it from a distance, you didn't notice anything different about it. It was a long strip made up of a group of shops. Cars filled the parking lot in front, with people going in and out of the various stores. A normal sight for a Sunday morning. It was only when you drove closer that you noticed something was off. Instead of the usual business names at the top advertising what shop you were about to visit, a sign stood dictating the *type* of shop.

GROCERY... DRESS... HEALTH... ELECTRONICS... WEAPONRY... Wait... did the last store say weaponry? I tried to crane my head around to see it again, but we were going too fast. The sign was already out of sight. That couldn't be right. I probably read it wrong. It must have been something like a winery.

We took a few more turns before reaching the next large building. The front of the building was made of glass. The only difference between this and the windows at Miguel's house was this glass acted as a mirror. They must have a coating on them to prevent you from seeing inside. I've been to a few stores like that. They get the benefit of natural light, but make the people inside feel more comfortable that strangers aren't randomly staring at them. Something that would put off anyone thinking about going to work out.

Like the plaza we passed, this one had a simple sign on top. *GYM.* I guess they liked to be clear and concise about what stores or places they were visiting. I wonder how they got the businesses to agree to this. Maybe the ability to have their stores inside a gated community guaranteed them continual business, so they were okay with following the neighborhood standards?

Dominic pulled into a spot farthest from the entrance. He probably didn't want anyone parking near his precious car. Derek, thankfully, didn't follow suit and pulled closer to the building. The distance didn't seem to matter because Dominic, Kyle, and Luke were already by the car before Derek, Emery, and I were out. Poor Emery was still climbing out of the backseat. I probably should've fought more to sit in the back. Derek popped the trunk and pulled out a couple duffle bags. I imagined they had their gym clothes in them. I wondered what they were going to do. Was I just going to watch them work out?

"You ready for this?" Kyle was nearly leaping toward the door in excitement.

"Alright, save that energy for inside." Dominic wrapped his arm around Kyle's neck pulling him in as he ruffled his hair. For the first time, Dominic actually seemed excited. Was that even possible for him? I thought the only emotion he was able to feel was discontent.

This was not the scene I was expecting to walk into. I have gone to a handful of gyms in the past. Every couple of months, Alicia would go on some type of health craze, which was typically followed by a new gym membership. Normally, you would walk in and be greeted by a few employees at the front desk. All very fit and usually very tan. Dozens of machines would fill the floor, giving different options like running, biking, skiing, rowing, lifting weights, pulling weights, or even pushing weights. If machines weren't your style, they would have rows of free weights or dozens of mats with large balls or bands scattered around.

This gym didn't have any of those items, at least on the floor we entered. How many floors did this place have? Instead, it had the floor roped off into four large sections. Kind of what you would expect when you walked into a gym that specialized in boxing or wrestling. Except each roped-off section was at least four times the size of one of those rings. They also weren't lifted like you would normally see. A mat still covered the floor, I guess to protect your body if you fell to the ground, but that was it. There wasn't much more to it. There was a row of bleachers against each of the walls facing one of the four sections. What would they watch in here?

A girl's voice interrupted my train of thought, "Took you guys long enough!" Hannah bounded from one of the corners toward us. "Oh, hi, Amy! I was wondering when you were going to join us!" Aiden followed closely behind.

Aiden was wearing a red shirt with the sleeves cut off. This allowed his full arms to be visible. The different muscles outlined perfectly down his arms. He was also wearing black basketball shorts that stopped around his knees. Another difference between this group and other athletes. Their whole bodies were in shape. Sometimes, people would focus on one area of their body, like their upper body. To ensure they had buff arms and a defined six-pack, but in doing that, they neglected their legs, which in turn would look like sticks straining to hold the weight. Or they would focus more on one side of the body. This typically happened to the ones who played tennis or golf. One side of their body would be huge, while the other would be noticeably smaller. But with them, they were always perfectly balanced. As if each work out consumed their whole body.

Hannah was wearing a cute pink tank top. She matched it with gray shorts. They had more of the windbreaker fabric to them than the mesh that made up Aiden's shorts. The girls weren't much different than the boys. Their whole bodies were toned. The only difference is they were more athletic than buff. More like Kyle and Luke in stature. Though I'm sure if you made that comparison to Kyle, he would have a fit!

"Alright, we just need to change, and then we can get started." Derek swung his bag behind his back. "Is anyone else planning on coming today?"

"I think Chris and Samantha are coming, but…" Hannah froze for a minute before responding. "I'm not sure about Becca." She followed by making a scrunched face. I wasn't sure what that was about. Didn't they all get along? Or was it because of me? Did she know I was going to be here?

"Amy, stay with Hannah. We will be back in a few minutes." I watched them all head toward the back. There was a small doorway between two sets of bleachers. That must lead to the locker rooms in the back.

"Are you excited?" Hannah's eyes were almost sparkling with excitement.

"I'm not really sure what we are doing." And nothing around me really gave any clues.

"They didn't tell you? Oh, you are in for a cool treat!" Her hands rubbed together in anticipation.

"What's *she* doing here," another voice interrupted us. I spun, almost colliding with the two people behind me. "Watch out!" She leaped back as if touching me would lead to her catching some horrible disease.

"Samantha, have you met Amy yet?" Hannah was unfazed, though that seemed to be her normal attitude. It seemed like it took a bit for things to bother her. Not like Kyle, who I think hit every emotion this morning alone.

"We have class together," I interjected. Hannah had a puzzled look on her face as if I had just spewed a complex riddle. "Gym," I continued. Though, did a specific class help?

"Oh, that makes sense." Hannah nodded. "Samantha's in the grade below us, so I wasn't sure how you two would cross paths."

I snapped my mouth shut. I couldn't stop it from dropping open. She was a year younger than me? Holy crap! She looked, well... what is the best way to put this? As Kyle differed from Dominic, I was the same comparison to Samantha. Okay, now I was thinking in riddles. I guess it was true. Girls do mature faster than boys. I remember Kyle mentioned something about him being the same age as her. And someone named Chris? I guess that's him.

"We should probably get dressed." Chris lightly touched Samantha's elbow before moving it to the small of her back, leading her in the directions the others went.

"Don't worry about her. She'll come around, but she's Becca's best friend, so she probably feels like she needs to dislike you."

"Yeah, I'm definitely not Becca's favorite person." That was clear even with her not in the room.

Hannah covered her mouth, hiding her giggle. "Well, in her eyes, you did steal her man." She followed with the most over-the-top wink. Her whole head bobbed with the movement.

Steal? What did she mean about that? They were still dating, right? "Did they br—" I tried to ask, but the boys came back whooping and hollering.

"Dominic, I'm going to whoop your ass!" Kyle jumped, wrapping his arm around Dominic's neck. He didn't even flinch before wrapping his arm around his back and flinging him to the ground.

"Save it for the ring!" A smile was breaking out on his face.

"Oh no you don't!" Derek interrupted. "Kyle, you're starting with Aiden."

"Awwwww!" Kyle responded, his eyes shooting annoyance at poor Aiden.

I don't remember the last time I blinked. I was sitting on the bleachers, my hands gripping the seat as I leaned forward. I couldn't believe what I was watching. Well. I guess my thought before was kind of right. The four sections were fighting rings. Except they weren't wrestling, boxing, or doing any martial arts sport I knew about.

Two of them each took up one of the rings. The only one not currently participating was Derek, but he was intently watching Aiden and Kyle sparring. They all held wooden sticks. I think I've seen things like this before. I think they are used as practice swords, so you don't have to use the real things. I guess that's safer, as you probably walked away with a few fewer gashes. Though watching them smack each other with them, I bet they still left some nasty bruises.

"Stop!" Derek shouted. They both leaped back from each

other. Kyle was huffing, clearly out of breath. Golden wings extended out of both of their bodies.

"Why... did... you... stop... us?" Kyle said between breaths. "I... was... holding him... back."

"Kyle, I've told you this before. You can't just go in swinging. You need to think one to two moves ahead. If you don't go in with some foresight, you just get stuck where you were." Derek was rubbing his head as he leaned against the rope of the ring. Clearly this was a topic he was tired of having.

"And what's that?" Kyle was finally catching his breath. He had dropped his sword on the mat and was leaning down to pick it back up.

"You get stuck focusing on just blocking the next strike."

"Isn't that the point? To not get hit?"

"And that's just going to lead you to getting struck!" Derek waited to see if it would sink in. Confusion just consumed Kyle's face. "When you strike block for block, you are just anticipating the next swing. You aren't thinking about how you are going to strike back at your opponent. While you're stuck on that, your opponent is going to use that against you and open you up for real vulnerability." He paused again.

"Aiden... switch with me." He leaped into the ring, his feet landing with a smack against the mat.

Aiden hopped out, tossing his wooden sword to Derek. In a flash, wings erupted out of his back. I was not going to get used to that scene. Derek suddenly charged at Kyle. With every swing, Kyle lifted his sword to block, but Derek was right. He wasn't returning any blows. He was stuck just blocking. Derek struck his sword forward, but just before the two sticks collided, Derek did a last-minute spin. This caused Kyle to lose his balance, as his sword now slashed the air while Derek's sword swung around the side, making contact with his side. A sickly slap followed.

"Damnit." Kyle held his side. I'm not sure if it was because of the pain or the frustration of getting hit.

"Now again, but this time, focus on how you want to hit me."

They went back and forth at least ten more times. Each time, Derek struck a different part of his body. His arm, leg, and back being a few of the places. Red marks were left on the exposed skin. But after each spar, Kyle was starting to pick it up, and a few times, he caused Derek to parry one of his swings.

"Good!" he said after Kyle returned a blow. "Now see how that pulled my focus to the left, leaving my right open. You can use that to your advantage."

I couldn't believe how good a teacher Derek was. No matter how many times he had to reshow a move or repeat what he was saying, he never got frustrated. I could now see why he didn't want Dominic sparing with him. I'm sure he would've snapped two spars in. It made sense why so many of them seemed to look up to him.

I looked around the rest of the gym. Dominic and Luke were in the middle of a match. Dominic had two swords. Was that allowed? Though did it surprise me with Dominic? I'm sure he would find any excuse to get more of something. Dominic would take a swing at Luke and, as he blocked, would bring the other sword around. Similar to what Derek was telling Kyle about. The difference, Luke was almost anticipating the other sword and instead of the swords being locked, he was almost bouncing the one sword off, freeing it to collide with the second. While Dominic used a lot of his brunt force, Luke seemed to be more agile, using his opponent's strength against him.

Emery and Chris were in the back right corner. They each were back to one sword, but I noticed that they were using their wings more. Wow how crazy was that? As Chris charged forward, Emery leaped into the air. He had to have gone at least ten feet up, his wings propelling him from the ground before flipping in the air and landing behind him. The other boy quickly spun, pulling his wing around and blocking the strike. Wait! They could use their wings as shields. Did that mean they were solid? They almost looked as if they were on fire. I wasn't expecting them to have a physical shape.

Samantha and Hannah seemed to be in a deadlock. Samantha, like Dominic, had two swords, but hers were smaller. The difference in size caused their fight to be in closer quarters. This caused Hannah's sword to be restricted in movement, as she needed more room to swing it. Hannah, like Emery, used her wings to pick her up as she pulled her legs forward, kicking Samantha square in the chest.

Samantha was pushed backward. Her wings flapped to stop the momentum, but that gave just enough space for Hannah to get enough momentum in her swing. Samantha brought up her sword to block, but instead of stopping her sword, the added force caused the sword to flip out of her hand across the ring.

"Okay, good!" Derek called out. My attention went back to their ring, which was right in front of my bleachers. I wonder if he picked that one on purpose. "Now Aiden, switch back. Kyle, this time, try and get a few strikes in." He jumped out of the ring, tossing the sword back to Aiden.

Aiden got it in one swift motion, returning to the ring. Before you could say go, they were already fighting again, but this time, Kyle seemed to be trying to focus on Aiden, not the sword like he was doing before.

"So?" Derek was standing in front of the stands, his hair wet from sweat.

"This is definitely… intense." I hope that was the right word to use. It was hard to look away, but I couldn't help flinching every time someone got smacked by one of the sticks. "But can I ask a question?"

Derek's eyebrow lifted. Almost like he was surprised I had a question. As if this was a natural occurrence. I guess it kind of is in his world. "Shoot," was all he said.

"Why are you fighting with swords? Isn't that a little medieval?" I sucked in air at the last question. I hoped that wasn't insulting. I didn't mean childish. It's just with the technology and advancement of weapons, swords weren't the first thing you would think to bring to a fight.

"Swords play an important role in how we fight." Derek hesitated. He was looking for the right words to use. Derek brought his right hand up. The light glinted off his ring. I thought he had one too. With his left hand, he covered it. It almost seemed like he was going to pull it off. Suddenly, a bright light erupted, and a large sword was in his hands. The dark metal glistened against the light.

"Holy crap! Where did that come from?" I was leaning back in the bleachers, keeping my distance from the huge sword.

Derek smirked, and with a quick shake of his hands, the sword was engulfed in the same yellow-looking flames their wings were made of. Thank God my eyes were attached because I'm sure they would've popped out from shock.

"These swords help us direct our energy. Almost like how lightning is attracted to those lightning rods?" Just as quickly as it erupted, the light was gone, and the black metal was back. The metal was unfazed as if nothing had happened. "If we didn't have them, our energy would be chaotic and hard to control."

"And what does your energy do? It looks like fire, so does it burn?"

"It's hard to explain since you don't really have a good comparison on your side." Derek stopped for a moment. Was this the first time he had to put it into simple terms? They all seemed to have it, so it was just a part of life for them. "I guess it resembles fire as it is fluid light. But it also harnesses a physical state we can control."

He paused again before flicking his wrist, engulfing his sword again. He looked across the gym, and I noticed a few shapes against the wall. They looked like people. No, that wasn't right. They only had the upper body of the human. They were those fighting figures you would use, so you didn't have to fight with a real person. With a swing of his sword, the energy around his sword shot out, following the momentum of the swing, colliding with one of the figures. It ripped it in two as if the sword had instead collided with it.

My jaw dropped, so that was what he meant as a conductor of their energy. The swords alone look sharp, but how deadly was it with the combined force. And here was a group of teenagers with this power. Suddenly, the sword disappeared just as quickly as it appeared.

"Wait, where did it go?" Swords couldn't appear and disappear in thin air… right?

Derek was playing with the ring on his finger. "These rings we wear. They hold our swords."

"How?!" That wasn't physically possible. A large, four-foot sword could not fit in a ring.

His response… that half grin. "I don't know the mechanics, but I guess it's part of our advanced technology. All I know is it's a convenient way to carry them around."

"Can I hold it?" What did it feel like? The metal looked so smooth, like glass. Was it hard to grip, or was it slippery? How much did it weigh? When he swung it, he seemed to use the same effort he used when wielding the wooden swords.

"No!" I flinched back from the change of his tone. Did I anger him? I think he noticed my surprise. "I'm sorry." His tone immediately softened again. "These swords are made from celestial metals. We can hold them with no problem, but if any other species tries to touch them, it will immediately burn them. That is another reason they are hidden in our rings. Our rings act as a shield against the metal, so if it touches anyone else, it won't have the same reaction."

"Oh." Swords that can magically shrink and transform.

Metals that can burn. How many other things did they possess that had such unusual powers?

"You broke my sword!" someone yelled. Luke was holding splintered wood in his hand. "I just bought this one!"

Derek rolled his eyes and turned back to their ring. Wings, sword fighting, magical powers, and weapons. How much more was I going to find out about them? This should frighten me, but for some reason, I just felt safer here with them. I hope I can continue to learn more about them.

SEVENTEEN

"Bye, Amy!" Hannah gave me a quick hug in the parking lot. "I'm so glad you came with us today!"

"Thanks, it was a lot of fun." It felt good to be included in this part of their world. They were all still buzzing from energy.

"Derek, I'll see you tonight. I'm going to head out with Dominic," Emery shouted over his shoulder as he followed the three boys to Dominic's car.

That left Derek and me standing alone. "So…" I broke the silence, biting my lip.

"There's a football game on. Do you want to go back to Emery's and watch it?" I didn't know Derek liked football.

"Sure!" Did I know anything about football? No, but I was happy the day wasn't ending yet.

In the car, we rode in silence. The radio quietly playing in the background. "So, your parents are okay with you staying with Emery?" This was my chance to find out if they really did have parents. I mean, they had to, right? They didn't just appear out of nowhere.

Derek's face tensed as he shrugged. Maybe I shouldn't have asked. I needed to stop being so nosey. "I wouldn't say okay, but for now, it's for the best."

So, at least, that was confirmation that parents exist. "Well, that's nice of Emery's parents to let you stay."

"It's just Emery. His parents are no longer with us."

"Oh… I'm sorry." My heart dropped for Emery. At least I still had my dad. I couldn't imagine losing both. "But wait… does that mean it's just you two?" I could see why Derek's parents weren't okay with the idea. I'm surprised they went with it.

Derek shrugged. "It's just where we eat and sleep. Trust me, we have a lot of supervision over the rest of our lives."

I wanted to ask more. Was he referring to the clan dynamics Dominic mentioned earlier? But I felt like this wasn't a topic Derek wanted to go into detail, so we sat in silence as we returned to Emery's. Now knowing it was just the two of them, the house seemed a lot lonelier when we arrived. Such a huge house for two people. Well, such a big house for one person. How lonely this had to be for Emery. How many rooms sparked memories of his family. I'm glad Derek was able to be there with him, at least for now.

I sat on the couch as Derek rummaged in the kitchen. His hair still wet from his quick shower. He came back with a large bowl of popcorn and two cans of soda. The football game had already started. All I knew was there was an orange team and a blue team. I wonder who Derek was cheering for. This game was a lot rougher than the soccer game. They intentionally slammed into each other, even when people didn't have the ball.

I awkwardly sat on one side of the couch while Derek sat

on the opposite side. It felt like a cavern between us. Why couldn't I stop thinking about it and why did the room have to feel so tense! Almost as if the air was electrified.

"You don't have to sit so far away," Derek said before taking a sip of his soda. "Unless you wanted to use the recliner.

I didn't even know the couch reclined. "I don't know if Becca would like that." Okay, that was me attempting to fish. Hannah's comment earlier had me thinking. Did they break up? Was it bad that I secretly hoped the answer was yes?

"Oh, we aren't together anymore." There was no emotion behind his statement.

"I'm so sorry to hear that." That was a lie. Oh God, I was going to hell. I wasn't fooling him, either. He looked over with a smirk across his face.

I bit my lip, scooting over next to him. This felt even more awkward. I had my knees pulled onto the couch as I sat on my legs. I tried really hard to pay attention to the game. Derek suddenly got up. Was this making him uncomfortable? I should've just stayed on my side. He returned with two blankets.

"In case you get cold." He sat back down, pulling his footrest up.

"Thanks." The blanket was nice. I pulled it over my lap, sitting back against the couch. The word touchdown covered the bottom of the screen. I wonder who scored?

The orange team now had the ball. They quickly kicked it down the field as one of the blue players was moving back and forth, waiting to catch the ball. Once caught, he rushed forward. He dodged one player spinning left. Then another came and tried to grab him, but he had quickly dodged him. He didn't see the one coming in from the left who leaped, grabbing his midsection and bringing him to the ground. They then dispersed, lining up on their sides.

After two tries, the blue team had been stopped both times as they tried to push forward. The third round came. One player snapped the ball back. The player who caught the ball was prancing back and forth, looking between the different players. That's when he seemed to make contact with one of them. He pulled his arm back, launching the ball forward, just before another player tackled him to the ground.

The ball soared forward without wavering in its path. That's when you saw the player he was aiming for running forward, his eyes on the ball. He caught it, pulling the ball to his chest and running even faster. Three orange players were closing in. Almost like lions chasing a gazelle on the African savannah. I really needed to lay off the nature films. The player, knowing they were closing in, leaped forward. Right on the white line. If his arms weren't extended, the ball would've been short, but instead, TOUCHDOWN covered the screen again.

Wow that was a rush! I looked over to Derek to see if he was happy with the play. I still didn't know who he was rooting for. He was fast asleep. I still couldn't get over how peaceful he looked when he slept. As if all his cares would wash away. I'm sure he was exhausted, after helping me, then having to go out again to talk to whoever he met.

I wonder who he would have to go get permission about me. Did he also see Becca today? I doubt he would make an early trip for that. I wonder when they broke up? When we talked last weekend, it seemed as if that wasn't even an option. From Hannah's earlier statement it clearly had to do something with me.

I jumped as the door creaked open. I quickly looked at Derek. He was still asleep. My eyes met with Emery's, who was about to say something. Scared he was going to wake him I mouthed he's sleeping while pointing to Derek.

"Oh," Emery whispered. He quietly walked around the

couch, looking over at him. Did he think I was making it up? "I can take you home if you want."

I didn't really want to leave. I don't know why, but it was nice just sitting next to him. But he really should get some sleep. Especially with school tomorrow. I nodded my head, carefully getting off the couch. My eyes didn't leave Derek to make sure he didn't stir from my movements.

I followed Emery outside as he walked toward Derek's car. "Will he be okay if we take his car?"

"He'll be fine. Unless you want to ride on the back of my motorcycle." He smiled.

My eyes widened as they looked over the black bike. I was definitely not one of those girls that swooned over guys on motorcycles. I would much rather take something with doors. "Uh, no, I think the car will work." I didn't know he rode a bike. I guess it fit. Did he ride it to school? I was trying to remember if I had seen motorcycles in the parking lot. I'm sure there were a couple.

"So, what did you think?" he asked as he pulled out of the driveway.

"Oh, it was so cool to watch. It reminded me of when you and Cole would pretend to sword fight." I froze in my seat. Where did that memory come from.

"I still can't believe he's gone." Emery's hands squeezed the wheel.

I needed to change the subject. I wasn't ready to talk about him, especially with Emery. The flashes of memories made me feel like I was not just forgetting them, but parts of my brother. "So, Kyle had said something about being left out. What did he mean by that?"

He was quiet for a few minutes. "Did Derek tell you anything about us?"

"He called you all Guardians, but that was pretty much it."

"And you remember what I said about the Shadow

Reapers." I nodded as a shiver spread through my body. I hated thinking about those creatures.

"Well… remember how I said our job was to protect you humans? Part of that job is to patrol the streets at night, making sure they aren't wondering around looking for their next meal."

"What, like your own police force?"

"Yeah, just like that. We are designated certain shifts and streets, sometimes we are also called to a sighting."

Was that what Derek was doing when I ran into him that night when I was walking home. Or that time, he rode the bus home with me. I was always wondering why he was out so late at night. Each of those times, was he looking for them?

"There is an arrangement," he started again.

"An arrangement?" They have an agreement with those monsters.

"Yes, there is no way to fully eradicate them, so there are rules on when and where they are allowed to feed," he spoke matter-of-factly. The food he was speaking about was us. Humans. "They can feed off those who are sleeping, as they feed off of their dreams, so the impact to the human is minimal. But if they are looking for people who are awake, not only are they creating emotional damage, but sometimes it leads to death."

I shuddered, thinking of the bridge. I guess I could see his point. When it's a dream, you chalk it up to an overactive imagination, but you can't do that when you are awake staring face-to-face with one of them. "But wait… Derek, when I first saw him, it was because they were in my room." That didn't make sense if that was allowed.

"Yeah… it's probably best if that stays between us."

So, he wasn't supposed to be there. Once again, he broke the rules because of me. I could feel my stomach flip. How many times was I going to put him in that position.

"We're here." He stopped in front of my house.

"Thanks Emery. And thank you for always being so open with me." He didn't sugarcoat things, which I appreciated, but he also treated me like an equal. "I'll see you tomorrow."

I walked to the door as he pulled away. Well, was that true? Would I see them tomorrow? Last time I was shunned once we were back at school. Would it be different now that they all know about me? Would we say hi to each other in the hall? What would Grace and Alicia think? Oh shoot! I never called Alicia back!

I sat on my bed taking in deep breaths. Okay, I better get this over with now. It will be worse tomorrow when I see her in person. Just let her know you were super busy, and this is the first moment you had to call her. But busy how? I couldn't say I was with Derek and his friends all weekend. Ugh... this was going to be torture. I clicked her name as the phone rang.

"Amy! Where have you been?! I've been waiting next to the phone all weekend!" Alicia whined. I could just picture her annoyed face having to wait so long for the juicy details of my weekend.

"I'm so sorry, I forgot my charger and I just finally got it charged." That wasn't a lie. My phone was dead all day because I didn't think to grab a charger. I also didn't expect to be out all weekend.

"You need to be more responsible with your phone!" she lectured. "But come on! Tell me how it went."

"It went... fine." I knew that wasn't enough. "The game was fun. I didn't realize how exciting soccer was."

"Well yeah! Remember going to the games when Mike played?" Oh yeah, I did go to games with her, but we never focused on the game. She spent the whole time gushing at Mike while he sat on the bench.

"Yeah, I mean, since it's been a while, I didn't think I'd remember how it went." Another lie. "Anyway, that was fun, but then there was a party we went to after at one of the player's houses. Out by the lake."

"Wait, you went?" she interrupted. "But that's only open for players! No one else is allowed to go. That's why Mike always had to go by himself."

I guess she did know about the parties, but that wasn't true, more than half the people there weren't players. Did they change the rules? "Oh, maybe they decided to finally open it up for everyone."

"Yeah... maybe." I wonder what she was thinking. Did Mike lie? Why wouldn't he want her to go? I thought back to the girls and their dislike of him. Was this why? No, I shouldn't jump to conclusions.

"Well, I need to get dinner started." I also was hoping to end the questions. I really didn't want to relive the party. If I told her I left last night she would ask what I did all day.

"Well, I want more deets tomorrow!" I hung up the phone letting out a sigh of relief. Okay, that wasn't terrible.

Maybe I should order pizza. I wasn't in the mood to cook. I grabbed my phone to look at the app and realized I had texts pending. They must have come in when I was on the phone. They were from Derek. I hope he wasn't mad I slipped out.

> Sorry I fell asleep, that was kind of rude. Can I make it up to you? How about I pick you up for school so you don't have to ride the bus?

I guess that answers the question if we have to act like strangers. I wonder if there is an open seat since he and Becca aren't together. Oh no. What's going to happen in gym! I had to pull myself out of the spiral. I wonder what Alicia and Grace would say if they saw me arrive with them? How would I answer those questions? My heart dropped. No, I couldn't.

> Oh no don't worry. I can't imagine how tired you are. I actually need to talk to someone on the bus tomorrow, so rain check?

Ok rain check. Cya tomorrow

That was for the best. I needed to be smart with our friendship. If I was going to hide their secret, I couldn't suddenly bring a lot of attention to them. Maybe acting like we aren't friends in public really is the better option.

I went back to the pizza app and started our dinner order.

EIGHTEEN

I stepped off the bus not ready for Monday. Luckily, Thanksgiving break was only a couple weeks away. I wonder how many people have ordered the special at Charlie's. New schedules would also be going out today. I wonder, with the additional help Mr. Johnson has been hiring, if my schedule would start shifting.

"Amy!" Someone called as I was walking toward the school. That's weird, Alicia and Grace normally waited until I reached our table. I looked around to see who was calling me.

Hannah came bounding up. My heart stopped. Well, this wasn't helping my keeping-a-distance approach. "Hi, Hannah," I meekly said as she reached me.

"I was so bummed you didn't ride with us. But Derek said you were going to join us tomorrow." She was chatting as if we were old friends.

"Uh… maybe." That was definitely not what I had texted. I should probably try and have a conversation with him at some point today.

"Well, come on, everyone is over here." She grabbed my arm, leading me toward their group.

I caught Alicia and Grace staring at me. Alicia's mouth

was hanging open. I wonder where they fell in her popularity chart. I doubted anywhere high because they stayed pretty isolated. Though how many students have had a crush on at least one of them. I was going to get grilled at lunch.

"Hey, Amy." Kyle waved as we got closer. I noticed three of them were missing from the group. Becca, Samantha, and Chris.

"Hi." I could feel my cheeks flushing. I wasn't expecting them to be so welcoming. Well as welcoming as they could be. Dominic barely looked up from his phone, not that he wasn't happy to see me, more like he didn't need to bother with a hello. "Umm...Derek... can I see you for a second?" I hope I wasn't being rude.

"Ooooooh. Already trying to get some alone time," Kyle chimed in.

"Knock it off, Kyle." Luke smacked his arm.

"Is something wrong?" Derek asked once we were far enough away from listening ears.

"I don't think this is a good idea." I was staring at the ground kicking at an invisible stone. I couldn't bring myself to make eye contact.

"Wait..." He ran his fingers through his hair. "Isn't this what you wanted? To be friends, right?"

"Well, yes, but what about all the questions this is going to raise? I'm not a good liar. What if I accidentally say the wrong thing and blow all your covers." Derek burst out laughing. Okay, that was not the reaction I was expecting.

He had to take a second to catch his breath. "Okay, let me get this straight. You think becoming our friend is going to be such a big red flag that people are going to immediately stop and think... wait, there is something off about them! They're obviously not human!" He continued to chuckle.

"Well... I guess." It did sound dumb when he said it out loud.

With his hand, he tilted up my chin so our eyes would

meet. My heart skipped a beat from the touch. His face was stern. "Amy, look. Yes, our secret is important. You can't go around talking about it, but I can promise you one thing. People aren't going to immediately think something outside of their normal is occurring. You humans live off seeking hard evidence before believing the simplest thing. Even if you were to end up telling someone, they would rather think you are crazy then believe there is something unhuman about us." The half grin appeared on his face. "Now us dating. That could be a pretty convincing conclusion."

"Dating…" I choked out. That word broke me out of the trance I had been in. Who would believe that someone like him, who was previously dating Becca, the hottest girl in our school, would immediately go from her to me?

He winked, and before I had time to react, he leaned down kissing me. My whole body buzzed, and it felt as if everything had stopped in time. Then just as quickly it was over, as if someone snapped their fingers, the world around me started again. The feeling of heat hit my cheeks first. Derek draped his arm around my shoulders, leading me back to the group. "I think it's the perfect cover," he whispered in my ear.

The bell rang, and we headed to class. I couldn't stop blushing as Derek walked me to class. "Lunch?" he asked as we stood outside the math door.

"I should probably sit with Alicia and Grace today. I'm sure they're dying with questions." I briefly touched my lips as they still tingled as I thought about the kiss. Though, maybe taking him up on the offer was a better option. No, Alicia would just bombard me at work. "I'll see you in English."

I was right. Alicia and Grace were anxiously waiting for me at lunch. Their food was lying untouched in front of them. Okay, stay calm. I set my lunch on the table trying to act as nonchalantly as I could.

"Hey, did you all have a good weekend?" I asked as I

pulled my food out, doing everything I could to avoid eye contact.

"Apparently ours wasn't as eventful as yours! Did you leave something out yesterday on our phone call?" Her arms were crossed while a firm frown covered her face. "And what happened to Ben? I thought you guys were an item."

Poor Ben. I was afraid I was going to hurt him, and that's exactly what I ended up doing. He avoided me today in gym. Derek was right, the rumors of us dating spread like wildfire. No one was questioning me hanging around them, though I'm sure there were a lot of questions about why me. Especially when his previous girlfriend was Becca.

Becca. That was also tense. She wasn't mean like she had been before. No, she just treated me like I didn't exist. I'm not sure which one was worse. Was there anything I could do to fix that? I mean, I didn't intentionally break them up. I really hope I didn't break up their friendship within the group. Would they have to choose sides? It kind of seemed like some of them already did.

"Well?" Alicia's fingers were tapping frantically across the table.

"So…" I had to think fast. "Remember how I said I went to the party. Well, I didn't know it was an overnight party. Luckily, Derek and his friends were nearby, and they were able to give me a ride home. And well… one thing led to another, and we started talking and realized we had a lot in common." I'm starting to learn the best lies are those built on a grain of truth. Dominic did get me from the party, and Derek and I had a conversation that night that secured our relationship. Even though it was about our friendship not dating.

"I can't believe you are dating Derek!" Grace squealed. "I mean, he is so hot!"

I could see the turmoil Alicia was experiencing. She was clearly still upset about not knowing about us, but she also wanted to know more about the relationship. "I thought he was dating Becca?"

"Oh, they broke up last week. I'm not sure why." I made sure to add that as Alicia would probably start a round of questions to pry, and honestly, I still had no idea.

"So, you're the rebound." Alicia nodded as if all the pieces were aligning now.

Because apparently that could be the only logical reason Derek would pick me. Anger filled my chest. Thanks Alicia, I sometimes forget what a great friend you are.

"Well, whatever the reason, I think you both look super cute. Alicia, did you see how Derek looked at her when they were hanging out front? He couldn't keep his eyes off her!" Grace was swooning. Though, I'm sure she was exaggerating. This was a cover. Right?

I barely had a chance to eat anything between all the questions. I don't remember being more thankful for the sound of the bell. I hope this wasn't an indication of how work was going to go.

THE REST OF THE DAY FOLLOWED SUIT. I COULD HEAR murmurs all around and knew what they were talking about, but luckily, Sally was the only person bold enough to ask. Well, outside of Alicia and Grace, but that was expected. English was the worst because we were both in the class together, and to make matters worse, Ms. Haines decided to change up seats again, putting Derek and I next to each other. Not only did that make the chatter worse, but I couldn't focus. I kept peeking over at him, aware of every moment he made. If this kept up, I was going to fail English. What if I had to repeat the tenth grade. I would never get into a good college then!

I finally felt relief walking into the diner. Yes, Alicia was still here, but at least I escaped the prying eyes of our class-mates. At least the ones who didn't come in for their afternoon snack.

"Alicia, Amy, can I please see you in my office," Mr. Johnson called out as we were getting ready to clock in.

"Did something happen Saturday?" I whispered to Alicia as we headed back. I was trying to think about my last shift. I couldn't think of anything out of the ordinary happening, and I was sure to stay within my scheduled time last week.

"Please have a seat." He motioned to the chairs when we walked in.

His office was super cramped. It barely fit his desk, and he still tried to have a couple chairs so anyone who came in could sit. I wonder if this was originally supposed to be a closet. His desk was cluttered with receipts, probably from the multiple deliveries he got through the week. A few pictures sat next to his computer. One was of him and his wife, then another with his whole family. He had three kids, one son and two daughters. The last picture was of his dog. It was one of those dogs that had that scrunched up face. The ones that looked like they ran into a door when they were little, and their muzzle just stayed compact from the injury.

"Is something wrong?" I asked. I could count the number of times we were called in here, and they were never good. Though most of the time it had to do with Alicia bailing on days or me working past my designated time.

He was clasping and unclasping his hands. Clearly not comfortable. This wasn't a good sign. "Look, I want to say that it has been such a joy having you both working here. You have helped us so much, but with the holidays coming it is getting harder and harder to try and schedule you both in. You know with your school schedule and restricted hours." I knew this was coming. "So, for now, I think it's best if you both just enjoy the holidays. I know you have a lot of vacation days coming up and the last thing you would want to do is work."

Were we getting fired? I could feel the sweat break out across my forehead. Maybe I was jumping ahead, and he was just referring to the next two months. "Do you mean just for the holidays or moving forward?"

His lips pressed tightly together. "Er… moving forward."

"Does that mean we don't have to work today?" Alicia was clearly excited to have her afternoon back. Not at all phased by the news we had just been fired.

"Yes. If you both want to just leave your uniforms with Beatrice." He was ready to be done with the conversation. He wasn't trying to be rude. He was just ready for this ordeal to end. I'm sure it wasn't easy for him.

"Thanks, Mr. Johnson, for the opportunity," I said before leaving.

I could feel the tears pricking at my eyes. What was I going to do? I wasn't like Alicia. I didn't have this job for the extra cash. We needed this money. Thank goodness for my savings, but how much of it would be used before I could find a new one? Most of the seasonal jobs that hired fifteen-year-olds had already been filled.

We both changed in the bathroom before giving Beatrice our uniforms. "You okay?" She squeezed my arm. "I tried to get him to change his mind. Or at least keep one of you." She glanced over at Alicia knowing it wasn't her job she was trying to save.

"Thanks, Beatrice. For everything. I'll be okay." I gave her a hug. I was going to miss her hugs. For a moment I imagined what my mom's hugs felt like. I needed to break away before I really started crying.

"Isn't this great!" Alicia announced when we were outside. "I was super bummed about having to work over Thanksgiving and Christmas, but this is perfect! Now my parents won't get mad about me not working right away!"

"Well, I'm glad it's working out for you," I snapped. I couldn't stop myself. Could she at least fake being upset when I was standing here. She knew I needed this job.

"What? You have savings, right? You'll find a job fast, plus were you really making a lot at the diner? I heard Mike's work pays double what Mr. Johnson was giving us. I'm sure Mike can put in a good word for us."

"Can we just stop talking about it?" If we continued, I knew I was going to say something I would regret.

"Yeah." She paused. "You can take the bus, right? I'm going to go hang out with Mike."

I nodded. That was probably for the best. I'm sure we would end up fighting if we spent any more time together. We barely said bye before she pulled away. I turned to head to the bus stop and my stomach dropped. Not today.

I noticed the familiar cars pull into the parking lot. Two of them being Derek and Dominic's car. "Hey, Amy!" Derek called. "I thought you were working today."

That was my breaking point. I covered my face with my hands trying to hide the tears. I stood there crying in front of all of them. I quietly prayed that Becca and her crew would not be there.

"Who wants pizza?" I heard Emery call out.

A strong hand gently squeezed my shoulder. "Let's get out of here," Derek whispered in my ear. All I could do was nod.

Once we were away from the restaurant, he pulled into a parking lot, placing the car in park. "What happened?" he softly asked, pulling my hand away from my face so he could look into my eyes. I'm sure they were already red and swollen from crying. Not exactly the sight I wanted him to see.

"I got fired," I whimpered between my quiet sobs.

"I'm sorry." He sat there just holding my hand that he had moved from my face.

"It's okay. I thought it was coming. I just…" I hiccupped,

"really needed this job." My sobs were starting to shake my body. How many times was I going to cry in front of him?

"Is there anything I can do to help? If you need help with money, I can give you some." I know he was trying to make me feel better, but we were just getting to know each other. I didn't want asking for money to make it more complicated.

"No, I'll be okay. I have savings for now." I wiped away some of my tears trying to clear up my vision. Maybe this was a good thing. Alicia was right the pay wasn't great. "Plus, this means we can spend more time together." I weakly smiled. Did that sound stupid? Why did I have to add that part in?

A big smile crept on Derek's face. "I like that result. Now, how about we get some ice cream? I heard that always helps with bad days."

I know our 'dating' was a cover, but I was falling hard for him. For once, I wasn't going to do the smart thing. This may be fake, but I was going to enjoy it. It's time I slow down a little and make some high school memories.

I just hope I don't get too hurt from it.

NINETEEN

"**Y**ou did really good today, Kyle!" I said as we walked out of the gym. He was really improving. He was even starting to get his own strikes in against Aiden. I think he hit him at least three times today.

"Now don't go around giving him a big head." Dominic walked up, ruffling his hair. "You know Aiden goes easy on you, right?"

"No, he doesn't!" Kyle smacked his hand away. Dominic chuckled before turning his attention back to Luke. They had been partners again today, and from the looks of it, Luke was giving him a run for his money.

"Dominic's just scared for when it's time for you to take him on because he knows you're going to beat him," I said, winking.

"HA!" he shouted from behind. I whipped my head, giving him the coldest glare. Did he always have to rile people up? He put his hands up surrendering for the moment.

"I know I'm getting nervous about having a match with Kyle again." Derek draped his arm over my shoulders. My heart was starting to beat faster. I still wasn't used to being so close.

"Really?" Kyle was starting to flush. I know that comment from Derek meant a lot to him.

"Yeah, you're really getting faster with your movements. You even had Aiden trapped a few times. Keep this up, and you're going to have Dominic sweating. Trust me." I wrapped my arm around his waist, giving him a thank-you squeeze. Kyle turned to tell Luke all about his praise.

"No school!" Hannah chimed in. "How are we going to fill the day?"

She was right. Thanksgiving break was this week. Normally, I would be working all week, getting as much time as I could since I didn't have school to compete with, but I still hadn't found a new job. Who was I kidding? I hadn't started looking. I decided to take a page out of Alicia's book and just enjoy the holidays. I did have savings, and if I just had a better budget next year, I could make up whatever I took. Maybe even find a bill to cut at home. Our grocery bill was already starting to go down since I'd been spending all my free time with Derek.

"Do you guys celebrate Thanksgiving?" I bit my lip, wondering if that was a stupid question. Did they celebrate the same holidays? Now that I was thinking about it, they never mentioned Halloween last month. Was it because monsters were real in their world?

"Or course," Emery said. "I mean probably not your same turkey dinners, but it is one of the few times we are all able to come together."

"What about you, Amy? What do you and your dad do?" Hannah was now sitting on Derek's hood.

"Well, we don't really celebrate holidays together." Crap... were they thinking I was hinting at an invite. "I mean, he usually works holidays since he's a janitor, so I usually hang out at home. It's the perfect time to start decorating for Christmas," I added, trying to recover. That wasn't true. We didn't decorate, but I didn't want to say sit at home alone doing nothing.

"Derek! She should celebrate with us!" She was clapping her hands in excitement. As if she came up with the perfect solution.

"I'm sure the elders would *love* that." Dominic obviously had to chime in. "Hannah, get off of his hood! You're going to put a dent in it."

"It doesn't hurt to ask." Hannah's arms were folded across her chest as she hopped down. She quickly looked at the hood to make sure it didn't really dent. "Plus, she's already like one of us."

"Would you want to join us?" Derek whispered in my ear. Chills went down my arm.

"Yes!" is what I wanted to say. Instead, I just shrugged. "I mean, if they were okay with it, I could come, but I'm really good just staying at home."

"I'll see what I can do." He winked. Hannah shrilled with excitement.

HERE I WAS, STANDING NERVOUSLY AT THE FRONT DOOR, anxiously pulling my purple sleeve while my other hand held the apple pie I had picked up from Charlie's. I had picked out one of the few nice dresses I owned. It was from one of those shopping trips with Grace and Alicia. I think it was for a school dance freshman year. I hope I wasn't too dressed up.

"You look great." Derek placed his hand on my fidgeting hand. He was wearing a dark blue suit, paired with a white shirt and patterned tie. It was weird seeing him so dressed up. "I'm going to be by your side the whole time."

I took a deep breath before entering. We had gone to one

of those store fronts that operated in their neighborhood. As common practice here, it didn't have a normal name above the entrance, so I wasn't sure what was inside. Though the names weren't very helpful regarding what store you were entering, as they were mostly generic to what type of thing you were looking for. And that one store that I thought had the word *WEAPONRY* on top? That was right. I guess that is where they could buy their special swords and whatever else they used.

I looked around at the tables scattered throughout. It looked like some type of banquet hall. I wonder if this is where they held all their important events. The inside was almost the same size as the gym. Though, you wouldn't have guessed that from the front.

"Derek." A young man and woman approached us. I was guessing they had to be in their late twenties, maybe early thirties. I couldn't help but squeeze his hand. This was it. I was finally meeting the adults of their group.

"Hi, Dad. Mom." My mouth momentarily dropped before I clenched it shut. They had to have been teenagers when they had him. His greeting was indifferent. If he hadn't said the words "Mom" and "Dad," you would think he was meeting complete strangers.

"Is this Amy?" his mom asked. She actually sounded excited to meet me. She was stunning, as if she walked out of one of those fashion magazines. I'm not sure what she did for a living, but a modeling career was obviously a missed calling.

With how Derek treated them, I expected them to be cold back. Instead, she wrapped me in a hug. I moved the pie out of the way just in time, or else we would both be wearing it. "Uh... hi," I mumbled as she squeezed me.

His dad was a little more reserved greeting me with a simple nod. Derek was almost a spitting imagine of him. Which made my heart flutter, it was as if I had a crystal ball

WINGS OF THE SECRET REALM

and could see into his future. His features were more enhanced as the boyish features had faded over time, making the already hard lines more defined.

"I brought a pie." I held it out, as if I was giving tribute.

"That is so sweet of you!" Derek's mom gushed. "Arnold!" she called out. Another gentleman appeared. "Can you take Amy's pie and put it with the rest of the food?"

"Amy!" I was starting to get used to Hannah's greeting. Every time she called my name, it sounded like she hadn't seen me in years instead of days.

"Hi, Mr. and Mrs. Adler." Hannah slightly bowed as she made her way toward us. That was a different type of greeting. Oh no. Was I supposed to bow to them? Was this how you showed respect to the adults? Or were these the elders? I smirked at that last thought. There was no way they were elders. I imagined an old man with a long white beard in black robes.

"Hi Hannah." His mom softly smiled. Pulling me back into the room. "Alright Michael, we better say hi to our other guests. It was good seeing you, Derek." She reached out squeezing his hand. A moment of sadness touched her eyes.

"That seemed to go well," Hannah said, smacking my back. The force made me stumble forward. Sometimes, I think she forgot her own strength. "Oops, sorry."

"Let's get a seat." Derek chuckled. It was good to see him relax again. I wasn't used to seeing Derek so rigid. When we were together, he typically acted like he didn't have a care in the world. I wonder what happened between him and his parents.

Even with everyone together, the kids still stuck together. I was surprised they didn't break off and sit with their parents. I was kind of looking forward to seeing whose parents were whose. What shocked me even more was Becca, Samantha and Chris were sitting with us. Were they putting on an act in front of the adults? Did they not want them knowing there was a rift between them? Would that cause problems? I'm sure they would understand if exes didn't want to stay friends.

I glanced around the room, now full of people. I was surprised at how normal it was. I don't know why, but I was expecting to see a room full of super models, probably because of how beautiful their kids were, but you had people in all shapes and sizes. And it was nice to see older adults, some completely gray, but still no long gray beards or wizard robes. I wonder if Derek's grandparents were here. Were they still around? I'd wait to see if he mentioned them. Alicia lost her grandmother last year and anytime she's mentioned you can see the sadness return on her face. The one shocking thing was that outside of our table, there were no other kids. Maybe there was an age limit to the dinner. Everyone was dressed to the nines, which is a little harder to maintain when you have kids running around and getting into things.

"So, Amy, are you having fun?" Was Becca speaking to me?

"Uh yeah." I started twisting my napkin in my lap. Why was she speaking to me. "It was cool to meet Derek's parents." I wonder about the type of relationship she had with them.

"Oh wow, starting out with the royals. That's pretty bold." She smirked as if I had just committed some faux pas.

"Royals," I nearly coughed out. What was she talking about? The table suddenly got quiet.

"Well, you know Derek is the next in line to be the leader of all of us. In your human society he would probably be seen as a prince or something." She flipped her hair as this was common knowledge. Well, I guess between them it was.

Wait, the next leader? Did that mean his parents were the current ones? But they were so young.

"Enough, Becca," Derek growled through gritted teeth.

"What? I assumed you would've mentioned it. I mean coming with a human date, how embarrassing for his folks."

Her eyes didn't stop holding mine. Satisfied with her announcement. "Well, I better go mingle, come on Samantha."

"Amy…" Derek reached for my hand. I pulled it away.

"I need to use the bathroom." I quietly excused myself, heading toward the labeled hallway.

I found an empty stall and locked myself in. I felt more embarrassed than upset. How did I not know how important Derek was here. I guess it made sense. Since we arrived, people hadn't stopped coming to the table to shake his hand or talk with him. And there was I sitting obliviously to it all. Plus, it explained how the rest of them acted around him. How he always took leadership in whatever they did, how Kyle and Luke were constantly seeking out his approval, but why didn't he tell me?

"I can't believe you did that!" a familiar voice echoed as a girl chastised the other one when they entered. I looked through the small crack between the doors. My breath caught in my throat. It was Samantha and Becca. I froze in place, afraid any movement would alert them I was there.

"I was just having a little fun." Becca smirked back. "Plus, can you believe what she was wearing? She looks like she's twelve!"

I could feel my cheeks flush as I picked at the end of my dress.

"You aren't going to get Derek back if you keep pissing him off."

"You think I'm worried?" The water was running as they washed their hands. "Let him have fun with his little pet. His parents will put up with it now, but we all know it's already decided who he will end up with. He knows it. He wouldn't do something that would jeopardize our clan. Regardless how he feels, I will be second in charge one day."

One of them ripped a paper towel. The sound of rustling followed by a quiet swish as it descended into the trash can.

The door thumped as they exited. My stomach dropped. Why should this upset me? We aren't really dating. This wasn't real, but why did it have to feel so real?

I opened the stall door and stared at the girl looking back. I did look like a kid. I should've asked Grace or Alicia to help me get ready. I'm sure they would've been thrilled to have a chance to ask all their questions about my relationship. Since Derek and I started 'dating' we barely saw each other. And we no longer had our diner shifts to catch up. I headed back to the table, where I sat quietly, replaying that scene in my head.

"Everything okay?" Derek asked as we drove home. His eyes darted between me and the road. "You were quiet the rest of the evening."

"Why didn't you tell me?" I tried to hide the anger from my voice, but it didn't work.

"Tell you what?"

"How important your family is!" Really, he didn't think that was an important detail. Especially when I was meeting them today. I felt like an idiot.

"It's not really that big of a deal." His grip on the steering wheel tightened. I could tell he wanted the conversation to end, but I wasn't ready to stop.

"If it wasn't a big deal, you would've said something." He tensed in response. He knew I was right.

There was a long pause before he answered again. "I'm tired of being treated differently." He pulled into a parking lot before stopping the car. He turned to face me, his eyes burning. Almost as if they were pleading with me. "I told you before. You're the only person I feel like I can be myself around. The only one who doesn't expect the most out of me or treat me like I'm on some damn pedestal." I wasn't used to him swearing.

"What about your friends? Emery, Dominic, Hannah. They don't treat you differently, do they?" That couldn't be true right? Or was I just that naïve. I guess if you think about it, they do always look to Derek for some type of approval. If Derek says something, most times they do it without argument. That's probably why Dominic helped me all those times. Because he knew he couldn't say no to him.

"How would you feel when you had to interact with someone you knew would eventually be the one who tells you what you can or can't do. It's just hard to forget something like that."

"Well," I grabbed his arm, squeezing gently, "I guess this is one of those times it's good that I'm human because you aren't going to tell me what to do." I smiled when he chuckled back. I wasn't any closer to understanding them, but I knew what my responsibility was to Derek. Whatever I could do to remove just a little of the weight he carried around.

That conversation between Becca and Samantha still bothered me, but one thing they said was right. We could enjoy our time together for now. Who knows what the future would bring, but if I spent too much time caring about it, I would miss out on us.

"Where are we going?" I asked as he started to pull out of the parking lot. Was he taking me home? It was only nine, and I didn't want to end the evening on such a heavy conversation.

"We have another Thanksgiving tradition I want to show you." He smiled at me before turning off onto a dirt road. Or what at least looked like a road. Would a community here have unpaved roads? A fire was lit in the distance as we drove closer. I noticed the normal crew huddled around the warm fire. A white blanket of snow covered the ground from the last snowstorm.

"Finally!" Dominic called out when we got out of the car.

"I thought you would never make it out of there! How many stiffs did you have to kiss up to?"

I smirked when I thought back to us leaving. An older gentleman with a receding hairline had stopped Derek at the doorway. It seemed with every statement he was slapping Derek on the back laughing. Oblivious to the subtle hints he was giving that we were leaving. It felt like an eternity before we were able to escape.

"Come on, can we just start?" Kyle pleaded. "It's freezing out here!" Always the impatient one. Though his excitement was intoxicating.

"If you think the gym is cool, you're going to like this!" Hannah nudged my side.

Swords appeared in their hands. They were all different shapes and sizes, but ironically, they kind of matched the wood swords each person used in the gym. I guess that made sense. Dominic and Samantha with their two swords, was that why Dominic wore all those rings? Was each ring a separate weapon? Everyone else held single swords, some were wider, while others were longer.

The only person standing out was Becca. Should that really surprise me that she would choose something to set her apart from everyone else? While everyone was holding swords, she was holding a long spear. Unlike a normal spear, the handle was made from the same metal as the swords, which was unique compared to the normal wooden handles that I saw in our history textbooks.

"Alright, you all know the rules, five against five. Aiden and I will be the team captains," Derek announced. They both stood on opposite sides, staring each other down.

"What about Amy?" I could just picture the smirk on Becca's face.

Derek's glare was enough to shut her up. I wonder if she realized she crossed the line tonight. My blood even ran a little cold from the look. He really did know how to take charge. He would make a good leader. I ran my finger nervously over my nails. I was doing just what he was worried about. I was already looking at him differently.

They finished calling the last person. I felt bad, Kyle was the last one chosen. I'm sure that was hard on him. Derek, Dominic, Hannah, Becca, and Kyle were on one team while Aiden, Emery, Chris, Samantha and Luke were on the other. My heart had dropped a little when Derek had called Becca's name, but I shook it off, they were still friends. Suddenly it started. Their swords engulfed in light. Their speed was breathtaking. You almost missed their movements as they were blurs against the dark.

They both chose well, as their teams seemed to be evenly matched. That was until Derek and Becca teamed up. I definitely underestimated her with her spear, she manipulated it with such ease. She spun it in her hands deflecting multiple sword attacks. The end of her spear could reach farther than anyone else, the distance was her best advantage. Derek and her worked in perfect harmony. Was that part of the reason they were best suited for one another?

I was starting to grasp the game. The goal was to make contact with a part of their body. They seemed to be hitting with the broad side of their swords, I'm guessing so no one would get cut. Becca spun her spear, pushing Emery and Chris back, this allowed Derek to rush in catching Chris off guard. His sword smacked his leg, and the slap of the contact echoed. He flung up his hands in defeat. Maybe they avoided serious injury, but they were going to have some nasty bruises after tonight.

Hannah was the next one out, then Kyle, followed by Emery and Luke. Suddenly it was three against two. Aiden flipped behind Dominic, smacking him in the back. He was not happy as a slew of curse words flew out of his mouth. Now it was Derek and Becca against Aiden and Samantha. Best friends against each other.

Becca's spear swung toward Samantha, but she stopped it between her two swords. They formed an X, almost like a vice grip. Becca was stuck. Was it bad that I internally cheered? Instead, she smirked. With all her might, she pushed the end of the spear forward. The motion swung the spear to the left. The momentum caused Samantha to lose her grip on her swords and they went flying. I jumped back as they landed just a couple feet in front of me. With Samantha unarmed, Becca spun the spear in a 360, colliding into Samantha's side.

"Nice!" Kyle cheered from the sideline. Two against one. The final standoff.

"Ready to forfeit?" Derek called out.

"You know me better than that," Aiden responded before rushing forward.

He jumped over the spear as Becca swung it toward him. Diving straight toward Derek. Their swords clashed together. The sound of metal hitting metal echoed. Aiden was holding his own. Between dodging Becca's spear and Derek's sword, I noticed he was doing exactly what Derek had warned Kyle about. His movements were stuck in blocking. He wasn't able to break free to plan his attack, and it looked like Derek and Becca knew this.

Becca spun her spear again. Aiden swung his blade to block it, but at the last moment, Becca's opposite hand caught the spear, stopping the momentum and causing Aiden to slash empty air. He lost his footing as he tried to recover from falling forward. Derek took advantage of this moment and leaped forward, his wings cutting the distance. In seconds, his sword collided with Aiden's shoulder.

"Out!" Dominic cheered. "Looks like our team won." He pushed Emery's shoulder as he gloated.

"Hey, Amy." I nearly jumped Becca was suddenly next to me. She must have flown over, but why. Did she want to gloat about how it was she and Derek who sealed the win? "I just wanted to apologize about earlier." Her face was surprisingly sincere. "It wasn't my place to say anything. I was being child-ish. Can you forgive me?"

Wow, that was an unexpected change. I wonder if she was making amends because of the look Derek had given her earlier. She knew she was going too far. "Oh, don't worry about it. I'm actually glad you said something." That part was true. It was good that I at least knew how important Derek was here.

"Hey, can you grab those swords and take them to Saman-tha? I didn't realize I flung them so far." I forgot they were still laying in the snow.

"Sure." Maybe this could be an olive branch to Samantha as well. I walked over and knelt down as I reached out to the first sword. My hand wrapped around the handle. Pain shot through my hand. It felt like I had just reached into the fire. I let out a loud yelp as I dropped the sword. My hand was already turning bright red.

"Amy!" Derek was at my side in seconds, his face twisted in concern. "What happened?"

"She grabbed one of our swords." Becca walked over effortlessly, picking them up. "You should really warn her about these. They can't be used by dirty humans," she spat out before she jumped into the air, flying back to her small group.

"Are you okay?" he asked, his eyes studying my hand. He picked up snow pressing it against the agitated skin. I winced at the touch, but it did provide a little relief. "I thought I told you not to touch these."

"I'm sorry, I forgot. I was just trying to help." More like I was tricked. Why was I so trusting? I should've known she was up to something.

"You should be okay. You didn't touch it for long, but let's get you back to Emery's so I can clean it up."

"No, I'm okay. I don't want you to have to leave." My

hand was still on fire, but maybe if I kept doing the snow trick, I could ignore it.

"Don't be silly. We're done." Derek waved bye as he led me back to the car.

"Is Amy okay?" Kyle jogged over to the car. It was touching to see how worried he was.

"She's fine. It's just getting late, so we should probably head out."

He pulled the car out, peeling down the road. Once we made it to the house, he had me wait in the living room when he got the medical supplies. He spread white cream over my hand. At first, it stung worse than the snow. I couldn't help but let out a miserable yelp.

Derek winced against the sound. "Sorry, but it will feel better soon, I promise."

He took one of the ace bandages and, holding gauze against my palm, wrapped my hand. He was right. The cream started to have a cooling effect on the skin, almost as if it was extinguishing the heat trapped in my hand. A few metal clips held the bandage in place.

"You should start feeling better tomorrow, but I would leave it on for at least twenty-four hours if you can."

"Thank you, Derek. I'm sor—"

Derek's hand tucked under my chin, lifting it up as he leaned in. My body felt like it was on fire as our lips touched. Not the same burning as when I had picked up the sword. This felt almost as if a primal emotion was taking over. His lips were soft and molded perfectly to mine. Almost guiding them in movement. A small moan escaped the back of my throat, and my good hand gripped the back of his head. My chest burned needing air, but I wasn't going to pull away first. When we finally parted, his forehead rested on mine as we gasped for air.

Well, that was unexpected.

Our first kiss was so unexpected, I was more in shock

when it happened. How many times had I imagined what it would be like when I kissed him? Well, one thing was for sure. My imagination did not measure up to the real thing.

"You shouldn't have gotten hurt on my watch."

I pulled his chin down, so our eyes met. Why was he beating himself up over this? This was my fault. "Derek, this isn't your fault! You warned me. I should've remembered, but hey, now I'll never forget. Sometimes, a kid needs to touch the stove before they listen to their parent's warning."

Finally, there was the grin I was waiting for.

We sat in awkward silence. I broke it first. "Derek."

"Yeah?"

"This may be a stupid question, but…" I was running my hand against the bandage. "Why was tonight a 'Thanksgiving' tradition? It didn't seem much different from your workouts." I could feel my face flush. I knew I was missing something.

He chuckled. "Oh that. Well, we aren't supposed to play with our swords, especially against each other. But since the majority of our parents are at the party, we can usually get in one quick game without being noticed."

I smiled, remembering how loud it was this evening between the clashing metal and their brute strength. Sometimes, it was easy to forget they were all still kids. I mean, battling monsters, wielding swords, clan politics, caused them to grow up fast, but it was nice to be reminded. I thought back to the sounds of the game. Though this was an elaborate neighborhood, it wasn't huge. I had my suspicions. The parents knew what was going on, but for one night, they let it slide.

"Alright, let's get you home."

Derek was starting to stand when I pressed on his shoulder. His eyebrow cocked in confusion. I brought my head back to his, our lips meeting again. This time, the kiss was a lot gentler, but my body still buzzed. "Just one for the road," I whispered as we broke apart.

I leaned my head against the seat as I attempted to catch my breath. I couldn't believe how this evening had unfolded. I not only met Derek's parents, but we shared our first real kiss. I was refusing to count the other one as our first. I bit my lip, this cover of dating is feeling a little more real every day. But how did he feel? Were his feelings changing as well? Are we crossing a line we won't be able to uncross?

TWENTY

I missed the sound of birds chirping outside my window. I was ready for the snow to melt away and spring to come back. One year, a bird built its nest outside my window. I remember tracking it every day waiting for them to hatch. There had been four eggs in total. Only three hatched. After they had hatched, I found the fourth egg splattered on the sidewalk. I wasn't sure if it was the parents or baby chicks that had knocked it out.

I started picking at the bandage on my hand. I wonder if it had started to blister from the burn.

"Leave it alone." I nearly jumped out of my bed. I sat up, pulling the covers to my chest.

Derek was chuckling as he sat in the old rocking chair. My face flushed as usual.

"What are you doing in my room!" I quietly yelled, praying the commotion didn't startle my dad.

"I thought we could get breakfast." A deep frown covered his face showing his disappointment.

"Have you not heard of a phone?" This wasn't normal. He couldn't just show up unexpectedly in my room. That gave major stalker vibes.

I was finally starting to register my surroundings. That's when I noticed Derek was still in his outfit last night. Minus the jacket and tie. His dark blue pants were wrinkled, and his white shirt had its sleeves rolled up and the top few buttons undone showing off the top of his chest muscles. I looked away so I wasn't caught staring.

Did something happen after I left? Why was he still in his clothes? I peeked, taking another glance, and once again, he looked exhausted. Sitting, looking like a dejected puppy. A pit grew in my stomach. I did tell him this could always be his safe place.

"Look I'm sorry." I held up my hand, still clutching my blanket. Thank goodness for my flannel pajamas, but I still felt naked without my bra. "But you can't just show up unannounced in my room when I'm sleeping."

His hand was rubbing the back of his neck as he nodded slowly.

"Don't get me wrong, I'm happy to see you." That was true. After the initial shock, my heart was beating faster for another reason. He looked like a Greek statue sitting in the chair. If I was trapped in my room, this wasn't a bad view. "Just… give me one minute. And close your eyes!"

He obeyed.

I jogged out of the room and into the bathroom. Quickly, I ran a brush through my hair, brushed my teeth, and threw on a cleanish pair of jeans. I had a shirt hanging from the washer that I had left to dry, along with a new bra. Finished with a few swipes of deodorant and a mist of body spray. I returned to Derek, frozen in the seat, eyes still closed.

My heart fluttered as I walked closer. Before I could say anything, a smile spread across his face, and he hooked me with one of his arms, bringing me closer to him. "Can I open?" he playfully asked.

"Yeah," I sheepishly answered, now self-conscious I didn't spend more time getting ready.

Opening his eyes, his grin turned more mischievous as he pulled me onto his lap. He nestled his face into my neck taking in a deep breath. Thank God I used the body spray. "Can we start over?" he mumbled.

"Yeah," I whispered, not wanting this to end. Sure, it was awkward, but it also felt safe.

"Good morning, I was thinking of stopping by. Do you want to get breakfast?" Pulling my hair back, he gently kissed my neck.

Goosebumps traveled down my arms. I didn't trust my voice, so I just nodded.

"Charlie's?"

I was expecting him to choose there. There weren't a lot of restaurant choices, plus it would be nice to see my old coworkers. "I don't know. Ever since Emery's pancakes, every-thing else seems to fall short." I was waiting for him to tense. Confirm they had a fight, but instead, he just chuckled.

"I'll make sure to give him the compliment. But I was hoping for a little alone time."

"Charlie's sounds good." I reluctantly got up, but I could feel his stomach rumble. Then I stopped again, looking at him. He was a little overdressed for breakfast. I nibbled on my lip, thinking of options. "Just give me a sec." I bounded out of the room before he could respond.

I quietly walked to the end of the hall, softly opening the last door. It was dark and disheveled. I let out a quick sigh of relief when I saw the bed empty. Which means Dad was prob-ably downstairs snoring. I walked to his dresser and pulled the last drawer open. I dug down to abandoned pants. Picking a few options and sizes. My dad's weight fluctuated a bit over the years, so hopefully, one of these would work.

Next was the closet. I pulled a nondescript black shirt and a hoodie that had some college logo on it. I jogged back to my room with my finds. When I returned, Derek had moved over to my small bookshelf, picking through the limited collection.

He was holding a picture in his hand. I knew which one it was. It was a picture of my mom, Cole, and I sitting on a park bench eating ice cream. My face was covered in the sticky cream.

I cleared my throat, holding out the array of clothes. Derek smirked as he looked down at his own clothes. "Good idea," he said as he reached for the clothes.

I sat on my bed as he changed in the bathroom. I grabbed my phone, seeing I had a missed call and a couple texts. Alicia and Grace had both texted wishing me a "Happy Thanksgiving." I was shocked to see I had received one from Ben as well. Maybe that friendship wasn't totally ruined. I was responding when Derek returned. A laugh escaped my lips before I could stop it. My hands rushed to my face, muffling the sound.

The outfit was, well, functional. The pants were a little loose, so he kept pulling them up. He was threading his belt out of his dress pants, hoping that would help. The black shirt was tight. He looked like a body builder, the ones who wore tight shirts to amplify their muscles, but one wrong move and you knew it would tear. He rolled his eyes as I tried to compose myself. He pulled the hoodie over his shirt, which was the one piece that fit well. With the attire, he could easily pass as a college student.

As we walked down the hallway toward the stairs, I stopped at Cole's door. "Wait."

"Everything okay?" Derek's eyes followed mine to the door.

I reached my hand to grab the knob, pushing the door open and taking a deep breath. I hadn't been back in since I had my mini breakdown. His stuff was littered across his floor. I needed to clean this up. My eyes caught Derek's as they looked at my questioning.

"You can't just randomly show up in my room. It isn't right, but if you need somewhere to crash, you can stay here. I want you to know you have a safe place to go."

He pulled me into his chest, his strong arms wrapping around my body. "Thank you," he whispered into my ear. My face, of course, flushed.

WHERE DID HE PUT EVERYTHING? I WATCHED ONCE AGAIN IN astonishment as he ate the last piece of pancake. That was on top of the six others he ordered, plus the hash browns, bacon, and eggs. As I was still picking at my two eggs over medium.

"So, what's next?" He placed his fork down and fished out his wallet.

Luckily, this time around, Norman had been our waiter, so at least no one was sliding him their number. Though I was a little disappointed, I wasn't able to see Beatrice. I wonder what she would think of Derek.

I shrugged. I wasn't good at being decisive. Plus, I wasn't sure what he liked.

"Well…" he prodded again, "what do you normally do on dates?"

"I think you have more experience with that. What did you and Becca do?" I immediately wished I hadn't asked that. His face went a little pink with the question, and I didn't want to explore why, but that didn't mean I wasn't already jumping to conclusions.

"How about a movie?" I blurted after sitting in awkward silence.

His eyes lit up as if I had suggested an exciting theme park. He made his way to the counter to pay as I took a final swig of water.

We decided on the new superhero movie. I wish I had known more of Derek's likes and dislikes, as he was no help at the movie counter. So, I decided this was the safer choice. We made our way to our seats, holding the large bowl of popcorn and two drinks, which I thought was overkill, but Derek insisted. I was surprised at how empty the theater was compared to how packed the parking lot was. When we made our way through the abnormally busy mall, I realized what day it was. Black Friday. It was a little encouraging to see how many people were out shopping, but that was probably because all the good online deals would happen on Monday.

I was surprised at how good the movie was. I was a little lost in the beginning on who the characters were—I hadn't followed the recent releases, and it seemed like they all built on each other—but I was able to catch up fairly quickly. I glanced over at Derek to see if he was enjoying it as well, hoping I made the right choice. My heart dropped when I saw his head cocked as he slept. I guess I picked the wrong one.

I kept my movements minimal, trying not to disturb him. I knew he was exhausted. I should've pushed him to go home. Was he doing this out of guilt? Did he think he needed to keep up the ruse of us dating so I would keep up the lie as well? As the credits started to roll, I moved my arm, purposely nudging him. He stirred in his seat. Slowly stretching his arms out.

"Well, what did you think?" He picked up his cup, taking a drink.

"I think we should go home," I answered dryly. Why was I so mad? I enjoyed it. I guess I wanted him to enjoy it as well.

"What's wrong?" I could hear the confusion in his voice.

"Nothing, let's go." As I started to rise, his hand took mine, pulling me back down. His eyes searched mine for answers.

"What's wrong?" he said a little more sternly.

I chewed on my bottom lip as I hesitated to respond. "If

you were tired, you should have said something." I exhaled my frustration. Damn, I sounded whiny.

His hand was rubbing his neck, which I started to notice was something he tended to do when he was nervous. At least I could add that to my Derek list. "I'm sorry, I didn't mean to fall asleep."

"No, it's fine." He was trying to make it a nice day. I was overacting. "Can we get out of here, though?" The lights were starting to turn on, and the attendants were making their way up the stairs.

He grabbed my hand, leading me out. I wondered if he was afraid, I would bolt as soon as we left. We dumped our drinks and popcorn in the trash on the way out. We didn't speak until we were out in the mall. I could tell he was looking for a quiet place to go, but to no avail. It was crowded. So, we settled in the food court.

I peered over at the chicken restaurant, and my body tensed as my eyes caught sight of Mike. Were we going to fight? If so, I didn't want to do it here and have my drama leaked back to Alicia.

"I'm sorry. I didn't mean to ruin our day." Derek's face was still defeated, which made me feel worse because he really tried today.

"No, you didn't ruin anything. I had fun." I bent my head down to try and catch his eyes, but he looked away.

His hand went to his neck again. "It was just a long night. We had an incident we had to take care of, and by the time we were done, it was already morning, and all I could think of was seeing you again."

My stomach flipped over the last part. "Oh," was all I could get out. My head was still taking in what he was saying. 'Incident.' Did that mean those creatures? I shuddered, thinking of them.

"I think we need to define what we are. And that will help with our expectations of each other."

Confusion spread across his face. "Define what we are?"

"Yes, you don't need to feel compelled to take me out on dates. I think as long as we hang out in school, maybe hold hands on occasion, we can keep up this dating facade."

"What are you talking about?" I could tell I lost him.

"You know…" I lowered my voice to a whisper, afraid someone would overhear, "Our cover, pretending to date."

"You're pretending?" His body went rigid. Was he hurt by what I said?

"No, I mean, yes. You said…" My words were jumbling together. I was really messing up today. I glanced over at Mike. Shoot, he was looking over at us. I just wanted to disappear.

"I mean, if you don't like me, I'm not going to force you to hang out with me."

"No, I like you!" How was this getting so jumbled? "But you don't like me that way. I mean, look at me!"

"I am looking," Derek said, his voice hard. His eyes holding mine. "Amy Evans, I am in love with you, and I have been since the first grade."

My mouth dropped. Did he just say—no, there was no way. "Derek…"

His hand grabbed mine. "I know. You don't feel the same way. Hell, you don't even know me. And I'm okay with that. Just give me time. Can you give me a chance?"

All I could do was nod. Derek just said he loved me. He was right, I didn't know him, but my heart was already consumed by him. Derek Adler, I'm falling in love with you, too. But I wasn't going to admit that. At least not yet.

Finally, that half smile I loved so much returned. "Glad that's over." He ran his hand through his hair. He was exhausted, and I wasn't helping.

"So now what?" I echoed his earlier question. I was afraid if I suggested going home, he would think I was still mad.

He sat back in his chair, his hand rubbing his chin as he

thought. "We have all week. We don't need to do everything on day one." I chimed in.

"Amy, I want a lifetime." I couldn't help blushing in response. "But maybe we should think of a more lowkey activity. Is going to Emery's too lame?"

That sounded perfect, but I wasn't ready to say that, so I just shook my head in response.

TWENTY-ONE

The rest of the week flew by. And it was one of the best weeks I've had in a long time. Most of the time was spent lounging at Emery's. We decided to continue the superhero theme and rented what I believe was all of them. I was starting to follow who each character was. It helped that each one has their own movie. Derek made it through 70% of the movies, and that was a generous rating. He had fallen asleep through a few more.

I was starting to understand why they had a reputation for sleeping in school. It's not that they didn't care about school. But it seemed like almost every night, they were being called out to a new sighting. I would see the sadness in his face when he got the text. It meant our evening was over, but I didn't take it to heart. It wasn't his fault.

Tonight was one of those nights. Unfortunately, the call came in a lot earlier than normal. It was only four when his phone buzzed. It was the last Friday of our vacation, so I wasn't ready to go home, so I convinced him to let me stay with Kyle and Luke, who were left out of the tasks each night.

Laying on the bleachers, I stared at the gym ceiling. *Ninety-seven, ninety-eight, ninety-nine,* I counted internally as my eyes passed over each ceiling tile. I hated to admit it, but I was bored.

"I can't believe they left us again!" Kyle whined. I pulled myself up, and my back screamed from lying on the hard surface.

"Come on, Kyle, the more you whine about it, the more you're showing them why we aren't ready." Luke scoffed, though he might not be verbally saying it, you could tell he was also disappointed. His elbows were on his knees while his hands cradled his face.

"Who needs them! We can have fun without them!"

Come on, Amy, what would Derek do in this situation? A grin spread across my face. That's it!

I walked toward one of the rings. I had both of their attention for the moment. My hand gripped one of the ropes. Wow it was a lot heavier than I thought. I guess it needed to be if one of them slammed into it. I pulled it up as high as I could, which was only a few inches, and slid inside the ring.

"Alright!" I turned around to them. "Who's going to spar with me!"

They both burst out laughing. Kyle was the first to leap off the bleachers, jogging toward me. At least he was smiling again. Luke got up, shaking his head. He may try and act a little more coy, but I could tell he was just as excited as Kyle.

"Do you even know how to fight?" Kyle was leaning against the ropes.

"Well..." I bit the corner of my lip while the other side turned up in a smile, "No, but come on, I have two really good teachers who can help me!"

That was enough prodding. They jumped into the ring with excitement burning on their faces. It had only been an hour, but my arms were on fire. Wow this was a workout. I was sitting cross-legged on the mat, catching my breath. Who knew sword fighting was so technical. First, they had me working on my stance, then how to hold the sword, and how to properly swing before fighting one of the human torsos.

"Tired already?" Kyle squatted in front of me, obviously getting a thrill out of teasing me.

"Alright, squirt, I'm doing pretty well as a human." I used my hands to help lift me back up. "Now, when are we going to fight each other?" I grabbed my sword. I tried to do a cool swing. Nope, it clattered back to the ground.

That did it. They both erupted into laughter. "Okay, Kyle, calm down. You have to learn the basics first," Luke mocked me.

I stuck my tongue out at him for comparing me to Kyle. Though, I can see why he was so anxious. I'm sure it was hard feeling left out and not good enough.

One of their cellphones chimed, interrupting us. Kyle jogged back over, fishing it out of his bag.

"Yes?" Kyle answered. "Uh huh... yeah, we know where that is... we'll be there soon." Luke and I both looked at him, puzzled. Go where? We were supposed to be waiting for the others to return. I'm not sure if they would be happy that we had left Emery's to hang out at the gym in the first place. A large smile plastered on his face. "Guys! They want us to join!"

"Really?" Luke asked as his brow furrowed. "Who called you?"

"I don't know, but they said Derek called them saying they needed us to come help them." He was already shoving his things back into his bag.

"What about Amy? Are we just supposed to leave her here?" Luke nervously looked over at me. "And how are we going to get there?"

"She'll come with us." As if that was the obvious answer. "And we'll just take the scooters we used to get here. Amy, you can ride with me!"

Luke hesitated for a moment before walking back toward

the bleachers. I grabbed my jacket, zipping it all the way up. This ride was going to be cold. Were they even allowed to ride them on the road? I kept my questions to myself. Kyle was so excited to be asked to join. I didn't want to ruin that for him.

"Alright, let's go!" Kyle bounded toward the exit. Luke and I just looked at each other. Luke seemed to have similar reservations, but we followed. The cold air bit our faces when we exited.

"KYLE, WHAT ARE YOU GUYS DOING HERE?" DEREK YELLED AS soon as he saw us.

We were standing on a quiet street. The houses were dark as everyone inside them was fast asleep. A couple of cars littered the street, but for the most part, it was empty. The only light being lit by the streetlights above.

"They told us you needed help," Luke tensely responded. He was biting his lip at the cold welcome we were receiving. The air felt thick, but it was quiet, too quiet. The eerie quiet you usually get before a big storm hits.

"You've got to be kidding me! You're the reinforcements?" Dominic had caught up to Derek. A large gash was bleeding from his arm. How did he get that? "We're so screwed. And why the hell would you bring Amy!"

"They're coming!" I could hear someone call. The rest of them were still a few yards back.

"Shit! You three just stay back. Kyle and Luke, no matter what, you better protect Amy!" Derek's voice was so cold. Wings erupted from Derek and Dominic's backs as they turned back around, rushing to join everyone.

At first, I thought something was happening to the lights, and they were just going out, like some type of electrical short. Pitch black started to cover the road. I couldn't believe how dark it was. Darker than I've ever seen it. And red? Bright red eyes started to fill the black. The air caught it my chest. It was eyes. Their eyes. Shadow Reapers. A swarm of them were coming down the street. How many were there?

I tried counting, but I was having a hard time figuring out where one stopped and another started. There had to be at least twenty, no more than that. Much more. They were being led by a couple of clouded figures, but they also had wings. More Guardians? No, they weren't right. Their wings were the same color as the creatures' eyes. Deep red, almost the color of blood. Were these the Tamers? A shiver ran down my spine as I thought of the bridge.

As if summoned by my thoughts, a voice called out, **"Amy... I was looking for you."** I grabbed my head. Why was it in my head?

"Don't worry, Amy, we'll protect you," Kyle whispered. I think he thought I was afraid. He grabbed my hand to try and comfort me.

I wanted to tell him about the voice, but when I looked at him, I saw the fear in his face. We made a mistake coming here. Clearly, Derek and the others didn't ask for Kyle and Luke. So, who called them and why?

"Quick, let's get over here!" Luke pulled us to the side of the road.

One of the brick houses had its entryway popping out from the main wall causing a perfect corner for us to back into. This way, our backs and sides were protected. Kyle and Luke angled themselves so they could see the opposite sides and defend against anything coming.

The eight others were standing in the road ready to meet the horde. Their drawn swords already engulfed with their energy. *Please, God, let them all be okay. Let us make it out of here.* I silently prayed. Then, the clash happened. My hands covered my ears as shrill screams erupted as creatures were slashed apart. The majority of them were fighting the floods of creatures coming. Right now, they were keeping them back.

Derek and Aiden had pulled out of the line. They were fighting one of the shrouded creatures with the red wings. It was too dark, and I couldn't make out what was happening between them. All I could see was the dancing of red and yellow light. If I didn't know it was a fight, it would've been memorizing to see. I prayed harder. Derek, please be okay. The only positive thing was the Reapers seemed to be avoiding their battle, it almost seemed as if they were being repelled from it.

It didn't help the rest of them. As soon as they killed a Reaper it seemed like another five would take its place. At first, the group held a line, so it was like hitting a wall, so it was easier to keep them at bay. But now, they were starting to break off, almost dividing the group.

"Hannah's in trouble." Luke grabbed Kyle's arm. "I need to help her. Stay with Amy." Kyle just nodded, moving so he was now in the middle of where they both were standing.

Luke was right. Hannah had been pushed back, out of the line. They were breaking her away from the group, and the Reapers were starting to circle her. It was like one of those nature documentaries. A group of lions targeting the weak water buffalo. First, they would break them from their herd, and then they would start circling. Confusing the animal, as it couldn't protect all sides. Letting the panic take hold. In seconds, Luke was pressed against her back. I didn't realize I was holding my breath. I gasped for air. The sound caused Kyle to tense. He was on edge like me. I hated to admit it, but they were right. He wasn't ready to be here.

With Luke at her back, it eliminated any blind spots, so they could focus on the circling reapers. Suddenly, one of the reapers leapt forward, but was caught by Luke's blade. They pushed off each other, slashing at the reapers, driving them back to the line. Hannah and Luke were able to take down the

Reapers, quickly rejoining the group. They were starting to push forward. Were the Reapers finally losing momentum?

At that moment, when I was finally feeling some confidence that we were going to be okay, a cold wind rushed down the street. A handful of the Reapers froze as their heads whipped toward us.

"Shit, they caught your scent," Kyle said through gritted teeth.

"What do you mean?" My hands pressed against the brick. If only I could melt into this wall. My scent? Did I smell bad?

"You're human. You're what they are out here searching for." His grip tightened on his sword. It started to blaze yellow. That's when I saw them coming.

A group had broken through the line. Everyone was still busy holding off the majority of them. No one could risk breaking formation to go after the stragglers without putting themselves in danger or allowing more to break free.

"Don't worry." Kyle turned, a smile of determination covering his face. "I got this." With that, he turned, letting out a loud scream, and rushed toward the incoming Reapers.

There was a total of five that had broken through. Kyle intercepted the first one. His sword swung, making contact with its side. His sword slid through as if the creature was made of butter. I couldn't help but think of my bedroom. The first time I saw Derek for what he was. When he was fighting the Reaper. With the same shrill scream, it dispelled. The second one came rushing in at the left. He turned just in time to collide his sword with its head. Its fangs were inches from his leg.

"Ha! Nice try," Kyle boasted.

"Your right!" I screamed. When Kyle had turned to fight the Reaper on his left, one of them had leaped on the side of the building, coming in at a blind spot. They seemed to be working together. How smart were these things?

I was too late.

The creature leaped from the building, colliding into Kyle's right side and knocking him to the ground. Luckily, he was still holding his sword. The creature leaped again, but he flipped onto his back, his sword held out front, intercepting the creature. It seemed touching the sword was enough to kill them. As long as it was still emanating the yellow energy. Was it the light that was killing them? Was that why one swing moved through them so easily?

Kyle was holding his side. He was trying to get up, but each time he fell back down. That's when I saw the blood.

"Kyle!" I had to help him. I ran out, dropping next to him. Red was covering his right side as the blood started to soak into his clothes.

I wrapped my arms under his shoulders, pulling him back with all my might as close to the building as I could. "Kyle!" I screamed again." He was losing too much blood, and he wasn't responding. His face was draining of color.

Panic was rising in my chest. There were still two Reapers left. It was up to me now. I had to protect him. This time I stepped in front of him. Would they come for me and leave him? Maybe that was our only hope.

I ripped the bottom of my shirt, carefully wrapping it around the handle of the sword before lifting it up. It was still so hot. I could feel the pain shooting through my hands, but at least it wasn't burning me like before.

"Come and get me!" I screamed. I wasn't going down without a fight.

The sword was too heavy and along with the pain in my hands I couldn't hold it for long, so I slammed the sword's tip in front of me, acting as a shield. Both my hands gripping the hilt of the sword. The heat from the sword was getting more intense as I gripped it, but I didn't dare to let go. I bit my tongue hard trying to focus the growing pain somewhere else. I had to clear my thoughts so I could focus on the Reapers.

But it was too much. I fell to my knees. It felt like the sword was pulling my strength from me. Was this part of the celestial metal? Was this how it was able to harness their energy.

Should I just drop the sword? But how else was I supposed to protect us? On my knees I just gripped as hard as I could. I blinked back the tears as the pain surged up my arms. My vision was starting to blur, but I could hear them getting closer. Their claws clicked every time they made contact with the sidewalk. They were too close, and there was more. More must have broken free.

Stay away. Just stay away from us. I pleaded internally. The sword was vibrating. Was this because my arms were getting too weak? No, this was coming from the sword, almost pulsating. It was reacting to something.

"Amy!" It was Derek's voice calling out.

No Derek don't come here. Don't put yourself in danger too. Why did I have to be so weak? Why couldn't I protect anyone? Can my sacrifice just be enough. Would it distract them enough to get away? Sword please just protect Kyle. "Protect Kyle!" I screamed.

Light erupted from the sword. Not the normal controlled light. This light exploded out. Like a wave, it pushed forward, colliding with all the Reapers in its path. As the light struck them, they instantly vaporized. It felt as if everything had been pulled from me. I couldn't hold the sword anymore. It clattered next to me.

I looked up, my vision was going in and out. Shoot I'm going to pass out. My hands reached out, catching me as I fell forward. Pain radiated through my body. A combination from holding the sword so long and catching the rough concrete. A soft thud landed in front of me. Did Derek finally make it? My head slowly lifted, looking at the feet, legs, torso, until it finally reaching the face.

This wasn't Derek. Was this finally one of the reinforcements that were supposed to come? No... the wings weren't right. They were what I saw earlier coming with the Reapers. Blood red wings. But why did they look the same? If the wings were the same golden color, I wouldn't have known the difference. What was I kidding, if he didn't have those wings, I would've thought he was human.

The man began to speak. "Glo…"

A flash appeared and something collided with the man ramming him into the wall. He crumpled to the ground motionless. Derek stood in front, his back to me as he stared down the man. He slowly turned to see me.

"Amy, are you okay?" He knelt next to me. My energy was gone. All I did was fall into his arms. For the first time, I felt safe. I didn't want him to let go.

"Kyle." My voice came out so raspy. "He's hurt really bad."

"Aiden," he called over his shoulder.

"I got them. I also grabbed Kyle's sword." Aiden flanked his side.

Grunting interrupted them as the man started pulling himself up. I grabbed Derek's arm. "Don't go." We could all leave. He didn't need to stay.

That half grin. Why did he always have to respond with that. "Don't worry." He paused, looking at the man. "I'll come find you."

Light exploded around him. It wasn't his normal wings. It was almost as if he was engulfed in his own energy. He rushed toward the man and grabbed him. Flying him back toward the group. I could barely follow him because of his speed.

Aiden carefully grabbed me and Kyle around our waists before taking off. He leaped into the air, carrying us away to safety. If it wasn't for the exhaustion or tension of the fight, I would've been amazed at the sights. Flying above the buildings, yellow glowed from house windows and streetlights. The cold air hit my cheeks, almost giving me new energy. Were they going to be okay without Aiden? They were now down two people. I didn't recognize where we were until we landed in front of the house. He had taken us back to Emery's. Where we should have just stayed.

"I need to get Kyle help. Are you going to be okay here?" All I could do was nod. His wings flapped, allowing him to lift back into the air. Then they were gone, and I was here. Alone.

I fiddled with the door handle. My hands barely working. Pushing the door open, I nearly fell into the entryway. They never believed in locking their houses. It was always open to anyone who needed to come by. Plus, who in their right mind would rob them. I swear I could still smell the pancakes. That surge of energy the flight gave me was gone. I fell to my knees. Why did I feel so alone? Alone and helpless. Was Kyle going to be okay? Just a couple hours ago we were sitting around goofing off. He was moping because he had been left out again.

What if he died trying to protect me?

I hugged my knees, the tears falling down my cheeks. I leaned against the wall, unable to move any further.

"Just come back to me," I whispered. "Please, Derek, just come back."

TWENTY-TWO

I felt numb. With each passing minute, I was playing the worse possible outcome in my head. What if they didn't come back? What if losing Aiden was too much for them? I should've fought to stay home in the first place. What business did I have going with them.

The door suddenly flung open as I was spiraling in my thoughts. "Amy…" Derek half whispered, half gasped.

Derek dropped to the floor, wrapping his strong arms around me. I felt like a broken ragdoll in his arms. A small whimper escaped as my hands got caught between us. He pulled away. No. I internally screamed. Don't let go yet. He pulled up my hands, examining them. I was still scared to look. I remembered the burn I received when just barely touching the sword. What about now? Would my hands be okay? What if I caused permanent damage.

"Let's take care of these." He looped one arm under my knees while the other wrapped around my shoulders and chest as he lifted me up. As if I weighed nothing. I laid my head against his chest. The beating of his heart was almost mesmeric. But his smell was off. That combination of his normal leather and sandalwood was replaced with the smell of sweat and the coppery smell of blood. My stomach twisted as I wondered whose blood.

Derek climbed the steps. Was he taking me back to the guest room? No, we were going down the wrong hall. He nudged the last door open with his foot. A queen bed was pushed against the farthest wall. I recognized his bookbag that hung over the desk chair. He carefully set me on the bed. He knelt next to me, pulling my shoes off. He froze as our eyes locked. His hand slowly raised, pushing the hair that had fallen in front of my face behind my ear. His other hand followed to the other side, cradling the sides of my head. Rising, he closed the gap and our lips met.

My eyes closed as I lost myself in the kiss. Suddenly everything just disappeared, and it was just us here. Pushing back everything that happened today. My hands instinctively moved to the back of his head. I winced from the pain. He pulled away, concern covered his eyes. He raised his lips, kissing my forehead gently.

"I'll be right back," he whispered before leaving. He returned with the bandages and salve. The same combination he used the last time.

He cradled my hands in his. I squeezed my eyes shut, biting my bottom lip, preparing for the stinging to start. The pain was ten times worse than before. As much as I tried to resist, I couldn't stop. I yelled out in pain. The tears ran down my cheeks. I could feel Derek's hands tense as he worked as carefully and quickly as possible. The pressure from the bandages wrapping was the first moment of some type of relief.

When he was done, Derek raised my hands to his lips, kissing the back of them. My heart felt like it was going to beat out of my chest. His hand rose again to my face, this time wiping the tears away. He kicked off his shoes before climbing in the bed.

"Derek…" I started to object.

"Just stay with me tonight." His voice was so tired. "I promise I'll be on my best behavior." He tried to give a reassuring smile, but his eyes were so sad. All I could do was nod.

He pulled me close to his body. His arm wrapped around my stomach. We just laid in silence. After what I felt to be an hour, I could feel his breathing starting to slow as his arm became heavier. Thank God he was asleep. He must be exhausted. My stomach flipped as I started to relive the evening again. Was this what it was always like for them? How could people send kids into such a horrific scene. I'm not going to lie, I always found their sparring sessions a little overboard, but now, was it even enough?

Time ticked by. Every time I tried to close my eyes, I pictured them. The Reapers. Their glowing red eyes. Those long white fangs were even more menacing against their pitch-black skin. Was skin the right word? They glistened as if the black was melting off of them. I shuddered thinking about how they must feel. How many of them were out there?

My heart beated frantically as I thought about how often they went out. How much danger did they put themselves in? And for what purpose? Was it really to protect us humans? If so, if they failed, what would happen to us? Were we worth it? Compared to them, we were just pitiful creatures. Why would they risk their lives for us?

Derek's arm slowly pulled away as he rolled onto his back. Making as little sound as possible, I turned, curling up next to him. I didn't want to lose the distance. At least being next to him I felt safe. I laid my hand on his chest so I could feel the beating of his heart. It was slow and steady, nothing like my heart at the moment. I jerked when his hand laid over mine.

"You okay?" He didn't open his eyes, just a reassuring squeeze with his hand.

"I didn't mean to wake you." I tried to pull my hand away, but he held on tighter.

A smile spread across his face. He turned his head so our

eyes could meet. "I'll always protect you, so you don't need to be afraid." His eyes were so intense I was sure they were going to start glowing again.

All I could do was nod. I wish it was that easy to stop being afraid, but for now I knew he was here. *Please don't take him away from me*, I prayed. Let this moment between us last. I closed my eyes, pushing the images away. Instead, I focused on Derek and me. What our life could be if we could just be together. What if their fighting could stop and he could just have a peaceful life? I focused on Derek's breathing, feeling it get heavy once again. At least he was okay. I just hope everyone else was. My eyes were getting heavy. The warmth of his body heat and the feeling of his beating heart was hypnotic as I let the exhaustion take over.

I awoke to the sound of a car driving by. I lifted my hand to rub my blurry eyes, but the moment it touched my face my whole body tensed against the pain. Oh yeah. Derek's arm did a quick squeeze, pulling me closer into his chest.

"Not yet," he murmured. "Let's just stay here."

I was happy he couldn't see my blushing face. I'm sure my whole face was beat red. How was this already the second time we woke up together. I rolled my lip between my teeth. What if he wanted more. I wasn't ready for that. Would that upset him?

"Come on, sleepy head," I said, scooting out from under his arm. The farther I distanced myself from his bed, the better.

We had fallen asleep in our clothes. Thank goodness. We didn't need any more awkwardness added to this. I walked to his door and froze. How long would it take for my hands to at least function again? I couldn't open a door, how was I going to function at school! I guess this is one of the moments I was thankful I no longer worked at the diner.

"Don't worry." Derek was behind me. His lips kissing my neck. Goosebumps spread across my arms, as my cheeks flushed. "Your hands should be better in a couple of days."

"I don't think so," I whispered. Why did he make my head so foggy? "We don't heal as quickly as you."

"You're right, but that salve is one of our special remedies. It speeds up the healing process on most living things." Why didn't that surprise me? "Alright, I guess we should see what Emery's up to."

I stopped in the bathroom. My hair was a disaster. I carefully pulled a few drawers open until I found a small brush. I bit my cheek as I pulled it through my hair as fast as possible. I'm sure I was going to have small dents left on my lip. I skipped brushing my teeth and instead gargled some mouthwash. Derek was at least right. I was surprised how much I could already use my hands. The pain was still intense, but as long as it was short spurts I could at least use them.

The downstairs was quiet. Not like the last time I was here. My heart dropped as I thought back to the first time I woke here. That's the first time I met Luke and Kyle. Did they have any updates? I needed to find out if everyone was okay.

I don't know why, but I was half expecting a full kitchen. Or at least Dominic with his stupid smug face. Instead, it was only Emery. His right hand was holding onto his mug, while his left was propping up his head.

"Good morning," I quietly spoke, afraid I was interrupting some deep thought.

He looked over, a small smile greeting me. "You sleep okay?"

I blushed. I wondered if he knew where I actually slept. I just nodded. He signaled to one of the chairs for me to sit.

I couldn't hold it in anymore. "Is everyone okay?"

"Yeah, everyone's okay. Scraped and bruised, but okay."
Emery took a slow sip of his coffee.

"What about Kyle?"

"Kyle's going to be fine. He'll be hurting for a few days,
but he will be back to his bouncing self, annoying all of us
soon." I know he was trying to stay lighthearted for my sake,
but he couldn't hide the concern in his own face.

"So, this is what you guys do? Almost getting killed!"
Before last night I thought they were invincible. Yes, I remembered Derek's injuries, but I thought that was because his own
kind did it to him. I never imagined they could be hurt by
those things.

"No." Emery was chewing on his thumb, back in deep
thought. "This isn't normal. I've never seen so many before.
And they were being led by—"

"Emery," Derek cut in. He was standing just inside the
kitchen. Whatever Emery was going to say, Derek wanted the
conversation to end.

A loud rapping echoed from the front door. Emery and
Derek exchanged a confused look before Emery headed to the
door. Normally their crew would just come right in, so this
had to be someone else.

"Derek," Emery called. His voice tense.

Derek lifted his palm up as I started to rise. "Stay here," he
said firmly.

He turned to join Emery and whoever was at the door.
The anticipation was killing me. I had to know what was
happening. Why did I have to be nosey? Why couldn't I just
listen? I heard them head into the living room. That voice, it
sounded familiar.

I tiptoed out of the kitchen and down the hall. I'll just sit
outside the living room.

"You might as well join us," a voice called out before I
even reached the room.

Shoot! What, did they also have super hearing? "Sorry, I

just wanted to see if anyone needed something to drink," I lied. Like I knew what there was to offer.

"We're fine." It was Derek's dad. Why was Mr. Adler here? This couldn't be a good thing.

I winced as Derek shot me a disapproving look. I should've stayed in the kitchen. His face softened as he scooted down the couch so I could sit next to him. He and Emery were on the couch, while his dad sat across them in one of the recliner chairs.

"What are *you* doing here?" Derek said through gritted teeth. His whole body was tense.

"I heard there was quite a commotion last night, so I wanted to check to make sure everyone was all right." Mr. Adler's whole demeanor was indifferent. I wonder why Derek reacted so negatively to him.

"We're fine."

"Really." Mr. Adler raised an eyebrow. "Because from what I heard, you have a kid checked in at the medical ward barely hanging on." Barely hanging on? I thought Emery said he was going to be fine. My chest tightened at the thought of him hooked up to a dozen machines. Like a coma patient on one of those medical dramas.

Derek's fist clenched. His dad wasn't as in the dark as he was trying to portray. "We ran into an ambush last night."

"We attempted to call in reinforcements, but no one came," Emery chimed in.

"Your reinforcements came," Mr. Adler stated matter-of-factly. "Kyle and Luke showed up, right?"

"You sent them in?" Derek leaped to his feet. His knuckles were turning white from clenching his hands so hard.

"What were you expecting? Why would I send in more people if you weren't utilizing your whole team?" He leaned back in his chair, not at all phased by Derek's outburst. "Though I'm not sure adding a human to the fight was the best idea." He shot a glance in my direction. My posture stiffened as I felt like I was silently being judged.

"They aren't ready to be out there yet! Don't you think I would know when they're ready? You almost got Kyle killed." Derek looked like he was about to punch someone. This wasn't good.

"I almost got him killed?" A dry laugh escaped his lips. This time his dad was at his feet, squaring off. "No. You should be asking yourself why they aren't ready. There is no excuse for them to be so behind! You aren't taking their training seriously. Instead, you are out playing around with that bastard child!" I winced at that last comment.

That pushed Derek to his limit. With both his hands, he shoved his dad back. His dad's fist slammed into the side of Derek's mouth. Blood started to run down his chin. A gash had opened up on his lip. I noticed red on Mr. Adler's fist. He was also bleeding, probably cut on Derek's teeth when he landed his punch.

"Stop!" I yelled, jumping up. Emery grabbed my wrist, pulling me back. Derek's dad's eyes burned with rage as they met mine.

A shiver ran down my spine. Derek was so strong, at times I forgot he wasn't invincible, but now I was seeing someone even stronger than him squaring off. Another reminder that these were only kids. How much stronger were the others?

"This is your last warning. Grow up and start taking your responsibilities seriously. You are DONE with playing house over here. I expect you home *tonight*." His gaze was back on me. "And you. I would be very careful where you insert yourself. There are a lot of innocent casualties during time of war." Emery's grip tightened around my wrist. Was that some type of threat?

"You're right about one thing." Derek wiped the blood away with his thumb. "There is a war coming. Donovan and Adam were leading the ambush last night."

"What!" Was that a look of fear on his face? He quickly hid his reaction, stiffening back up.

"I don't know what they were planning last night, but whatever it was I doubt it was a one-time thing. If I were you, I would increase patrols and maybe… if someone calls for back-up actually send some." He turned to face Emery and me extending his hand out. "Let's go, Amy."

I tried to walk confidently, but my whole body shook as we walked past his dad. I could feel his eyes burning into my back. I don't think I took a breath until we were in his car. Derek's hands gripped the wheel as we sat in the driveway.

"I thought I told you to wait in the kitchen," he said through gritted teeth. He was angry with me.

"I know… I'm sorry." I couldn't look at him. He was right to be mad. Why couldn't I just listen for once? Such a great start to the day had turned so quickly, and it was my fault.

The car jerked out of the driveway as he sped off. I tried to think of a dozen different ways to bridge an apology, so we just sat in silence until I built the courage to say something. "So…" I swallowed hard, "are you really going to move back home?"

At first, I didn't think he was going to answer. He just stared silently at the road. "I don't really have a choice." His voice was flat.

"Why?" He shot me a look. My body tensed. This wasn't helping. His shoulders sank a little. Even when he had every right to be angry, he still tried to be soft with me.

"It's just the way it works in our world. His word is law."

"And if you go against it?" I kept my eyes on the road. Afraid I would lose my nerve if my eyes met his again.

"You're cast out. Stripped from everything and ostracized from everyone."

"But you're his son. He couldn't do that to you." I know parents get angry, but a dad wouldn't just throw out his son.

Right? My mind then went to my mom. I guess we are some-times disposable.

Derek shrugged. "He did it to his own brother. Family means little to him."

His own brother? Was that why Derek was so cold to them? How hard was it to live your life in fear that at any moment if you made a mistake, you would be tossed away like garbage? I know that's what Derek was describing, but that couldn't be right. It had to be for something big to receive that type of punishment. I wonder what happened?

"That was him last night." Derek shifted in his seat.

"Who?" I was trying to think who we met.

"My uncle. Donovan." That name was the same one he said to his dad.

"Wait. The ones with the red wings? They are Guardians? I thought they were Tamers?" I stopped looking out the window and now was locked back onto Derek. I knew they looked alike.

"I don't know how they got wrapped up with Shadow Reapers, it doesn't make sense. They were Guardians who were banished from our clan. Adam was the first one, since I've been alive, to be sent away." Derek's hands tightened against the wheel as he continued. "He was the one who came after you last night. I don't really know why he was forced to leave; it happened when I was really little. But apparently it never sat right with my uncle. A little over four years ago a group of them confronted my dad about it. Demanding to let Adam back in. Well... my dad took it as a sign of mutiny, and they were all forced to leave. Emery's parents were part of the group."

"I thought they were dead." My hands were starting to fidget as I tugged at the seatbelt. That's what he said earlier right?

"I said they were no longer with us. But they might as well be. They aren't allowed to have any contact with any of us ever again. I don't know how Emery was able to cope so quickly with the loss. I think it was fear. Afraid if he didn't accept it, he would be banished as well."

"I see." I didn't really. Separating a family with no regard for their son. Left alone to raise himself. I thought back to that big house. How lonely it must be for Emery to live there. "So, if they are Guardians or ex-Guardians, why are their wings red?"

"I don't know." I could tell he was wrestling with something. "To be honest, this is the first time we've seen someone after they left. And why are they with the Shadow Reapers? It doesn't make any sense. We are their enemies. How can they work together? How are able to control them? Only Tamers are able to." I knew he wasn't expecting me to answer. He had his own questions he was trying to work through.

He pulled in front of my house. I can't believe how open he had been with me. "Amy." He hesitated, not making eye contact. "I think it's best if we end this now."

"What?" I gasped as the air escaped my lungs. I felt like I had been punched in the gut. What was he saying?

"I told you before. I was fine with us having a friendship as long as it didn't put you in danger. That clearly didn't work."

Why did the word friend sting so deep. "Are you going to sit there and say we are just friends? Because in my book friends don't go around telling each other that they love them!" I was focusing on the wrong thing. I needed him to stay with me, he couldn't throw us away so easily, right?

"Amy…" His hands grabbing tighter around the wheel. I was afraid he was going to rip it off. "It's over."

"I'm sorry, Derek. I should've listened. Please, give me one more chance." Here I was sitting there begging. Fear filling my chest. This couldn't be the end.

"Bye, Amy." My body froze when he leaned close. Was he going to kiss me? Was this how he was saying goodbye? He grabbed the handle, popping the door open. He then looked forward, refusing to make any more contact. My hope shattered. He was making it clear. There were no more arguments. If I tried to fight anymore, I knew I would lose it. I had to get out of this car.

Can your heart actually break?

I refused to look back at him when I got out. All I heard was the peeling of the tires as he sped away. I could hear the television blaring as I reached the door, so my dad was up. It didn't really matter. He didn't say a word when I entered. Not a question of where I was or why I was clearly upset. Could you at least acknowledge my hands? Ask why they were bandaged. Just play the concerned parent for once.

I shut my door, climbing into bed. It couldn't be over, right? He just needed to cool off. There had to be some feelings there. He couldn't just turn them off. I pulled the covers over my head. At least no one was here to see me cry now.

TWENTY-THREE

I t had been a few weeks since I rode the bus. Christmas music played over the radio. Two weeks and we would be off again for winter break, which meant exams were coming. I stared at my hands. I had taken the bandages off this morning, replacing them with band-aids on the worse areas which seems to be where I cut them on the concrete. They were already showing signs of healing. Hopefully, this would bring less attention.

I shuffled off the bus. Should I approach them this morning and act like nothing happened? Maybe if Derek saw that I wasn't going to leave so easily he would change his mind. I mean, this friendship was a two-way street, right?

They hadn't arrived yet, so I decided to stop by and see Alicia and Grace. I haven't really had a chance to talk to them.

"Well, look who's here," Alicia called out. "Where are your new friends?" She was hurt. I couldn't blame her. I did suddenly vanish on them.

"I just wanted to stop and say hi." Maybe this wasn't the best idea.

"You missed your appointment." Grace didn't even look at me.

"My appointment?" What appointment did I have?

"Yeah, for your hair." Shoot, I think I did have a reminder call on my voicemail. "Do you know how embarrassing it is when it is one of your friends who is a no-show!"

"I'm sorry. Money is a little tight right now." My voice was almost a whisper. Why was I such a bad friend? Why didn't I call and at least cancel?

"Yeah, it always is, isn't it? I need to get something out of my locker." Grace stood, grabbing her things.

"I'll go with you." Alicia followed her into the school.

That couldn't have gone worse. I threw my bag on the table, placing my hands against the cold metal. Then I heard his car. Alright, I'm going to go talk to him. Show him that I wasn't going to leave so easily.

I watched as he pulled in. My heart sank. Becca exited the front passenger seat. After letting Hannah out of the back, she loped around, grabbing onto Derek's arm, parading him through the crowds toward their normal spot. It was as if nothing happened between them. Why did Derek smile at her like that? I think I'm going to be sick. I grabbed my bag and ran to the library. At least I can hide here until the bell rings.

Everyone stopped talking the moment I entered math. I prayed for my name to be called over the speaker. Any excuse to turn and flee their staring eyes. I quickly made it to my seat, sinking as low as I could. My eyes not leaving the board.

Mr. Bellows walked across the room, dropping off worksheets at the desks. His eyes were full of pity when he reached mine. "Hi Amy." His voice was thick with sympathy, as if he just found out my grandma died. Oh God, he even knew. How fast did news get around!

It took me all of fifteen minutes to finish the worksheet, but my eyes never looked up. Instead, I just doodled on the back for the rest of class. Wings of all sizes filled the sheets along with hearts, which I then scribbled out.

"Did you see Derek with Becca today?" I heard someone whisper.

"I knew they would get back together! I mean, who would go from Becca to Amy?" another person responded, not even attempting to whisper. I refused to look. I was firmly scribbling out one of the hearts I made. I'm surprised I didn't rip through the paper.

"Shhhh... she'll hear you," the first person responded in an even lower voice in hopes of encouraging the change of register.

"What do you think she doesn't know? I wonder if he just started dating her to make Becca jealous," they responded, unfazed.

The bell rang and I rushed out. I'm not sure if I was the first out because I was so quick, or people were stepping out of my way. Afraid they would have to pretend to show some type of pity.

The whole day, whispers continued to follow me both between and in class. High schoolers were ruthless. They didn't care if the person they were talking about heard. I actually think some people got joy out of knowing they were inflicting more pain. I skipped gym. So, I hid in the nurse's office complaining of an upset stomach. It wasn't a lie, just the thought of having to see Becca made me want to hurl. Her concerned eyes drifted to by bandaged hands.

"I was running too fast and fell on the sidewalk. My hands caught my fall." I sheepishly held them up. Thankfully, she bought it and left me alone.

I spent lunch in the library. There were still wandering

eyes, but at least people weren't allowed to talk. The library during lunch was usually filled with the outcasts of the school. People who didn't feel like they belonged anywhere. A place where you didn't have to be fearful where you sat. The fear of rejection you would face in the cafeteria when just trying to find a seat. No one was going to anger the librarian by speaking and risk being sent back.

In chemistry, Sally was quiet and was the first person to act like nothing happened. I appreciated that. Instead, we focused on the assignment. Lighting a light bulb with potatoes. We were one of the few tables that actually had light. I wonder if I should stock up on potatoes at home. Just in case.

In art class, I was able to find an easel in the corner. I just stared at my canvas. It was due next week, and it still looked like a muddled mess. I took black paint and just started covering the painting. I couldn't stop staring at it. I screamed. My stool clattered as I flung myself back. The whole class was silent, staring at me. I couldn't catch my breath as I continued to stare at the painting. I couldn't stop seeing the red eyes.

"Amy?" Ms. Kelly placed her hand on my shoulder. I jumped at her touch.

"I'm s-s-sorry." I knelt down picking up my stool. Oh great. What were people going to say? Probably how I had a psychotic break.

"Maybe you should go see the nurse." I could tell she didn't know what to do. "I'll call Ms. Nelson and let her know you are coming."

Their eyes felt like lasers as I gathered my things before leaving the class. Becca was in that class. I refused to look in her direction, but what was I afraid she was going to say? If only I had a car, maybe I could sneak out to the parking lot and drive away.

"Amy," Ms. Nelson said as I entered, "do you want me to call your dad?"

"Do you think I can just lay down until the buses come?"

We only had one period left. Plus, I knew calling my dad was pointless.

"Sure." She led me to one of the beds that was isolated with some standing curtains. The same bed I used when I came during gym. She hesitated. "If you need to talk, I can get Ms. Wilkinson."

Ms. Wilkinson was the guidance counselor at our school. She was a middle-aged woman. She wore thick black glasses and always came to school in a business skirt and jacket. As if she was going to some swanky business job rather than a school. Apparently, she originally went to school to become a psychiatrist, but for whatever reason she ended up working at a high school. So anytime there was some type of student crisis, she would be the first one to jump in to help. I was actually surprised no one had called her yet.

"Thanks, but I think I'll be okay. I think I just need some sleep." I gave a pitiful attempt at a smile. I just wanted her to leave so I could be by myself. She actually seemed relieved as she left. Maybe she was required to offer the guidance counselor for these occasions, but she didn't seem like she was any happier to see her.

"Amy!" Alicia called out as I was heading to my bus. "We missed you at lunch!" She was catching her breath when she reached me. Why was she sprinting across the parking lot? "Do you want a ride home?"

"I thought you were mad at me?" What the heck changed in the last seven hours?

"No, I was just backing Grace up. She called me super upset yesterday." Okay. I guess. I followed her to her car. At least I would get home faster. All I wanted to do was lock myself in my room and end this day.

"So…" Alicia glanced over after we left the school. "What happened?"

There it was. There was new gossip, and she was just as lost as everyone else. I wonder how many people came up to her today, trying to get the inside scoop? I'm sure she was loving that and wasn't about to give up the chance at the spotlight. Even if it was at my expense. I played coy. "What do you mean?"

"With you and Derek. I can't believe he is already back with Becca! What an asshole." At least she was pretending to be the outraged friend.

"Yeah, I guess we weren't as compatible as I thought. We decided it was best if we saw other people."

Alicia nodded. "Yeah, you have to be careful with guys who just went through a breakup. They tend to date the first girl that walks by. I was afraid he was using you as a rebound." That stung, I'm sure that was what she was going to spread tomorrow. Her poor naïve stupid friend let herself be the rebound chick.

"I guess." I was ready for the conversation to be over.

Alicia then droned on about her and Mike. Apparently, they did Thanksgiving together this year. She decided for Christmas to get him one of those expensive watches from the jewelry store. She was going to engrave their dating anniversary. I wonder if she was doing that so he wouldn't forget the day. I jerked at the thought. That was mean to think.

"Thanks for the ride," I said as I got out. I closed the door with my elbow. My hands were killing me.

"If you need to talk, you know you can always call me," Alicia called through the window.

"Thanks." She did mean well at times. Even if sometimes it was self-serving.

The house was quiet. Which was a little unusual. I looked out the window, I didn't realize my dad had already left. I wonder where he went. It wasn't grocery shopping day. He typically did that run on Friday, so he had enough beer stocked for the weekend.

"**Hi, Amy**," a voice called out.

No, not you. I screamed in my head. "W-w-who's there," I stuttered instead, trying to hide my fear.

My body froze as I waited, I couldn't remember if the door was locked when I got home. Did someone break in? Why did it sound like that voice? I slowly turned, but no one was there. I stood still waiting. Waiting for the voice to return, but it was just quiet.

Great, now I was hallucinating. Maybe I was having some type of psychotic break. Secretly hoping that the voice had returned, because then, just like in the past Derek would come barging in to save me from it. I just needed to get to my room. I would lock my door, crawl in my bed and maybe never get out.

I stopped at Cole's door, slowly opening it. What I would give for him to be here. To run into his arms for that protective brother hug. The type that pulled you in and you knew they would fight the world for you. I pictured how angry he would be when he found out what happened today. He would probably storm over to Derek's house, threatening to beat him up for hurting his sister.

I froze at the sight. His room was still trashed from my tantrum. That felt like ages ago. When I found out the truth about them. The truth about our past. How much about our childhood did I block out, and why? Was Cole mad that he had to give up a close friend? I walked in, picking up a couple books and placing them back on the shelf.

"*They left because of you*," the voice echoed again. "*Everyone leaves because of you*."

"Shut up!" I grabbed my head. I didn't want to think about it. I didn't want those memories back. I just wanted to forget about all of them.

I couldn't stay here. I left the room, slamming the door behind me. I went to the bathroom and opened the medicine cabinet. I was looking for some ibuprofen for my hands. That's when I saw the bottle. It was an old prescription given to my mom after Cole's accident. The label was hard to read. If I remember, it was something to help her sleep at night. Maybe that would help me today. I popped the lid off. There were only a couple pills left. The directions were also hard to read. Did that say one or two pills? Two should be fine. I just wanted to sleep and get these voices to stop.

I grabbed one of the paper cups, filling it with water. I popped the pills in quickly following it with water, so they didn't start dissolving. Didn't help. They still tasted nasty! At least now I should be able to block everything out, at least for a little bit.

I yanked my drawers open, rummaging through my pajamas. That's when I saw them. The blue tank top and black pants. The clothes Hannah gave me. I pulled off my clothes and changed into them. I climbed into bed. Pulling my covers up. I rolled, staring at the side of my bed. Would I ever forget the memory of Derek laying there? How peaceful he looked when he slept. Stop! I turned away. My eyes were starting to get heavy.

"*Goodnight, Amy... we will see you soon,*" the voice called out. Wait. I couldn't move. My body was too heavy, and everything was fading away.

Twenty-Four

"Amy!" It felt like someone was shaking me. Why couldn't I respond? I couldn't open my eyes. "Why isn't she waking up? What's wrong with her?" The voice was frantic. Why did they sound so familiar?

"What is she doing out here?" another voice joined in. "Did you find Derek yet?"

Derek? Derek was coming. Why? What did they mean, why was I here? I was in my room. If anyone here has any questions, it should be me! I tried again with all my might to open my eyes, but it was like I didn't have control of my body.

"Relax Amy. It's not time for you to wake yet." That voice was back. ***"We need him here."***

My body was paralyzed. Was he doing this to me? What do you mean, he needs to be here? This voice. It had to be connected to the ambush. Was this another trap? I needed to warn someone. *Please body…* I pleaded to myself. *Please just wake up.* Wake up! As if I found the switch, I felt control coming back. It was like I was drudging through deep muck, but I was able to finally gain a little control. My eyes shot open.

"Emery!" I saw Hannah leaning over me as she screamed. "She's awake!"

"T-t-t," I tried to speak, but it wasn't working. I couldn't get the words out.

"What's happening?" Emery was now in view. I couldn't turn my head. Why did I see stars? My feeling was starting to return, and I felt cold. I could feel cement under my hands.

"She's trying to say something." Worry filled Hannah's voice.

"T-t-t-r-r," I tried again. I was straining inside. I felt like I was rattling inside a cage.

"Just relax Amy. Derek and Dominic will be here soon." Emery's hand rested on my arm. My arms were bare. The cold was starting to fill my body. Why was I outside in my pajamas? No, I needed them to listen to me.

"T-t-t-t-r-r-r-r-a." Damnit! I locked on with Hannah's eyes. Come on Hannah, I need you to figure this out. My eyes pleaded with her.

"Emery... I think something's wrong. She's trying to tell us something." I could see she was trying to put it together. I watched her eyes expand. Yes, Hannah come on! "Oh my God. I think she's saying trap! I think this is a trap!"

Panic filled Emery's eyes. "Quick, take her to Derek's house. I'll find Derek and Dominic and we will meet you there."

Strong arms picked me up. They were smaller than Derek's, but they picked me up with the same ease. Wind pushed against my skin. We were flying. The farther we flew, the more my body loosened. As if we were leaving whatever was controlling me. I gasped when I finally felt control of my breathing.

Hannah fumbled with the unexpected movement. "Just stay still, Amy. We will be there soon."

I wanted to test out the rest of my body, but I didn't want to put Hannah in danger, so I stayed still, until I felt us finally descending. By the time we landed, my teeth were chattering as my whole-body shook. How long was I outside for? The flight didn't help as the air was arctic as we flew.

Derek's mom was waiting for us at the door. "Quick, come inside."

Mrs. Adler led us into their living room. A large fire was burning. They pulled a rocking chair in front of the fire before sitting me down. A large quilt was wrapped around me.

"Hannah. There is a kettle on the stove with some hot water. Can you please pour Amy some tea?" She was making sure my whole body was wrapped. I could feel the warmth on my face from the fire, but the rest of my body still felt like ice.

"Where is she?" I heard someone yell. The door slammed behind them. I knew that voice from anywhere. Derek.

"She's in here," Mrs. Adler calmly spoke, still playing with the quilt.

"Amy!" Derek dropped in front of me. His eyes were erratic. "What happened!" His head snapped back toward the door.

I followed his gaze, which was now set on Emery, who was in the doorway. "We don't know. Hannah and I were following the Reaper and it's like it led us to her. Hannah thinks it was a trap, so we thought this was the safest place to go."

"Amy was trying to warn us." Hannah was back holding a mug. I tried to speak, but my teeth were chattering so much I couldn't get a word out.

"Come, Hannah. The tea should help and warm Amy up." Mrs. Adler waved her in. Derek didn't move.

I struggled to get my arms out. Mrs. Adler had swaddled me tight. When I did, the quilt fell, exposing the top half of my body. I'm glad I had decided on the tank top and yoga pants for pajamas tonight.

I cautiously took a sip of the tea, hoping to not scorch my tongue. The tea was bitter. If I had made it, I would have filled half the cup with sugar, but I could feel the hot liquid coursing through my body, warming it from the inside. I took a couple more sips before my teeth finally slowed. Enough for me to speak again.

"The voice…" I chattered out, "it… was back."

"Voice? What the hell is she talking about?" Dominic impatiently probed.

Derek shot him a look. Dominic crossed his arms, slumping to the couch. Everyone wanted answers, but Derek was making it clear he was the one who was going to ask the questions. He gently placed his hand on my arm. It jolted against the cold. "What voice?"

"The one from the bridge." I took another sip from my tea as my teeth started chattering again, but this time, I'm not sure if it was from the cold or having to remember that voice.

"Shit!" Derek cussed out.

"What does that mean?" Emery asked.

"Donovan," Derek said through gritted teeth. "Amy… it's very important… you need to tell me exactly what happened."

"I-i-it didn't h-h-happen until I got h-h-home." I couldn't stop from stuttering as my teeth continued to chatter. "H-h-his voice was in my head-d-d again, so I went to the b-b-bath-room and…" Oh no. Should I tell him about the pills? Maybe it wasn't him. Maybe they were the reason I was hallucinating. Was this just a bad side effect from them? No, because his voice came before I took them.

"And what?" Derek gently urged.

"I found a c-c-couple of my mom's p-p-pills and took them." I couldn't make eye contact with him.

"Great, Derek! You made her suicidal!" Dominic threw his hands up.

"T-t-that's not it! I just wanted-d-d the v-v-voices to stop and just forget-t-t about everything. T-t-they were something my mom took to help her s-s-sleep, so I thought they c-c-could help me…" I may be cold, but that didn't stop my cheeks from flushing. "The next t-t-thing I remember is w-w-waking up to

Hannah and-d-d Emery. But I c-c-couldn't move, and the v-v-voice said he needed someone t-t-there."

"That bastard," a new voice joined. Derek's dad was in the doorway. "He used those pills to take control of her. He knew using her would bring you all out to him."

"C-c-control m-m-e?" A shiver spread through my body, that didn't help my chattering. I pulled the blanket closer.

"Some Guardians have special skills. Donovan is able to use someone's soul energy to manipulate them. His specialty is manipulating a person's thoughts. Though, if someone is weak enough, his manipulation can sometimes control their whole body." Derek spat out.

"We need to call a meeting with the elders," Mr. Adler spoke. "Derek, I expect you to be there." That wasn't a question.

"I'll take care of Amy," Mrs. Adler interjected.

I could see the concern in Derek's eyes. "I-I-I'll be okay," I said, trying to be reassuring.

"Fine." Derek got up, spinning toward his dad. "But Dominic and Aiden are coming with me." Derek and his dad squared off.

"Twenty minutes and we leave." Mr. Adler stormed off, clearly not happy with the insubordination his son was displaying.

"Emery. I want everyone to be here tonight. No excuses. I don't know what is going on, but they are targeting us." His eyes flicked to Dominic. "Let's go, Dominic. We need to get Aiden and fill him in." Dominic leaped from the couch, clearly ready for some action. I was a little surprised Derek was taking Dominic, maybe he did know how to hold his tongue.

Mrs. Adler returned. I didn't even know she had left. She almost floated when she walked. It made her movements silent. "Amy, I drew you a bath, if you want to follow me."

I was in such a daze when I entered, I didn't have a

chance to look at the house, but once I was in the foyer, I could tell the house was huge! It reminded me of the museum. With two marble staircases leading upstairs. Once upstairs, the hallway followed the perimeter of the room, each corner breaking off to its own corridor. A large chandelier hung in the middle of the room.

We took the hallway in the upper left corner. Halfway down, we entered a large bathroom. White marble covered the walls with a matching vanity. There was a large porcelain clawfoot tub filled with steaming water. All the faucets and knobs looked like they were made from gold. Everything held an air of elegance, as if it was designed for a king and queen to wash in. Though, I guess in their world this family was it.

"The bath should help you warm up more. Those are clean towels." She pointed to the towel rack. The fluffiest white towels were hanging. The type of towel you would picture at a five-star hotel. The ones that would usually end up in someone's suitcases.

"Thank you," I meekly responded. Not only had I pretty much barged into their house, now I was being catered to. How pitiful I probably seemed.

She stopped for a moment. Her eyes caught mine. They were the same hazel as Derek's. I could see sadness in them. "I'm sorry, Amy."

"It's okay." I rubbed my arm nervously. My teeth were finally still. How fragile I must seem to everyone. No wonder I'm seen as such a burden.

"No, you shouldn't have been dragged into this. Your mom did everything she could to avoid this, and yet you still got sucked back in."

"You knew my mom?" My whole body froze. How did she know my mom? What did she mean my mom tried to avoid this?

She pursed her lip. "Yes, I've known your mom for a long time."

"How! How did you know my mom? Do you know where she is now?" My words were stumbling over each other as they rushed out.

"We can talk about it later. Your bath is getting cold." Her hand was already on the golden doorknob. She was going to leave.

"Wait—"

Her look cut me off, her voice turning stern. "I'll come get you in a little bit. I expect you in the bath."

Okay, I'll take a bath, but we are talking after, I told myself.

The bath was heaven. I felt like an ice cube being dropped into that cup of tea I was served earlier. My frozen body felt like it was melting. I slid down until only my chin was exposed. My hands initially stung when they hit the water. Was something added to the water, maybe bath salts? An intoxicating aroma filled the air that put a calm over my body. I closed my eyes, pushing out everything that had just happened. There was only one thing on my mind right now. My mom. What other secrets did my past have? Is my mom's friendship with her another memory I forgot? And if so, why?

TWENTY-FIVE

A gentle knock rapped on the door. "Amy?" Mrs. Adler's voice called out.

I was already done with my bath. I wonder if she had heard the water draining. I only had my pajamas to change back into. At least they were technically regular clothes. "You can come in," I called back.

The door slowly opened as she peeked in. "How was it?"

"It was fine." I sounded ungrateful. "Thank you for taking care of me." I tried to give her a smile. I was grateful for her helping me, but I had so many questions.

"I'm glad. You already look a little warmer." She was eyeing me up and down. "Though you could use some warmer clothes."

My arms were crossed around my chest. I quickly dropped them. I didn't want to waste time searching for clothes. "I'm actually okay. The water was pretty hot, so these clothes are helping me to cool down." I hesitated, chewing on my lip. "Can you tell me about my mom now?"

"How about we get some food?" She was already turning from the door.

"Wait… can we talk first?" My stomach was in knots. There was no way I could eat anything.

Her head turned as she shot a glance over her shoulder. "I didn't say we wouldn't talk, but at least we can talk over some good food."

I silently followed her down the hallway and back to the stairs. My feet were cold against the marble floor. How far had I gone with bare feet? They were a little sore from walking across the rough concrete. I wonder where they found me. She led me between the two staircases down the hall that opened between them. We passed a room with French glass doors. I peered inside. It looked like some type of study. We passed another room that looked like a giant library. How cool it would be to have a room surrounded by books.

Mrs. Adler must have spent the time I was in the bath preparing the food. Or did they have a chef on staff who cooked for them? They had to have people who help with the house. I couldn't imagine Mrs. Adler tugging around a vacuum and mop or scrubbing toilets. The dining room table was lined with food. More food than two people could eat. I felt guilty. I hope they didn't make all this for me.

I wonder where everyone else was. Maybe they were joining us, and that was why there was so much food. My heart dropped. Would that mean Mrs. Adler wouldn't answer my questions? No, she said we would talk over food.

"The others will be here soon, so I thought they may be a little hungry." She shot a reassuring smile.

Mind readers, I thought. Goosebumps spread over my arms. That is what they said Donovan could do. Right?

The table was huge. It could seat sixteen people comfortably, probably even more if people squeezed together. I wonder how many dinners they have had here. It was usually just the three of them, right? I don't think Derek had any siblings. I can't believe I never asked him. If I was being honest with myself, I've never really asked him anything personal about himself. Sure, a lot of questions about what they were, but not much about him.

We sat across from each other. I picked a few items to fill my plate. A roll, some mashed potatoes, and a chicken breast. My stomach gurgled. I did miss dinner, plus the food smelled amazing. My mouth was watering, maybe I could get a couple bites in.

"So…" I started after swallowing down a mouthful of potatoes. "How do you know my mom?"

Mrs. Adler was looking into her mug, swirling the liquid around. I'm sure she was thinking about how to respond. "I met her a little before she became pregnant with Cole. When she first fell in love with your father."

She knew my mom and dad? "Do you still talk to my dad?" I was diverting the topic, but I wasn't expecting her to mention him. Were they still close?

Her lips pursed with that question. I wonder if she even liked him. My parents had such a tumultuous marriage, I wonder if she had disapproved of them. Maybe that disapproval is the reason I never met her before. "No, I haven't seen him a very long time."

I needed to get back on track. "You said my mom wanted to keep me away. Did that mean she knew the truth about what you guys are?"

"Yes. She knew about us early on. It wasn't known to many that our secret was out, but I trusted her." She set her mug down, meeting my eyes. I wonder what she thought about me knowing their secret. Did she trust me?

"Is that how Derek and I became friends?" Could she help me piece together my past?

"Since we had kids close in age, we used to plan play dates together. You, Cole, Derek, and little Emery. You all were as thick as thieves." A smile lit up her face as she thought of the memory. I wish I could remember. "But those were simpler times. As you all grew older, it was harder to ignore the differences in Emery and Derek."

All I could do was nod. I knew this. Well, I knew we had been friends. I didn't know Derek's mom was involved in our friendship. I wonder why? Why would she encourage a friendship with her son and humans? If they were as important as everyone made them out to be, wouldn't this be like socializing with the lowest class. Or was Becca right in that we were just pets for them to play with?

"So, what happened between us?" If everyone was okay with us being friends, why did it change? And why don't I remember?

"As kids, there was the risk of our secret getting out. Your mom was worried about the consequences. Partly the risk it puts on us if people were to find out about us, but also the risk it put on you, being labeled an outcast. People tend to ostracize people who talk about things that don't make sense to the majority." Mrs. Adler had picked up an apple. She was rotating it in her hand. As if she was trying to find the perfect spot to take the first bite.

"So, everyone went their separate ways?" I mean that was a sensible solution, but then why did it seem like this was all still a big secret? "But if it was that simple, why don't I remember anything? You made it sound like my mom did something extreme to keep us away. Two families growing apart happens all the time."

Mrs. Adler didn't answer right away. She signaled to my plate. I obediently took a few more bites of the chicken. It wasn't until half my plate was cleared that she was satisfied enough to continue. "You and Derek had a hard time letting go. Your mom and I didn't realize how close of a friendship you both had created, especially at such a young age. It was hard on Emery and Cole, but they were old enough to understand the why." The apple froze in her hand as a smile pulled at her lips. "You both would find the most creative ways to sneak out and see each other."

My body tightened, almost as if it was trying to warn me something bad was coming. "So, what did you do?" I whispered.

"I asked Donovan for help." Regret filled her eyes. The apple resumed its spin.

"Donovan!" I yelled. There was no way she was talking about him. The same Donovan who was currently stalking my brain and trying to hurt her son.

She wasn't fazed by my outburst. "Yes, it was different then. Donovan is Derek's uncle, so my husband, Michael, is his brother. At the time we were very close, and his abilities came in handy at times."

"You mean his ability to mess with a person's mind," I spat. I dropped my fork. My appetite was gone. "How is he even able to do that? Are you saying everyone can pretty much mind-control us?" I paused.

I could tell she didn't want to have this conversation. This was moving away from my mom and getting more into the secrets about them. I guess she didn't really trust me.

"I'm sorry. I'm getting us off track." I picked up my fork, pushing my potatoes around. I didn't want to say the wrong thing and end the conversation, but I felt like with each new revelation I had ten more questions appear.

"You don't need to apologize. I know this is all confusing for you." She paused again, examining the apple. Was she ever going to take a bite? I wonder if she was using it as a distraction. Was that why she wanted to go eat? So, our focus could be pulled elsewhere if needed. "I'm going to put it as simple as I can. As you probably heard we can control our energy. Which we refer to as your soul energy or souls. Well, it doesn't just stop there. Every living thing around us is made up of energy as well. The plants, animals, humans, Reapers, and Guardians. We can also pull the soul energy from others, but that is a lot harder."

"Like the Reapers?" I remember Emery talking to me about how they devour our souls, in order to become stronger.

"No, nothing like the Reapers. They must feed on souls in order to survive." A disgusted look spread across her face by the comparison. "Guardians must work hard to specialize in that skill, which most tend to focus on their own soul energy and how it can help them fight. The ones who use other souls tend to be our healers. They use outside energy to help speed up the healing process or help to shift emotions to calm others in times of high stress."

A door closed somewhere in the house, and she jumped in her seat. I wonder how much of this was taboo to say. I needed us to get back on track before someone had the chance to interrupt us. "So, Donovan specialized in this technique?" I think that was the gist of what she was saying. To be honest, I was lost. I had so many questions about this energy she spoke of. The others used that word a lot too. How did you utilize it? If this was a common thing, why didn't we learn about it? I'm sure if humans knew there was another type of power, we would capitalize on it. Which wasn't always a good thing. But that had to be for a different time. I had to know why Donovan was so important to this story.

"Yes, I know they mentioned it earlier, but he can use your soul to project thoughts into your mind." I shivered in response. I didn't like to hear anyone could mess with my head.

"So, he can hear my thoughts?" How could we be safe from that?

"No, he isn't a mind reader. All he can do is give suggestions." Okay, I was lost again. She knew she was confusing me, so she started again. "It's more of a trance. He can only do it when he's in close proximity to someone.

Almost like he hypnotizes the person into having those thoughts."

I'm not sure if that sounded any better. I thought of those magicians on television. The ones who picked people in the audience and, at the end, had them strutting around like a chicken clucking at people. Were magicians just Guardians in disguise? Stop I'm derailing, stay on topic.

"Oh," is all I could say.

"We were running out of options, so we brought you to Donovan. It took a couple days, but he was able to convince your brain to seal those memories. At the end when you walked out, we were all strangers to you."

I shuddered. How could someone do that? Did they really think that was the best choice? What were the memories they sealed? Were they just of them, or did Donovan seal other things away? I felt violated. I also felt like part of me was missing. Could I ever recover them? How could my mom think that was okay.

A door slammed, followed by yelling. Mrs. Adler's and my eyes met. Our conversation was over. I still wanted to ask more about my mom. Did they stay in contact after? Did she know why she left or where she went? But that would have to be another time.

"I don't care what you say! I'm not going to let that happen!" Derek was yelling at someone.

"That's enough, Derek. You will not go against the elder's decision," Mr. Adler boomed back.

I pushed my chair from the table. I had to see what was happening. I needed to make sure Derek was okay. I looked over at Mrs. Adler to see if she was going to stop me, but she was also up. Her lips were pursed into a fine line. I'm sure she wasn't happy with her son and husband yelling at each other. I followed her out of the hall toward the screaming voices.

"What is going on in here? You both know better than to be using such loud voices inside," Mrs. Adler sternly said when we entered the foyer. I stood a little stiffer with her tone, as if I was also being lectured.

There was a group of people huddled around. Aiden and Dominic were standing behind Derek, who was once again squaring off against his dad. I was starting to think this was a common occurrence between the two of them. Was this how their relationship always was, or was it because of me?

I didn't notice the rest of our friends were also there. Wow. I think that was the first time I referred to them as our friends. Everyone but Kyle. My stomach dropped, was he ok? But there were others here, too. People I didn't recognize. They were also much older. Even older than Derek's parents. Had I met any of them during Thanksgiving? They stood behind Mr. Adler as if sides were being drawn. I didn't like this at all.

"Nothing." Derek was still gritting his teeth. "I'm taking Amy."

He took a step toward me, but his dad's arm grabbed his shoulder, pushing him back so he was facing him. "She is staying here." Derek's dad growled.

"Over my dead body," he spat back. If I thought his dad got angry before, it was nothing compared to what was happening now.

Electricity was sparking in the air. It almost felt like when a little kid shuffles across a carpet in socks, gathering all that static electricity before they find their poor target to shock. Was this what Mrs. Adler was saying about manipulating the energy around them? This wasn't going to end well. Something had to be done.

"I would be careful about what you are asking," Mr. Adler spat through his clenched teeth. One of the men behind him started to step forward.

No. They are going to hurt him again. I can't let him get hurt again because of me! "Please, Derek, stop!" I screamed. My legs took off on their own. I wrapped my arms around his body. Trying to act like a shield. I know I was no match for them, but I needed to do something.

"Amy..." Derek's voice whispered in my ear. My heart raced. There was such fear in his voice.

It took all my courage, but I turned around to face his dad. I spread my arms to continue to shield Derek as best as I could. Mr. Adler's eyes were so cold. I lifted my chin, trying to prove I wasn't afraid. My little act of defiance. All I knew was this had to do with me, and I couldn't keep having Derek fight my battles.

"I'm not going anywhere." I had every intention of saying it confidently, showing I wasn't afraid. Instead, my voice trembled with every word.

"Aiden and Dominic. Please take Derek to his room." Mr. Adler's gaze never left mine.

"No!" Derek hollered.

I heard them scuffling behind me, but I refused to turn around. I knew they would protect him. The longer Derek stayed here, the more likely he was going to do something he would regret. How many chances was his dad going to give him before something bad happened to him? The wounds on his back were a warning, what would be considered a punishment for such disobedience. Would he be ostracized like the others? As Derek had said, it didn't take much, and it looked like he was walking that fine line.

I waited until the footsteps disappeared. I closed my eyes, taking a deep breath before opening them again. I don't know what's going to happen, but I knew it wasn't going to be good. "What do you want from me?"

For the first time since I met Mr. Adler, a smile appeared on his face. It wasn't the smile I yearned to see from Derek. Goosebumps covered my arms. This smile was of someone plotting.

And I was the main character.

TWENTY-SIX

"Do you understand?" Mr. Adler asked after he finished going over the plan.

We were sitting in his study. The only people here were Mr. Adler, three of his men, who had been standing behind him during the altercation with Derek, and Becca. Out of everyone, why did it have to be Becca?

Who was I kidding? She was the only one who had no problem going against Derek's wishes. Especially when there was the potential of getting me out of the picture. She'd already got him back. She'd won, but I guess this was the cherry on top.

"Yes sir." I understood one thing. I was going to be the bait. I was being used to lure Donovan out. Their plan was to ambush him. Apparently, they believed he was the ringleader behind everything that was going on.

"Do you have any questions?" His hands were clasped together on his mahogany desk. I felt like a little kid sitting in the principal's office.

I had a million questions. The plan was very vague, but I knew that was because Mr. Adler didn't trust me. I'm sure he believed I would blurt out their plan at the first sign of trouble. "I just have two." Mr. Adler's eyebrow raised.

It reminded me of the first time I was at the gym with Derek when he had asked if I had any questions after watching them spar. When he wasn't angry, I could see the resemblance between the two of them. Derek had his mom's eyes, but the rest of his features came from his dad. I had no doubt he would almost be his double in a few years.

I swallowed hard. I'll start with the easy one. "What about school? According to your plan, I'm not allowed to go to school until this is over. If this goes on too long, how will I be able to catch up? I have tests happening in two weeks."

Mr. Adler pressed a button on the phone sitting at his desk. It was like the phones you would see on TV whenever they shot scenes in an office. A loud buzz followed. "Please send Agnes in," he spoke into the speaker." Who was Agnes? And how was she going to help with school?

The door creaked open. "Yes, sir?" a shrill voice spoke.

That voice. I know that voice. I spun in my chair. I was suddenly staring at Ms. Haines. What was my English teacher doing here? I snapped my mouth shut. At some point, it had dropped open. How many reveals were going to happen tonight? Did this mean she was a Guardian as well? She stood out against the rest of them. She was much older. They all looked between their thirties and forties, and she had to be at least sixty. And I was being generous with her age.

"Agnes will cover for you at school. She will make sure you are granted extensions on any assignments you miss." Mr. Adler spoke as if this was the obvious solution. As if it was well known that she was part of this plan. Well, I guess I was the only one who was surprised. "And your second question?"

"I want you to promise me that nothing is going to happen to Derek." This time, I was staring him down. This was something I wasn't going to waver on.

"That isn't a question," Mr. Adler responded. Our gazes

didn't break, though his was different than before. It wasn't the normal anger or annoyance. Was it a bit of fear?

"I'm serious. You must promise me that nothing will happen to Derek. Nothing physically, and no matter his reaction during this, you won't banish him." I knew he was going to be angry, and I was afraid of what he was going to do with that anger. I didn't want him to do something that had consequences that couldn't be taken back.

"You have my word." I know what the look was. It was a father's look. He wanted the same thing for his son. He didn't want to lose him either.

"I don't want him involved at all in this plan." I wasn't dumb. I knew there was a large risk for me. I don't know what Donovan wanted from me, but I know, in their eyes, humans are disposable. I doubt he was just going to let me go. Especially when he finds out, I'm the key player in this plan. If that happened, what would Derek do? Would he throw himself in the middle of danger to try and help me?

"I think this is going to be one of the few times we are in agreement." Mr. Adler looked around the room. "Alright, everyone. Our plan will start tomorrow. For now, please go home and try and get some rest. I need everyone at their best tomorrow." His eyes returned to me. "Amy, you will go with Becca. She will make sure you are where you need to be."

I pushed the chair out from the desk. Why did it have to be her? But there were no arguments. I agreed to follow their plan. She turned and was about to walk out of the two French doors before I even made it to her. I sluggishly followed behind her. Down the hall and into the foyer. I slowly turned to look at the marble steps.

I'm not sure where Derek's room was. It could be anywhere in this mansion. What I would give to just say bye. For him to wrap his arms around me in his strong embrace. The only place I recently felt safe, but I knew if I saw him, he wouldn't let me go, and I don't know if I would have the strength to leave either. Just please, Derek. Don't be mad at Dominic and Aiden. They did what they had to do to protect you.

"Ready?" Becca's voice dripped with annoyance. Some things don't change. You would think agreeing to sacrifice myself for everyone could win me a couple brownie points with her.

A car was waiting in front of the house. It was a red sports car. One of those expensive types. It only had two seats and was low to the ground. The type I would be scared to drive. Afraid that the moment I took it out, I would get its first scratch. Was this Becca's car? It was even flashier than Dominic's car. Though his was more of a muscle car, this one was built for speed.

We rode in silence. Well, we didn't say a word to each other, but she had the radio blasting the entire ride. I wonder if she did that to ensure we didn't speak. Luckily, the ride was short. Becca didn't live far from Derek. Her house was big, but it was similar to Emery's house. Actually, now, looking at the house, they looked almost identical. There were a couple bushes out front that were different. Emery's house had more of a gray stone on the front, while Becca's house was tan, but the overall look was the same. I wonder if the houses meant anything.

"I'll show you to your room." Those were the first words Becca said to me since we left the house. I just nodded and followed. I was afraid she'd make me sleep outside if I angered her.

Even the inside of her house was the same. The living room was on the left. I imagined if I followed the hallway back, I would run into the kitchen. The staircase leading upstairs. I obediently followed Becca up. She pointed out the bathroom, still the same as Emery's. The guest bedroom was different, but that was probably more the residence preference.

"I'll come get you in the morning," she firmly said before closing the door and leaving. I guess she doesn't want me to wander on my own.

I walked over to the bed. A beautiful purple quilt was spread out. It went perfectly with the gray walls. A couple purple flower paintings were hung complimenting the color palate that was chosen. I sat on the bed. It folded a little under my weight. The bed was nice, but Emery's bed was much comfier.

I laid my head on the pillow, staring at the ceiling. I watched the fan blades spin around and around. I wasn't going to be able to sleep. I wonder what time it was anyway? I didn't think to look at the clock at Derek's, and my phone was still sitting at home. The sun was still down, so we still had a bit before people would be up.

If I had to be alone with my thoughts, I knew what I was going to think about. I closed my eyes, thinking of him. I pictured Derek's face. I wonder how he was. Who was I kidding? He had to be fuming. I hope Aiden and Dominic were at least still with him. Was he mad at me? Mad that I wasn't listening to him yet again. Maybe he was happy he was rid of me. Just like he tried to push me away, maybe he realized this was what he really wanted in the end.

I opened my eyes, shaking my head. No, I'm not going to waste my time worrying about the unknown. He was safe. That's all that mattered. I might not like his dad, but from what I took from being around him, he was a man of his word. Hopefully, his word to a human meant something to him.

I closed my eyes again. This time, I replayed our memories together. At least the ones I could access. I thought about the first time I saw him in his true form. In my bedroom, protecting me from that Shadow Reaper. How I first thought that was just a dream. When it was crazy to think people could have wings.

I thought about him riding the bus with me. How annoyed he was that I wouldn't just get in his car. His scent. The combination of leather and sandalwood. I smiled thinking about the text he sent me when I got home.

Then, I thought about him laying bandaged on my bed. How he got those wounds. The first time he put himself in danger because of me.

I thought about breakfast, and the museum. I knew those annual passes were going to be a waste.

My mind continued to replay our adventure. It might have been short, but I cherished these memories.

My lips burned as I thought of his lips on mine. I imagined his arms were wrapped around me as we laid together in this bed. Knowing that when I was with him, I felt not only safe, but wanted. Something I haven't felt in a long time. Abandoned by my family, I had been going through the motions. At least these last couple months I was reminded what it was like to love. I wish I could've told him that. I don't care how he felt about me.

I loved him.

I awoke to pounding on my door. "We're leaving in ten minutes. I can't be late to school," Becca barked from behind the door.

"I'm glad one of us gets to be there," I mumbled under my breath. "I'll be ready in a few minutes," I said a little louder.

"Fine, just meet me in the car." I heard her footsteps stomp away.

I walked to the door, grabbing the knob. I froze with my hand on the handle. I was expecting the jolt of pain to shoot out of my hand, but it didn't happen. I pulled my hand away looking at it. They were still healing, but the last of the open sores had finally closed. I've never had a wound heal so quickly. Especially one this severe. Their medicine was incredible. If they shared this with everyone, how many people could be saved? Do they keep it to themselves because they are afraid it would spark too many questions? Or because they didn't want to waste the energy on us? If they cared so little about humans, why did they risk their lives night after night fighting the Shadow Reapers?

I wasn't going to get the answers now. I silently laughed. Who was I kidding? I'll probably never get my questions answered. I opened the door and walked toward the bathroom. A hairbrush and toothbrush were lying on the counter for me. I was surprised to see a folded stack of clothes with a pair of sneakers sitting next to the vanity.

I pulled on the clothes. It was a simple black T-shirt and a pair of jeans. They must be Becca's because I had to cuff the bottom of my pants, so they didn't drag on the floor. I pulled a gray hoodie over my shirt, enjoying the warmth it provided. The sneakers were a gray color with pink strips running down the side. I sat on the edge of the bathtub, fixing the laces.

I walked down the stairs. Family pictures lined the wall as I walked down. Why was this the usual place to hang them in houses? When you walked on stairs, you usually had a purpose, so why did we think this was the perfect place for people to stop and look at your family mementos? There were a lot of pictures of Becca.

Becca holding her spear.

Becca's back as she sat on a pier, the sun setting in the background.

Becca in some type of graduation outfit, maybe middle school graduation?

I stopped as I looked at a picture of Becca with what I assumed, were her parents. Her dad was on the left. He had broad shoulders and a stern look. Did any of these parents ever smile? He was wearing a business suit. Her mom, or what I think was her mom as she could pass as Becca's sister. She had the same blonde hair. She was shorter than Becca and her dad. She wore a white floral dress. Becca was in the middle, wearing a cute purple sundress.

A horn honked. Becca was getting impatient. I stepped outside. The cold wind whipped against my face. I crossed my arms, trying to save my body heat. The warmth the sweater was providing was slowly disappearing. I wonder if there was any way to stop at home first so I could grab my jacket.

I slid into the car, thankfully the heat was already running inside. I couldn't believe how low this car was. It almost felt like we were sitting directly on the road. Becca stepped on the gas, jerking us forward. One thing that was common with all of them, they liked to go fast. The music was still blaring in the car. I think that was Becca's way of saying she wasn't up for small talk.

I looked out the window as we drove down the road. We stopped at the entrance as the black iron gates squealed open. Becca flipped the lever next to her steering wheel, engaging the right blinker. After a moment pausing, she turned right. She followed the road until it led us onto the highway, taking it into town. I realized why I had never seen their neighborhood. Though it was part of our town, it was on the off skirts. You had to jump on the highway to get to it, and once you got off you had to follow a maze of winding roads to finally get to it. Something you would have a hard time stumbling onto. Plus, once you found it, it led you to the menacing black gate.

Once we got off the highway, the buildings started to look familiar. She pulled into one of the business building parking lots. It was a smaller building with only three floors. The sign out front listed a couple of businesses. I wasn't familiar with any of them. I recognized the building as my bus would typically pass it when I rode home from the diner.

"We are here." Becca placed the car in park. She stopped

in front of the entrance. She wasn't about to park and help me inside. "When you get in, turn left, there will be a pair of elevators. Go to the third floor and stop at the receptionist. She will know you are coming."

I slowly nodded. I took in a deep breath before getting out. I closed the door without looking back. The tires squealed as Becca left. She didn't even wait for me to get inside. The doors swished as they sensed my motion and opened. I wrinkled my nose against the chemical smell. A mixture of cleaner and air fresheners. Once I was inside, I turned left, trying to remember Becca's instructions. I saw the silver doors of the elevators a few feet away.

Standing in front of the doors, I stared back at my reflection. I pressed the up arrow, and the button lit up. A dinging sound filled the hallway as the lights above the door blinked, signaling the elevator was coming down. A final louder ding followed before the doors on the left opened. I stepped inside. The sound of smooth jazz filled the small room. I grabbed one of the bars as the elevator jerked up. I was always uneasy riding these things. I've heard so many horror stories of people getting stuck inside. The fire department having to be called to break them out. An inspection card was posted above the buttons. At least it looked like it was inspected in the last few months.

Inside dinged as we made it to the third floor. The doors once again swished open. I quickly jumped through the opening. Again, the back of my head thought about the possibility of it suddenly dropping, chopping me in two. Why did I have to have such an overactive imagination? After looking both right and left, I spotted the receptionist's desk. A young lady was sitting, tapping away at the keyboard. I swallowed hard as I walked toward her. Alright this was it, there was no going back now.

"How may I help you?" the lady automatically responded.

I wonder how many times a day she used that phrase. She didn't even look up from my computer.

"Hi," I awkwardly started. Crap, should I have said hello? Was that more professional. "I'm Amy. I was told to come here." More like I was dropped off here.

She stopped her typing, finally looking away from the screen. Here eyes gave me a quick once over. "You can have a seat." Her hand signaling to the row of chairs against the wall. That was it, she went back to typing.

I walked over to the chairs. They were black metal chairs with plush cushions on the back and seat. An end table sat next to the chairs with a handful of magazines. A typical waiting room, but what was I waiting for? I wonder what business they did here. To be honest, I wonder what any of them did. Did they all have normal jobs? Apparently, teaching was one job.

I sat staring at my hands. For the first time since leaving Derek's house I felt like I had a second to think about what was happening. What I agreed to. I felt my stomach drop. What difference did they really think I would make? Me. Only a human. Was Derek, okay? Would he eventually forgive me?

"Amy?" a familiar voice called, bringing me back to reality.

"Emery?" I stood on my feet. What was he doing here?

"Follow me," was all he said. He waited at the door, holding it open so I could walk through. I then followed him down the long hall to another room. He led us into an empty conference room. A large, polished table sat in the center of the room. Twelve black office chairs surrounded it. In the center was a black telephone. Almost identical to the one that was on Mr. Adler's desk. On the opposite wall, there was a large television that had been mounted.

This is where we sat. Waiting.

TWENTY-SEVEN

"Why are you here?" I didn't expect to see him again. Actually, I didn't expect to see any of them.

I accepted the next eight hours I would be surrounded by strangers. That was supposed to be the next part of the plan. I was going to pretty much be in their custody. Donovan wouldn't try and come for me when I was around them. This would give Mr. Adler and his men the time they needed to formulate their plan and get everyone in place. Once school let out, I would be taken home, and there the trap would be laid. When I asked for Derek not to be included, I assumed that would apply to everyone else. I guess I was wrong.

"You didn't think we would just up and abandon you." Emery's chin was resting on his fist. He was slowly looking me over, probably trying to figure out where my current mood was.

"We?" My chest grew tight. Was Derek also here? I'm not sure what I wanted more. For his dad to honor our agreement or the chance to see him again.

"Can you believe you have to *pay* for the snacks here?" Dominic stormed through the door.

Him! Out of all the people to bring, it had to be Dominic. He grabbed the seat next to Emery and slumped into it. Dark purple circled his left eye. I couldn't help but stare. When did he get that?

"That's what I get for pissing off your boyfriend." Dominic smirked, rubbing the side of his face. "I'm not his favorite person at the moment."

"I'm sorry." My head dropped. I just stared at my clasped hands. "Is he okay?"

"He feels a little like a caged animal right now." Emery was still staring at me. Like I was going to pop at any moment. Did they think I was going to bolt? Were they here to make sure I went along with the plan? Thinking that I would be more compliant with them?

"I wouldn't be surprised if he busted out and came and found us." Dominic smiled. He was apparently picturing something amusing.

"You better hope he doesn't find you first." Emery smirked. Was that him attempting to make a joke?

Dominic on the other hand did not. His smile quickly vanished. "Hey, I agreed to watch out for his girlfriend! This has to count for something."

"I'm just messing with you. He knows you did what you had to. And I know he wouldn't have chosen anyone else to be here." Emery lightly punched his arm in an attempt to cheer him up. At times it was easy to forget that we were just a bunch of kids, so it was nice seeing moments like this.

"Thanks, guys." A tear ran down my cheek. I quickly brushed it away, hoping they didn't notice.

"Oh great, now you made her cry." Dominic pushed back in his chair.

What I would give to kick him in the shins right now. "No, I'm just thankful for both of you. I'm going to miss this." I could feel my cheeks growing hot. I just stared at my hands. I couldn't look at them. If I did, I may really start crying.

"Nothing is going to happen to you, Amy." Emery's voice dropped. His face stern. I wasn't used to seeing him so serious.

"Yeah, you think this shiner is bad. Derek will kill us if we let something actually happen to you." Dominic was leaning back in his chair. His hands behind his head. "Plus, no Reaper can get past us!"

I wanted to feel better, but I still couldn't shake the feeling that this wasn't going to end well. I wanted to get us off this topic. "So, what is this place?"

"It's an office building," Dominic answered frankly. Thank you, Captain Obvious.

"Yes, I saw that." That was my polite way of saying no shit, Dominic. "I mean what do they do here?" Was this where they had all their secret meetings? Is this the room they use to meet with the elders?

"They work." Dominic looked at me like I had a screw lose. "You know to make money."

My face dropped. Yup, I was going to strangle him. "Okay, what kind of work do they do here?" I asked through gritted teeth.

"Amy thinks all we do is go out and beat up Reapers," Emery interjected. It seemed he was clearly enjoying the back-and-forth banter. "We have to get jobs too. This business is actually run by my neighbor. They sell life insurance."

I had to snap my mouth shut to avoid it from dropping open again. Life insurance. Was there a more ironic business they could get into. Not only were they protecting our lives every night. Why not sell insurance for it as well.

The door opened and a middle-aged man walked in. He was wearing a business suit and holding a notepad and pen. "I'm here for lunch orders." He clearly did not want to be here. I wonder if he picked the shortest straw.

"Sweet! I want steak!" Dominic rubbed his hands together. "With a side of mashed potatoes and…" His fingers were at his lips as he intensely thought. Like this was one of life's most important decisions. "Actually, I'll take double potatoes."

"Subs. We are ordering subs." The man was not amused. His lips were pressed, probably holding back some snarky comment. "You have a choice between turkey and ham."

"Ham…" Dominic crossed his arms, pouting. "Can we at least get chips and a drink?"

"Fine." The man scribbled something on his pad. I was just thankful he wasn't preparing the food.

Emery and I both ordered turkey. The man left without a parting word. I crossed my arms over my stomach as it gurgled. I didn't realize I was getting so hungry. It didn't help that we skipped breakfast this morning. I wonder what time it was. If they were ordering lunch that means it had to be close to noon.

If that was the case, there were just a few more hours left. I chewed my lip. Was I really ready for this? Was Donovan going to really fall for it? Thinking it over more, he had to know something was happening. What if we spooked him and he decided I was too much trouble and changed his plan?

It felt like an eternity before the sandwiches finally arrived. I don't know if it was the fact that I was starving, but this was the best sub I ever had. I was actually a little sad when I finished it. They even threw a cookie in with the chips and drink. I smiled as I turned the cookie in my hand, and I thought about how much they all liked their sweets. I thought of the diner. They would always order milkshakes and desserts. I let out a soft chuckle when I remembered the pancakes. How they all drowned them in syrup. Kyle swiped his plate with his finger, trying to lick up as much of the sweet, sticky liquid as he could.

"What's funny?" Emery's eyebrow was raised. Intrigued at my sudden mood change.

"I was just thinking about how much you all like sweets." I started chewing on my lip again. Was that rude to say?

"Why is that funny? We need the sugar," Dominic mumbled through a mouth full of food.

"I mean sugary food is good, but I wouldn't say it is a necessity." I'm not sure how their parents would feel about them making that statement. Though, with their active life-style, they didn't have to worry about the extra calories.

"What Dominic means to say, is we tend to eat sugary food because it gives us the most energy." Emery could see the confusion on my face. He paused to think of a good example. "You know when you eat a lot of sugar, your body will go into a sugar rush? You have all this energy all of a sudden."

I nodded, thinking about all those Halloweens when I was little. Stuffing my face with a fistful of candy. Then, bouncing off the walls non-stop until I finally crashed.

"Well, it's like that. Except our bodies thrive off of that sugar rush. Your body utilizes it right away, our body will build up on the sugar. It helps to replenish our bodies especially when we harness the soul energy."

"Oh." I felt bad laughing about it. Being with them, it was hard to remember they were different from us. Of course, that would mean their diets were different as well.

"So, you want to share your cookie?" Dominic was staring at it in my hands. Emery elbowed him in the side. "Ouch! What? She's just playing with it."

"Here." I held it out for him to take it. It was gone in seconds. If that would give him more energy for today, I'd try and find them both a dozen cookies.

The food at least provided a little distraction for us, but soon we were back to awkwardly staring at each other. What I would give for a simple pack of playing cards. Something to divert our attention.

"I'm so bored!" Dominic whined. He was now pacing the room. Who did he say was acting like a caged animal?

"Would you rather be in school?" Emery sighed. We were

all bored, of course Dominic would be the one to voice it. "We can just bring things tomorrow to entertain us."

"Tomorrow?" I bit my lip. They want us to do this again?

"Well, I mean…" Emery stopped midsentence. I knew what he meant. If Donovan didn't come for me tonight, we would have to keep trying.

"Why would they have us come back here, though? I thought being here was deterring Donovan from making a move." I couldn't understand why that would be part of the plan. It gave us such a small window.

"Well…" Emery paused for a moment, I'm sure he was under orders not to give details on the plan. "We want to flush Donovan out… but we need it to happen at night. There are too many… witnesses around if we try during the day."

"That makes sense." It did. I thought back to when they were ambushed. How intense that battle was. There was no way that could happen in front of humans and their secret still being safe. But that meant Donovan wasn't the only one we may encounter. Would he bring the Reapers with him?

The door creaked open, and all our heads jerked in unison. "You can take the girl home now." It was the same man who had taken our order. He did not look any happier. I guess he was the designated babysitter.

"Finally!" Dominic stood, stretching his arms over his head. "Let's get out of here!"

"You doing okay?" Emery asked once Dominic left the room.

The concern on his face touched my heart. Even though it was a short time, it was so nice to have people who I felt really cared about me again. I couldn't discredit Alicia and Grace. They had been there for me during my lowest point, but our friendship has definitely changed in the last few years as we have each grown, I could tell we were growing apart. Well… I was growing apart from them.

"I'm okay." I tried to give a reassuring smile. I was okay. I was content with my decision. This was my one chance to help them. "Though will Dominic make it?" That last part was a joke. Sort of.

Emery chuckled. "Alright, let's get you home."

We walked down the same long hall, back into the waiting room. The receptionist was still furiously typing away. Whatever she was working on must be important because she barely acknowledged us. That or she didn't care to interact with a group of kids.

"So, Dominic is going to drop you a couple blocks from your house," Emery advised as we were waiting for the elevator. "This way, it looks like you are just walking home from school."

I stared at my reflection, rubbing my arm nervously. I nodded in response. *I can do this,* I was telling myself over and over again in my head.

"If Donovan doesn't come tonight, you will meet me there so I can bring you back here." Dominic was now giving the instructions.

The elevator pinged and the doors swished open. We stepped back into the jazz filled room. A smile pulled at the corners of my mouth. At least if something happened in the elevator this time, I knew I was safe with them. I couldn't stop picturing Dominic with his two swords hacking away at the door to free us.

I WAS BACK IN DOMINIC'S CAR. "SO, I GUESS YOU ARE STUCK driving me around still." I remembered our last ride together. When he rescued me from the lake house. How annoyed he was that he was forced to be my driver once again.

"Would you trust anyone else?" Was that a smile on his face? I could feel my cheeks flushing. I was expecting an annoyed response.

"I guess not," I meekly responded. I just stared at my hands.

We drove in silence, until Dominic pulled to the side of the road. This must be where I was being dropped off. I made a mental note of the street sign for tomorrow. Would there be a tomorrow? I chewed on my lip as the nerves started to hit.

"Amy…" Dominic was clenching the steering wheel.

"Yeah?" Did I do something wrong? Why was he so serious all of a sudden?

"Just don't do anything stupid, okay?" Was he worried about me? "I mean… Derek will have all our hides if something happens to you, and I'd rather not get punched in the face again."

"I'll try not to…" I stepped out of the car. The cold December wind whipped around me.

It must have snowed today. My feet crunched against the snow on the sidewalk. My arms wrapped around my chest. I walked faster. I was anxious to get home. Anxious to see what was waiting for me.

The television was playing when I opened the door. That was a good sign. At least that meant my dad was home. For now. I took a deep breath. Alright this is it. The house was the same. Nothing was out of place, but it felt different. Every creak or rattle made me jump. I had to get to my room. I doubted my dad would notice anything off, but I didn't want to risk it.

I stopped at Cole's door, remembering my last conversation with Donovan. I continued to my room. I needed to act normal. On a normal day I would avoid this room. I needed to go to my room and work on my homework. Or at least pretend to do homework.

The time ticked by. It was hard to focus on anything. I kept pausing, almost wishing for the voice to speak. "This is hopeless," I muttered. I closed the book I was working on.

I grabbed my phone from my nightstand, pulling the charging cord out of it. It had of course died after not being charged for two days. I quickly booted it up. I wonder if Alicia or Grace had reached out. I wonder what they thought about my unexpected absence. I'm sure they assumed I locked myself in my room, crying about Derek and my break-up. To be honest, if last night didn't happen, that wouldn't be far off from the truth.

My phone started pinging with incoming messages. I was right, I had a message from Alicia and Grace. Grace was short, but sweet. Just a simple text.

> U ok?

> > I'm ok. I think I caught some kind of bug.

The break-up excuse was good, but if this lasted a few days I needed a better reason to miss school. A day or two recovering from a break-up sure, any longer would cause too many questions. Now Alicia's text.

> Grl r u skipping w Derek? U back 2gether??? I need deets!

> > No. I caught some kind of bug. Idk about Derek we haven't talked since the breakup

So, Derek wasn't at school either. I guess that made sense. He was probably still under house arrest. His dad was probably afraid the moment he was let out he would try and screw up their plan. Or was that his dad's way of ensuring he held up his end of our bargain to keep him away?

My breath caught at the next messages. They were from Derek. This time there was a string of them.

> Amy pls don't do this

> Emery and Dominic are meeting u. Just tell them u changed ur mind

> Call me!

> Why is your phone off?? Call me when you get this!

As soon as I read the last message, my phone started ringing. It was Derek. How many times has he tried my phone since I left? I dropped it on my bed, biting my lip as I waited for it to stop. I couldn't bring myself to talk to him. A few minutes passed before it pinged again. He left a voicemail. I held the phone up to my ear, my heart began to pound as I waited for his voice.

"Amy..." There was so much desperation in his voice. Tears started to well in my eyes. "Please call me back. I just need to know you are okay."

I held the phone to my ear, half hoping there was more to the message, but it went silent. I needed to let Derek know I was okay, but I didn't trust myself to talk to him. I think deep down I was hoping for an out. A reason not to go through with this plan. How easy I would make it for Derek to talk me out of it. I went back to the messages. A text was better.

> I'm OK. This is my decision plz don't be mad at Dominic & Emery. They can't talk me out of it. Just know I love you and I'm sorry

Once the message was sent, I turned off my phone. Partly because I was afraid Derek would try and call again, and partly I was afraid of his response. I finally told him that I loved him. If this doesn't end well, I just wanted him to know. Was that selfish of me? Was I just hurting him more?

I flung myself down on the bed. My arm draped over my eyes. Tears running down my cheeks. "Okay, Donovan!" I yelled. "Come and get me. I'm ready for you!" I waited, but there was nothing.

Nothing but silence.

TWENTY-EIGHT

Three days had passed, and still nothing. Waking up, pretending to get ready for school, but instead of walking to the bus stop. I would walk the four blocks to the corner of First and Bell St., patiently waiting for Dominic to pick me up in trusty ol' Callie. We would then drive to the same office building, where we would spend the next eight hours waiting in the same conference room. At 11:15, on the dot, the same man would come get our lunch orders. Dominic would get ham, Emery and I turkey. Remember when I said it was the best sub I ever had? Well, that ended on day two.

Then we would leave. Dominic would drop me off at the same spot, and I would walk home. Then more waiting, but this time alone. Waiting for Donovan to do something. To make some type of contact. Lure him out, so the others could act. To finally end this monotonous cycle.

At least we learned from the first day. The conference room was cluttered with books, games, and movies. Dominic had even brought his game console and hooked it up to the television. We spent hours playing a racing game. The type where you play against each other, not only trying to be the fastest car but there are also items you can collect to increase your speed or hit other players. Emery and I would gang up against Dominic, though even as an unofficial team, he would still beat us.

"So, what happens tomorrow?" I asked, setting the book I was reading down. It was getting close to the end of the day, but tomorrow was Saturday, so I didn't have school to pretend to go to. Would we still be stuck here?

"We still have to stick together. We don't want Donovan coming for you during the day." Emery leaned back in his chair, thinking as well. I don't think anyone thought it would take this long.

"I need to go to the gym." Dominic interrupted, his eyes glued to the screen. He was now playing some war game.

Of course it wasn't a question. Though to his credit, I wasn't the only one locked up. Emery and Dominic both were stuck in the same cycle, I'm sure they both were going stir crazy.

"We are not—" Emery started.

"Actually…" I interrupted, "I think the gym would be fun. Plus, it's another place we know Donovan won't go to."

"You sure?" Emery was shooting Dominic a look.

"Yeah. Do you think the others will come?" I was starting to get excited about this plan. I missed seeing everyone. Would we be able to at least pretend things were back to normal?

"I don't know if that's a good idea."

"I mean…" My eyes were pleading with him. Did he think I was hoping to see Derek? Was I?

"Chill, Emery. We have to do something. At least this stupid building is closed on the weekend. Awww crap I got sniped!" Red covered the screen as it brought him back to the main screen.

"Great! So, Dominic will just pick me up in the usual spot tomorrow." I wanted to finalize it before Emery had a chance to object.

Then I let my mind wander. Was Derek still under house arrest? Would he come if he could? I had kept my phone off since that text. I carried it with me just in case I needed it, but I was too big of a chicken to turn it on. Afraid of what message was now waiting for me. I still can't believe I said I love you. Or texted it. How cruel could I be?

"You can take her home." The same guy, giving the same message, allowed us to leave the building once again.

"See ya tomorrow!" I called out as we arrived back to the meeting spot. It was nice to be excited for something again. That moment of happiness didn't last long.

"Where have you been?!" My dad boomed as I entered the house.

I jumped back, almost colliding with the closed door. I'm not sure what shocked me more, him yelling at me or that he was actually acknowledging my presence.

"S-s-s-chool…" I stuttered out. Why was he so mad?

"If you were at school, then do you want to explain why I just received a call saying you've been out since Tuesday?"

"Uhhh…" Crap! I didn't expect the school to call. I guess it made sense. Didn't they usually call to let parents know when you missed a day? But why wasn't he getting calls before this? I wonder if Ms. Haines was intercepting them.

"Are you seriously cutting school?" His face was red, and his hands were clutched by his side. I could feel my heart pounding in my chest as I was reminded of the fights my dad had with my mom before she left. "What about work? Are you skipping out on that too?"

"No! I got fired last month!" My hands flung to my mouth. Why did I say that? How was this making things better?

"What?!" Yup, that definitely made things worse. "What did you do? Don't you understand we need that money!"

"I didn't do anything!" I was getting mad. Of course, what he really cared about was money. "They cut me and Alicia because they needed to make room for full time waitresses. Something we can't do since we go to school."

"Well, apparently, you don't go to school anymore, so I guess that isn't a problem anymore."

"I am going to school. I just…" Come on Amy! Make up a lie! It shouldn't be this hard. "I needed a break."

"Ha!" There was no humor in his voice. "A break from what? Here I am busting my ass for us, and you're running around town doing who knows what! Are you doing drugs?" I could feel his eyes searching for some sign that I was high or drunk.

"No…" I was losing steam. He had every right to be mad at me. What parent wouldn't be? But why did he have to take the role of doting dad now?

"You need a break!" His hand was rubbing his forehead as he shook it. "Here I am, stuck with you. Stuck raising a kid I never signed up for that has brought me nothing but trouble. And you're here telling me you need a break."

"Dad…" My whole body drained. This was my fear. This is why for the last four years I was fine keeping the distance between us. Because deep down I was afraid he really didn't want me. Afraid he didn't love me, so I just stayed out of his way. If we avoided each other, we wouldn't have to say what we both felt.

"Don't call me that!" He scoffed. He pursed his lips together after he spoke almost as if there was something else he wanted to say. "Just get out."

I didn't need another invitation. I grabbed the handle and flung the door open, running back outside. I ran as fast as my legs could take me. I didn't know what direction I was going, and I didn't care. I just needed to get away from him.

I'm not sure how far I ran, but I ran until my lungs were on fire. I stood on the sidewalk, my hands on my thighs as I gasped for air. Trying with all my might to block out the fight.

Once I caught my breath I just mindlessly wandered as the

sun started to set. Just letting my feet take me wherever they wanted to go. I just wanted to get as far from home as I could. Far away from everything. I walked until I was on the bridge. I wasn't surprised this was where my body led me. My hand traced the plaque. Why did you have to go?

"Hi, Amy."

No…not now. I wasn't ready to face him now.

"That was a pretty intense fight with your dad."

"Go away!" I shouted. Had he been in my house? Was this his doing? Or was that me just hopelessly wishing that it wasn't really how my dad really felt?

"Now, Amy. You don't mean that. You and your friends have been waiting for me. Isn't that right?"

He knew. Of course he knew. "I don't know what you are talking about." My eyes were darting around. Where was everyone? Were they waiting for Donovan to reveal himself? "Why don't you come out and talk to me? Stop being such a coward!"

"Hi, Amy."

My whole body jumped. I spun around and was face-to-face with him.

He towered over me. Taller than Derek, and broader too, but their similarities were uncanny. Which made sense, being his uncle and all. His hair was a dark brown almost black. It was tied back into a ponytail. I wonder how long it was. He also had a dark, but well-trimmed beard that covered his face. His whole body was bundled. The only skin showing was his face. A cap was pulled down.

Wait… I recognize that cap. He was that man who helped me with my phone that night I tried to walk home. Oh God… how long had he been following me? And why? But that was before I was close with Derek. If his goal was to trap me to lure everyone in, it wouldn't have worked back then.

My hands clenched. Alright, I did my part. I lured

Donovan out... so where is everyone? *You all can come out anytime now,* I internally called.

"Something wrong?" His face was smug. Did he do something to them? Why wasn't anyone coming?

"What do you want?" I could feel the fear rising in my chest. The sense of doom looming over. This wasn't right.

"You. Like I told you before, you are a very special girl, Amy." A smile spread on his face, there was something sinister about it.

"If I'm so special, then why try and kill me!" He wasn't going to fool me. He tried to run me over with a car! Well, more like having me jump in front of a car.

His shoulders raised as he shrugged. "Circumstances change."

"What do you mean?" Why was he talking in circles? The more he talked, the more questions I had, but I had to keep stalling him. Give them time to get here.

"You changed from a liability to an asset. And you can thank your new friend Derek for that." He sneered.

"Amy!" My name rang out.

Yes! They were finally here, but his attitude didn't change. No, just the opposite. That stupid smug smile returned to his face.

"Hi, Michael." Donovan was looking past me.

I slowly turned my head to see who was there. What I would guess was about twenty feet away were five people. Mr. Adler, then Dominic, Emery, and two others I didn't recognize.

"Donovan." Mr. Adler's voice was ice. His stare was just as cold.

"I was wondering when you were going to finally show up. I'm actually surprised you were so willing to bring a human into this. On second thought, they are just pawns to you, right? Just disposable." He placed his hand on my shoulder. My whole body tensed under his touch.

"Don't touch her!" Dominic growled, taking a step forward. He was ready to fight.

"Tsk tsk. I wouldn't come any closer. Unlike you. I'm not afraid to let our secret out." His eyes were back on Mr. Adler. Almost prodding now for them to make a move. His opposite hand was clenched. Red sparked from it as a car passed.

Mr. Adler raised his hand, signaling Dominic to stand down. Why was he stopping them? This was their chance!

The sickly smile returned to his face. "That's what I thought." His hand gripped harder on my shoulder, pulling me back toward him. "There is one thing I want to leave you with, Michael. I hope this is a lesson to you that these humans you look down on, they're more valuable than you think." With a final jerk, he pulled us over the side of the bridge.

"No!" I screamed. I squeezed my eyes shut.

As I felt the free fall from the bridge, my stomach lurched. The same way it did when I rode one of those tall roller coasters. The wind whistled in my ears as it whipped around my body. My whole-body, tensed waiting to collide with the icy water. Was this the end? Was this how he was going to kill me?

We jerked again, but it wasn't the impact I was expecting. Almost as if we were slowing our descent. Another jerk, as if we were now going sideways. I slowly opened my eyes. Blood red wings extended out. We were flying. I tried to look around, but it was dark. We were in some kind of cave. Instinctively I gripped tighter to Donovan, afraid he would let go at any moment.

Inside, we traveled through a maze of tunnels. Illuminated only by his wings. He didn't say a word as he flew. At first, I tried to memorize the turns. Hoping, if given the opportunity, I could find my way out. Though, I don't know if that was even possible. The floor was covered in water from the river I was expecting to hit. With how icy it was, I wouldn't be able to swim far.

Finally, the floor seemed to start to rise, the water finally disappearing, and a rocky floor was now visible, so at least that meant there were some dry areas. Donovan descended, dropping us onto the floor. My feet slipped against the slick, wet floor, and I fell backward. Pain shot up through my back as it collided with the ground.

Donovan yanked me up, I was surprised my arm didn't rip from my shoulder with the force he used. "This way." His harsh words echoed inside the cave. His patience was clearly gone. I obediently followed. There was nothing I could do now. I couldn't outrun him, and if I did, the icy water was all that was waiting for me.

"Where are we?" How did I not know there was a cave around here?

"Home," was all Donovan said.

My body shuddered as I thought about my conversation with Derek. When Guardians get excommunicated, was this where they ended up? Was this why no one ever saw them again because they were forced to live their lives out underground? Were Emery's parents here?

The tunnel started to open. Donovan's wings vanished as we entered a room that was lit with artificial light. The light was a muted orange. I looked behind us. Darkness. Another disadvantage. There was no way I would be able to maneuver through the tunnels without some type of light source.

The light started getting brighter as more lamps hung to the wall, but it was still a deep orange color. Was that because of the cave walls? I looked around, now that I could make out the details inside. Steel doors lined the walls. My stomach lurched. What were those for? A shrill scream filled the tunnel. My whole body ran cold. What was this place? Those doors. What was behind them? Donovan yanked me forward.

We stopped at one of the doors. Jingling in his pocket he pulled out a key. Why were the doors locked? He pulled the door open. The room was bare. This had to be some kind of old jail. There was a toilet and sink on one wall. In the middle of the room was a bed. Ice ran through my veins. There were straps on the bed, and it was facing another door.

"Donovan?" Someone spoke behind us, so there were more people here. No... not people. Guardians. Or more like fallen Guardians. "Another one?"

"Strap her down." Donovan released my shoulder.

This wasn't good. I had to get out of here. I spun, making a feeble attempt to run. It was no use. The other Guardian was in front of me. It was a woman. Her hands grabbed my arms as if they were made of steel. I tried to break free, but her thin fingers dug harder. Tomorrow I was sure I would have five finger length bruises on each arm.

She picked me up effortlessly, throwing me against the bed. Pain flooded my body from the impact. There was very little cushion on the bed, so it felt like I was making direct contact with the metal frame. The large leather straps flung across my body, biting into my body as they were tightened. I couldn't move.

"Cassandra," Donovan's voice echoed. I couldn't move my head to see him.

"Yes, sir," she responded.

"You are not to tell Adam what happened here. Understood?"

"Yes, sir."

My arm tensed as something sharp pricked it. I could feel something cold spreading into my arm.

"No," I weakly protested. "Please don't turn off the lights." The room was fading as darkness took over.

Twenty-Nine

"Amy, it's time to wake up," a warm voice called.

"Ugh, five more minutes." My head buried farther into the pillow.

"Come on, sleepy head." A hand softly shook my body.

I opened my eyes. The sun was shining in my room, and I could hear the birds chirping. My mom was sitting on the edge of my bed. A smile spread across her face. "Hurry up. You don't want to be late for school." She pushed herself up from the bed. "Isn't Derek picking you up?" She winked before exiting.

"Derek?" Why did that name sound familiar?

"You don't remember your boyfriend?" She chuckled. "I'm not sure if you should tell him that."

I stretched, looking around my room. Why did I have this sense of dread? It must have been a bad dream. I pulled jeans and a sweater out of my drawers before heading to the bathroom. Clothes littered the floor. A wet towel was hung over the shower. I kicked the jeans away from the sink. Did my dad change in here? That didn't make sense.

I walked downstairs. The sound of clanking came from

the kitchen. The smell of freshly made pancakes hit my nose as I entered.

"Why are you wearing that?"

I froze and looked at my outfit. "What's wrong with it?"

"Uh... it's going to be like eighty degrees out," the muffled voice called out. Obviously full of food. I turned to see who was speaking. Tears filled my eyes. Cole was sitting at the table, stabbing a stack of pancakes.

Why was I crying? It was just my big dumb brother. And he was right. It was almost summer vacation. Why did I think it was going to be cold outside?

"Cole," my mom chimed in. "What have I said about talking with your mouth full?"

"Sorry," he mumbled back, his mouth still full. A smile tugged at my mouth.

"Honey, I think you're going to be too hot in that. How about you change into something cooler."

"Uh... yeah... sorry." I climbed back up the stairs. I must still be drowsy from the dream. Maybe I was dreaming about something cold.

I opened my drawer and looked inside. I was staring at a folded pair of black yoga pants and a blue tank top. Why was my heart racing? I shook my head, grabbing a pink T-shirt instead. A stack of chocolate chip pancakes was waiting for me when I returned downstairs. I grabbed the syrup and started pouring it over them. Suddenly, the cap fell off and the sticky liquid gushed out, drowning the pancakes.

"Careful, honey!" My mom grabbed the bottle right siding it.

I just stared at the pancakes. "Sorry, Mom. I'll give them to Derek. He likes a lot of syrup."

"Oh, now you remember him?" She smirked back.

"Thanks, but I'm not a fan of syrup," a voice interrupted us. "And what do you mean 'now she remembers me?'" Derek was standing in the doorway.

Why was my heart pounding so hard? "You don't like syrup?" That didn't seem right.

"I'm not big into sweets." He pulled a chair next to Cole.

"Shouldn't a girlfriend know that?" Cole teased. "Or at least a good one?"

I stuck my tongue out in response. He threw his dirty napkin. It landed in the mess of pancakes in front of me.

"Enough you two." She was using her warning voice now.

"We should get going." Cole got up, dumping his plate into the sink. "We don't want to be late for school."

"Here." My mom wrapped a chocolate muffin and handed it to me.

"Thank you." I hugged her goodbye. I didn't want to let go so I just squeezed a little tighter. Why did this hug feel so good? Like it had been years since I had one?

"You okay?" Concern was now in her voice.

"Yup!" I responded a little overly cheerful. I wiped a tear from my eye before she could see.

I followed Derek to his car. He opened my door before walking to his. He hesitated before getting in.

"Everything o…" He tilted my head toward him, kissing me before I could finish my sentence. My whole body burned. My hand drifted to the back of his head, pulling him closer.

"You remember me now?" He huffed as we parted.

"I think it's coming back." I slyly smiled before kissing him back.

A honk interrupted us. "Can you all stop smooching for two seconds and let me out? I'm not enjoying the show!"

Derek chuckled as he started his car. He was parked behind Cole, blocking him in the driveway. "Sorry!" Derek called back.

"Amy!" Samantha ran up, giving me a hug once we got to school. "Derek, you need to stop hogging her all weekend. I missed her!"

"Uh… I'm sorry." My body was stiff against the hug. Why

was she so happy to see me? "Where's Becca?" Wouldn't she get mad to see us so close?

"Becca?" Confusion spread across her face. "Who's Becca?"

Where did I know that name from? My memory was so cloudy all of a sudden. Why did I think she was Samantha's friend? No, we were best friends. We have been since elementary school.

"You okay?" Derek whispered into my ear. His hand felt warm on my back.

I nodded. What was wrong with me today? Before I could shake this feeling, the bell rang. Derek wrapped his fingers between mine as we walked to class. I let him take the lead. Afraid I was going to make another mistake. Would he think I was going crazy? I could feel my palms starting to sweat.

I followed him to class. We sat next to each other while Samantha sat on my other side. Kyle behind and Cole in front. Wait. Why was Cole in my class?

"Thanks for joining us, Dominic," the teacher called out.

All of our heads whipped to the back. Dominic was coming through the door. The tardy bell had already rung, and the teacher was in the middle of writing on the board.

"Any time." Dominic smirked, pulling a seat next to Kyle.

The class laughed, but was quickly silenced by the teacher's look. "See me after class," was all he said before returning his focus to the board.

"What's with the wings?" Samantha whispered, staring at my paper.

Before Dominic's interruption, I had been mindlessly doodling on my paper as the teacher was droning on. For some reason I had scribbled wings all over my paper, but why? Without warning, the lights went out. Darkness filled the room.

A scream filled the classroom. Four black creatures appeared in the room. Their eyes bright red. They looked almost fake. As if someone was pulling a prank and had dropped Halloween decorations into the room. No, they were real. White long fangs were baring at the students.

Derek grabbed my hand, yanking me up. "Run!" He yelled, pulling me to the back of the class.

Everyone was trying to get out, a barricade of bodies formed as everyone tried to funnel out of the small door. Derek shoved through them, pushing toward the door.

"No!" Samantha screamed.

My head whipped back. One of the creatures had leaped, knocking her to the ground. I pulled toward her, but Derek pulled me back toward the door. My free hand covered my ear, trying to block the screams. My heart was racing.

We finally made it to the hallway. Cole, Kyle, and Dominic were close behind.

"What are those things?" Kyle's voice trembled.

"I don't know." Derek was leading us through the hall. Why did it feel like a maze?

We stopped short. Two more creatures were in our path. They leaped into the air. One collided with Kyle, its mouth biting into his side. A blood curdling scream escaped his mouth. The other launched toward Cole.

"Cole!" I screamed, but it was too late. The creature was on top of him. It opened its mouth. Fire escaped. Cole's whole body erupted in flames.

"No!" I screamed. Derek yanked me again, pulling me away.

"This way!" Dominic called.

He was holding something metal in his hand. His sword. No, it was a metal bat. Why would I think he had a sword? We continued through the maze of halls until we finally saw the front door.

"No!" I cried. Two more creatures dropped from the ceiling, blocking the door.

The two boys stood in front. Derek's body spread out

acting as a shield. The first creature leaped toward Dominic. With one hard swing, his bat connected with the creature, sending it crashing into the lockers. It vanished from the impact.

"HA!" Dominic cried out, but he celebrated too soon. The other creature leaped before he noticed. It knocked him to the ground.

Clicking echoed behind us. We turned, locking with the creature. "Run," Derek whispered.

I shook my head. I couldn't leave him.

"Run!" Derek pushed me back toward the door before running toward the creature. He picked up the bat that Dominic had dropped.

I turned and ran as fast as I could. I closed my eyes as my body slammed into the door. I froze. I was expecting to be blinded by the sunlight. Why did I think that made me safe? Was the light going to protect us? I opened my eyes, and my heart dropped. I was back in my house.

"Amy?" my mom called out. "What's wrong?"

Suddenly, the lights went out.

"No!" I screamed.

Creatures flooded through the doorways. All I could see was the horror in my mom's eyes. Before I could even blink, a creature leaped, striking my mom. I dropped to the ground, covering my arms over my head. Trying to provide any type of protection and waiting. Waiting to be the next victim, but nothing happened. It was quiet.

I opened my eyes. I was in my kitchen, but the cheeriness was gone. The cabinet doors were disheveled, a few hanging from broken hinges. The paint peeling. Dishes piling on the counter. The smell of pancakes was replaced by old musty water.

"What did you do?" another voice rang out. "They're all dead because of you!"

"No." A sob slipped out.

My dad was standing over me. "This is all your fault! They're gone because of you."

"Stop!" I screamed, covering my head again. "Please stop!"

"Who would ever love you?" His voice faded as everything went black.

I GASPED. WHY DID IT FEEL LIKE I COULDN'T BREATHE? I couldn't move. I was bound, but it was like my energy had also been zapped away.

"She's awake," I heard someone call out.

My eyes weren't focusing. Tears were running down my face. "They're all dead," I mumbled.

"That's enough for now," another voice responded.

A shadowy figure hovered next to me. I could hear rustling next to me. My body, which was stiff, felt like something was restricting it, started to loosen. I could finally move my arms.

The sound of metal clanked behind me before something heavy slammed. My body jumped against the sound. I tried to move, but my body wouldn't respond. I had no energy. I couldn't move.

The metal sound returned again. First, the jingling, then the loud thud of something slamming shut.

"Hello, Amy."

Donovan.

"What did you do to me?" I gasped out. It took all my might to just respond.

"What? You didn't like it?" Donovan chuckled. He walked around the bed, so he was in my sight. "This is called surviving."

I couldn't respond. I didn't have the energy. That didn't stop Donovan, he was excited to share.

"You see. Behind this door." He tapped on the metal door that was facing the bed. "Are the Shadow Reapers. Instead of sending them out to the city, we are bringing their food to them."

My heart dropped. All those doors I passed. Were there people in them? Fear was spreading across my face. This seemed to delight Donovan.

"Unfortunately, we haven't had too much success. We can only get two to three cycles out of a person before they become unusable. And something about only using those who deserve punishment. Which is kind of hard to find in a quiet city, but not impossible."

"Unusable?" My voice was raspy. I needed water.

"Well, before they could die. But Amy, you're special. I think you are going to be able to help us break that succession! You could help us make the perfect weapon!"

"No..." I whispered. I couldn't hold on any longer, my energy was leaving me. I couldn't hold back the darkness.

"Don't worry Amy. This is for the greater good." Something tightened around me. I couldn't hold on any longer. The black was taking over again.

"Amy, it's time to wake up," a warm voice called.

THIRTY

I gasped for air, the surroundings coming into focus again. Damn, my body felt so weak.

"We need to give her a break."

"We can't, Cassandra. Donovan wants at least five more Reapers fed today," a voice echoed.

"Well, he's going to be more upset if we lose her first," Cassandra shot back. She was unstrapping the large leather bands.

"Fine!" the other voice reluctantly agreed. "But you're telling him!"

The thud of the door echoed in the room.

The whole room was stuck spinning. I lifted my arm, covering my face. Wait... I was able to move. They didn't strap me back down before they left. How long have I've been here? I was getting lost in the cycle. Dream, wake, unstrap, check vitals, re-strap, then I was back to dreaming. Shit... was this just another dream?

No, they always started out cheery, before horror would ensue. I wonder if they did that to get the biggest reaction. This was real. This may be my only chance to escape. If I could just move... With all my willpower I rolled my body.

Too much. I rolled off the bed. A loud thud echoed in the room as my body hit the hard rock floor.

"Ow…" I sat up, leaning against the bed. I patted my body to see if I was bleeding. At least nothing is broken.

Okay, I can do this. I used the bed to stabilize my feet. I took a step. That wasn't so bad. Another step and I released from the bed. Nope. I fell to my knees. More pain as the rocks cut into my skin. I can't do this. I don't have the strength. My eyes burned against the tears. Why did I have to be so pathetic? I laid my head against the cold floor as I slowly closed my eyes. Maybe if I could just rest a little bit.

"What the hell!" My body jerked awake. Oh no… they're back. I'm out of time.

"What's she doing here?" The voice was so angry, but why did it sound so familiar?

Arms wrapped around me. "No…" I weakly protested. "Don't put me back."

"It's okay." The voice was still hard, but kind. Their movements were gentle. Completely different from Donovan.

"We were just following orders, sir," the same woman from earlier responded.

Footsteps. We were moving. I braced myself, ready to be strapped back to the bed. Nothing. We were still moving. I only made it a few steps. It shouldn't take this long. I slowly opened my eyes. I blinked against the light. Everything was still coming in blurry, but what little I could make out, I could see we were no longer in the same room. We were back in the hallway, but where were we going?

I couldn't keep my eyes open any longer. The warmth of this person's body was making me drowsy again. I couldn't fight it. I was losing consciousness.

I WOKE UP WARM. SOMEONE HAD LAID THICK BLANKETS OVER me. As the room started to come into focus, I was able to look around. This room was different. Though, it still had the same rock walls, but it was cluttered with things. Someone lived here. A stack of books was in one corner next to a pile of folded clothes. Two chairs were on the opposite wall of the bed. A rug rolled on the floor, something soft to combat the cold stone floor. A sleeping bag was rolled out as there seemed to be only one cot in the room, and I was on it. Someone was fast asleep.

I attempted to sit up. The movement caused my head to spin. I sat still holding it as if steadying it would make the room stop spinning. Luckily, it was beginning to pass. I finally had a little strength back, but my body still felt weak. My stomach gurgled. When was the last time I had something to eat? I can't focus on that right now. I needed to get out of here. Would I be able to sneak past this person without being detected?

The man rustled, turning on his side. His sleeping face was now facing mine. My heart skipped a beat in my chest. "Cole?" I gasped.

No, I was dreaming again. I never made it out of that terrible room. My chest tightened. But this felt different. There was too much pain to be a dream.

His eyes gradually opened, locking eyes with mine. So, if this wasn't a dream, there was no way it could be him, but why did this person look so much like him? His hair was too long. His skin paler, as if it hadn't seen the sun in years. But those were his eyes. Those same piercing blue eyes. Just like our moms. He pushed himself up with his arms. The muscles flexed against his weight. Cole had always been long and lanky. He had a high metabolism that allowed him to eat whatever he wanted without gaining a pound, so he saw no use going to the gym. This man had muscles almost matching Derek's.

Three large scars covered the left side of his face. The top one starting from his temple, ending right before his top lip, the other two spaced almost an inch apart, stopping at his chin. A chill ran down my spine. They looked like claw marks. The air was thick as we stared at each other.

"Hi, Mya."

My nickname. This person knew my nickname. Tears welled in my eyes. Before I could think, I leaped out of the bed into his arms. "Cole," I sobbed. His arms wrapped around my body as the sobs shook me.

We just sat there on the floor. My head pressed into his shoulder. How could this be real? How was Cole here? Why was he here? I sucked in air, pushing him back. "Oh God... I'm dreaming again."

"Mya..." Cole reached his hand out to pull me back in, but he froze before dropping it to his lap. "You aren't dreaming."

A dry laugh escaped. "Then explain to me how my dead brother is sitting across from me." My hands grabbed the side of my head. I just want these to stop. Reality and dreams were now blending together, I couldn't determine what was real and what wasn't.

"It's complicated."

I let out a humorous laugh. "Nothing you can say will surprise me." How much has changed in the last few months? He could tell me he was brought back from the dead and was now a zombie and I wouldn't be shocked. Oh no... please don't let that be it.

"How about we get some food first?" He responded as my stomach gurgled again.

"Is it safe?" He had just broken me out. Weren't we in hiding? What if someone found me, would they make me return?

"Yes, you are safe now." Anger flashed on his face.

He stood extending his hand. I grabbed it as he helped me

to my feet. I wobbled for a moment. When was the last time I stood on my own? Afraid I was going to fall, Cole wrapped his hand around my waist, helping to steady me.

He led me out of his room. I froze at the sight. It was nothing like what I'd seen since coming here. Unlike the prison from before, this felt lived in. We were now standing in a large room which was lined with similar doors. But these doors were different as they were made from wood, not like the steel ones from before. In the center were a group of large wood tables. People were constantly moving around. How were there so many of them? Some sitting at the table, others going in and out of the rooms, and a few were walking through the hallways that led to, what I assumed, more room.

"Who are all these people?" I counted at least fifteen. Were they people? Were these all prisoners like me? If so, why were they allowed to move around so freely?

"That's… also complicated." He was leading us to one of the tables.

"Guardians…?" I quietly guessed.

Cole froze. "How do you know about Guardians?"

My body stiffened, his arm still tight around me, guiding me forward. "You can say… I have a few friends." The side of my mouth tugged as I thought about them. Would Cole be excited to hear about Emery?

"You can't be friends with a Guardian…" he almost hissed out. He continued toward the table. Cole signaled to the bench, and I obediently sat.

"Well… then what are they?" I motioned to a group that was seated at the opposite table.

"I wouldn't call them that. They lost the title of 'Guardian' a long time ago. They're more outcasts. They call themselves the Fallen." He started to walk away.

"Wait!" My chest grew tight with fear. I didn't want him to leave.

"Relax, kiddo. I'm just getting some food." He smiled.

He returned with an armful of sealed pastries. "Where did you get these?" With the looks of everything, I was expecting a more apocalyptic atmosphere. The type where they had to salvage their own food. Making delicacies scarce. But these were items you would find in the bakery section of a grocery store. And all packed with way too much sugar to be nutritious.

"The store?" Great, I was now getting Dominic style answers. He read the confusion on my face. "Everyone here is free to come and go. This is just a safe place for them to live. Where they aren't forced to be alone. They aren't supposed to be together, but here no one will know."

"Yeah, safe." I grabbed a Danish and ripped open the plastic wrapper. The middle of it was yellow, probably lemon flavored. Did this give the illusion that they were eating fruit?

Cole gripped my arm. "I'm sorry, Amy." He stopped for a moment. His eyes were so sad. "That never should've happened. I don't know what Donovan…"

"You know Donovan?" The Danish dropped to the table.

"Yes. He is one of the leaders here."

"What a great leader." I shoved the food away. I had suddenly lost my appetite.

"Amy…" Cole only used my name when he was being serious. "Eat."

I obediently took a bite. We sat in silence as we both ate. I wonder what time it was. There were no windows to the outside. Only the orange lights that lit up the room. Since he grabbed pastries, did that mean it was breakfast? Or, because they were the easiest items to quickly grab?

"Why didn't you come home?" I broke the silence first. I was picking up the crumbs from the wrapper.

Cole noticed and pushed another Danish over. "I couldn't."

"Why!" That wasn't an answer.

"It wasn't safe. It's better if I just stayed dead."

"That doesn't make any sense." Why couldn't, for once, someone be honest with me?

He let out a loud sigh, his hand running through his long hair. He had always kept it so short, but now it hung just below his chin. I tugged on my own hair which was almost the same length.

"You know about the accident." Cole was staring at his hands. His thumbs were slowly rotating.

"Yeah…" I rubbed my forehead as the images flooded in. The scenes of the car wreck. The funeral we had. The dreams that followed.

His eyes lifted for a second, catching mine before dropping back to his hands. "The accident isn't what it was made out to be. It was a cover up to disguise the truth."

"What do you mean the truth?"

"We were attacked." His hand lightly touched his face. Was that how he got his scars?

I could feel my eyes widen. Who would attack my brother? And why?

"We were attacked by these things called Reapers. They are creatures that lurk in the darkness and hunt people. I don't know why they were on the bridge that night. But before I could react, they had run in front of my Jeep. I swerved, nearly missing them, but I slammed the car into the side of the bridge. Before we knew it, they were attacking us." His hands clenched into fists. "I watched as they killed my friends. I would've been next if Donovan and Adam hadn't come when they did."

This made no sense. Why would Reapers attack humans? They fed off their soul energy. If they died, they wouldn't be able to feed. "Reapers don't kill people," I whispered.

"How do you know what a Reaper is?" His eyes were cold. A cold chuckle left his lips. "Let me guess… Your Guardian friends?" His hand ran through his long hair. "Reapers will do anything to evoke fear, and the ripest fear is when a person faces his own death."

I then remembered the conversation with Emery. He had told me how they liked to influence the soul. I guess I had blocked that part out. That was why they hunted them at night. He said that once Reapers stopped feeding off dreams, they could be dangerous for humans. Is this what he meant? I shuddered.

"So, what... they then torched the car and kidnapped you?" I scoffed out. That sounded like Donovan's MO. "Did they also turn you into one of their dream slaves?"

"No." Cole's voice was sharp. "The Guardians did that. They were there. Just watching us. Hiding in the shadows like the cowards they are. Doing nothing to save us. If Donovan and Adam hadn't come when they did, I would've also been killed."

"You don't know that." I whispered. I didn't believe it. I refused to believe it. If the Guardians were there, they would've saved them. They were here to protect us.

"HA!" His laugh was cold. "I saw them. I saw them drag my friends into my car, pour gasoline all over, and light it on fire."

"But there were four bodies..." My voice whispered out. I pictured the four coffins. The closed lids. "Okay, so say what you said was true, why didn't you come back? Why did you abandon me?" Didn't he think about what his death did to us? Didn't he care?

"I wanted to." Sadness replaced the anger in his voice. "Once they reported me as one of the victims, they thought it was best for me to stay hidden with them. They were afraid if I turned up, it would spark too many questions, and the Guardians would have me killed."

"That's ridiculous!" I stood up. "I don't know what lies they are filling your head with down here, but the Guardians protect us. They wouldn't kill a human!" Anger ran through my body. What did they do to my brother down here? Did they brainwash him? The Cole I knew wouldn't be surrounded by such cruel people.

They must have. Didn't he remember Emery? He was his friend! I thought of the times he had talked about my brother. The sadness in his voice, knowing he would never have a chance to see him again. What other lies were they telling him?

"Well, that's humorous." My body froze at the voice. Donovan. "Relax, Amy. My plan for you was... well... vetoed."

"You should've told us first." Cole's face was dark, refusing to look in his direction. He made it sound like they were friends, but you wouldn't believe it looking at their interaction now.

Donovan raised his hands in surrender. "It was all for the greater good, but I suppose..." His eyes were back on me. "It's back to the drawing board."

"Great," I spat back. "So, you can let me go."

A twisted smile spread across his face. "Not quite yet, dear girl. We still have some use for you." My body shuddered.

"Donovan," Cole hissed.

"Relax." He placed his hand on Cole's shoulder. He stiffened against his hand. "She won't be harmed. Hasn't she told you yet? She has befriended the prince himself. And from what I've heard, he is desperately searching for her."

"I won't be your pawn!" I jumped from the table. My head was spinning. They were going to use me to get to Derek. I couldn't let that happen.

"You are more than welcome to return to your room." My body froze in fear.

"Enough!" Cole barked. He stared icily at Donovan "HE wants to talk to you."

Donovan's hands raised as if showing he wasn't trying to fight. Like when a dog rolls on his stomach in submission to the larger one. A smile spread across his face. "I guess it's time for me to get my scolding." With that, he left.

"This is who you trust?" My eyes pleaded with Cole.

"Yes." He pushed away from the table, but I could tell he was conflicted. "Just... please go back to the room." His head tilted back to the wooden door before he turned to follow Donovan. Leaving me behind once again.

The Danish felt like a brick in my stomach. I was alone again in this strange place. Were we even still in town? Was what Donovan said true? Was Derek looking for me? I shook my head. Of course he wasn't. His dad wouldn't allow it. I had failed. No one would come and save me. They would think of another way to lure Donovan out. Something that didn't involve a pathetic human.

I was standing in front of a makeshift bookshelf, looking at the various names on the spines. These were all new books. I picked up a fantasy one. It was being adapted into a movie this summer. Was Cole right? Did they waltz in and out of the world with no worry? How did they pay for these things? Did they have jobs?

I shook my head, returning it, but as I did, a paper fell out. I knelt to the ground, picking up the yellowed paper. I felt the glossiness as I turned it in my hand. It was an old picture. My breath caught in my throat. She was younger, but I immediately recognized the young woman. It was Mom. Her hand held the hand of her young child, a blond little boy. I recognized him from our own family pictures. It was Cole. He was so young. It must have been taken before I was born. But that man standing with them. He was a stranger. It wasn't Dad. But why did he look so familiar?

"How is she?" The voice was so sad.

"Who?" I slid the photo back between the books.

"Mom." The words stuck in his throat.

"How would I know?" I stomped to the bed, refusing to look at him. I didn't want to see him sad over *her*.

"What does that mean?" Cole was shuffling the books, probably ensuring the picture was safely returned. Out of everything, that is what is kept? Not a picture of me or our Dad? The two people who actually stuck around.

"She left. Deserted us shortly after you did." I spat out. I was getting angry. Yes, I was happy to know Cole was alive, but that meant he purposely left me too.

"That's impossible." Cole spun, his eyes meeting mine. Those blue eyes searching for the lie. I watched as his face dropped. Realizing it may be true. "That's not possible." His voice was so low, if I didn't see his lips move, then I wouldn't have known he spoke.

I shrugged. "She left for a better life I guess." I hated talking about her. I pulled my knees up, wrapping my arms around them.

"We were her life." Cole said dryly. Why was it so hard for him to accept?

"Maybe *you* were." The words felt like knives cutting into my chest. Reminding me how disposable I was. He was right. She wouldn't have left if he was there.

"Something's not right." Cole paused, his eyes searching me once more. "I'll be… right back." He turned to leave.

I stared at the bookcase. Why did we have to speak about her? Was Cole mad with me now? I didn't want to fight. I chewed on my lip. Extending my arms, I pushed myself off the bed, walking back to the books. I stretched my hand, pausing before tugging on the picture again.

I sat on the bed, staring at it. My fingers tracing over her face. Why did I still miss her? I hated her! No, that was a lie. That is what I told myself to stop the hurting. I could feel the tears running down my cheeks. I just wanted to go back. Back to when we were a family.

"Find something interesting?" The picture dropped from my hand as I jumped. Why did it have to be *that* voice? My head slowly turned, begging that Cole was next to him.

My breath caught in my throat. He was alone. "Where's Cole?" My voice trembled. Was he so mad that he sent Donovan back?

That sickly grin returned to his face. The one that made my skin crawl. "He's busy, but don't worry, we decided what to do with you." His hand grabbed my arm, the fingers wrapping around like a vice.

With one swift pull, he yanked me out of the room, ripping me away from my brother once again.

THIRTY-ONE

"No!" I yelled.

My hands had been bound together. A piece of cloth wrapped over my eyes, acting as a blindfold. Was this so I couldn't lead anyone back? Donovan was leading whatever *this* was. He had five of his own Guardians and ten Reapers. One of the females was carrying me. I had recognized her before they blindfolded me. Cassandra, I think someone had called her that.

How did this plan go so wrong? We were supposed to have the upper hand on Donovan. Now, I was once again their pawn. "Please don't be looking for me," I silently prayed. "Please don't fall for this trap."

"Here!" Donovan shouted. Even blindfolded, I could feel the descent as the wind had started blowing from below.

My blindfold was ripped off. They were standing in an open field. Behind us was a dense patch of trees. I swiveled my head as I tried to look for a familiar landmark, something to give a small hint on where we were. The arm was still wrapped around me like a vice. My body hovering above the ground. They probably chose this place since it had such little light, aside from the pale glow of the moon. I wonder how long they would have to wait. It wasn't like they could just call them up. Or could they?

"Now!" Donovan called out.

Cassandra dropped me. With my hands tied, I couldn't catch myself. I landed hard on my side. Luckily, my hands were bound in front, so I was at least able to sit up. With her now free hand, she raised it straight into the sky. Red sparks were flying from her fist. With a loud crackle, four large red bolts shot into the air. Just as Derek had mentioned. Without the sword, their energy was so chaotic.

Everything became still. A little sigh escaped from my mouth. How long had I been holding my breath? See, they weren't looking for me. They weren't wasting their time trying to find a human. My heart dropped as Derek's face flashed before my eyes. No, this is for the best. Their plan wasn't going to work.

How long would they wait before they gave up? My chest tightened at the thought. But if they did, what would happen to me? Unless I could figure out how to make a run for it. I squinted my eyes against the dark. Trying to get some lay of the land. Did I even have a chance at outrunning them?

The air was thick with anticipation as everyone waited in silence. I couldn't believe how quiet it was. My body was beginning to shiver against the cold. I wish my hands weren't tied. I pulled my elbows closer to my body, trying to conserve any precious body heat. How long would they wait? I stared up at the sky, trying to see if there was any way to tell how long it had been since we landed.

"No," I whimpered out.

I could see specks of yellow light up in the sky. My heart raced as I counted. Eighteen, nineteen, twenty. The ground began to crunch around me as the Fallen and Reapers ascended into the trees, leaving me alone. Once again, I was the bait. A low chuckle carried behind me, as they disappeared.

"Turn around!" I cried. My lungs were starting to burn against the cold.

Of course he had to be the one to land first. Agony covered his face when he saw me. He took a step forward, but Mr. Adler landed next, gripping his shoulder. The look of agony was quickly replaced by rage.

"Stop!" I called again. "It's a trap!"

Derek brushed his dad's hand off his shoulder. "Good," he hissed, "let them come."

Menacing laughter erupted as Donovan was the first to reappear. "I guess there's no point in hiding. We should've gagged the girl." His foot slammed into my side, knocking the wind out of me. I lay on the ground, gasping for air as pain radiated through my body.

"Don't touch her!" Derek leaped forward, but before he could collide with Donovan, something pulled him back. The rest of the disgraced Guardians were starting to flank Donovan. The Shadow Reapers stood like their own personal attack dogs. Creating a wall between us.

"Now, now, hasty aren't we?" Donovan continued his taunts.

"What do you want?" Derek spat. It was his dad that had pulled him back. At this point, the rest of the Guardians had arrived. It was a mix between familiar and unfamiliar faces.

"We're just looking for a simple compromise." Donovan's hands raised, as if he was showing he was no threat. Similar to what he had done with Cole. "We're tired of hiding in the shadows. We want to find a way to live our lives in peace." He was attempting to play the role of peacemaker instead of the instigator that he was.

"Come, brother, you aren't one to negotiate so easily." Mr. Adler was now the one speaking. A smile on his face, but his eyes ice.

Donovan shrugged in response. "Well, living in exile for so long can do that to a person."

Mr. Adler scoffed. "You want to come back?"

"Well, wouldn't that be the dream, but we aren't naïve. We know that isn't on the table. All we want is a place we can call our own without having to constantly look over our shoulder. Afraid to break this unspoken rule."

"What, for you and those creatures?" Mr. Adler's eyes moved to the Shadow Reapers.

"Brother. Always afraid of what you don't know. How could we not think of our pets?" Donovan stretched out his hand, almost as if he was scratching one of their heads. I swear, its tail wagged.

"And if we did agree, what are you offering?"

"Well, first, we have the lovely lady here." His arm was motioning to me. I was still trying to catch my breath. Why was it so hard to take a deep breath. I was pretty sure I had a few broken ribs from that kick.

Derek took another step forward, but his dad stretched his arm out, holding him back. A smile crossed his face. "Though, a tempting offer, as you can tell, she means a lot to my son. She is just human," he spat back. "Plus, judging by our numbers, I feel as though you are the ones who are at a disadvantage, so how about we go by these terms? You give us the girl, and we won't immediately execute you."

"And that is part of your problem, brother. You shouldn't be so quick to underestimate your opponent. Because sometimes, there is more than meets the eye. You see, we've learned something. If you take time to ensure your Reapers are fed, they have incredible abilities and are extremely loyal." With that, Donovan let out a loud whistle.

Suddenly, the ten Reapers started shaking, and within seconds, they started transforming. They were growing three times their size, and for once, their liquid skin was starting to harden. Almost as if they were becoming stone. They started to resemble the gothic gargoyles people used to decorate old stone buildings.

"You should've taken my deal." And with that, chaos erupted as the Reapers and the Fallen leaped into battle. Donovan stood behind me, almost as if he was guarding me. He still had plans for me. I was forever the last trap.

I watched in horror as the Guardians were being pushed back. For once, their swords had little effect on the Reapers. As if they were deflecting off their new skin.

"Donovan, please, you have to stop this!" I pleaded. "Someone is going to get killed!" He stood unfazed. "Cole said you were good! He believes in you, but he's wrong. You're evil!" I screamed.

"Evil, you say." His body went rigid. "You know nothing of our world. If you did, you wouldn't be so quick to judge."

An explosion erupted to the left of us. The sound of something hard hitting the ground. My heart leaped, but Donovan just stood smiling. "Looks like phase two is already here." And before I could make out what happened, he grabbed my waist, hoisting me into the sky.

A bright light also launched, chasing us. Donovan quickly spun to face the incoming light. It was Derek. His wings spread out while his whole body was engulfed in the flame. I had seen that only once, back during the ambush.

"I knew you would be the one to break through." Donovan smiled, unfazed by the new encounter. As if this was another planned move in this ongoing chess match.

"Let her go." Derek's teeth were clenched, his sword extended.

"She is getting a bit heavy, maybe I should just drop her." His arm shifted around me, causing me to briefly slip.

"NO!" Derek yelled, leaping forward.

An evil laugh erupted from Donovan as he tightened his grip around me, jumping back to keep the distance between them. "That's what makes you special, nephew. That is why we have hope that there can be change."

"I'm not my dad. I'm not going to sit around and waste time on negotiations that will never be honored. Give Amy to me, or I will kill you!"

"So, once again we are at an impasse. Is the only option to exterminate us? Would you be willing to kill Emery's parents? All over the death of one human." His grip was starting to loosen with his threat. Was he finally done bluffing? Was he finally going to drop me? My hands were still bound, I had no way to grip him. I kept my body bent, afraid that if I moved in the slightest, I would fall.

"No, just you." He was done talking. He leaped forward, but Donovan was ready. Just as quickly as Derek moved forward, Donovan matched his speed, launching himself back. The same dance as when they met on the bridge.

I yelped as I slipped. But the arm instantly tightened, holding me in place. Derek froze, only his wings moved, keeping him steady in the air.

"Careful now." Donovan cooed. "If I'm distracted it would be so easy to lose my grip."

"Let her go. This is between us." Derek snarled between gritted teeth. "Or are you that scared to face me?"

"Taunting now? You are starting to sound like your dear ol' Dad." Donovan's grip began to loosen again. "But all this for a human?" Donavan's eyes held mine, the sickly smile spread across his face. "Would you be willing to take her place?"

"Yes!" There was no hesitation in his voice.

"Derek, no!" I screamed back. "Don't say that." I yelped as Donovan's arm squeezed around me, putting extra pressure on my already injured side.

"Donovan, please." Derek's voice faltered; the earlier conviction was dissipating. "I'll do anything you ask. Just please, let her go."

"Drop your sword." Donovan's eyes shifted to the golden sword that Derek was grasping.

"Derek don't." I pleaded. "It's a trap. You can't trust him."

His eyes caught mine. There was so much pain there. "I can't lose you again." His hands dropped to his side, releasing his sword.

"No!" I screamed as it fell.

"Sorry Amy." Donovan whispered. "You have just turned back into a liability."

"Amy!" Derek's scream ripped at my heart.

My body was being pulled backwards. The darkness surrounding me as Donovan drifted away. I closed my eyes. I didn't want to see Derek's face. I didn't want to see him in pain. I felt the same rush as when Donovan pulled me off the bridge. The same sick feeling in my stomach as the wind rushed past my body. The whistling of the wind in my ears. But this time would be different. This time, I would hit the ground. I just prayed it would be quick.

A loud crash erupted above me. I squeezed my eyes tighter. I was a coward. I didn't want to see the fight. All I could do was pray. Please don't kill him. Whatever your plan for him is, just keep him alive. My body stiffened, waiting for the impact of the hard ground. Would I feel it? Or would my death be instantaneous? Before I could dwell anymore, my whole body jolted. Pain radiated, but not to the level I expected. Almost as if something had stopped me. For a moment my body was being pulled back upward, but then the descent started again, slower this time.

I opened my eyes, and my heart jumped. Kyle had caught me. He was slowly descending before awkwardly releasing me. He grabbed my wrists, cutting the binding with his sword. Before the cloth even hit the ground, my arms wrapped around him. The sharp pain spread through my side as I collapsed to the ground, his arm looping back around, keeping me slightly upright.

He was okay. I hadn't seen him since the attack. But he was okay, and he was here. How proud he must be to have been included. But I couldn't think of that now, my attention was back to the sky.

"I've never seen him like that." Kyle whispered.

I stared upward. It was so hard to make them out. They were so high. My stomach flipped thinking how far I had fallen. The two lights squared off. The red light from Donovan's wings, and the blazing light next to him. A white light replaced the normal yellow glow. It was so bright I had to look away. Was that Derek?

"His sword!" I gasped, grabbing Kyle's arm. "He dropped his sword. We need to find it!"

Obediently Kyle nodded, leaping forward, his wings extending out as he searched the area. Was it possible to find it? How far would it have fallen?

A loud crack caused my head to spin back to the open field. Blinding yellow light erupted from one of the Guardians in the direction of an oncoming stone reaper. An explosion rattled the ground as the reaper exploded from the impact, both allies and enemies braced against the stone shrapnel. But the pause only lasted a second before the fighting continued. I tried to count, but they were moving too fast. It was hard to see who was winning.

That same humorless laugh echoed from above. My eyes left the field back to Derek and Donovan. It was hard to follow the lights, they moved so fast. Streaks of light flashed across the sky as they brawled. Suddenly, the white light slammed into the red. A loud crack echoed through the sky, if I hadn't seen them collide, I would've thought it was thunder. The white light was driving the red towards the ground. At the last second they both broke away, nearly missing impact. Red bolts erupted from Donovan, but it seemed to be absorbed by the white light that was surrounding Derek.

Derek rushed towards Donovan again, this time the

impact pushed Donovan into a row of trees. The sound of splintering wood filled the air. A couple trees started to fall, slamming into the ground.

"I found it!" Kyle yelled, lifting the sword above his head. I couldn't believe how far it had fallen. I had to be a couple hundred feet away. If a normal human would have searched for it, I doubt it would have been found.

I took off running after Kyle. We had to get his sword back. My arm lifted, covering my face as we got closer. The light was blinding I could barely make Derek out.

"Derek!" Kyle called, lifting his sword. No reaction. Derek was stood frozen staring at the woods. Waiting.

"Derek!" This time it was another voice that called. Two people dropped next to him. Emery and Dominic had made it. Was this enough? Could they defeat him?

Derek didn't acknowledge his friends. He was still standing frozen in place. His glazed eyes fixed on the trees.

"Hey?" Dominic's hand grabbed Derek's shoulder.

If I had blinked in that moment, I would've missed it. Derek's arm swung out, colliding with Dominic's chest. The blow launched Dominic into the air before he collided with the ground.

"What the hell?" He coughed, lifting himself up.

"Well, this is unexpected." The voice coughed out. Donovan was slouched over, holding his side. His other hand propped up against a tree.

Derek growled as he launched himself towards Donovan. Donovan's wings erupted from his back again, dodging. He kicked backwards, disappearing back into the woods. Derek froze at the tree line, scanning. Trying to find him.

"**Amy.**" Donovan's voice returned inside my head. "**Fix him**." There was urgency in his voice now.

"Derek!" Emery was next to him. "Snap out of it."

Derek's arm swiped at him. A loud smack erupted as it made impact with Emery. Throwing him to the side as if he was a simple rag doll. Something was wrong. Why was he attacking his friends? My legs started moving, as if they had a mind of their own. Before I knew it, I was running at full speed towards Derek. Something was wrong with him.

I lifted my arms to my face, covering it from the blinding light. The air around me was growing heavy as I got closer. As if it was trying to push me away. "Derek…" I whispered. I was standing in front of him. My eyes searching for his eyes.

I sucked the air between my teeth when I found them. His eyes were replaced by burning white light. His face was emotionless.

"Derek!" I yelled, but nothing registered.

My heart raced as I pushed closer. The air was crushing around me making, it difficult to stand. He was as still as a statue. My hand reached towards his face. Was he going to attack me like he did the others? I wouldn't survive a blow like they did. I didn't care. I needed to touch him. My hand brushed his cheek, as I tried to find some way to get his attention. I quickly pulled my hand away as it made contact. It was wet. He was… crying.

"Derek…" I reached my hands out, cradling his face. I just needed him to look at me, but his face wouldn't move. I leaned forward on my toes to close the gap. My eyes closed as our lips touched.

At first, they were hard. Unmoving. I felt my stomach drop. What an idiot. What did I think was going to happen? This wasn't a movie. As I was about to pull away, I felt a shift as they started to soften. His arms finally moved, wrapping around me, as his lips molded against mine.

"Amy…" He huffed between breaths. His forehead pressed against mine. "Is it really you?"

I was the first to break away. The blinding light had dissipated. His eyes had returned, but they were still filled with such sadness.

"Derek!" His voice was called out behind us. "Donovan escaped!"

Finally, his head turned in recognition. As I turned to follow, I felt my legs begin to buckle. The world was spinning around me as everything started to blur.

"Am…" the voice was fading away.

"Don't leave…" I gasped out.

Once again, I was consumed by the dark.

THIRTY-TWO

My nose wrinkled against the smell of alcohol. But this alcohol smell was different. Not the same stale odor from piles of beer cans, but more of a clean alcohol smell. The smell of antiseptics. There was also this annoying reoccurring beep that wouldn't stop. It wasn't my alarm, but just as annoying. Why won't it stop? I reached out my arm, searching for my nightstand, in the hopes of finding the sound, but instead my hand collided with something hard. "Son of a..." I muttered out.

My eyes blinked against the bright light as the room came into focus. My breath caught as it did, which caused the beeping to increase. I tried to sit up, but a sharp pain erupted through my side.

"Welcome back, Amy," an unfamiliar voice greeted me. A nurse was standing over my bed. My nose scrunched against the smell of disinfectants.

My heart dropped. I was alone. The nurse reached over, pressing a couple of buttons on the machine.

"Someone's here to see you." She sweetly smiled. The beeps quickened as my heart fluttered.

"Hi, Amy." With that voice, my stomach became agitated. Mr. Adler entered the room.

"Mr. Adler." My voice was raspy.

"I'll get you some fresh water," the nurse chimed in, leaving us alone.

"We can't find them." The formalities were over, as he started pacing around the floor, his hand running through his hair. "I need you to tell me where they are! How many were there, what are their plans?"

I had never seen him so frantic.

"I... I don't know." I was barely awake, my memory still clouded, probably from the drugs I was on. I glanced over at my IV drip. What were they pumping into me?

"You were there for three weeks!" he said, his voice exasperated. "You must have stumbled on something during your time there."

"Three weeks..." I choked out. It hadn't felt longer than a couple of days. How long had I been trapped in that room? Stuck in the loop of dreams. My teeth were cutting into my bottom lip. I knew I needed to tell him what had happened to me. My brain was still stuck in a fog, but something else was also holding me back. Cole's face appeared in my head. If they found them, what would happen to my brother? Would he be killed as well? Was he really in danger?

I shook my head. "I'm sorry, they kept me locked up. I wasn't able to see anything." My voice was quiet.

My body jolted against his laugh, but there was no humor behind it. "And that's what happens when we put our faith in a human." He threw something across the room making a loud clatter.

Without another word, he left. I sat dazed for a few minutes. Three weeks. I had been gone for three weeks. I hesitated. No, it's been even longer now. Did anyone know I was here? Did anyone care? My stomach twisted at the thought.

That's when my eye caught the side table. A collection of

cards and flowers filled the surface. I picked up the closest one and opened it. Alicia's handwriting was scribbled on the inside. There was one after another from Grace, Sally, Ben, and even the waitresses from Charlie's Diner. As I reached for the next one, a sound echoed into the room.

"Amy?" the voice cautiously called out. My head turned, catching his sad eyes.

"Derek." My voice caught in my throat, as tears sprung to my eyes. He stayed frozen in the door. Was he still mad? Was this his way of making sure I was okay before leaving? The machine started beeping furiously.

His head whipped to the machine. Worry spread across his face. "Are you hurting?"

I shook my head, afraid to speak, not trusting my voice.

"You've been pacing nonstop these last few days, but now you're going to act like she has the plague." The nurse chuckled, pushing her way in again. Dutifully carrying the glass of water to my bed. "Don't let his coy behavior fool you. He's barely left your side since you got here." Her eyes darted in his direction.

Pink spread across his cheeks as he slowly walked into the room, standing awkwardly at the foot of my bed. Before another word could be said, whooping and hollering erupted through the hall. A group of people stormed in.

"She lives!" Dominic declared as he entered. The nurse shot him a scolding look. His hands shot up in defense. "She lives…" he said quieter.

Derek's whole body tensed. I bit my lip as I watched him shift farther from the group. Something was wrong. Was he still mad at them? But my worry was brief as my eyes still lit up when they entered. It wasn't everyone, but it was who I wanted to see. Dominic, Kyle, Luke, and Emery stood by my bed. My heart swelled at that moment. They wanted to check on me. They still cared.

"How're you feeling, kid?" Emery asked, nudging my leg.

I cleared my throat, hoping my voice didn't crack as much. "Good!" I tried to sound enthusiastic.

"When're you getting out?" Kyle asked, bouncing on his toes. "I finally creamed Aiden on a one-on-one!"

"HA!" Dominic boomed.

Kyle glared at him. "I did! See Amy, this is why you need to come and see, so you can tell them!"

"Ahem." The clearing of his throat interrupted the chatter. My heart sank as I looked at Derek. Why did he have to look so stern?

"Alright, we should probably let her rest." Emery was starting to corral everyone out. "Get some sleep. We'll come back later." He threw a quick glance in Derek's direction before bowing out.

"That was rude!" I chastised Derek as they left. They had just gotten there.

I watched him nervously chew his lip as he shifted his weight between his feet. Why was this so awkward? "You don't have to be here if you don't want to be," I choked out. I grabbed my water to hopefully cover the cracking of my voice from just being dehydrated instead of being on the verge of tears.

"I should leave..." Derek's body slumped into the recliner next to the bed. I felt as if I had been punched in the stomach. "That would be the smartest decision. Make a clean break, let you recover, and move on with your life." His hand was now rubbing his face. "God, why do I have to be selfish?"

He leaned forward, grabbing my hand. They were just as I remembered them. Rough with callouses, but warm, and most importantly, they made me feel safe.

"Why don't I get a say?" I was surprised at how confident my voice sounded. "Your word isn't law here!" That's what I needed to be for him. I wasn't going to follow blindly like everyone else around me.

Sadness flashed in his eyes. "I thought I lost you." My heart leaped as his voice caught on the end.

"Hey, I'm tougher than you think." I tried to make a muscle with my arm.

Derek gently tugged my arm forward, bringing me closer to him. His other hand lifted my chin before he brought his mouth to mine. My arm wrapped around his neck as we kissed. My body felt like electricity was running through it. My body tensed against the pain in my side. He jerked away in response. That look of worry returned as he looked back to the machine. As if it held all the answers.

"Alright, you two." The nurse was back, her back leaning against the doorway. "Amy needs to get some rest."

My hand tightened around his. I wasn't ready for him to go. "Can we just have a couple more minutes?" I pleaded.

The nurse held up her hand as she mouthed, "You have five," before she headed to the next room.

I needed to get this out. "Derek, I need you to know I'm not sorry." His body jerked, but he continued to hold my hand. "It was my choice, not yours, not Emery's, your dad's, or Dominic's." My lip began to quiver as I continued, "So if you need someone to hate, it should be me."

"I could never hate you," he said, his voice ragged. That's when I saw the exhaustion in his eyes. How long had he been waiting for me?

"So does that mean you forgive Emery and Dominic?" I peeked into his eyes. His jaw tightened. "Derek?" I urged.

He sat back, rubbing his neck. "We're fine." He saw my skeptical expression. "We're *going* to be fine," he clarified.

"Promise?" I wrapped my pinky around his, the white cord connected to the small plastic clip on my index finger dangled between us.

He chuckled. My heart leaped at that simple sound. "Promise." He brought my hand to his lips as he kissed each finger. The machine frantically beeped again. I cursed at it under my breath.

"I love you, Amy Evans." His eyes burned.

"And I love you, Derek Alder." His hands cradled my face as we kissed.

The nurse returned too quickly and ushered him out, but finally, as I fell asleep, I was happy.

Maybe, for once, I would have a good dream.

Epilogue

"Find anything yet?" Derek peered over my shoulder as I continued to scroll through the job postings.

I was chewing on my bottom lip as I read each description. "No," I answered defeatedly. Why was it so hard to find a job?

He pulled the laptop toward him. "What about this?" He started reading the ad out loud. "Hard worker. Check. Detailed oriented. Check. Time management…" He paused. "Half check."

"Hey!" I pulled the laptop back. "This is an accounting role! You need a college degree."

He shrugged. "You never know. Maybe it's negotiable."

I chucked my pen at him as I closed my laptop. "Maybe, I can go out this weekend and just hand out my resume."

"That's the spirit! Don't leave until they give you the job!"

"What happened to my table!" Emery gasped as he entered his kitchen.

I looked around as our books and papers cluttered every inch. I was still trying to catch up on all the homework I missed. Derek was supposed to be helping, but he had missed almost as much as I did. Thankfully, since my grades were already in a good spot, I got a medical waiver to excuse the mid-terms, on the caveat that I passed the finals with a C or higher. I wonder how much Ms. Haines had influenced that decision.

"Sorry," I sheepishly responded, trying to organize the clutter into more condensed piles.

"Your table?" Derek bellowed. "I thought this was OUR house."

Emery threw a towel at him. "Once you actually start cleaning around here, I *may* allow you to claim ownership. On some things."

Derek threw the towel back as I spied the mound of dishes behind him. I couldn't help but laugh, which earned me a glare from him. I was happy to see them back to normal. While I was in the hospital, Derek had moved back in. And since getting out, they all seemed to be back to their normal selves. Though, I worry that there might still be a small rift between them.

My smile started to drift away as I thought about my own home. Since returning, my dad had turned into his own type of ghost. He avoided me at all costs. He barely returned home, and when he did, it was conveniently when I was at school and gone before I could return. The only communication was a pad of paper in the kitchen that consisted of a grocery list and what bills were due.

"The boys are asking if you both are going to the gym tonight?" Emery glanced my way. "Apparently, the big event is finally happening. Dominic is finally sparing with Kyle."

"We wouldn't miss it!" I nearly leaped from the chair. "Do you think he has a chance?" I lowered my voice, even though it was only the three of us.

"I mean, there is always a chance." Emery shrugged. "I mean, probably the same probability of you finishing this homework." He gestured back to the chaos of the table.

"Hey!" I gasped. My hand clutching my chest as if he had

just stabbed me. "I'll finish this!" I stared at the papers. I swear they were multiplying.

"You better grab your stuff." Emery's head jerked to Derek. I think they want us to be there by five."

"Shoot, you're right." Derek jumped up from the table. He stopped next to me, tilting my hand up. A sly smile spread on his face as he dipped down to kiss me.

"God knock it off!" Emery whined. "Can you all go five minutes without making out."

Derek smirked. "I'll be right back."

I watched as he loped out of the room. I waited until I heard the door upstairs close. "Well?" My voice dropped to barely a whisper.

Emery's head just shook as my shoulders sagged. It had been two months and still no sign. Emery was the only person I decided to confide in. I knew I shouldn't be keeping this from Derek, but it didn't feel right yet. Emery was in the same boat as me. He had the same desire to find them first. Because he and I both knew, if the Guardians found them first, his parents... Cole... they would be killed.

"We'll keep searching. They lost a lot of comrades. It will be a bit before they make another move." Emery's eyes were distant.

Donovan was the only survivor that night. Four casualties don't sound like much, but when you only have twenty to twenty-five people, compared to the hundreds of Guardians, it is a pretty significant hit. My body shuddered as the picture of their bodies spread across the field entered my mind. The Guardians had lost a few as well, but they were part of Mr. Adler's crew. Everyone I knew was okay. I felt bad being relieved. My mind continued to spin. What was their plan?

"Ready?" Derek was holding his duffel bag. His eyes darting between the two of us.

"I think I deserve a break." I stretched my arms above my head.

"Wait…" Emery glanced back at the table. "You're just leaving this here?"

I leaped from my chair, bounding to the door. "Sorry, I can't hear you!" I laughed.

"Just think. If it was OUR table, I could help you out," Derek hollered back as he ushered me out of the door.

We climbed into the car, gasping for air between the laughs. Derek leaned his head against the seat. His head turned as he just stared at me.

I could feel my cheeks flushing as I pulled on my sleeve. "What?" I sighed after a painful minute.

"Have I told you lately how beautiful you are?"

"Shut up!" I pushed his shoulder.

He grabbed my wrist, pulling me across the seat. His other hand cradled my cheek. My free hand tangled in his hair as our lips touched. No matter how many times we kissed, my body still exploded as if it was our first. His lips pushed mine apart as his tongue slowly brushed over them. A small moan escaped my throat, which caused him to pull me closer.

His forehead leaned against mine as we gasped for air. Could you die from kissing? Derek lifted my hand as he kissed each finger. "I have something for you." His voice was raspy.

He opened the middle console, pulling out a small blue velvet box. My chest tightened as he lifted it between us.

"I'm not asking you to marry me." He chuckled, lifting my chin so our eyes would meet. "But this is a promise. As long as you wear this, you will be protected." He popped open the box, exposing a silver ring.

He picked up my right hand as he pulled the ring out of the box. The cool metal slid effortlessly onto my ring finger. I pulled my hand closer to my face, examining the details. It was so similar to theirs. Not a perfect circle like your typical ring. You could see where the two ends of the metal overlapped, but around the edge was an embroidered vine of leaves.

"Now you're one of us." He kissed the ring.

"I love it." I wrapped my arms around his neck. "I love you."

That half smile that always made my heart flip returned. I glanced at the clock. We have time for one more kiss. Kyle would forgive us if we were a little late tonight.

But at this moment, it was just Derek and me.

About the Author

K. E. Deyarmin lives in sunny Florida with her husband and a small squad of mischief-making cats and law-abiding dogs. She graduated from the University of Florida with a degree in Elementary Education, but her true education began the day she picked up her first manga and fell headfirst into the world of fantasy.

In college, when "adulting" started throwing curveballs, she discovered the ultimate escape, which was building magical worlds of her own. These days, whenever life gets too real, you'll find her tucked away in her home library, recharging with a favorite fantasy book and a fuzzy feline or two.

This is the first book in her debut series. One that she has been dreaming about since those cramped dorm room days, where a mystical world made more sense than the looming day of graduation. The day she would be summoned to the ultimate task of becoming an adult.